I0604915

Arguing her Heart

Ada S. Blunt

A message from the author:

Within every true story lies an untapped masterpiece poised to ignite motivation. Whether woven from reality, born from fiction, or both, each narrative is a unique tapestry capable of stirring and inspiring the depths of our being.

This book is a tribute to the countless incredible women whose names may be unsung but whose impact resonates. To those remarkable women, you know who you are! Any resemblance to other real-life experiences is entirely coincidental, acting as subtle echoes, highlighting the profound influence embedded in the art of storytelling.

Before embarking on this literary journey, pause to acknowledge the remarkable women who have shaped your narrative, contributing to the richness of your character and the depth of your existence.

May this reading experience not merely be a passage through pages but a wellspring of inspiration, motivation, and fulfillment. May it empower and encourage you, serving as a guiding light along your journey.

Ada S. Blunt

Prologue

"Good news. You are about seven weeks pregnant. We'll know more after the ultrasound," Doctor Wong said as he removed his vinyl gloves. Ava propped herself up into a sitting position. And her expression? One of confusion and disbelief. "Oh! You don't look so happy about the news. I understood you already knew from the pregnancy test," the doctor continued.

"Truth is, I don't know what I was hoping for. I ... I guess I hoped you'd tell me it's some cyst or hormonal something that could give a false positive result on those tests. You probably remember how badly I wanted to have a baby years ago. And we couldn't make it happen. Why in the world now? I guess I thought I was too old to get pregnant," her voice faded.

Doctor Wong scoffed. "Old? You're not old."

"Are you sure you're looking at my file? Doctor Wong, I'm forty-nine. So yeah..." her voice cracked, and she appeared crushed.

"I've been in this profession for over two decades. I've seen pregnant women in their fifties. What can I say? Babies have their own schedule. They come when and if they want to. I see you're in a bit of shock right now. You probably need some time to process the news. I'll give you a requisition for blood tests and an ultrasound, just to know if everything is okay and determine what protocol we need to follow. Why don't you go home, talk to your husband, and decide? If you choose to continue with the pregnancy, schedule the tests, and I'll see you in a week or so." Doctor Wong tried to diffuse the shock of the news, noticing how devastated and confused she appeared.

He had a hunch that there might be more to it. But he didn't know much about her life in the past few years. Not since she made peace with her fate and gave up on trying for a baby.

After the doctor left the room, stooped, Ava stumbled to the chair where her clothes lay. She dressed on autopilot, while a million thoughts flooded her mind.

How? Screw this! I know exactly how. Why? Why now? Should I tell him? How would I? Do I want this baby? Will I have this baby? Or will it just be another loss to add to my long, dark list of losses? She bit her lip, as her mind went on and on, and if you listened closely, you could hear the wheels spinning and squeaking.

Shuffling her feet under the weight of the latest, unnerving news, she left the clinic.

A horn blared, and she froze. As if life wasn't done checking her reflexes. Again. Wide-eyed, she glared at the driver, who managed to stop just inches away as she began crossing the street.

From deep within, a wave of responsibility for another life washed over her, and she instinctively placed a hand on her belly.

Right then and there, she knew. She had to have this baby. A baby she wanted so badly and had been trying for so long without success. It was her last chance to have someone she could love and who would love her back. Unconditionally.

She had the means to raise a baby on her own. And she still had so much love left in her to give. To have someone to make her life meaningful again? That was something she was willing to take on.

Well ... babies have their own schedule. They come when and if they want to. If this baby chose me, then so be it.

She got into her car and sat there for a few minutes, glaring at the fallen leaves rolling, dancing, and twirling across the parking lot. Her mind wandered, trying to make sense of the life she was living at that very moment.

"If anyone told me a year ago, when I first literally bumped into him, that I'd be here today, carrying his child, I would've laughed my head off," Ava muttered to herself, letting out a deep exhale as her hand touched her belly again.

Her upper lip arched in a bitter yet hopeful smirk.

Is this a nightmare? Or a dream come true?

1. That bad, huh?

Some disturbance on the street below Ava's window woke her up. Honking cars and tires screeching, followed by even louder arguments that she tried to make sense of, pulled her out of bed.

Sitting on its edge, she looked around, scattered, and finally remembered where she was. Days bled into each other as if she travelled back and forth in time. Despite her sorrow, mixed with excitement about the trip, Ava couldn't wait for it to end so she could go home.

Over the past week, each day, she's found it harder to get out of bed. Crossing so many time zones in such a short time wasn't something she was used to anymore. Her weary body felt like running on fumes. Then, she remembered. She needed this. She needed closure. And this was the choice she made.

She glanced at her fitness tracker and checked the time. Instantly, the heavy feeling that she was late for something took over her. *Oh, please! Calm down, girl! You're on vacation. You're not late for anything. Le Louvre has been in the same place for hundreds of years. I'm sure as hell they won't tear it down in the next few hours*—she tried to reassure herself, rolling her eyes at the noise outside.

Still in slow motion, she dragged her depleted body into the shower. The small loft she had rented for a short—*or was it too long?*—stay in Paris was conveniently located close enough to almost everything she wanted to visit. She was reasonably picky, thinking about stuff other people would consider trivial, when choosing a place to stay while on vacation.

The small and cozy loft had everything she needed—a clean bed, a roof, and hot water. A whole, expressive experience of the places she visited was what she always sought. Just the simplicity of a hot shower felt invigorating.

The craziest thing, otherwise true for other people, was having a washing machine. So, she could do some laundry. After all, this adventure was more than just a few-day trip, and you can only carry so much with you. Hence, she planned it carefully.

I'll likely have enough clean clothes to last for the rest of my vacation. Well, we'll see about that—she mused.

Now, Ava gave herself a proud pat on the shoulder as she remembered to take her laundry out of the washer before leaving for the day. Exhausted, last night she crashed before the cycle was over.

Under the hot whips of water, the inexplicable feeling of being late for something returned, only to nag her once more. *Shit! That guy ... the actor! He said around eight at the café. Right! Like he'll be there*—she dismissed the thought as quickly as it came to mind.

"Nah ... Just making conversation. Probably trying to make me feel better about the whole incident. That's something to be appreciative of, actually," she muttered, trying to reassure herself.

Then she pouted as another thought crashed in. *Unless it was pity that he felt! Huh ... I'd hate that!*

Ava was past that time in her life when she felt the urge to rush into anything. Or would be easily impressionable. Not anymore. And definitely not today.

She caught so many curveballs life threw at her, she now knew. *Life is short.* Slowing down and enjoying it was probably best. And being comfortable in her own skin? That was right up there, too.

Getting overly excited about small, ordinary things was more her vibe these days. *Stop and smell the roses! This is it!*

She stepped out of the shower and checked the time again. Then, she pulled the laundry out of the washer and spread it across the chairs and the shower rod. Sort of stacked, but it will dry. And, exactly when she thought she was done, she noticed the ingenious pull-out clothes-drying system above the shower.

"Duh! Of course! They have a washer. It only makes sense to have some system in place so one can hang their clothes," she muttered, rolling her eyes at her own absurdity. Hence, she started figuring out how that works, and now, "Let's do this again! Hanging clothes to dry. Now, the proper way."

She exhaled in relief and rubbed her palms together. "Okay! What's next? Coffee! Bien sûr, it's coffee. Well, first things first— a little makeup..." Then, of course, she had to remember the guy again.

Already seven-forty. Ten minutes—makeup. Another nearly ten minutes—trying to get into something that wasn't wrinkled. When Ava left Madrid, she had to deal with a bit of a mishap. The consequence? Things were shoved into her suitcase in some sort of orderly chaos.

At eight precisely, she was on her way to the café with only one thing in mind—*vitamin coffee.*

Since arriving in Europe, she had been counting down the days until she could see Sandra. Today was supposed to be the day. Ava's high school friend made Paris her home just a few years after they graduated.

Disappointment washed over Ava when she called the night before. Sandra couldn't take the day off.

Ava sighed, realizing their reunion would be limited to just Sunday. A one-day catch-up while wandering around the French countryside. Today would be hers alone to explore Le Louvre by herself.

The previous day, Thursday, her first morning in Paris, ended in a failed attempt at making coffee. She just used what she found in the loft's kitchenette. The result? Disappointing, to say the least. So, she set out in search of a place to get a decent cup of coffee.

That shouldn't be too hard. It is Paris, right?

Determined to find the best coffee in Paris, she began towards Trocadero Square. Her ambitious plans for the day included, among other things, a visit to the famous Eiffel Tower. *Well, not before coffee. Priorities, you know…*

It rained most of the night and was still drizzling, but Ava enjoyed what, in her opinion, was a short walk. She wanted to see, to absorb as much as possible—nearly everything. Otherwise, the traffic is the same everywhere: congested.

The weatherman announced it will be sunny later in the day. *Yeah! Define later.*

Ava welcomed the day with optimism. The clouds were already beginning to part. Lifting her eyes, she was blinded by the sun peeking through—beams of light occasionally piercing the clouds.

Then, she sniffed it: the haunting smell of freshly baked French pastries wafting down the street. Like a hound dog, she picked up the aroma and chased it, hoping it would go hand in hand with a great cup of coffee.

When travelling, Ava gravitated toward local restaurants and other mom-and-pop shops, all of which reflected the local culture. Eventually, old traditions, too. Suddenly, she found herself standing in front of the place where the scent trail stemmed from.

The small, picturesque bakery and coffee shop exuded the vibe of a family business. Exactly what she looked for. *They probably still follow old recipes passed down through generations.* Or so she liked to imagine.

Then she looked up and almost laughed. "And look at that! Chez Martin. It's like predestined. It's calling my name," she muttered and pushed the door with a hopeful smile.

The bell above rang like a good omen on a gloomy morning.

Once inside, Ava realized she might be in the right place. A long line of customers waiting for their respective cup of coffee, and a croissant or something, told her this must be a popular spot. The grin persisted. She felt lucky to have discovered this gem before even more disappointment struck in her 'need coffee' department.

She peered around and noticed a few people sitting at the tables, sipping coffee with whatever choice of pastry. Most had their noses in their cellphones. Probably reading the news or ... who knows what? *They're in no hurry*—Ava concluded, and she waited in line.

When her turn came, she ordered a medium coffee 'to go', in a large cup, topped with two espresso shots. It wasn't long before she'd heard her name. With the large cup of her prized hot coffee in hand, she was ready to leave. And that's when it happened.

Reeling back, Ava felt she had stepped on something higher than the ground, and she lost her balance. She squeezed the coffee cup, and the lid popped ... and flipped, and... she estimated, nearly half of the life-supporting liquid burst into the air.

Some fell on her, and the rest? Everywhere else. She was absolutely sure she'd done a quick shoulder check before stepping away from the counter.

But there he was! Right behind her. *Where the hell had he appeared from?*

"What the..." she started cussing as she kept turning to see what she had stepped on, when a pair of solid hands grabbed her arms. The stranger's sudden grip didn't help regain her balance, as he probably intended. Instead, another splash of coffee shot from the cup. "... fudge!" she blurted, frozen in place, pushing to remain upright.

"And she speaks English," the stranger's remark arrived, probably aiming to undo the whole incident, knowing full well he shouldn't be standing so close behind someone. Especially when hot drinks are involved.

Somehow, her intuition told her it wasn't a gallant observation. *Great start to the day!* Ava thought, rolling her eyes. She recognized his accent was likely British. Or maybe Australian? Or … whatever you could make out of just a few words. All she knew? The hot coffee didn't burn as badly as the embarrassing moment.

"Yes, she does…" she grumbled, succeeding in remaining on her two feet and finally turning around. "And you do, too. For the life of me, I couldn't remember how to apologize in French right now. I'm … terribly sorry. I … didn't see you standing there," Ava muttered, avoiding his gaze.

Concerned, her eyes flicked up and down, searching his outfit for eventual damage from her coffee erupting. *High-quality trench coat. Looks like an expensive one. Probably a businessman*—she appraised. Luckily no trace of coffee on him.

The stranger swiftly reached and grabbed a bunch of napkins off the closest table. "Here. Are you okay?" he asked, voice tinged with concern, while studying her features.

"I'll be fine," she mumbled, still evading his gaze, rather preoccupied with assessing the damage to her own outfit now.

"I'm truly sorry. I shouldn't have stayed that close behind you. Are you sure you are alright? I'm certain the coffee was hot," the stranger said.

"Not hot anymore. I appreciate your concern. Great!" Ava muttered in annoyance. "At least this time, I managed to create a disaster that affected only me." A quasi-smile mixed with disappointment on display, she waved her hands up and down, pointing at herself and her coffee-drenched dress. "Gods must love you, protecting you from a klutz like me."

She peeked around, trying to find a washroom where she could continue the scrubbing process away from prying eyes. Or whatever she could do to make herself look somehow adequate before hitting the streets of Paris.

Fortunately, she made a wise choice this morning: a black

casual dress with white stripes on the top only. As her leather jacket was still zipped up, the coffee only stained the black bottom part of her dress. The rest? Landed on her jacket. Miraculously, her white sneakers remained unstained.

Once in the ladies' room, Ava assessed the damage. *Not too bad*—she reassured herself. With one exception—the coffee smell. Well, that was something she'd have to learn how to live with for the rest of the day.

The water helped some, but not entirely. After a brief deliberation, she pushed back the idea of returning to the loft to change.

Nearly fifteen minutes later, fearing her wrinkled ego would suffer even more, she convinced herself that whoever witnessed the incident must've already left the café. With one last look in the large mirror, she sucked in a deep breath and stepped out rather confidently.

She trudged towards the door with only one goal in mind: leaving, not anticipating she'd get another coffee. *Not from here, anyway. I'll find another place. I made a fool out of myself in front of these people ... Do I want to look them in the eye again? The answer is 'definitely no'. It's too much for one day. Even for me*, she thought, pacing valiantly towards the exit.

Her eyes on the door—her escape—she marched bravely past the tables when a hand reached out, gently grasping her right arm above the wrist. "I think you're forgetting something," the same stranger said, flashing an eccentric smile as he lifted a cup of coffee off the table.

When he handed her the napkins earlier, the stranger offered to hold the cup, so she had two free hands to wipe the coffee off her jacket. Mainly. Too late for her soaked dress.

"Oh, I completely forgot about it." She forced herself to maintain a stoic expression.

"Please, sit down. It's still cold, and you may not want to go out there in damp clothes … unless you have somewhere to be," the stranger added. *Some cues from her would be nice,* he thought.

She couldn't argue—his statement was spot on. It was a chilly October morning in Paris. Afternoons were nice and relatively warm, but mornings opened quite frigid. Especially after rain.

Hold that thought. No need to attract more attention by making an awkward move, Ava dismissed the idea of running for that door.

"No, I don't need to be anywhere right now," she said, her voice low. "I guess staying here for a bit may not be such a bad idea." She succumbed to the invitation and sat across from him.

The stranger looked at her with curiosity, trying to guess her. "I must apologize again," he said as he reached across the table and placed the coffee in front of her.

She gently nibbled her upper lip. "Oh, my goodness! That's so precious! No one ever apologized to me for my own clumsiness. I'm glad my spilled coffee didn't get you, though."

"Are you okay? Any burns, blisters … besides the obvious damage to your dress?" His tone beamed with sympathy.

She half-squinted and tilted her head slightly, pressing her lips briefly to conceal a smirk. "Does my ego count?"

"Absolutely!" he approved with an amused grin.

"Then, yes … that. Well … also, I'll have to spend the rest of my day in the world's capital of perfume, smelling like plain damn coffee. How original of me!" She rolled her eyes as she puffed softly, aiming to appear stress-free.

The stranger laughed. "You have a wicked sense of humour. I don't know anyone who'd go through something like you just did, with more grace than you did."

Ava lifted the cup to take a sip. "I hope this coffee is worth the experience, at least." Her gaze shifted to the cup in her grip, gauging it. "This is not my coffee. This cup feels full, and I'm sure mine had less than half left when I was done splattering every soul in sight," she said, and stared intently into his eyes for the first time, gnawing at her bottom lip.

Those eyes ... those features... perfectly fitting the rest of him. Of all the shiny shoes in Paris, how the fuck did I manage to step on his?

The stranger laughed softly. *She is something else. Clever and mockingly funny*—he mused, before continuing out loud: "Well, I thought it would be a shame to go through what you did and not have a good cup of coffee, at least. I ruined your day ... Doing something to sweeten it up a bit seemed just right. Luckily, Jean-Pierre remembered what you ordered." His gaze flipped to the guy behind the coffee counter, and Ava assumed that must be Jean-Pierre. "So, here's your replacement coffee. Sadly, it may not sweeten your day. I just figured you take your coffee black. Still, it's the least I could do." He shrugged awkwardly.

"Oh ... so you disapprove of black coffee. The good news is that, once it dries enough, I hope the stain won't be visible any-more. I guess there's something good in that." She smirked, rais-ing a casual shoulder.

His lips curled a little, amazed by her practical logic and the detached way in which she looked at all that trouble. "As a matter of fact, I approve of black coffee. It just so happens that we have the same taste ... At least in coffee." He paused. "Are you always this positive?"

"Well ... let's say I'd gladly trade any of the bad, or very bad days of my life, for a day in Paris when all I need to do is wear my damn coffee. Wearing some or a whole cup of coffee doesn't sound as intense as the alternative. Yet, I got a coffee, which is a plus." She smiled. "So, this turns out to be a good day. Thank you for the coffee, by the way. Here's to good days." Ava raised her cup in a toast, aiming to sound emancipated while remaining evasive.

She then took a sip and sighed in satisfaction. The coffee was good—possibly all that incident-worthy.

The stranger smiled. *And she's original*—he made a mental note. "Sorry. I'm such a fool. Allow me. I'm Caden. Caden Hamil-ton." He extended his hand across the table while scrutinizing her face, as if trying to catch her reaction.

Displaying a mocking smile, she reached across the table, her fingers barely touching his. "Ava. Um ... Ava Martin. Ironically, making a fool out of myself at Chez Martin."

"I guess you are visiting Paris, Ava?" His tone radiated sheer curiosity.

"Yes, one quick stop in Paris, among other places."

She didn't feel like sharing more and opening her soul in front of a stranger. He had a name now, but was still a stranger.

"What are your plans for today?" Caden asked, his interest escalating.

"Well, perhaps predictably, the first would be a stop at La Tour Eiffel. Once that's done ... I'll see. I have a few things on my 'to-do when in Paris' list. Not sure how much I can accomplish today, but it's only my first day here." She deliberately continued to be somewhat evasive.

Revealing too much about herself wasn't something Ava believed in. The world has been a strange place lately, and she was travelling alone. Until Madrid, she met and toured around with friends. But from Paris on, she was on her own for the next two weeks or so. Being more guarded was now part of her itinerary.

Then she noticed some unusual commotion. Her heart raced, and she peered around discreetly. Looking for clues why the uncomfortable feeling she had was spreading at an alarming rate. A knot of unease twisted in her stomach, growing stronger with each passing moment as she sensed something was off, although she couldn't tell what. Caden kept talking, and she'd heard nothing.

When her exploration proved futile, she squinted back at him and asked, "Who exactly are you, Caden Hamilton?"

He arched a brow. "What do you mean?" a touch of hesitation in his voice.

Leaning closer, she looked straight into his eyes with an inquisitive expression. "As a matter of fact, I know I'm nobody, and I'm so darn sure wearing my coffee doesn't make me any more popular, or some sort of celebrity. Yet, I noticed several cellphones emerging from pockets and pointing toward this table. Taking pictures, I assume ... Since I'm nobody, that leaves you. So, who are you?" she whispered with a rehearsed, steady smile.

"Quite observant, aren't you? You really don't know who I am?" Caden whispered back, somewhat entertained by her reaction.

Ava cocked a brow, staring into his blue eyes. "Sorry to disappoint. Should I ... know who you are? God, I hope I'm not making a bigger fool out of myself today. Well, why don't you enlighten me?" Her teeth grazed her bottom lip.

"Um ... I'm sure not everybody knows me. I was absolutely certain that we had met before, although I can't quite pinpoint when or where. So, if you were pretending, I found you were good at it. But you say you have no idea who I am. I could be wrong, and we haven't crossed paths."

Who the hell is he? Where is he aiming with this 'we met before' line? Is he a con artist? Nah, that wouldn't explain the pictures taken by all those people. Con artists keep a low profile. He must be 'somebody'. Who? Beats me! Ava mused as she held his gaze.

She leaned closer. "I don't think we've met before, and I'm not sure I'm comfortable being here anymore. The last thing I want is my picture out there, associated with—"

"Me?" he interrupted, his voice low and his eyes wide with surprise as he leaned forward, staring into her green eyes. "Well, it may not be as bad as you imagine. Who do you think I am? Humour me, please. I promise I'll tell you who I am if you don't guess."

She nibbled at her upper lip. "Huh ... So, we're playing truth or dare now. Okay, I'll take this challenge, then I'll be out of here."

"No. I'll take you out of here. If you don't mind, walk with me for a minute ... or a few. And I'd suggest you take this offer," Caden insisted, sensing she was about to back away. Biting her lower lip, Ava gave him a cautious look, trying to understand the message he was trying to convey. *We'll see*—she thought to herself. "Don't get me wrong. I enjoy talking to you, that's all. So, humour me. Please..." he added with a playful twinkle in his eyes as he continued gazing into hers.

Elbows resting on the table's edge, she squinted as she held her chin. "Oh-kay. So, let's see. Politician? No. I don't think you are. You're missing your security detail. Not a gangster—nobody would dare to take a picture of a gangster. Your physique may suggest an athlete, although your outfit says otherwise. Um ... singer, maybe?" After a quick appraisal, she added, "Nah. You're not."

"Why not?" he asked, amused and somewhat intrigued.

"Um ... Not sure... Something about you doesn't scream... rhythm, I guess. Am I wrong?" Ava paused, curious to hear his answer.

He looked at her, absorbed. "No. You're correct so far. I like your logic."

"Are you ... an actor?" Her eyebrows raised as if she'd just had a revelation, and she leaned back in her chair, away from the table's edge.

Caden also leaned back as his lips curled upwards, amazed and pleased at the same time. "Wow! I'm impressed. Well, I promised I'd take you out of here ... Ready?"

"Oh, I'm sure you have better things to do. I'll be on my way. Nice to have met you, Caden Hamilton."

"Ah ... It's Caden James Hamilton, a.k.a. CJ Hamilton. Everybody calls me CJ, which I go by as an actor, in case you feel compelled to look me up... I suppose it's only fair for you to call me CJ. Everyone does." As they were getting ready to leave Chez Martin, he added, "I still have an hour to kill. I need to be somewhere at eleven. I don't mind walking with you for a bit if you don't have to be anywhere soon. However, letting you head out alone is probably not a good idea."

As she zipped her jacket, Ava raised her eyes to meet his, astonishment clear in her expression. "Wow! Are you always this full of yourself?"

"Trust me. You could be harassed if you walk out that door alone."

"Really?! That bad, huh? Well, I'm a grown woman. Don't worry about me. I can handle myself." Her tone was flat but cocky.

"Oh, I'm sure you can. However, I wouldn't forgive myself if I allowed anything remotely unpleasant to happen to you. Please trust me." CJ pressed.

"Do I really look like I need any rescuing?" The cocky tone persisted. "Except from coffee, of course."

He laughed softly and insisted, "Well, you still have time, and I hope you'll change your mind. I'm walking out that door with you, anyway."

2. So, you really are an actor...

Meanwhile, the rain stopped. A few speckles of fluffy clouds still floated lazily in the sky. Steam rose from the trees and streets, where the sun shone. That only heightened Ava's eerie sensation that she had stepped into another world. *The weather guys are right in France*—she quickly reflected after checking the clear skies.

A subtle glance to her right revealed another unsettling scene—a few youngsters positioned as 'innocent' bystanders. Yet, with a very interested air, their cellphones pointed at Chez Martin's entrance. *For sure, taking pictures. Probably videos too*—Ava thought. *Oh, no! What have I gotten myself into? I don't like this*—she blamed herself.

Discreetly, CJ guided her to turn left. Her shoulders tensed and squared; a clear sign she had already noticed the strategically placed group of prying onlookers. CJ didn't miss the change.

"*La Tour Eiffel* is to the left. We'll also avoid those guys if you walk with me." His lips barely moved as he spoke.

"How do you know they won't follow?" she asked, reasonably mystified by the circumstances.

"One or two may be more determined, yes. They are mostly interested when they suspect I may be romantically involved with someone. I'd suggest we walk for a while. Hopefully, we'll lose them. Then, we'll hop in a taxi, and I'll drop you off wherever you want," he said. Her head buzzing, Ava quickened her pace. *Romantically involved? Is that supposed to be reassuring?* "Ava, you don't have to worry. I'll take care of this," CJ added after just a few steps.

"I'm not worried," she pushed back.

"You're running … almost."

"I walk. This is how I walk," she countered.

CJ slowed down, subtly grabbing her forearm and gently guiding her to match his pace. "Please, running isn't a good idea. It might seem to others like we have something to hide. You have no idea what kinds of rumours they can start. You're married. Running could make it look bad. Especially for you. You don't want that, do you?"

"Married!" she winced, prompted by his affirmation.

"Well, if you want to pretend you're not, you probably shouldn't be wearing that engagement ring and wedding band. I'm sorry, I couldn't help but notice them."

Her lashes drooped slightly as she subtly glanced at her left hand, biting her upper lip. "Oh, that! Yes, right!"

"If I were your husband, I wouldn't let you travel alone. Paris is the city of romance, after all. However, none of my business. Please, just keep up the pace and act as if you're doing nothing wrong. And don't look back. No shoulder check, nothing. Okay?" CJ said with a slight grin, as if he were casually talking about the weather.

Ava nodded with a sour-bitter smile, shifting her eyes as if weighing whether his suggestion was the right move. "Oh-kay." Her stomach clenched with anxiety, irritated by the whole situation. *How lucky I am you're not my husband! Not that you'd want to be. You are at least ten years my junior, buddy. And you're so damn right. It's none of your business!*

"So, you travel alone. Where from?" He tried to steer the conversation towards something more mundane and ease her tension.

For reasons she couldn't understand, she suddenly felt

safer and more relaxed. "Many places." She gnawed at her upper lip. "I live in Canada. That's where this trip started. However, as you probably guessed from my accent, I'm from Eastern Europe. More specifically, from Romania. I was born and raised there," she continued, thinking there was no harm in sharing some details.

"Romania? Interesting," he commented.

"You think? We're not all descendants of Dracula, you know?" she replied, entertained. It was what most people knew about Romania.

He sneered, glancing at her. "Oh, I know. I was in Romania. For work. Nice people. And funny, just like you."

"Ha … funny, yes. You got that part right. About Romanians, I mean. If I must go further back, I'm part Austrian, part Hungarian, and probably more. Who knows?"

"I see. Suppose you don't mind me asking … When I mentioned you were married, your reaction was a bit… I don't know… You acted… um… surprised. Almost like you just remembered that … little *detail*?" he asked with a nosy air. "You know … never mind. I can see I made you uncomfortable, which wasn't my intention. I shouldn't have asked." His tone flipped.

After a few seconds of hesitation, she glanced up at him, trying to evaluate whether sharing anything with this stranger was a good idea. He looked out for her, making sure she was safe. And he seemed honest. *Most likely, he wouldn't do anything stupid to damage his career or public image.* Then, she decided she'd never see him again, so … what *the heck!*

"About that…" She glanced down at her left hand. "I'm not married … sort of." She broke the silence, her voice faded.

"Sort of!" Almost laughing, he looked at Ava again and noticed some hurtful thoughts clouding her expression. Instantly, he knew laughing might not be the most appropriate response. "So, it's a prop."

"A prop?" she asked, surprised by his statement.

"A prop … You know… Like in movies and photo shoots. Something just for show. Probably to keep away pesky guys …

like me?" He theorized nearly smugly while trying to offer her a line to escape his interrogation.

Ava fiddled with her rings. "I know what a prop is … but no. It's… not that. It's not a bad hypothesis, though. I'll keep it in mind. It may work that way, too. I'm a widow," she quickly added in a dim voice, without looking at him. "I lost my husband over a year ago, during the pandemic. I couldn't bring myself to take these off," she continued in one breath, voice catching in her throat. "This trip … this is me in search of closure. And these rings will probably come off at the end of it. At least, this is the plan."

"Oh, my! I'm so sorry for your loss. I'm such a dork. I shouldn't have asked. I'm … I'm terribly sorry." He nearly stuttered, genuine regret for his insensitive question evident in his tone.

Ava halted and turned toward him. "No need to apologize. Three years ago, my late husband, Dan, and I set off on a trip across Europe, just as the world was on the brink of the pandemic. We didn't get very far. The day we landed in Europe, Italy went into lockdown, and Italy was part of our travel plan. Rumours were that other European countries would also impose lockdowns. We reassessed our options, cancelled everything, managed to get on a flight back to Canada, and that's how our legendary European adventure came to an end. Almost a year later, Dan fell ill and passed away. Now, here I am, finishing alone what we began together."

His gaze darkened as he exhaled. "Oh, my!"

"Though this time, I'm going backwards. I didn't want to complicate things by having to explain to every customs official all over Europe about the powder I was 'smuggling' in my luggage. I took my late husband's ashes to Romania." Ava explained the powder reference. "This is where I'm coming from. I've already made it through four countries, and I'm on my way out of Europe and back home to Canada. That's home for me, now." She sighed, forcing a smile.

"Wow! That's … so brave of you!" Thick stillness fell between them as they took a few more steps. "I don't mean to pry, but … do you have kids?" CJ broke the awkward silence.

"Do you see any around?" she asked, a little irritated, before re-evaluating her attitude. "No. No kids. They would be with me, I guess. I just buried my husband, who would've been their father … Sorry, I didn't mean to be rude. I'm just a bit…"

"It's understandable. I'm sorry I asked," his tone, full of empathy. "It seems like today, making conversation isn't my strong suit. I keep asking all the wrong questions."

"It's not you. It's not like you run into pathetic souls every day."

Ava had already decided—there was no reason to put any more effort into exploring the kids' theme. The topic was even more difficult for her to discuss and open her soul about. Not to a stranger, anyway. That would be a story for another place, another time … if ever. They walked in silence for a few moments.

Why do I feel like an idiot today? CJ pondered what to say. What subject wouldn't touch another sensitive side of hers? Or re-open another wound?

Ava was the first to break the awkward silence. "Well, enough about me. How about you?"

CJ cocked his head, looking at her, somewhat surprised. "Me?"

"Yes, you … Same questions… Your questions. Where are you from? What are you doing in Paris? I suppose you're not married. I don't see the seal of the deal on you. So, no need to answer that." She looked at him, displaying a soft smile.

"Seal of the deal … I like it!" he exclaimed in an elated tone. "Well, I'm from the UK. Born and raised. London is my home. And you're correct, I haven't sealed any deals in the marriage department yet. I'm in Paris because I imprudently agreed to partake in an audition. That's where I must be at eleven. Unfortunately, I can't go into any details about it. I mean, I'm not allowed to share details about the project."

"Oh! So, you really are an actor," she teased.

"Sort of," he teased back, clearly intending to replicate that moment when she said she was not married, 'sort of'. Both burst into genuine laughter. "You can discover more about me on the big wide web. Possibly a lot more than I'd like to share. And not all of it is true," he finished in a cheeky tone.

She chuckled. "Right?!" her voice, a bit too affected. "Hmm ... the web... You know... detecting what's real and what's fake can be time-consuming. I believe you are the most educated source of information on yourself. So, I'm tempted to stick with the source. I prefer to form my own opinion about people, rather than rely on others' assessments or speculation. I can only imagine there's plenty out there. I'd probably look you up and watch or read some of your online interviews. I'm sure I'll find some. That should still count as coming directly from the source, correct?" she said in a rather amused tone.

"That's correct! I truly appreciate it! Most people would choose the easier route." He smiled at the thought—*She's not the type who falls for gossip.* "That's my taxi." CJ pointed to the street corner, about fifty yards from where they were. "La Tour Eiffel, you said? I can drop you off there. If there's any trace of anyone still following, we'll lose them now. Before getting in, may I ask what your plans are for tomorrow?"

Ava's eyes widened, her eyebrows raised, as she chuckled, half-surprised, half-uncomfortable. "Tomorrow! Why are you curious about my plans?"

"I was thinking ... After today's audition, I'll be in Paris for a few more days. I'm not sure exactly why they booked me for five days. If I get the part, I presume they have in mind a meeting for dinner, drinks, or both. In the meantime, I'll be in Paris with no plans other than keeping my evenings open for a potential meeting. So, what do you think about coffee tomorrow? Same place? Same time?" With an arched eyebrow, he looked at her, seriousness shining through his tone.

She gave a puzzled scowl. "And ... what time was that? I have no clue what time I was at Chez Martin. The place is easy to remember; it has my name on it, and my friend, Mr. Google, will give me directions if I get lost. I just bumped into it by chance..." She paused as if she had changed her mind. "You know what? I can't promise anything. I'm on vacation. Just taking my time and playing it by ear, mostly. I travelled through a bunch of time zones in the past month. I'm a tad discombobulated. I don't want to say I'll be there, then won't show up because I can't kick myself out of bed. I'm sure you can find better things to do in Paris." She digressed.

His mouth opened and closed. Then he quickly followed an idea that just popped into his head. "Do you have a cellphone?"

"Duh! Who doesn't, in this day and age?" She giggled.

"Do you mind passing it to me for a second, please?" he continued in the same serious tone.

She pouted, flashing a skeptical gaze through squinty eyes. "Why would I give you my phone?"

Seriousness still there, he pressed, "Just want to put my number in your phone, that's all. It's totally up to you if you want to text me, so I'll also have your number. All I can promise is that I'm not a weirdo. I won't be stalking you..." He grinned.

She laughed half-heartedly, her hesitant hand reaching into the aqua-green backpack slung over her shoulder. Tugging at her lower lip while considering her thoughts, she fished out her cellphone but paused, lips pressed together.

Sensing her reluctance, "No obligations, okay? If you don't want to text, you don't have to. We say goodbye, and that's it." He shrugged, a hint of regret passing over his face. "It's entirely up to you to text, keep my number, or delete it. That said, I'd like you to text." His lips curved into a genuine smile.

She tilted her head, teeth grazing her lower lip, but handed over her cellphone. "Oh-kay."

"Great. There you go." CJ returned her cellphone after punching in his number. "Whenever you decide, text me and say who you are. Just don't call. I don't answer unknown numbers, and ... remember? I don't have your number yet. I won't stalk you.

I promise," he mentioned again with a reassuring grin.

"Oh, I can block you if you do," she countered teasingly.

He laughed, clearly entertained. "See? You know what to do."

"Before you gave me your number, did you stop to consider … what if *I am* a stalker?" she continued taunting.

He snickered, slightly raising a shoulder. "Well, you just gave me the recipe for that."

"So, you said you don't answer unknown numbers? Would you—?" She paused for a few seconds. His cellphone began ringing. "—answer this?" Arching a brow, Ava flashed him a spirited look.

"I guess I'll have to make an exception. Just this once." He picked up with a crooked smile, bringing the phone to his mouth while holding her emerald-green gaze. "It wasn't that hard, was it?"

CJ held the taxi door open so Ava could get in. The cab driver, a man of no particular age, probably over forty-five, and who knows what, greeted in Italian, "Ciao! Benvenutti!" his tone upbeat, eyes sparkling dark from under bushy eyebrows against an olive-toned face.

"Ciao, Paolo," CJ said, hopping through the opposite door into the taxi's back seat, next to Ava.

Paolo glanced at Ava, probably trying to guess the relationship between his long-time client and the woman he was with. Ava herself was trying to figure out the relationship between the two men.

Way before they arrived, CJ knew this was his taxi, waiting for him, and the two seemed to be on relatively friendly terms.

And why is this important? She gave an internal shrug and dismissed her own curiosity.

The taxi driver continued chatting with CJ in Italian. "So, I can see you have a new girlfriend," Paolo commented, appraising

Ava through the rear-view mirror.

Without flinching, Ava nibbled at her upper lip as if she didn't get what he said. After a quick glance at her, CJ concluded she didn't understand the driver's forward remark.

"Just a friend, Paolo. Not my girlfriend," he replied in Italian.

"*Si-si* ... *For* now, maybe. You should make her your girlfriend. She's pretty and smells good," the meddlesome driver continued, checking Ava out through the mirror again.

She appeared preoccupied, re-examining the dress, and the quick assessment gave her some satisfaction. *One can't even see it when I'm walking. Standing still may be a different story, but I'll be on the move. So...*

The nosy driver kept chatting in Italian—part of their agreement, so CJ had the chance to practice and improve his Italian. Whenever he was in Paris for business or travel, Paolo was his on-call driver. The two had grown quite close a few years earlier, during CJ's second visit to Paris after he became a celebrity with 'full privileges', easily recognized everywhere. Therefore, public transportation or other means were no longer desirable options for him.

CJ stole another quick glimpse at Ava, observing her demeanour. By now, he knew Paolo could be quite straightforward in his comments.

She flashed him a broad smile. "He's quite chatty, eh?!" she asked, feigning ignorance about the discussion between the two.

"He says you smell good. And I must admit he's right. So, I guess that 'damn coffee' did the trick." CJ winked and smiled back, probably intending to distract her attention from the dress she kept inspecting.

"I guess it did. Well, coffee is a note in some fragrances. Between the perfume I put on this morning and the coffee, I must smell like nobody else in Paris." She gave a vague smile before biting her lower lip and shifting her gaze out the window.

"So original of you," CJ mocked.

Her gaze returned to him, a smile lighting up her face once again. "Right?!" she asked rhetorically.

Ten minutes later, the taxi pulled over near Trocadero Square. Before she could reach for the door lever to get out of the cab, CJ's lips curled into a gentle smile. "So … See you tomorrow morning at Chez Martin for coffee? Please message me … only if you can't make it."

"Okay. No promises, though, other than … I'll try," Ava said as she exited the taxi. "Thank you for the coffee … and the ride." She leaned in before shutting the taxi door. "And … break a leg."

On the curb, she blew a soft sigh as she looked ahead. The Eiffel Tower stood majestically before her. She glanced over her left shoulder for a moment, watching the taxi pull away. CJ looked back and waved at her. In response, she smiled with a raised hand.

"What a morning!" she muttered, letting out a deep sigh of relief.

She started toward the monumental Eiffel Tower, trying not to be self-conscious about the stain on her dress. Not visible anymore to the unadvised. However, continuing to check it might prompt others to notice it. *Whatever! Nobody knows me in Paris. There are better things to look at right now. I can stare at the damn stain when I get home. It'll still be there. Eventually,* she brushed off her own uncertainty.

In her favourite, comfortable, white platform sneakers, every step took her closer and closer to the Eiffel Tower. She had imagined this breathtaking moment her entire life. As she got close enough, she stopped for a minute to admire the magnificent masterpiece in front of her, take some pictures and remind herself to breathe.

Finally, here! She sighed.

3. She's walking with a purpose

That Friday morning, after wrestling to get ready and mostly succeeding at getting tangled in organizing and reorganizing the laundry and such, Ava finally walked into Chez Martin for coffee. For twenty minutes, she worked on her doubts, ironing out her confidence as she followed the landmarks to get there.

Just like the previous day, her nose picked up the same trailing flavours. Unlike the day before, this time, she also detected the aroma of coffee, mixed with that of freshly baked French pastries.

She had already made up her mind. *He won't be there. For sure, he forgot about my existence the minute that taxi took off.* So, she stepped inside and waited in line. Surprise! The queue was much shorter than the day before. She viscerally hated standing in line. *I guess Parisians don't drink coffee on Fridays! Fine by me.*

While waiting in line for her turn, Ava scrutinized the activity behind the counter, trying to find out if the same staff were working today. To her disappointment, the answer was 'yes, same staff'. She scoffed quietly. *Well, the coffee was good, so it's worth staying. And cross my fingers, they won't recognize me.*

In just a few short days, she'll make room for another fool to take her place, so they can laugh at someone else's expense. Until then, she wasn't about to take any chances on her coffee fix.

She already knew she was a bit of a snob when it came to coffee. Or 'such a snob!' as others would say. Hence, she decided to stay and face the … whatever.

Uneasy, she shifted her weight and peered again. She caught a brief exchange of gazes between one guy behind the counter—Jean Pierre, if she understood correctly the day before—and someone else. The people in line obstructed her view, so she couldn't see who the other person was. She glanced at her fitness tracker and checked the time. Eight twenty-two. As if she had anywhere to be. She stifled a giggle at her own silliness.

A sudden, gentle grasp at her elbow caused her gaze to shift to the right as she slowly lifted her lashes. Concealed beneath a flattop, CJ stood beside her, discreetly motioning with his head for her to follow. Before Ava arrived, he sat at a table, sipping his coffee and waiting patiently.

As if hypnotized, she began following him back to his table. But she stopped after only a few steps, her gaze flicking to the queue she had just left. *I'm here for coffee.*

"Your coffee is coming, don't worry about it," he said as if he read her mind.

Ava tugged at her upper lip, cocking an eyebrow. He began to understand, somehow, that she bit her upper lip when she wanted to say something but wasn't sure if she should. And she bit her lower lip whenever she tried to digest something she'd just heard and wasn't sure what to make of.

"How did you know I was coming?" Her voice dripped with curiosity.

He raised a shoulder, his gaze carrying something deeper, as if he knew the future. "It's the best coffee in Paris, in my opinion. I noticed that, just like me, you are a coffee enthusiast. I thought you wouldn't miss the opportunity to have the perfect coffee," he replied with a nearly brash smile. "Plus, you didn't text. I figured there was hope you'd show up. Unless you were still asleep."

Ava's gaze stilled for a split second. *Right! He asked me to text if I couldn't make it. Oops! I completely forgot. Well, I made it. And here I thought ...* She concealed a slight cringe as she turned to hang her jacket on the back of her chair, embarrassed by her biased judgment.

"So, I just happened to stumble upon the best coffee in Paris?" Ava asked mockingly.

"I guess you did. Although I'm not claiming I tried it all."

It turned out it was Jean-Pierre, indeed, who had been watching for her arrival. *Huh! So much for hoping I wouldn't be recognized.* Just a few minutes later, Jean-Pierre floated past customers and tables with two cups of coffee and set them in front of Ava and CJ. The allusive smirk he flaunted triggered a twitch in Ava's eyebrow.

"How did yesterday go? Did you have time to check off a lot of the things on your 'to-do when in Paris' list?"

Ava's evasive reply, "Some," fell quite plain.

"Aha ... Some. Any plans for today?"

"Yes, I have quite a plan. It may require more coffee, and I'm armed with some protein bars for lunch on the go. Today is not just about 'going up and down a tower'. This one will take a few hours, depending on how long I last..."

CJ tilted his head, displaying an officious expression as he waited to hear more. "And ... may I ask... what? I'm trying to make it up to you for yesterday, but you keep your cards close to your chest, and I'm a bit hesitant to ask. Yesterday, my questions didn't go so well. How about you tell me about yourself? If you feel like sharing your plans for the day, I think that would be a good start." His shoulders rose in a quick, uncertain motion.

With a faint shrug, she shook her head as if chasing away a bothersome thought. "I'm sorry. Yesterday I was a bit out of it. Bad memories, or what would've been some kind of memories."

Over two years earlier, Ava and her late husband, Dan, began their European tour in London. Their idea of an extravagant vacation. Their plan? Continue through Europe, up to Romania.

In the city of romance, by herself, the love of her life wasn't with her. That was enough heartache.

Ava exhaled sharply, fingers curling around her cup. *This was supposed to be my quiet, solo adventure, and this stranger popped out of nowhere to muddy the waters with his questions. And … my God, he's relentless! Keeps showing up like a bad penny! Whatever!* Paris should have been Dan's surprise for her. Now, it was just her and this stranger.

Ava's chest tightened as random echoes of earlier days attempted to take over her mind. Uninvited. *Memories are good, but when you get stuck in memories, you're not living anymore.* And she wanted to live. In the present. Looking forward into the future.

She had learned to push grief aside, but some days, it still coiled around her like a snake. Yet, she became an expert at hiding the pain. She didn't want to hide it anymore. All she wanted was not to feel it. Ever! If only that were possible! She was learning to live with it.

She shook off her thoughts, forcing a smile. "Well … my day, you'll probably find, will be… boring. But I'm a big sucker for art, history, archaeology … all ancient and uninteresting things. But they speak to me." She paused, glaring at CJ as if she were just about to reveal some horrendous detail. "You probably wouldn't guess, but Le Louvre is on my 'to-do when in Paris' list for today." He stared at her, arching a dazed eyebrow. "Yup … I was sure you'd find it insipid. No surprise there," she gently drew the conclusion.

"Why do you think I'd find it insipid?" His voice rose a note.

"Well, your face said it, not me. You seemed surprised by my choice."

"I, indeed, am surprised … but not by your choice. I have the same kind of attraction to all things … how did you put it? Ancient and uninteresting? I'm quite passionate, actually. I thought you might prefer to go … I don't know… maybe perfume shopping? Do you mind if I tag along?" He seized the opportunity with a disarming smile. "I haven't visited Le Louvre since high school. I'm sure I'll see much of it with fresh eyes now, so many years later."

"Oh! You really don't have anything better to do in Paris, eh?!"

He flicked a hand. "Maybe a day at Le Louvre is better than what I would've picked."

"Ha. Well, as long as I don't have to carry you ... It's entirely up to you if you want to tag along. Just don't blame me if you get bored to death, okay?"

Once at Le Louvre, Ava revealed she already had two admission tickets.

"So, you were going to invite me?" CJ's curiosity was barely concealed behind a half-brazen smile, although his tone sounded teasing.

"Please don't get ahead of yourself. I got the tickets months ago. My plans changed last night. I'm just glad the extra ticket doesn't go to waste. And if you get bored, you won't have anything to regret but your time. Oh, wait! Time killed is time killed, so it shouldn't matter how, as long as the murder gets done, right?" Ava's reply dropped promptly, just as teasing as his.

"I'm actually really excited ... Almost like I was when I first visited Le Louvre. And this time, I enjoy the company. I wouldn't call it killing time but rather spending some quality time—getting to know you, for instance."

The subtle undertone in his voice ... Ava didn't know what to make of it.

Brows arched in surprise, she scoffed, "Ah, please. No need for flattery with me. I must warn you. Flattery makes me grow suspicious. So, if you want us to remain on friendly terms, please refrain from saying anything that even slightly resembles flattery."

"See? I'm already learning about you. So, no flattery. Even if it's the truth, which may sound like flattery only to you?" He beamed a mischievous grin, earning a deadpan glare from Ava, meaning, *what wasn't clear about what I just said?* "Okay, okay! I get it! You come with a 'user manual'. Is there also a 'fine print' I should be aware of? I suppose getting to know you will be interesting. Luckily, I don't mind 'interesting'." His tone carried bold determination.

"Fine print! Huh," Ava wondered genuinely, a smirk tugging at the corner of her mouth as she slowly bobbed her head.

Tough cookie. I'm not sure I like being put in my place like this. Why don't I mind it, though? She's challenging but refreshing—CJ thought.

It had been nearly two hours since they had stepped into the wonders of the history and art displayed at Le Louvre. Amazed and overly excited, like a kid in a candy shop, Ava barrelled from room to room, CJ barely able to keep up with her excitement.

She paused in awe to admire certain items on display that intrigued her the most. Absorbing every architectural detail. Getting close, checking out the strokes in the paintings. Well, as close as the museum's rules allowed her.

A group of teenagers, as 'unnoticeable' as kids that age can be—in a museum or anywhere else—approached.

Most visitors passed their time in silence, lost in admiration. Either that or, just like Ava, set out to discover and absorb everything quietly, as if afraid they'd disturb all those centuries-old wonders. Or they'd cause Mona Lisa to toss them a crooked look or smile. A different look and smile than those that made her famous. But not these kids. They elbowed each other, subdued comments and not-too-subdued giggles echoed, bouncing between the walls and the exquisite ceilings of the palace.

A couple of older individuals, part of the same group—probably teachers—huffed and puffed, rolling their eyes in annoyance. The tour guide kept talking. Just doing his job, seemingly unbothered by the few youngsters focused more on goofing around than showing any interest in history and art. In fairness, most of them paid attention. Some even tried to straighten up their pals—the 'peace disturbers'.

And then it happened. The 'peace disturbers' spotted CJ and began sharing their discovery with the group. United, they abandoned the tour guide talking to himself and charged down the long hall to where Ava and CJ were. As twelve to fifteen snoopy teenagers instantly surrounded CJ, asking for selfies and autographs, Ava stepped aside.

CJ's quick cast toward her read like a cry for help. Tossing a demi-smile in reply, she shrugged and kept walking, leaving the too-noisy cluster behind.

Minutes later, finally escaping the curious bunch, CJ began searching for Ava. But she was nowhere in sight. Glancing at all the nooks, crannies, and chambers, he marched through the vast halls of the palace as if he were the king himself.

One last look in one of the rooms, then suddenly halted, pivoting on his heels. With an arched brow, he scrutinized up and down before considering the opposite direction. Then he frowned, scrambling to understand if he was going the wrong way.

It probably isn't where she went. Although he could've sworn that's where she was headed last time he saw her. *Did she dump me?* Just then, some slight rustling behind made him turn around.

There she was! Reeling backward as she exited the next room, her head tipped back, admiring the ceiling and taking pictures. With a precise turn to her right, her pacing determined, Ava headed toward the next chamber.

An 'Aha!' moment nudged CJ. Right there, in front of him, was his clue.

"Rome," his thought materialized out loud. Louder than acceptable in a museum.

Eyes wide, Ava halted in her tracks, completing it with a perfect one-eighty. "Oh, so you are alive. They didn't lynch you."

His laughter propagated like thunder under the high, intricate ceilings. "I don't believe lynching me was their intention."

Ava snickered, displaying a lively smile. "You looked a tad ... um, maybe the word 'stranded' isn't the right one? But for a second there, I could swear you were asking for help."

"And you didn't offer any. I thought you were my friend, but you left me stranded there," he replied with a playful smirk, perfectly in sync with his tone.

"Oh! So, I was supposed to rescue you! Sorry, I thought that what happened over there was a job hazard, and it's your duty to deal with that part. Am I wrong?" She motioned toward the other end of the hall.

"Actually, they were sweet and enthusiastic. And you're not wrong. However, Rome?" CJ reiterated, dropping a questioning stare straight into Ava's deep green eyes as his lips arched in a half-smile.

She peered around, her eyes wandering and searching for a Roman artifact. "Huh? Where?"

He chuckled, "You said you're travelling through Europe and have visited a few countries. Were you in Rome two weeks ago?"

"I-um ... sounds about right." She blinked, nearly stuttering, stupefaction clear in her expression. "Yes, I ... was in Rome... two weeks ago. How ... did you know?"

"I knew I saw you somewhere before yesterday. Your outfit today ... I mean, the same cute red sneakers, the same blue rain jacket, the one around your waist... You wore them in Rome, am I right?"

Visibly puzzled, she cringed, scrambling to remember. The last two weeks were a blur.

"Well, I travel quite light. I believe I wore this jacket and these shoes in many places around Europe. I'm not sure who you saw exactly."

"Oh, no ... I'm sure it was you. When you walked out of this room, the same thought that crossed my mind in Rome when I first saw you popped in again." Confidence radiated from his tone.

"Thought! What thought?" Ava's eyes rounded in astonishment as the words left her lips.

"She's walking with a purpose. That's what I thought when I saw you in Rome. More precisely, in Piazza Navona."

She puffed, amused. "Where?!"

"Piazza Navona. The historical centre of Rome. I was having a coffee at one of the many cafés in the piazza."

She untied the jacket from around her waist and shoved it into her backpack. "Yeah, it probably wasn't me. Doesn't ring a bell. Then again, I'm sure all places have names, but a big chunk of the time, I had no clue where I was. Besides the major objectives on my list, I didn't take the time to register much. Well, except for the memories captured in the pictures I took."

"Oh, yeah, you were taking pictures. Lots. Just like today."

"I didn't see you, though. Or ... I didn't notice you."

He scoffed. "That's because you were looking up. I remember thinking you should probably watch your step. I'm not surprised you didn't see me. Or anyone else."

Her eyes squinted, struggling to determine which day it may have been. "Was I alone?"

"I believe you were. I didn't catch anyone near you to make me think you were with someone, and the place wasn't particularly busy. Like I said, you paced with a purpose and crossed the piazza." CJ's words continued to flow with passionate conviction, each sentence more fervent than the last.

"If it was me you saw, it was probably exactly two weeks ago, in the evening. Or the following morning. My friends had trouble with their car and arrived in Rome a day late. After that, I wasn't by myself."

"Oh, it was evening."

"Well, it was my first day in Rome. Don't expect me to know where I was wandering. Exploring without a clear target. I only hoped I'd find my way back to the hotel," Ava giggled.

4. Where have you been my whole life?

After a few more minutes of quietly strolling through the museum, Ava asked in a near whisper. "By the way, I meant to ask you earlier, how did your audition go yesterday? Only if you're allowed or want to talk about it."

"Oh, I can tell you about my performance. I just can't reveal any details about the project. It went well. Maybe too well, I'm afraid."

"Too well … you're afraid! How come?" Ava chuckled.

"Well, let's just say I have a feeling I might be selected for the part. However, I'm not certain it is what I want. Not now," CJ replied, leaning close to her ear. He then pulled back and quickly stepped in front of Ava, facing her. "Can I ask you something? I need your honest opinion."

"Oh! Sure. Ask away." Her stomach clenched as uncertainty swept over her, and she wondered if her answer was the right one. Hopefully, he won't ask another question that might make her regret encouraging him.

Hesitant, he shifted his weight from one foot to the other. "What should I do? Take it? Not take it?"

Ava blinked, scowling in confusion. "Take what?"

"Take this part? It's a leading role, actually. I'm still looking for a good reason to turn it down. Yet, I don't have enough solid reasons to take it, either." His upper lip arched with doubt, letting out a small exhale.

Incredulous, she looked at him for a moment, tilting her head. "Are you asking *me* for advice on where to take your career? You can't be serious. You just met me yesterday. Literally!"

"Well, I know. See...? I mainly rely on advice from family. More often than not, they tell me what they think I want to hear, probably not wanting to hurt my feelings. My manager is all about making money, so I know exactly what he'd say." He fidgeted a bit. "You strike me as an honest person. You're not afraid to speak your mind. I could really use those qualities of yours. And this isn't me flattering you. It's the truth. And the truth must be told. I probably need to be shaken to my core right now, and no one I know would have the guts to do it. So, I'm asking you," CJ said it all at high speed, an uncomfortable sneer matching the doubt in his tone.

Wary, she pouted. "Huh ... So, you think I have the guts? I'm not sure it's my place to offer any advice on how to go about your career ... or hurt your feelings."

"Please hurt my feelings. I need an honest opinion right now."

She chuckled, pausing for a moment as if considering her response. "Well ... Could you share a bit about your career so far? What are your goals? What's this role about? I understand you can't disclose too much, but I'd still need some general points to go by."

"So, you didn't look me up?" Curiosity took a toll on him.

Her expression twisted into a bashful grimace as she shrugged. "Sorry to disappoint. As I said, I prefer to form my own opinion. Besides, I fell asleep before my laundry was done. And ... honestly? I didn't expect to see you again."

His mouth opened and closed before forming what seemed like a pleased smile. "Alright. Fair enough. Even better. Clean slate. So, about me ... Like most actors, I began with supporting roles. I did a bit of everything. However, in recent years, I have mostly played leading roles. I've mainly been cast in adventure, mystery, sci-fi, and fantasy."

She raised an eyebrow, trying to grasp the source of his uncertainty. "Oh-kay. I take it this new opportunity is a bit different from what you're known for?"

"Exactly! I knew you'd understand." His eyes sparkled with excitement.

"What's this role about?"

"It's about war, heroes, a bit of romance … It's somewhat new territory for me. And it's not that I don't want to take on this kind of role…"

Ava leaned in, intrigued. "And, if you don't mind me asking, why did you audition if it's not your thing?"

"I was invited. I truly hope I'll get the chance to prove myself in this area, just not at the minute. This is what I'm struggling with."

"I see. So, you were invited." Lips pursed, she appeared to ponder. "Question is … why?" Ava speculated as she browsed the exhibits, contemplating what she could—or should—say.

"I don't know why. Well, what's your take?"

"I'm thinking … when is it too early, too late, or just the right time to change something? Is there a universal guide for it? Because if there is, I'd like a copy. Take Bill Braun's career, for example. The guy dominated the big screen for years. He dabbled in other genres, which, personally, I find he excelled at. But ultimately, he boomeranged right back to what made him famous. Classic move," Ava sneered. "And then … he retired. Though not before spending his last few years in what I can only describe— affectionately, of course—as senior abuse. I mean, seriously … he flipped from being the leading guy to mere supporting roles. Literally, glorified cameos. Of course, he helped launch the careers of younger actors by doing it … Good for them! But as a lifelong fan of his? I found it really heart-wrenching. I'd sit through entire movies, waiting for yet another Bill Braun experience, only to find out he was in the film for what? Seven minutes? Fifteen, if I was lucky. And yet, there he was, listed first in the cast, like some kind of publicity bait. I don't know why he did it. Maybe for the art, maybe for the love of film, or perhaps because he needed cash to support a candy habit ... Who knows? But from my side of the screen, it felt like getting hyped for a gourmet meal, only to be served a stale bagel. I felt betrayed."

CJ's gaze lingered on her, a slight smile tugging at the corner of his mouth. "Interesting. I never thought of it that way. I was one of those younger actors you mentioned. He's a great actor and an even greater human being. The story goes a bit differently, but it's not my story to tell. Let's just say you were right in understanding that there may be other, deeper, quite sad reasons, in fact."

Ava winced. "Oh, it makes sense. And you're right, he's great. I truly admire his work. Excuse my rant. I didn't mean to be judgy."

"No worries. I totally get your frustration. However, there's too much passion out there. Therefore, most of us choose to keep our private life ... well, *private*."

"Yet, you are putting yours at my feet, asking me to step all over it..."

"Go for it, please!"

"Alrighty, then," she giggled. "May I ask you a few questions? But let's get one thing straight. You're on your own here. This is *your* career, *your* decision, and if it all goes south, I won't be the person you call at two A.M., wailing."

She flashed a vague, noncommittal smile. The kind that said, *I'm here for the drama, but I won't be held legally or emotionally liable for what happens next.*

"Oh, I take full responsibility. I know I have the last word. If you give me any advice and I go with it—and let's say it doesn't go as expected—ultimately, it's me taking your advice. Don't worry, I won't blame you."

"Fair enough. No advice, though. Just questions for you to consider. I don't even want to hear your answers. So, how long do you plan on being the master of the same old roles? I mean, do you expect Hollywood to keep the same opportunities available to you forever, or do you think they might just drop you? Seriously, take a look around. The industry is like that friend who ghosts you at three in the morning without warning. I understand you don't want to ruin your fans' favourite show, but honestly, would they really flip backwards if you decided to broaden your portfolio? You might even pick up a whole new fan club. Look at me. I'd probably be the first in line. From what you've said, this movie is inspired by historical events, and guess what? I'm basically a walking encyclopedia of history. I also have a soft spot for the genre you mentioned. So, why not try something different? You might surprise us all! Just saying." She shrugged casually.

"Have you watched my movie with Bill Braun?"

Ava blinked. *Is he still fifteen questions behind? Did he hear what I just—?* She raised a shoulder, making a long face. "I ... don't know. Maybe I didn't ... maybe I did, and you just left a fuzzy impression. I'm terrible at this sort of thing, so forgive my selective memory."

He flashed a beaming gaze. "Fair enough."

"Anyway, back to your question. Here's the deal. Your career isn't just about keeping your loyal fans happy. It's about you and that ever-evolving portfolio of yours. So, what's it gonna be? Are you planning to add some new chapters to that portfolio, or just leave it as is? And if you're thinking about adding to it, when exactly? Right now? Later? How much later? After you've had your third cup of coffee? Seriously, when is the best time to try something new? Let's break it down. Where do you see yourself in five, ten, or twenty years? When should you stop lurking in your comfort zone and start working on those big ideas? Have you asked yourself why you were invited to this audition in the first place? Was it because you're a superstar? I don't know ... Are you a superstar?" She breathed a chuckle. "Is this a win-win situation, or are you just the guy they use to benefit themselves? Remember, the future is a one-way ticket, and ... spoiler alert, you're not exactly getting any younger. Nobody is. So, score those opportunities now, because trust me, missed opportunities will haunt you like that embarrassing photo you wish you could erase," Ava ended the ad hoc rant. Then she turned to CJ and shrugged, sulking as she cast a gaze that implied: *This is all I've got.*

He stared at her for a long moment as if he saw an apparition. "What photo?"

She rolled her eyes. "Don't we all have a skeleton in the back of our closet? It was just an example ... If there really is an embarrassing photo, you should know better..."

"Where have you been my whole life?" He broke from the trance. "This is what I needed. A wake-up call. You nailed it. And, oh, my! Everything's much clearer right now. Thank you, thank you, and thank you! I have to hug you. I must." Without waiting for her approval, he hoisted her into a hug.

CJ's embrace took Ava by surprise. Totally unexpected! "Wow, the bear hug!" She chuckled sheepishly when he released her from the strong, swift heave that briefly lifted her off the ground. "And please, don't thank me. I only challenged you, merely offering a different perspective. The decision is still yours to make."

"You have no idea how much you helped. I knew I needed fresh eyes on this 'doubtful me' situation. Someone to challenge me the way you just did. A different perspective, as you said. Now I can see the forest." His eyes sparkled with excitement.

"Now you can see the forest," she repeated, entertained.

"You know, it's a saying ... You can't see the forest for the trees! When someone is too close to something or too involved, and they lose sight of the bigger picture..."

Hmm ... Another one who thinks accent equals stupid—she thought before she continued out loud, "Oh, I know. We have the same saying in Romania. And in Canada. Well, I'm glad I could help. At least, I hope I did."

"You absolutely did. And I'm sorry. I should've known you got it. You are too brilliant for me even to think you didn't understand what I meant by the forest thing. Yet, I believe I've just made a friend for life! I owe you big time!" he continued as if he had read her mind again.

"Hmm..." She stopped to admire the Nike of Samothrace statue. *Magnificent!* "What do you think about this?" Ava asked, turning toward him.

"Fabulous!" he said, jumping like a schoolboy caught cheating.

Are we talking about the same thing? Was he looking at my ass? Pretending she had to adjust her shoelaces, Ava crouched and let him gain a few steps—his opportunity to reflect on what she said.

"What are your plans for tomorrow?" The question fell out of nowhere when she caught up with him. "I still need to keep my evenings open. Well, coffee in the morning, of course. That's already *tradition,* so to speak, and I hope you agree we all need coffee. What would you say about lunch as well? Of course, if you don't have other plans ... I see you're pretty well organized and have it all planned ahead." One could tell he was hopeful she'd say 'yes'.

"Tomorrow would be my shopping day, meaning nothing concrete, other than ... probably perfume shopping as someone suggested." She flashed a shrewd smile before continuing. "Not planning for a full shopping experience. I don't want to go over the luggage limit. It'll probably be just a little something to remember Paris by. Otherwise, just a relaxing day. Sleeping in ... wandering, browsing and checking out things. But, as you just said, one needs coffee and food. So, I guess lunch is fine."

Enthusiastic, he made the characteristic motion with his arm and fist as if she had just given him the answer he was hoping for. "Yes!"

*Dammit! All I wanted was some peace and quiet, not this daily game of Guess Who's Coming to ... lunch now? Well, I brought him here. My mistake—*a thought crossed her mind, holding a poker face as she said, "However, just so we're clear, you don't owe me anything."

They continued through Le Louvre, and the conversation shifted toward the history of the place and the artifacts before them. He seemed more relaxed, and his gaze didn't appear to wander anymore.

Nobody bothered them after the group of teenagers drifted away. Possibly, nobody else noticed him. Most people seemed to do exactly what they were there for—dive into the palace's history and the exhibits. For many, it was probably the same as for Ava, a once-in-a-lifetime occasion to see up close all those history-filled wonders. Or maybe slip back in time and feel like a monarch. And who knows, it may have been just another item to be checked off their bucket list.

About twenty minutes later, CJ pulled the vibrating cellphone out of his pocket.

He glanced at it, scowled, and said, "I need to take this call," before quickly stepping out.

The day at Le Louvre was getting close to an end. His expression beamed with anticipation as he scurried behind Ava and leaned into her ear. "I got it."

Ava jumped when his whisper sent a blow of warm breath that tickled her, shivers coursing down her spine, and she turned her startled gaze to him. "Got it? Do you mean—?"

A wide grin spread across his face as he nodded. "They just called me. I said yes, in case you're wondering. I'll meet them for dinner tonight. We'll go over everything else—financials, timelines, and so on."

"Wow! Well then, congratulations. I'm so happy for you!" Ava reacted, genuinely thrilled.

"And guess what? All of a sudden, my tomorrow evening just opened up. So, how about celebrating with a nice dinner? I mean coffee, lunch, dinner ... Everything? You're my lucky charm."

She chuckled quietly. "Do you always get this excited? Not

that it's a bad thing. Not at all. I was simply thinking that you might want to celebrate with people closer to you."

"Right here and now, you are the closest to me. You're the one who helped with this decision. So, who would be a better fit? However, I may need to head back to my hotel and prepare for the meeting right now. I'll likely need to leave in about twenty to thirty minutes. I can drop you off wherever you need. I've already called Paolo to pick us up."

"Great! I think it won't be longer than twenty minutes."

Half an hour later, Paolo picked them up. While driving the two to Le Louvre in the morning, he mostly listened and didn't say much, as Ava and CJ were deep in a conversation. But now, he was quite chatty. Naturally, CJ carried on the discussion with Paolo in Italian. Ava gazed out the window, saying little in response when CJ translated and asked her opinion.

This Paolo didn't leave a good impression on her. He was prying, and his questions were far too personal for her liking. Or maybe she was mistaken. Perhaps he acted this way only around CJ since they had known each other for a few years, as she understood. Ava sensed that keeping her distance was the only way to avoid Paolo's intrusiveness. She didn't feel the need to disclose that she speaks and understands Italian very well.

And sure enough, Paolo couldn't help but ask CJ, "So, still not your girlfriend?"

"Well, it's complicated. I must admit, though, I'm tempted to. Now that I've gotten to know her a bit, I can tell she's amazing. We'll see how this goes," CJ responded, giving Ava a quick glance.

In her corner, she cringed, her eyes launching lasers from behind the sunglasses. *Good for you, CJ. Make him shut up!* She thought. A few minutes into their ride, she asked to be dropped off. Without a clue of where she was, she only knew she needed something to eat. Then, another one of her friends, Miss Guiding People Safely, as she liked to call it—aka GPS—would take her back to the loft.

CJ's cautious fingertips lightly grazed her shoulder as she

slipped out of the taxi. "Hey! Text me in the morning when you wake up. And thanks so much for today."

"No. *Thank you* for spending time with a damsel in distress," Ava replied with a sincere smile. "And … I'll text you when I'm up."

"Promise?"

"Cross my heart."

She shut the door and waited for the taxi to drive away before beginning to understand where she was. Then she checked the map, only to realize she was far from where she needed to be. *No rush.*

Coming across several restaurants, she looked them up on the 'big wide web,' checked the menus, and read some reviews, trying to find something appealing that fit her specific diet. Too specific, she figured, in the last few weeks since she was travelling.

If nothing fits, I'll have to find a grocery store and cook again—she sighed. But she wasn't in the mood to cook. Eventually, she found a lovely restaurant close to her loft. Nothing fancy, but some nicely spiced chicken and a massive salad to satisfy her hunger.

Already in her jammies, sprawled on the bed, Ava was sifting through the cluster of pictures on her cellphone. Deleting the crappy ones and saving the outstanding captures of the day. The shots worth keeping began transferring from the cellphone to her laptop. *This may take a while*—she thought, reeling into the kitchenette and pouring herself a glass of sparkling water.

The well-known notification sound of a new text message made her glance toward the bed. She scowled and dismissed it as just another sound. Nobody would message her.

Unless one of her friends, who knew she was travelling alone, checked on her well-being. They promised they would if they didn't hear from her daily. She hasn't messaged anyone since yesterday. Her gaze shifted to the clock above the door. *Hmm …*

Almost ten. Wow! They really freaked out. It's been less than twenty-four hours. Even the police wouldn't open a missing person case this soon.

Ava arched a baffled brow as she glared at the cellphone she picked up from the bed. In disbelief, she tapped on the new message. From CJ.

> You sleeping?

Ava replied promptly,

> Not yet.

> Can I ring you? I need to talk to you. It's important.

> Sure.

I wonder what happened. She was just moments away from finding out.

Sprawled back on the bed, Ava quickly tapped the screen when her cellphone rang. "Is everything alright?" she asked.

"Yes and no. I mean, the meeting went well."

"Oh! That's good, right?"

"Yes, all is fine in that regard. However, I got a call about thirty minutes ago from Rob, my oldest brother. My mum broke her leg."

"Oh, my goodness! I'm sorry to hear this. Is she okay otherwise? Other than the leg, I mean?"

"Yes, but knowing my mum, she's probably fretting over a million things right now. However, it turns out I'm the only one available to be there for the next few days until my sister returns from vacation and takes over. Meaning, unfortunately, I'll have to leave Paris tomorrow morning. I'm really sorry about everything we had planned. I'll have to take a rain check on it," he jabbered without taking a breath.

"Don't worry about it. Family comes first! Go, take care of

your mom. It was great meeting you. And ... thanks for letting me know about the change in plans."

"Oh, it's just for now. I'll make it up to you, I promise." Seriousness came through in his tone again. "I'll be in Canada next month for a couple of weeks. Working. I might show up in Edmonton for a day. Possibly a whole weekend."

"You know that's easier said than done, right? Canada is a big country," Ava giggled. "Not sure where you'll be working. It may not be conveniently close to Edmonton, but that's okay. You really don't need to worry about that."

"You don't want me to visit you?" As he asked, CJ's voice conveyed a palpable sense of dismay, as if something had deeply affected him.

"That's not what I said. I meant if it doesn't happen, it won't be the end of the world. Really, you don't need to go to any lengths to try. You'll be busy working."

"Alright. As long as you don't tell me to 'go to hell' ... you'll see. I keep my promises. Always!" he said, a smile tucked beneath determination.

Ava genuinely chuckled. "Okay, I believe you. There's plenty of time to make plans, change them, and come up with new ones. Now, first things first ... think about your mom. Go and take care of her! Have a good night, and I'll see you when I see you."

"Until I see you, can I call you? I'd like you to challenge me sometimes. I'd really enjoy chatting with you every now and then. We remain friends, right?" he asked, a bit too eager.

"Absolutely! You're my only celebrity friend. I have no pets, no kids ... What would I talk about when it comes to small talk? You know I'm kidding, right? I don't need that kind of attention, so you can be sure I won't talk or gossip about you." She chuckled again, entertained. This reminded her she was contemplating getting a dog. She needed another soul around so she wouldn't talk to herself anymore and appear as if she were crazy. "And if you ever come to Edmonton, don't be a stranger. Call or drop by for coffee, lunch, dinner ... whatever time of the day may be. You might be surprised to find that I can make a decent cup of coffee, easily navigate the kitchen, and am pretty good with my pots and pans. Well … despite what a certain coffee cup may have suggested about me."

He laughed. "So, see you soon. And expect a call from me before I see you. When I visit, I'll bring what goes in those pots and pans, and we can have a cook-off. Once again, I'm truly sorry. Good night, and safe travels!"

"Take care of your mom and yourself, okay? Bye now, and good night." She hung up. "Well … guess who's not coming to dinner?" She muttered to herself.

Ava enjoyed the mundane life of the metropolis for two more days, doing a bit of shopping, a bit of this and a bit of that—nothing extravagant. But, hey! Who leaves Paris without a new perfume? Especially since she collects them, which she 'failed' to mention. She adored all the nice-smelling things. So, this was just another chance to add to her collection. Many wouldn't understand her perfume 'addiction'.

Ava saved her last evening in Paris for a stroll along the Seine esplanade, occasionally pausing to admire the scenery and, of course, take more pictures. How else? She had to capture her memories.

She sat on a bench, scrolling through the images on her cellphone. *The city of romance...* Her mind drifted back to those days when she and Dan travelled with two hefty cameras, a pile of batteries and lenses, chargers, and a sturdy tripod—an arsenal needed to freeze memories in time.

Today, all you need is a cellphone and a stick. She smiled, extending her arm and admiring the last shot. *National Geographic* … she stifled a chuckle.

Years ago, while on a cruise in Alaska, Ava, and Dan attracted some hype.

"Are you from National Geographic?" asked Mike, timidly, one evening.

Wendy, his wife, mustered her courage and approached as well. That's how their friendship with the Florida couple began.

"National Geographic?" Ava tittered. "What makes you think that?"

"We've been watching you since you boarded the cruise. All the cameras and stuff ... We thought—"

Ava laughed. "Oh, that? No, it's just a hobby."

"Impressive. Are you always travelling armed like this?"

"I wouldn't have it any other way." She spoke too soon.

Here she is, just a few years later, with a camera just the size of her palm, taking pictures.

Photography had been woven into Ava's being since childhood. Her parents' close friend, a professional photographer, often turned the lens on her.

At the age of ten, Ava's fascination deepened when she joined a photography art class for young students. That's how she learned the secrets of the trade, each lesson enchanting.

She spent countless hours in the red-lit room, where the air was thick with the smell of chemicals and creativity. She eagerly helped develop the film and, watching images mysteriously appear on photographic paper under the red light, always left her breathless.

There was a mesmerizing wizardry in the old technology, a tangible anticipation as each picture developed. She held her breath, her heart pounding, waiting to see if the exposure was perfect or flawed. Setting the photos, hanging them to dry, and retouching with delicate brushes demanded patience, a virtue Ava always struggled with. Her impatience ruined many a photo, but each mistake served as a lesson learned. Cutting images to size and framing them—each step was a labour of passion.

Back then, every click of the shutter was a well-thought-out decision, a moment captured with intention. A time when the scarcity of film made each shot precious compared to today's selfie-saturated world.

Now, that magic feels almost lost. You turn a bit, a quick tap on the screen, and you snap a picture. Crooked, slanted, poorly lit, or perfect by chance ... but who cares?

With a critical eye, Ava methodically sifted through the day's captures each night, sorting the wheat from the chaff, deleting most but cherishing a few.

Low battery. She shut her phone, stowed it in her backpack and strolled back to her loft.

5. We don't like stalkers around here

The rain seemed to follow Ava. Or was she following the rain? *It is fall, after all. Typical*—she thought to herself. *And it's Scotland!* She remembered this joke she once heard. *Want to experience four seasons? Come to Scotland on a day trip!* It sounded quite a lot like Edmonton weather. *Don't like the weather? Just wait five minutes.*

She couldn't stop all those old memories from flooding her mind. Each vacation she and Dan took. Almost every single time, the weather forecast looked intimidating until they left. But they stuck to their plans, no matter if the elements had their backs or were against them. Was it their determination or their good hearts that always brought out the sun?

Well, I'm going to make this vacation memorable, too.

When she sought refuge from the rain in this Tea and Biscuits place in Glasgow, she hoped Yelp reviews held some accuracy. Ava knew she was in the tea drinkers' territory, but she hoped coffee was just as good. According to Yelp reviews, it must be.

Her confidence surged as she stepped into the place and looked around. *Wonderful!* Small and lively, yet not crowded, the essence of the past lingered in all those old details preserved intact, interwoven with the notes of the present.

Her eyes took in the bright display cases, filled with all sorts of mouth-watering shortbreads, Scottish biscuits, a large variety of freshly baked goodies, and modern coffee machines. The haunting scents challenged her olfactory senses. Among other tantalizing aromas, the air was laced with bergamot—likely from the Earl Grey tea—deliciously intertwined with the flavours of coffee, butter, cinnamon, and vanilla. *Yum!*

Ava flashed her best grin, positive that she was about to immerse herself in another unforgettable experience. After a quick glance at the coffee menu, she ordered the strongest coffee, topped with two shots of espresso. Black. Invariably, her morning coffee recipe. The rainy morning called for extra energy.

On her first drizzly day in the Lowlands of Scotland, she planned a train trip to Edinburgh to meet Eliza, her best friend's daughter. Enrolled in a master's program at the Law School in Edinburgh, and in the middle of midterms, lunch with Ava sounded like an excellent opportunity for a break. The last time they saw each other, Eliza was still a teenager.

They shared fond memories of the days when Eliza called Ava her second mother. To Ava, Eliza was the daughter she'd never had. She smiled nostalgically as her mind wandered back to those times.

Water splashed from beneath CJ's feet as he raced in the rain, speeding past his cousin's tea shop. Hoping to catch a glimpse of Cindy, his gaze shifted toward the large windows. *She may be in the back, organizing the bakery or another yummy batch of biscuits or scones*—came to mind when he failed to see her. And he kept running, intending to stop and say *hi* after the pharmacy business.

The thought of a fresh biscuit ended in a big gulp of his own saliva, threatening to choke him. His sprint came to a sharp halt. Reeling backwards theatrically, he stretched his neck and peered inside, trying to get a clearer look at the woman sitting at a table, her back slightly turned to the window.

His brows pulled together, intrigued, as his shoulders squared, muttering to himself, "No way. Can't be her."

CJ's eyes darted from the rain jacket he had seen her wearing twice and stopped on the cellphone in her hands. The same blue case, just like her jacket. Like the one he had in his hands just a few days ago. Eyebrows knitted, uncertain of what he was looking at, he scrambled to remember if she had mentioned Glasgow. *I would've remembered, for sure.*

Oblivious of her surroundings, sitting at a table and sipping her coffee, Ava didn't hope the sun would come out from behind the ceiling of clouds today. Somehow, she knew it. *I'm in Scotland. What are the chances? Minimal. If not zero.* The prospect of meeting Eliza was exciting enough, and Ava needed nothing more than just that to enjoy her day, rain or whatever else came her way.

She only wanted to ensure she wouldn't be late and disrupt Eliza's school schedule. Meanwhile, she took advantage of the place's Wi-Fi to double-check the train schedule.

"Oh, please tell me you're not stalking me, are you?" A familiar voice brought her back to reality.

Sudden awareness of her surroundings flooded her as her spine straightened, and she cocked her head, slowly lifting her lashes. Across the table, wearing a massive smile, stood CJ. Her eyebrows arched nearly to her hairline as Ava's eyes widened in surprise.

"Stalking you? Aren't you full of ideas now? Besides, I could ask the same, you know?" A blurry, slanted smirk tugged at the corner of her mouth. "Well, hello there. What are you doing here?"

"I'm home. I figured you'd be home by now, too. In Canada." He smirked.

She still had a tangled look plastered on her face as her teeth raked at her lower lip. "Home! Didn't you say you live in ... London?"

"I did. I live in London. But I was born and raised here. My um … my parents still live in Glasgow. So here I am, helping Mum just like I said I would."

She set her phone on the table, switching back from the entangled state. "Oh, I … didn't know that. Anyway, how's your mom doing?"

"She says rainy days aren't the best for broken bones. Otherwise, she's managing surprisingly well, thank you for asking." He paused briefly. "I was headed to the pharmacy next door to fill Mum's prescription. I couldn't believe my eyes when I thought I saw you here. I had to come in and see for myself. You know what? Please don't move. I'll just drop off Mum's prescription, and I'll be right back." A quick glance into Ava's coffee cup gave him some reassurance.

She smiled, catching the motive behind the glance that checked out her coffee cup. "I'll be here for a while. I'm not going out in the rain yet. Go ahead. Do what you need to do."

From behind the counter, a striking, dark-haired, blue-eyed woman, seemingly in her mid to late thirties, watched the scene unfolding at the table by the window. Her gaze? Serious. Scrutinizing. Evaluating. The woman's face lit up with a broad smile when CJ turned to leave.

"Hey, CJ! I was wondering if that was you. Come on over. I'll put together a care package for Patti. How's she doing?"

"Oh, hi, Cindy! Mum's getting there. I have to run now, but I'll be back in a few," he tossed over his shoulder, storming out the door.

Ava glued her eyes back on her cellphone and kept planning her trip to Edinburgh. Just minutes later, displaying a curious look, the woman behind the counter approached.

"How do you find your coffee?" she asked.

A smile spread across Ava's face as she raised her eyes. "It's excellent, thank you."

From experience, Ava knew the server would usually leave at this point. She buried her nose back in her cellphone to continue her Internet search.

Cindy didn't move, though. She continued in a sharp, uptight manner, and a matching tone, "You know … we don't like stalkers around here."

Ava's gaze lifted back at the woman, a genuine smile blossoming on her lips. But when their eyes met, something else struck Ava. Although she didn't fully grasp it from the tone at first, the woman's gaze conveyed it clearly. She wasn't joking.

As her smile faded, Ava frowned and bobbed her head, trying to understand the meaning behind the woman's words. A muscle ticked in her jaw, but she didn't say a word. Probably not the best time to start defending herself. Creating or maintaining a scene wasn't on her list today.

By the sound of it, this woman had already made up her mind, and the verdict was out and final. No point in starting an argument. Not since people kept flocking in, likely drawn by the aroma of the fresh batch of scones that Cindy had brought just a few minutes earlier.

After a brief evaluation of the awkward moment that sent icicles down her spine, Ava finally opened her mouth. "You know, I guess you're right. I don't welcome bullies in my life, either. I'll gather my shit and will be on my way. Thank you for the coffee. It's excellent. I mean it." She tossed her cellphone into her backpack, grabbed her scarf off the back of the chair, and, coffee in hand, trudged toward the exit.

Just as she was about to grip the handle, the door swung open, and she nearly bumped into CJ. Instinctively, Ava stumbled back for him to enter. A vision of the Paris scene flashed in her mind.

Relieved that, this time, her life-supporting coffee remained safely in the cup, Ava grumbled: "I'm sorry, I have to go," then squeezed between him and the door frame and out of there.

Staggered, CJ lingered by the door, blinking in confusion,

trying to process. *Why the change?* He looked around, his inquisitive glare stopping when he met Cindy's.

From behind the counter, with an air of justice, she said, "What? We don't like stalkers around here."

"What?!" he asked, perplexed, before mouthing 'Fuck!'. "It was a joke," CJ continued loudly and stormed out the door. "Ava! Ava, please wait!" he called, speeding down the sidewalk.

She halted but didn't turn, staring aimlessly, still fuming. *People rush to judge and label. What a crazy world we live in! So, this is how it feels.* Ava swallowed her frustration. She didn't want to project it onto CJ. In a way, she felt sorry for him, who may deal with trolls every day. *In his world, they probably walk in herds, not one at a time.*

Nearly out of breath, CJ spoke quickly, gesturing broadly. "Ava, I'm sorry. I apologize for whatever happened in there. Cindy is my cousin. She misunderstood our conversation. Please, come back!"

Only two years older, Cindy always took it upon herself to look out for her little cousin.

The significant age gap between CJ and his siblings often led to different interests as they grew up. The result? Their relationship was far from tight. Things changed as they all became adults. But growing up, Cindy was his closest playmate, and their bond remained strong.

Ava shook her head, raising an awkward shoulder. "I doubt that putting her and me on the spot is a good idea. I'm sure she won't feel comfortable. I know I wouldn't if I were her."

"Cindy's not a bad person. Not sure what she said, but I can imagine. She's always been protective of me. She's a lot like you. Reasonable, doesn't get intimidated, speaks her mind, and she's all about justice. It makes sense if you think she used to be a lawyer. Please come back in. Once you get to know her, you'll like her. I promise," he furthered.

Lips pressed, her eyes showed an unconvinced look as she tilted her head. "You need to know ... the brief exchange of words between me and her was not pleasant. I don't think she wants me back in there."

"Cindy's one of the most reasonable people you'll ever meet. I'm sure it was just a misunderstanding. And she never holds a grudge."

"Well, I guess she and I have something in common, then."

"Please..." He held out a hand, his tone endearing.

A reluctant Ava turned around and walked beside CJ. Reserved, she stepped into the tea shop but avoided looking around. She remembered—indirectly, she called Cindy a 'bully' just before leaving.

The table in the corner, by the window, where she sat earlier, was still unoccupied. He took her to the same spot. Tension crackled in the air as Ava made herself as comfortable as she could, considering.

CJ shot a telling look at Cindy, mouthing 'Darn!' Just a minute later, with a deflated smile in tow, she approached their table.

"I'm sorry for my behaviour earlier ... calling you a ... stalker. I may have only heard part of your conversation, and I must've gotten it all wrong. CJ says he was kidding. In my defence, I've never known him to be a jokester. So, there's that," Cindy apologized.

"Oh, I figured that much. I mean, he's not the jokester type. He tries, though." After a quick glance at CJ's surprised mien, Ava shifted in her seat and continued, "I wasn't too civil either. I couldn't understand what was going on. I'm sorry I called you a ... bully."

"Well, I kinda asked for it," Cindy replied in a conciliatory tone.

A spectator to all this, CJ kept blinking, his eyes darting between the two, straining to understand what exactly had happened in his short absence. "Oh, dear! When exactly did you two have time to say all that?" he finally managed.

"Oh, my dear cousin, you got the wrong idea about strong women. We can cause a lot of damage with minimal use of words and in nearly no time. Take it from a lawyer. None of that took longer than a minute. Right, dear?" Placing a hand on Ava's shoulder, Cindy chuckled, hoping to ease the tension hovering above them.

"Right you are!" Ava approved with a breezy, broad smile.

"I'm Cindy, by the way. I'm CJ's cousin and best friend. Or so I like to believe. Oh, and Bully is not my name," she added, extending her hand with a sincere smile and a wink.

"Ava. Nice to meet you." She shook the other woman's hand.

"More coffee? A scone? Anything else? Peace offering. It's on the house." Cindy tried to entice her.

Ava's eyes lit up with an indulgent smile. "Just coffee, thank you."

"Are you sure?" Cindy insisted. "Not to brag, but this is where you can have the best scones in Glasgow, if not entire Scotland. Just saying, so you know what you're missing."

"I'm sure it is. I'll stick with coffee only," Ava replied, her gaze reassuring as another broad smile spread across her face.

"Okay, I'll be right back with your coffee ... And yours. And your favourite," Cindy said to CJ before disappearing behind the counter.

The tension had eased somewhat, and she now felt more comfortable.

6. You must be an alien

"So, I'm not the jokester type to you, am I?" CJ asked Ava after Cindy left.

"Oh, I thought you already knew you weren't," she giggled.

"Ha! What's your perception, then? Of me?

"Well, your cousin, slash best friend over there, just said it. I'm sure she knows you a lot better than I do."

"Well, family and friends, you know ... not that their opinion doesn't matter, but yours has proved to be quite ... refreshing. So, please tell."

She flashed a playful sneer and shook her head. "I don't think you want to hear my opinion. Not on this."

"Oh, I do. Believe me." He gave a subtle wink accompanied by a cheeky smile.

Ava stared at him, amused, tucking a strand of hair behind her ear, weighing whether venting the impression he left on her was a good idea.

"Well, you come out a little ... conventional?" She puffed with hesitation, crinkling her nose. "I could tell you were trying hard to act funny in Paris. But it's quite obvious that's not who you usually are. I could only guess that your natural way of being is ... serious? And there's absolutely nothing wrong with it. You are who you are, and that's okay. I was just thinking how you're not the typical celebrity." She wiggled in her chair before continuing. "Or maybe I got the wrong idea in my head. At the end of the day, celebrities are just people and come in many types, like the rest of us, regular dudes." Ava shrugged with a cramped, tentative smile.

His head kept tilting as he listened, then he scoffed. "That's right. We are just people. You know what we-um ... well, at least *I* appreciate?" Curiosity flowed from her expression as Ava shook her head before he continued. "When others realize I'm not special and I'm treated like a regular dude, as you said, not as a big shot celebrity. When I have a normal, open, friendly conversation with someone. Like you and I are having now." He paused and squinted. "Do you think I come across as condescending by being serious? Should I try to crack jokes more often?"

"Oh, no! I mean, you can be quite funny when you remove your shield or whatever it is that you are hiding behind. Just don't start overdoing it suddenly if that's not what you're known for. I'm sure you don't want to turn into a clown overnight. Probably your fans didn't sign up for that. They like you for who you are. Funny, in a geeky kinda way."

"Some think I'm too serious in my social media posts. As you said, a geek," he made a funny grimace.

"I didn't mean it in a negative way. You're not alone. Thinking now ... I follow a few celebrities. I can tell some are too serious, while others are funny as hell. But that's their charm. Us, people, are a colourful bunch, like a box of crayons."

Cindy returned with their coffees and some cheese scones. CJ's *favourite*, as Ava figured out.

"And don't eat them all! Share," she nagged CJ after placing the basket with the lip-smacking scones in the middle of the table.

"Yes, ma'am!" CJ replied, saluting military-style. He then turned towards Ava and asked, "Have you had the chance to look me up? Skimming through my social media, at least?"

"Well, the chance may have been there. But the curiosity was not. So, no, I haven't looked you up." She checked the time.

"You didn't say you were coming to the UK," CJ said.

"No, I didn't mention it. That's another sensitive topic, and I didn't want to start another awkward moment. I mean, I always wanted to visit Scotland. Dan wanted London. We compromised, and London won the first time. It turned out to be neither. We were just in a hotel room—true, in London—for two long days before we returned to Canada. So, this time, London wasn't on my itinerary for all the reasons you can imagine. Otherwise, I probably would've said something when you said you're living there. Just probably." With a half-smile, she looked into her coffee cup. "I still have about ten days left, so I'm not going home yet."

"How do you do this?"

"Like everybody else. Airplanes, trains, road trips, hotels ... And ... I think you weren't asking about how I travel." She burst out laughing when she noticed him blink, looking confused.

He laughed too.

"I was more curious about ... You've been through what you've been through, yet you are funny, owning the different circumstances. Cindy had read you perfectly in one minute, better than I had—a strong woman."

"Huh. Everything I've been through! Have you ever wondered if some people are good at acting on the big screen while others act throughout their lives? However, I'm not quite sure 'strong' is the right word. I guess it's determination. Resilience, maybe?"

"In my book, determination and resilience mean strength."

"May very well be."

*If only you knew all I've been through! If you think my sarcasm is funny, you probably need to know it's just a coping mechanism. I have failed and smacked my face on the ground so many times, but I got up and kept going. Not because I was expected to, but because I chose to. Or maybe I had no other choice—*Ava contemplated, watching him take a bite from one of the cheese scones on the table and savouring every single crumb.

"Please, have one!" he urged Ava. "They're delicious."

"I'm sure they are. They look irresistible, but I can't have this stuff."

"May I ask why? No. Let me guess. You must be an alien and can't eat Earth's food. Seriously! I haven't seen you eating anything. Do you ever eat?"

Throwing her body against the chair's back, Ava laughed again. "What? Of course I eat! How about at Le Louvre?"

"Yeah, birds' food. Nuts and seeds. Oh, and protein bars. I seriously think you might be an alien."

Still laughing, Ava said, "As an alien, I'd probably have tools to adapt to Earth's food. I accepted an invitation to lunch ... and dinner. Unfortunately, there's a different reason. My curse—I'm celiac."

"Oh, and I eat in front of you! Sorry for being inconsiderate." CJ placed the scone back in the basket and wiped his hands.

"Gosh, please, enjoy. Yes, it is tempting sometimes. It's been so long, though. Just ignore me. Besides, I have delicious recipes to replicate almost everything I used to love. I told you I'm good with my pots and pans."

"About your pots and pans. Until we get to use them, I was wondering if you have time for that dinner. You know, the one I had to cancel in Paris. Not tonight, though. I promised my mum I'd be home for dinner with the family," he said.

"You have my number. So, whenever you have time ... I'll be here until Saturday."

"Saturday! Didn't you say you have ten more days?"

"I did. But I won't spend all of them in Glasgow." She re-checked the time and started gathering her things, preparing to leave. "Well, it was nice seeing you again ... and unexpectedly. I must go now. I have a train to catch," she said as she wrapped her scarf around her neck.

"What train?"

"I have to be in Edinburgh by noon. I'm meeting someone

there."

"A friend?"

"Yep. My best friend's daughter. She's attending law school in Edinburgh. Meeting her for lunch."

CJ quickly checked the time on his cellphone. "I could do better than the train," he furthered. "My mum's prescription must be ready. I'll run next door to pick it up and will return to get you. We'll stop by my mum's and drop off the meds, then I can drive you to Edinburgh. We'll be there by noon."

She squirmed, flicking a hesitant hand. "Oh, no. I couldn't. Your mom needs you here."

"I must return some books to a friend in Edinburgh. They are long overdue. Emily, my sister, is back. She's basically moving to Mum's for the next few weeks. There's not much I can do at this point, anyway. Mum can't wait to take a proper shower, and Emily can help. So, giving them some space might be a good idea," he insisted.

"I don't want to take you away from your mother. I already have a plan. I'm fine," Ava objected.

"You're not taking me away. I offered. Besides, if not today, I'd probably take this trip tomorrow," CJ pressed. Uneasy, Ava glanced at Cindy, behind the counter. "Don't worry. She's all bark and no bite. And I figured you are quite capable of holding your ground, so—" he flashed an expressive smile.

"Oh, I'm not worried. It's just— I hope you're past the feeling you owe me something. Because you don't."

"Okay. I don't owe you anything. Let's just say I prefer your company over ... my sister's. I'm not exactly thrilled to be under the same roof as her." He grimaced, rolling his eyes.

"Oh! I can't imagine why you'd say this about your sister. You can't possibly be too different."

"Yeah, though sometimes I could swear she was found on the doorstep. We can talk about this later, on the way to Edinburgh. Please wait for me here."

A little unsure but also intrigued, Ava gave in. "Oh-kay."

When he returned, a few minutes later, the two women were chatting and giggling.

"Well, this picture is much better," he remarked.

Only then did they notice him.

"Ah, you're back," Cindy said. "Here." She grabbed a bundle from the counter. "I packed some goodies for Patti and Don. Also, those cheese scones, for you. For the road. I hear you're going to Edinburgh."

CJ hugged his cousin, kissing her on the left temple. "Thank you, Cindy. Mum will be thrilled."

Arms open, Cindy turned to Ava and gave her a warm embrace. "Come back. I promise I'll act civil," she teased.

"If you decide to chase me away, please do it after I get my coffee," Ava tittered. "The coffee is exquisite, so you can be sure I'll come back for more."

Cindy saw them to the door and whispered in Ava's ear before leaving. "Be careful. He's not only charming and a heartthrob. He's a big, fuzzy teddy bear at heart. Just don't get on his wrong side."

Ava vigorously shook her head, giving a muddled stare. Before she could respond, Cindy had already stepped away, leaving her with the unsettling feeling that she'd just been given a warning she didn't know how to process.

Patti sat comfortably, her injured leg propped up on a padded ottoman. When CJ pulled into the driveway, she raised her eyes from her book and glanced out the window. She didn't fail to notice the woman sitting in her vehicle—the one CJ was driving.

"Why didn't you invite Louise in?" she asked when CJ walked inside.

His jumbled stare turned to his mother. "Did you say ... Louise?"

"Aye, Louise. You know, my leg is broken, not my eyes. You didn't say you two got back together."

"Mum, what are you talking about?" he chuckled.

Patti pointed through the window. "That's Louise, sitting in my car, right?"

"Mum ... no! That's not Louise. Ugh, Mum! Louise is ancient history. Besides, last I heard, she was engaged. She's probably already married."

"Hmm ... whoever that is, sure looks like Louise. A lot. Who is she? Why didn't you invite her in?"

"She's a friend, Mum. Just a friend. Is Emily here yet?" CJ swiftly changed the topic.

"No, dear. Emily is stopping by the store for groceries. We are cooking supper, and Finn is joining us tonight," Patti mentioned, fully aware of the cat-dog relationship between her two youngest children—CJ and Emily. However, CJ and Finn, his brother-in-law, shared many common interests and enjoyed each other's company.

"Ah, great. Cindy sent you some goodies and says *hello*. She said she'll stop by tomorrow to visit."

"Hi, CJ!" Don greeted his youngest son as he returned from the garden with a basket of carrots and potatoes. "What's the fuss?"

"CJ didn't invite in his 'just a friend' lady. She's waiting in the car." Patti couldn't hold back a tease.

Don's brows lifted. "Really? In the car! Why?" After setting the basket on the small console in the hallway, Don paced toward the window, intending to peek outside.

"Dad, Mum's just exaggerating a bit. Dad! Please, don't spy." CJ stepped in front of Don, blocking his path.

Don narrowed his eyes, suspicious but amused. "Who is she?"

"I promised Ava I'd drive her to Edinburgh. I must return those books to Ian. Mum, I got your meds, Emily's on the way ... Do you need help with anything right now?"

"I'm fine, dear. If you give me a glass of fresh water and the painkillers, I shall be fine until Emily arrives. Go and visit Ian.

You'll be back for supper, won't you?"

"I'll be back, Mum. Ava has a lunch meeting in Edinburgh. I'll meet Ian in the meantime and will be home by four. Call if you need anything," he hollered from the kitchen.

"Okay, dear. You can go now. Hey! Why don't you invite this girl over for supper?"

"Absolutely not, Mum. And you know why."

"Okay-okay … as you wish." Patti exhaled, rubbing the arm of her chair.

Always unpredictable when things would explode again. They'll all have dinner tonight and will share the same roof for a few days. She prayed that, for once, the truce would hold.

CJ rolled his shoulders, already preparing for his sister's inevitable sharp comments.

Just keep quiet—he reminded himself. *Don't give her ammunition.*

7. It's not about the bloody doll

A frowning CJ returned to the car and tossed the books onto the back seat. His fingers drummed against the car roof, unease clear in the way his gaze swept up and down the street as if expecting something, or someone, to appear. Finally, he slid into the driver's seat and pulled onto the road. The sullen look of concern persisted, and Ava stayed quiet.

The thick silence threatened to percolate into awkwardness, and she had to break it, unaware that she was about to open a can of worms. "Is your mom alright? Was your sister there yet?"

"Mum's okay. Emily wasn't there," CJ's reply fell quite sharp. Another moment of awkward silence passed. "Can I ask you something? As a friend. I hope you can help me untangle this mystery."

"I'll try," she answered in a subdued voice.

"It's about my sister."

Surprise and confusion flickered across her face. "Your sister? I thought you said she wasn't at your parents' yet."

"She wasn't. It's an old story. I'm not sure why Emily acts the way she does. It bothers me."

"And what does that have to do with me?"

"I was hoping you could help me understand. You know ... what it looks like on your side?"

"You give me too much credit, you know?"

After a quick glimpse at Ava, he looked back at the road and continued, "I'll ask anyway. I must. For my mum's sake. She doesn't deserve to be caught in the middle of my sister's nonsense. But Emily has no filter or consideration for any situation."

"Oh, I don't know what this is about, but I believe I'm not the right person to ask. I have no siblings. I can choose who my friends are, and I avoid people I don't want to interact with. It's different when it's family, though, and the options are limited."

"Tell me about it." He shifted in his seat, as if he were physically uncomfortable.

"You make it sound so bad, and it probably isn't."

"Hmm." A muscle ticked in his jaw. "You sound like Cindy. Did you know I was in boarding school?" His eyes remained on the road.

"Wow! I didn't see that coming. Why? Wild kid? I have a hard time picturing you as a wild kid."

"Not me. I also have two older brothers. Somehow, we are all six years apart. Emily's the youngest. First disconnect. Six years younger and the only girl. Throw in the boarding school, and here you have the perfect combo of an interrupted relationship. As kids, we weren't close to my older brothers. Too cool to waste their time with us, the babies. As adults, that has changed. Never with my sister, though. I suppose she refuses to grow up and get over certain events from our childhood. I don't know. But she gets along just fine with my older brothers. I seem to be the only one she can't stand," CJ blew a deep sigh.

Ava arched a curious brow. "And why do you think this is?"

"Like I said, old story. I'm not sure it's the real reason, but it's the only reason I can think of," he continued with a thwarted smirk. "See, when Emily was three, Luke was fifteen, at the peak of his rebellious phase. Rob had already joined the Army. Mum was juggling a moody teenager, a handful like me, and a toddler. Boarding school for me was the solution to keep a closer eye on the 'problem child' and the baby."

"Did you feel you've been punished?" Ava asked in a small

voice.

"There was a time when I thought that, yes. I felt alone and somewhat abandoned. I was only nine, homesick, and I didn't have any friends at first. I managed to attract some bullies, though..." He sneered. "Funny enough, one of the bullies is my best friend now. I'm meeting him in Edinburgh in a bit."

"I see," Ava's reply trailed off.

"Anyway, I adjusted to my home away from home. Until one Christmas break, when I came home and found my room ransacked. Emily had taken some books and scattered the rest. I made quite a fuss. Was Mum impressed? Nope. Said the books were for all of us and meant to be passed down. Fine, but my room was my sanctuary, not a free-for-all. That Christmas, Grandma gave us something to remember her by. Something about our time with our grandparents. Grandpa had passed a few years before, and she was battling cancer. It was the last time I saw her. The next time I came home was for her funeral."

"Oh, I'm so sorry."

"Thank you. It happened a long time ago."

"What did you get?"

He nodded slowly, as if recalling a memory. "Grandpa's chessboard with handmade pieces. A real work of art. I used to play with him. Emily got Grandma's porcelain doll. She wasn't even two when Grandma caught her climbing the wardrobe to get it. Too young, Grandma said. She thought she'd break it. But before she passed, she made sure Emily got it. Anyway, when I came home for summer break, all my books were in Emily's room. Mum 'solved' the issue and left me one shelf mostly filled with games and encyclopedias. One day, while Mum was out with Emily, I went to get my books back. She moved everything, even my sci-fi and fantasy books. I bought those with my pocket money. They were mine, right?"

"Absolutely," Ava agreed.

"A blood-curdling scream split the house after Mum and Emily returned. The bloody doll was on the floor, shattered. I swear, I didn't even touch the damn shelf it was on. I didn't touch anything. Just grabbed my books from the other bookshelf and got out of there."

"Let me guess. Emily blamed you for breaking her doll."

He clicked his tongue. "Exactly! She didn't speak to me the whole summer. Even when I had to babysit her, she'd go into her room and wouldn't come out until Mum or Dad returned."

"And how long ago was this?"

"About … eighteen years."

"How old was your sister?"

"Around nine."

Ava studied him for a quiet moment before turning her gaze to the passing scenery, letting out a pensive hum. "I don't know … seems ancient. Do you think she still holds a grudge? Have you apologized to her?"

"I didn't think I had to apologize for something I didn't do. It didn't feel right. Would've been like admitting I did it."

"Well, true. Yet, you apologized to me for something you didn't do."

"Isn't it too late? I was a kid, too. Only fifteen. And being accused of something I didn't do was unfair. Back then, I suspected she did it and blamed me. I now know she didn't, but—"

"Why don't you sit and talk? Clear everything up? You are both adults. I don't see why you couldn't discuss and relieve the tension. I know it's hard to prove you didn't touch that doll. But, even if you need to apologize for something you didn't do…" Ava suggested with an indefinite shrug. "Then you can move on and have a normal relationship. Maybe that's all it takes."

CJ ran his fingers through his hair, pushing it back, revealing deep lines of concern etched on his forehead. "I talked to her at some point—"

"And?"

"She said she got over that incident a long time ago. Her words. I really don't understand her."

"What's your family's take on this?"

"Mum says it's all in my head. Dad quiets up when things get stormy. Rob casually changes the topic while Luke barely says anything. Shannon, Luke's wife and Lisa, Rob's wife, promptly follow. Even Finn, Emily's husband, hops on that bandwagon. They all insist it's not about the bloody doll and say Emily always speaks kindly of me. I have to admit, when she chooses, she can be surprisingly decent. Actually, she never attacks me personally." The frustration in his voice was raw. Unfiltered.

Ava cocked an intrigued eyebrow, looking at him. "If she doesn't attack you, personally, I don't get it."

"Now, whenever I bring a girlfriend home, Emily attacks. She doesn't care if she hurts others. Irony, overreacting, nasty and allusive comments about my girlfriends in front of them ... This is Emily. Not sure what she wants to prove. Luckily, I'm single now. So, chances are, this time— But you never know when it comes to Emily. And she's pregnant. So, between hormones and Emily being Emily, I really don't know what to expect."

"Hmm. So she's attacking your girlfriends, not you." Ava pressed her lips, scrambling to compute.

He glanced briefly at her before turning his eyes back to the road. "What? Say it, please."

"You're not with those girlfriends anymore, are you?"

"Like I said, I'm single now."

"Take it with a grain of salt, but I suspect Emily may have told the truth. I believe it's not about that old 'doll story'. Just saying."

Tilting his head, CJ stared at her, absorbed. "Are you sure you didn't talk to Cindy about this? She made almost the same comment when I asked her."

"Well, women have a sixth, seventh—you pick a number of your choice—sense. She probably saw certain things in your girlfriends. Something you may have missed? I haven't met your girlfriends, but—"

He snickered. "Trust me, you didn't miss anything."

Ava gave him a half-smile. "Hmm. Anyway, I guess you were

probably too close and involved to see those flaws or whatever Emily saw. You didn't see the forest. But, for whatever reason, they're no longer your girlfriends. Did it occur to you that Emily might have just been protective? Just like Cindy, when she chased me away. Emily may lack diplomacy, but I believe she cares about you."

His grip tightened on the wheel. "Rubbish! Why does everybody say she cares about me? If it's true, she sure has a strange way of showing it," CJ blurted in anger before adjusting his emotions. "I'm sorry. I'm quite upset right now. I keep seeing one thing, and all I hear is everybody coming up with excuses for *her* attitude."

Ava reached out and placed a hand on his arm. He didn't shake her off, but he didn't relax either. "Well, I can't be certain. It's … just a theory. Based on what you told me. You probably need to sit down and talk to her. If she is as you described—that 'no filter' side of hers, you know? I think she won't have any problem telling you where she's coming from. Maybe it's just her protective mode kicking in. You could ask her to share her opinion next time. In private. I assume not only the targeted person feels uncomfortable."

"You think? However, I'll give it a try. Nothing to lose, right?" He let out a loud exhale that blended into a grunting sigh.

"Just try not to get confrontational. I'm sure she'll appreciate you asking to talk. And yes, pregnant women can be weird and may seem difficult, but they're not irrational," Ava's words wrapped around him, almost calming.

"How would you know?" In an instant, his jaw flexed, and his lips pressed in a thin line, biting his tongue.

Unstirred, Ava said, "Same as you, been around a few," casually raising a shoulder. As she began laughing, he joined in.

When the laughter died down, CJ sighed and said, "I'm sorry. I guess I was just my sister's brother. You know, Ian, the friend I'm meeting in Edinburgh, dated Emily for a while. He also confirmed that she looks up to me."

Ava shrugged again. "Well ... There's only one way to find out."

"You know what I find remarkably interesting? You're the first person who hasn't met Emily, yet intuitively, you seem to have the same opinion as everybody else. I'm convinced. I'll talk to her. Not tonight, but soon. Now, tell me about your friend. The one you'll meet in Edinburgh," he changed the topic.

"Eliza? She's my best friend's daughter. I used to babysit her. She calls me her 'second mother', and I like it. We've been together through thick and thin. A 'one of a kind' friendship. Something you cannot find easily." Ava paused, her gaze dropping as she carefully chose her words, deliberately evading the painful details.

He glanced at her. "Sounds like she's very special to you."

"She is. Her mom, too. She's my amazing baby. Well, she's a mature, smart, and beautiful young woman now."

"Probably not too different from you. You said she called you her 'second mother'. So, like mother, like daughter, right?" A tentative smile tugged at the corner of his mouth.

Ava turned an intrigued gaze at him. "Whatever that means. Eliza was the flower girl at my wedding. A great kid and so adorable." She smiled faintly at a fond memory.

"I'm sure she is. We're almost there. It's just around the corner. How long before I should pick you up?"

"Um ... two hours. Is that okay? If you need more time, I can wait, or I could take the train back to Glasgow."

"No way. Would you let me get bored to death driving back alone? I'll be back in two hours. I'll text you when I'm on my way. Well, here we are," said CJ as he pulled over.

Two hours later, Ava returned to the same spot, appearing entertained and laughing with Eliza.

Parked across the street, CJ swiftly exited the car when he saw the two women. "Ava! Here," he shouted.

"Is that—?" Eliza's jaw dropped, her voice laced with incredulity.

"CJ Hamilton? Yes. Do you know him?"

"I wish I did! Is that the friend who's picking you up? How do you know him?"

Ava scoffed. "By chance? I bumped into him last week in Paris. And he seems to resurface everywhere I go."

"Now, that's some chance!" Eliza tried unsuccessfully to conceal her excitement. "Please tell me where you are going next. Forget about school. I'll come with you!"

"Sure! Come along," Ava said, both bursting into giggles.

After she introduced Eliza to CJ, the two women embraced and said goodbye. Ava was still turned, waving at Eliza as the car pulled away.

"So, it looks like you had a good time," CJ alluded.

Ava puffed a nostalgic smile. "I had a great time. So many memories, so much life happened..."

"Well, I was wrong. She's nothing like you. She seems nice, but different."

"She's her own person," Ava's unbiased reply arrived.

"A bit of a Goth...?"

"Oh, I admit it was a little shocking. Haven't seen her in a few years. I'm sure it's just a phase she's going through. It's probably the influence of this place. Didn't the Goth subculture start here, in the UK?"

"You're right." He raised a curious eyebrow, glancing at her. "Would you? Or have you tried?"

"I once dyed my hair the darkest black, and I wore dark clothes, combat boots, and dark makeup. So yes, I guess I did, even though I had no idea what a Goth was." Ava made a funny face. "Or maybe I was a Punk? Make whatever you want of it. Just don't laugh, please. How about you?"

"Are you kidding? I would've been expelled from boarding school. The rules were extremely strict."

"Oh ... What about after? Did you have any wild

inclinations?”

“No, not really. I’m probably more open now to acting wildly. But not that. I suppose I missed the window for it.”

She looked at him, almost laughing. “Is that right? Is there a window?” Ava asked, gripped. She appeared to ponder for a second before continuing, “Thinking back, I was probably about Eliza’s age when I—” She flinched. “Well, you may be right. There might be a window.” Both burst into laughter. “About Cindy...” Ava diverted to a different subject when the laughter faded.

Intrigued, CJ glanced at her. “What about Cindy?”

“You mentioned she was a lawyer. She’s young. I suppose she didn’t retire. I don’t mean to pry, but I’m curious. What made her switch from being a lawyer to running a bakery?”

“Now, that’s a story right there. It’s good you’re sitting,” he continued, telling Cindy’s horror story.

“As happy as Cindy seems now, I’m sure the ghosts of her past still revisit her,” CJ began.

After graduating from the same law school as Eliza, Cindy received an offer from one of Glasgow’s most prestigious law firms. Motivated by ambition, she invested countless hours in her work. Made a good name and reputation. Some of the most challenging cases landed on her desk. Yet, each time she stepped into the courtroom, she didn’t feel any joy.

Her dream had always been to bring justice and be a voice for the voiceless. But more often than not, she found herself defending those who didn’t deserve it.

Each time she had to fight for lighter sentences for ‘all sorts of crooks’, she took the punch of disappointment. And each case was just a step further away from her original ideal. But she clung to the prospect that she might find a path back to that passion. She held onto the hope that one day, she’d get to do what she dreamed of when she chose to pursue a career in law.

“... At the peak of her career, a few years back, she was close to getting a reduced sentence for a criminal. The victim's family wasn't your ordinary victim's family, though. They weren't thrilled about the direction the trial took." CJ continued as Ava listened. Speechless. Almost holding her breath. Afraid to interrupt, like she was watching a mafia movie unfolding. "The story involved a criminal background on both sides. Things were about to get vile. and eventually turned that way."

"I don't think I like where this is going," Ava said.

"Cindy and her husband, Sam, were threatened, and Sam was kidnapped. Somehow, the partners at the law firm figured it all out, and she was taken off the case. Around that time, Cindy found out she was pregnant."

"That's insane."

"... It was massive and ugly, but it ended well. Sam returned home, and a few months later, Sophie, their daughter, was born. Sophie is five now, and the brightest little spark. Mum still has the newspaper clippings. I'm sure you can find the story online," CJ wrapped up the tale.

Ava shifted in her seat, hesitating before asking, "So ... she never went back? I mean ... I don't blame her."

CJ shook his head, exhaling sharply. "She never talks about it like she regrets it. Just that ... she wanted something different. Something safer. Aunt Lynn wanted to retire, Cindy stepped in, and— Anyway, like I said, happy ending."

"Wow! That's something you only see in movies," Ava murmured, more to herself.

8. I guess we are friends

Before dropping Ava off in downtown Glasgow, CJ asked, "What are your plans for tomorrow? I bet you have some. I thought we could have dinner tomorrow."

"Tomorrow, I'll be visiting some of the famous castles of Scotland. An organized tour. If everything goes according to plan, I should be back in Glasgow around six."

"Organized tour, you say? Hmm … I believe I can do better. I'll take you around Scotland and give you a private tour. I'll take you to some castles. Better ones. Not open to organized tours but rather for private events and individual groups. We could also stop at some of those included in the tours, and worth your time. What do you think?" CJ rushed to advertise his 'better' offer.

"Gosh! As tempting as it sounds, I must decline. I won't take you away from your mother's side. Dinner, yes. But a whole day?"

"My mum's in good hands. Emily's there to help."

"You said Emily's pregnant. She probably can't do as much as you hope. Your family may need you. Instead, you'll be driving a stranger to some old castles. I'll be absolutely fine taking the organized tour," Ava reasoned, her voice firm.

"Okay. Then, we'll do it this way. Tonight, I'll ask if I'm needed tomorrow. If they can handle one day without me, I'll let you know. You can cancel the trip, and I'll take you around Scotland. How about that?"

Her lips briefly pursed, and her tone lowered. "You never give up, do you?"

"Nope," CJ vigorously shook his head.

"But you'll ask in a way that gives them options, right?"

"Absolutely!" his tone playful, but final.

Ava's lips stretched into a crooked smirk, and she slowly bobbed her head. "I ... guess I'm quite okay with that. I just hope this is not you trying to avoid your sister again."

"Well, there's a bit of that. But really, you won't regret the experience. I promise. It will be so much better than any organized tour."

His honesty felt somewhat unsettling. Real, not scripted.

"Well, first, see how things go tonight. It's too late to cancel the tour anyway. And if you can't go tomorrow, that's fine. I've got everything covered, okay? Please don't make me regret accepting this. If I were your mother and figured you'd rather spend time with a total stranger instead of being there for the family when they need you, I'd be upset."

"Oh, I'll have no problem calling you and rescheduling if Mum needs me. I did that in Paris, didn't I?" He felt he had to agree to her conditions.

"Yes, you did," she smiled. "Okay then. I'll wait for your call."

"You were right. As much as I don't know what the organized tour would've been like, today's experience was ... Wow! I'm sure I'll remember it for the rest of my life," Ava said after a long silence, overwhelmed by everything. "And the dinner was wonderful. Thank you so much. No stranger has done anything like this for me. Ever."

"I like to believe I'm no longer a stranger. I thought we agreed we are friends, right?"

"I guess we are friends, yeah," she nodded, smiling.

"I'm glad you liked it. I hope I delivered as promised."

"Well, you did, so you may brag about it," Ava teased.

"Here we are," CJ said, pulling over in front of her hotel. "Will I see you at Cindy's for coffee in the morning? I heard you said you'd go. Or do you have other plans?"

"No special plans. Too exhausted." She pressed her palms against her eyes. "I might sleep in. I'll go for coffee, though not sure when. I may get a pass for one of those hop-on-hop-off city-sightseeing bus tours, just wandering around Glasgow. I'll see how I feel about it."

His blue eyes lit up with mischief. "Hmm ... You know what? Text me when you're up, and I'll meet you at Cindy's for coffee. I have something in mind. A surprise."

"You're not plotting to be away from your family again. They'll hate me without even knowing me." Ava's voice carried genuine concern.

"Oh, my! No way. They have no reason to hate you. I probably gave you the wrong impression yesterday. So, are you going to text me in the morning? Not like Paris. I know you forgot back then," he teased.

"Was that obvious?" she asked, laughing.

"Sort of. Did you really?!" Dismay dripped from his voice.

"Was it a trap question, and I just admitted?" Her eyes rounded, and they both burst out laughing. "I thought you forgot the incident right after I got out of the taxi. You had bigger things on your mind. So, yes, I didn't really expect you'd come back to the crime scene. Not after all the havoc I created."

"You've got to be kidding. But you went back."

"What can I say? I'm a big sucker for good coffee, and I hate to take chances when it comes to it. Then again, I am nobody worth remembering, right?! And I don't plan to return to Paris anytime soon. So, I couldn't care less if they had another good laugh at my expense, as long as I got my coffee." Ava fidgeted a little. "I should go now. It's almost midnight. Thanks again for everything, and I'll see you in the morning."

With a toothy smile, he nodded, gazing into her eyes, lost in a blend of admiration and intrigue. *You are somebody worth remembering.*

She slipped out of the car and entered the hotel. He stayed there for a while, dreamy eyes lingering on the glass doors that swallowed her. *She really is something else. She knows her worth, and she's confident in her own skin. I wish I could be as carefree as she is,* he thought to himself.

Despite Ava's protests, CJ took her back to Edinburgh the next day. The surprise he had in mind. The pretext? She hadn't visited Edinburgh properly. Just as he promised, he delivered again.

As she lay in bed that night, Ava was debating which city she preferred—Glasgow or Edinburgh? She couldn't decide. She had yet to explore Glasgow, and she missed her opportunity.

The following day, she visited the famous Botanical Garden in Glasgow and checked off a few other spots on her 'to-do when in Glasgow' list. She needed to give both cities equal chances before ranking them among her top favourite places.

Of course, her tour guide was CJ, which somewhat spoiled her plan to try the hop-on-hop-off, charming red double-decker buses—trademark of the UK. She had ridden them at Niagara Falls years ago. But experiencing them in the UK? Just like having an espresso in Italy or buying a perfume in Paris.

Ava knew she couldn't ask CJ to get on the bus. By now, she understood he was trying to stay low and fly under the radar. Otherwise, it was surprisingly easy to go unnoticed and avoid people, even in crowded places.

It took some effort, but CJ managed to convince her he could do just as well at showing her the most popular locations in Ireland—her next and final destination in this adventure.

When she refused, he leaned forward, eyes bright with confidence. "Ava, I know Ireland like the back of my hand. My mum's Irish. I grew up exploring every corner. I can take you to spots no organized tour would cover." Ava's lips puckered with reluctance, but CJ pressed on, a playful insistence in his tone. "Look, I'd be off to London on Sunday, anyway. Just leaving a day early. Nothing is waiting for me in London except for Bella, my dog. And she's at my brother's. I have no work engagements right now. I'm free until next month, when I'll be in Canada. So, I'll see you tomorrow in Dublin."

Somehow, he had already become part of the journey. Her journey wasn't only hers anymore. That night, Ava packed her suitcase, getting ready for Ireland.

When she landed in Dublin, with a humongous smile on display, CJ was waiting. He couldn't find a seat on the same plane, and he caught an earlier flight. At least, that was his excuse. Ava suspected he deliberately aimed to keep her away from prying eyes.

He understood her 'don't need or want anything to do' with the kind of attention he was attracting. Parked in a secluded area of the parking lot, a rental car was ready to take them away.

"You're travelling in style," he commented, picking up her suitcase.

"In style?" she scoffed.

"Good quality suitcase and everything else."

"Gosh! It was a long trip. I needed something durable to survive all the unforgiving handling. My suitcase had been destroyed once. The suitcase itself was still fine, but the pull-out handle was damaged. You don't want to know what's playing in my head when I pack."

"What's playing?" he raised a curious brow.

"This really bad luggage-handling scene from an old movie. Just don't ask me what movie. You should probably learn that I couldn't remember movie names if my life depended on it. Unless I watched it five times or more. No offence," she chuckled.

"None taken. So, stylish and practical," CJ continued, amused.

"Or more on the lines, I learned my lesson and did my homework. I guess that would sum it up."

"Well, let's take you to your hotel first. Where are you staying? I need to put the address on the GPS," he said as they got into the car.

"Another thing you'll learn about me: when I travel, I keep away from chain hotels at all costs. And not because of the cost. For a full experience, I choose more picturesque places with a personality specific to the location. Glasgow was somewhat of an exception. But Kimpton is symbolic of Glasgow."

"Okay, I love that. Let's see what you picked in Dublin. If I like it, and they have rooms available, I might stay there, too."

"Well, I can't promise anything. I only went by reviews and internet pictures. Hence, it's going to be a surprise for me as well. It is done, and it's only for a few days. I'm not planning to spend the rest of my life here. I'll survive. Not sure about you, though," Ava said nonchalantly.

"We'll see. So, the address is—"

When they pulled up before a Guest house, the place looked picturesque and revealed a true Irish character. A subtle smile curled CJ's lips as the place brought back good memories from his childhood.

An apartment and a room were all they had available, and CJ chose the room. *It should be enough.*

"This is yours," the bellboy said, opening the door to Ava's room and pushing her luggage inside.

"Wait. May I see the other room first?" CJ asked after a quick, inspecting glimpse into Ava's room.

"Sure." The bellboy released Ava's luggage, crossed the hallway, and opened the other room.

CJ stepped inside and peeked around. "Well, I'll take that one. The lady can have this room. It looks more suitable for her." He smiled at the bellboy as he turned and walked out.

A fazed Ava stood in the middle of the hallway, her eyes darting between the two, scrambling to follow.

"Okay." With no further comment, the bellboy turned around, grabbed Ava's suitcase, and pushed it across the hallway.

"We'll talk later," CJ answered Ava's unspoken question, tipping the bellboy for his trouble. "Make yourself at home, and I'll see you in about an hour. Text me when you're ready. I need to take a shower and change. I'm getting hungry. I know the right place where we can get a bite to eat," he continued, slowly closing the door to his room.

"I need a shower, too," Ava replied with a vague smile and a reproachful headshake.

She could've booked a more 'suitable' room if she wanted. However, offering grounds for speculation by arguing his decision in front of the hotel staff wasn't on her agenda.

"I'm sure you could've booked a more suitable room. I'm also sure you already did. They always feel like they need to spoil me, and I hate it. If I took the apartment, I'm convinced you'd be in the room you are in now," CJ replied to Ava's question while waiting for their lunch.

Her entire demeanour screamed doubt. "I don't think so."

"Oh, I know so. Believe me. Did you see the lady at the reception when we left? Her face, her sneer? She still had feathers on her chin from the canary she ate."

"Huh!" Ava muttered, still finding it hard to believe.

"Well, you'll still have your full experience. I hope I didn't ruin that part." His voice arrived warm and reassuring.

"Thank you. I feel bad that you have to stay in that room," she added, a sense of feeling poorly recognizable in her voice.

Just like his tone, his position remained unaltered. "I could've upgraded to the apartment if I wanted to. But, as someone incredibly wise told me, 'I don't plan to live here for the rest of my life. So, I'll survive. Don't worry, I have a good plan. We won't spend too much time in our rooms."

Ava studied her hands as she took the last sip of her after-lunch coffee. "Well, I hope you don't have any plans for this after-noon. I'm in dire need of a mani-pedi. I hope to find the right place somewhere around here."

"No plans. We can do whatever we want for the rest of the day. I have dinner planned, though. Find what you need for now. I also have something in mind and will see you at dinner time," he said when exiting the cozy restaurant, parting ways with Ava.

"What were the odds? See you later." She pointed at a mani-pedi place right across the street that she had missed when they arrived, then stepped off the curb.

Later that night, after a nice dinner and back in her room, Ava took a shower, getting ready for bed. Still in the bathroom, nearly finished with her bedtime routine, she looked in the mirror, think-ing—*It's been a long, interesting day.*

A faint knock made her pause. She turned off the water and listened, unsure if it was at her door. With an open ear, she stood there for a moment, listening. Her brows drew together, wondering if she'd appear nosy if she snooped around.

A second knock—louder this time. It was at her door. *Some-one probably got lost.* Quickly wrapping the bathrobe around her, she scurried over. When she cracked the door open, her curious eyes were met by CJ's, leaning against the door frame with a bottle of wine in hand.

"Do you have glasses for this? I had to drive after dinner, but I could now have a glass of wine. I thought I'd be really pa-thetic if I drank alone. I always get this wine when in Dublin. It's mead, actually. Made from fermented honey. One of my favour-ites," he said in one breath.

A wide smile split her face from ear to ear as she opened the door all the way and waved him in.

She reached for the bottle in his hand, closely studying it with a keen eye. "Let's see what you have here. I had mead before. Years ago, I visited a winery in Alberta. I remember enjoying it.

Well, let's try an Irish one. Part of my Irish experience." She set the bottle on the table.

CJ pulled up a chair and started unsealing the bottle. To his disappointment, it was a corked one. And ... surprise! No corkscrew in the table's only drawer.

"Do you happen to have a corkscrew?" he asked Ava, busy fetching the glasses from a cupboard.

"Oh, no! I knew I left something out when I packed. Then again, I never planned on getting all *pathetic* and drinking a bottle of wine alone." She returned an amused beam. "Well, I guess we won't need these glasses now," she mocked.

"I'll call the reception. I'm sure they have one."

"Oh, no-no-no! Please don't give them any ideas. Thanks to being a smoker, I think we can try the trick I saw on Instagram. Let's see if it works," Ava said as she dug in her backpack and produced a lighter.

And it worked. She knew it would. She wasn't the first to try heating the neck of a wine bottle with a lighter, only to have the cork slide and pop right out.

CJ watched her, fascinated. "So, that's what you do on Instagram."

Amused, she winced. "Oh! Did you think I was just keeping up with the Kardashians?"

"I wouldn't have pegged you for one of those." He laughed while pouring wine into the glasses. "To new friends!" CJ raised his glass.

Ava took a small, shy sip. "It's good. It's really sweet. Almost ... hurts your teeth, sweet." She peered around. "Do you mind if I lie down on the couch? I'm starting to feel this trip, and I might have a funny and undesirable reaction when combined with the wine. I mean, the mead."

"Well, it's your *home*. Do whatever you want."

"Okay..." She lounged comfortably on the couch and tucked a pillow under her neck. "Well, I think I've exhausted all the topics about myself in the last few days. You've heard all the ridiculous stories I've had to share." She yawned. "I believe it's your turn to tell me something about yourself. Mind you, my tongue will probably be completely tied after a few sips of this. Here's your chance to talk," Ava suggested.

"So, you want to hear *my* ridiculous stories? Ha! I have quite a few of those. If you're thinking of posting any ... well, for full disclosure, some are already out there. Everything else, I'll deny," he teased.

She giggled, took another sip from the glass, and slowly placed it on the floor by the couch. CJ continued to talk, vividly describing some funny or embarrassing events from his past. Ava listened, laughing when he laughed or making short, spirited comments. After a while, he switched to telling stories from his childhood. He looked down into his glass as he spoke. Two stories later, as he lifted his gaze at Ava, she was asleep.

Bobbing his head, he puffed a smile. "Well, I guess I have another talent I may have to look into. Bedtime storytelling," he muttered to himself, getting up from the chair and browsing around. Then he picked up from the floor Ava's glass with only two sips missing. "Too bad this has to go to waste," he added in the same subdued tone, tossing the contents into the sink.

After rinsing the glasses and placing them on the counter, his hand on the door handle, he was ready to leave. Head tilted in thought, he squinted once more at the couch. *Well, I guess that's gonna hurt in the morning.*

He paused, glancing around and quickly assessing the situation. First, he pulled the covers off the bed, then stealthily walked to the couch and lifted Ava's body carefully so she wouldn't wake up. After gently laying her down, his fingers gingerly brushed a rebellious lock of hair from her stunning features, smiling as he gawked once more at her peaceful expression. Managing to make no noise, he turned off the lights and tiptoed out of the room.

"I must apologize. I guess I made a fool out of myself last night. I must've gotten so drunk, I don't remember anything. I don't even know how or when I got in bed," Ava uttered when she met him at the rental car to leave for the day.

"I don't think so. I guess I'm a good storyteller." He flung a grin. "You fell asleep after only taking two sips of that mead, and I dumped the rest so you wouldn't trip over it. You were sleeping peacefully when I left." The grin persisted with an added hint of mystery that she completely missed. He also failed to include that he knew how she got into bed.

A nervous simper warped her expression. "I appreciate you trying to protect my feelings, but you don't have to. I'm a firm believer that everyone has the right to get drunk at least three times in their life. After last night, I still have one left."

He chuckled. "I think you still have two left. Really, you weren't drunk. Believe me, I'd know. I think you were tired, fell asleep, and absolutely missed your chance to get drunk. How was your first time?"

A little mystified, Ava raised a brow. "My first time?!"

"Um ... the first time you got ... drunk?" he stuttered.

"Ah! It's been many years since. I can't even tell if I was drunk or maybe it was just food poisoning. If you say I missed my chance last night, I have nothing to compare it to. But back then, I got so terribly sick. I didn't have much to drink. Just a beer, a sip of vodka and a couple of sips of champagne ... Strangely enough, unlike last night, I remember everything I did to this day. But for three days after, I couldn't eat or drink anything. I couldn't even hold plain water longer than three minutes. So, ever since, I choose my poison wisely. I swore that night that I'd never mix booze again. I'm not much of a drinker, and when I drink, it's no more than a glass ... maybe two. I really don't know what happened last night."

He puffed. "Nothing happened last night. You just fell asleep."

"Well then, I believe you. The good news is that I feel terrific and rested today. So, what's the plan? I threw mine out the window."

Ava fell in love with Ireland. There was something magical, something surreal, about the Emerald Island.

On the day she left, at the airport, Ava sighed as her heart sank with mixed feelings. Excited to go home, she also wanted this vacation to last just a little longer.

It was the end of one chapter and the beginning of another in her life. And she had no idea what the new chapter would bring. She had no plans, and she didn't want to make any. Every time she made long-term plans, life got in the way and destroyed them. Like clockwork.

One day at a time. Now, this, right here, sounds like some sort of plan—she hummed inside, her hand gripping the luggage handle.

"Thank you so much for everything. It was a wonderful experience. Now, I'll run through those doors before I start bawling my eyes out." Ava forced a smile, pointing to the doors leading to the terminal after she said 'Goodbye' to CJ.

"Come here," CJ held her close in a long hug. "Take care of yourself. I'll see you in a few weeks." His hand glided on her arm until it reached hers, brushing his thumb against her fingers. He cringed with a muted gasp, looking down at her delicate hand. "You forgot your rings. I have time before my flight. I'll get back to the hotel, and I'll return them to you when I come to Canada."

She flashed a knowing smile. "I didn't forget them. I took them off this morning. Remember, I said I'd probably take them off at the end of this trip?" she said, fishing one of her necklaces from under her shirt. Her rings were now a necklace. He heaved her into yet another hug. "Now I have to run."

Ava marched through the doors, taking one last look back and waving at him, mouthing another 'thank you' as she lowered her hand and placed it over her heart.

9. I have a trained eye

Startled, Ava opened her eyes at the sound of the cellphone vibrating. As usual, it was charging on the console in the hallway just outside her bedroom. She checked her fitness tracker: just a bit after five.

It had been quite a while since she had started putting some order in her life and habits, including not sleeping with her cellphone in the bedroom. *If someone died, they'd better still be dead two hours from now. If they're not, then it can only be good news.* Ava flipped in bed, annoyed by the awkwardly timed call.

She knew better. Sleep was important. Besides, her friends, who lived all over the world, called at odd hours of the night, claiming they were confused about what time it was in Canada. *Yeah right! How about asking Mr. Google?* Then again, this could be just another spam call.

She wasn't about to get out of the comfort of her bed. Not yet, anyway. Not that she could sleep afterwards. The sun was already shining through the window, and she had forgotten to close the blackout curtains when she went to bed the night before. Ava refused to get out of the comforting bed to do even that. She lay there, half-awake, dozing in and out, hoping to get more sleep. And she probably did.

She liked the new 'work from home' trend since the pandemic. Otherwise, on the days she had to work in the office, she'd wake up at five. Dan used to say that the pandemic would give everyone what they wanted. *Is that true? What did you get out of it, my love? What did I get out of it?*

The fitness tracker alarm went off at seven. Only then did she roll out of bed, dragging her feet to the kitchen, with Fox, her trusty German shepherd, on her heels. Her companion since last Christmas, Fox, always followed her around, like a shadow.

"I should've named you Shadow," Ava mumbled as she made a quick detour by the back door and let Fox out into the backyard.

Standard morning. Later, they'd go for a walk. *But not before coffee.*

She took her favourite cup from the dishwasher and pressed the button on the espresso machine. A quick shower, contact lenses in, her morning facial routine … and now, she finally can have her coffee.

Swinging by the living room, she turned the TV on and grabbed a cigarette. She contemplated quitting a few times. Something out of the ordinary always happened, making her understand that *life is short anyway.* Each time, an unexpected event would pop out of nowhere to alter or derail her life's trajectory. If there was one thing she enjoyed, it was her morning coffee, accompanied by a couple of cigarettes.

Why give up on the only thing that brought some kind of normalcy to this craziness? Or maybe she just wasn't ready and always found excuses? She gave it an indifferent shoulder and pranced into the kitchen. After grabbing her coffee, Ava rolled outside.

The morning was unusually chilly for the end of July, and she failed to pay attention to the weather channel playing on TV. Watching Fox running around the backyard drew a smile from her. She sipped her coffee. A chill followed suit, and she returned inside to get a sweater. The annoying call this morning came to mind as she grabbed her cellphone from its charger. *The audacity! Who could've been?*

Her brows scrunched together as she looked at her phone. "Huh. CJ? This early?" she muttered, playing the new voicemail.

"Ava. Sorry, I didn't realize what time it was. I believe you might still be sleeping. Please call me when you get this message. I need to talk to you about something important. And before you freak out, just know everything's fine. I've been extremely busy with work lately and didn't have time to call. I have a fascinating offer for you. If you're interested, of course. Talk to you soon."

Nearly two weeks had passed since she'd heard from him. For the last ten months, since they first met, his twice-weekly phone calls have been a staple in her life. Just like the ad hoc visits, every few weeks.

CJ always had something 'important' to ask or just called to check on her. Or some other pretext to call or show up when she least expected it. "Hey, I need your opinion on something important..." he'd say.

Like last time, *important* meant whether oat milk was a crime against coffee. And, of course, it was.

She wondered and dialled back.

"Ava! I'm so glad you called."

"Good morning to you, too."

"Yes, sorry ... Good morning. I have some exciting news for you. Not so exciting how we ended up in this mess. It's actually quite tragic. But I hope you can help." CJ shot straight to the matter, spilling it all in one breath.

"Help? How? What is it?" she asked disorderly.

"Remember that movie I auditioned for when we met in Paris? We started filming. Well, not exactly, but we're already at the location. We begin shooting next week. However, something terrible happened. Our historical and Eastern European cultural consultant was in a serious accident. He's stable now, but recovery will probably take months. We need a replacement A.S.A.P., and I recommended you." He spoke fast.

"Me?! What are you talking about? Is this some kind of work-from-home job?"

"Actually, no. You have to be here, on the set. But you work from home, right? We can arrange for you to do your other job while here."

"I'm afraid I can't. I can't work from Europe. Only from North America."

"We're filming in California. So ... North America."

Her lips briefly puckered. "Are you trying to trick me into accepting this?"

"Are you trying to find excuses? I know you're perfect for the job. Please," CJ insisted, his tone endearing.

Lips still puckered, Ava arched an interested brow. "And ... what exactly am I supposed to know? What do I have to do as a consultant?"

"Thank you. I knew it."

"Hold your horses. I didn't say 'yes'. First, I need to know what I'm getting myself into. So, please tell me what I have to do. I'll let you know if it is fascinating and if I'll consider it. And why in the world did you recommend me without asking?"

"Ava, you're so brilliant. I know you can do it," he pressed further.

"CJ! Do you remember how I feel about flattery?"

"Yes, I do. But truly, I believe you can do this. You are perfect. You have all the qualifications for the job. You come from an Eastern European culture, worked in TV, and are an Army brat, so you know the ranks. Bonus, you are a walking history encyclopedia, as you once said. Plus, you are good friends with Mr. Google."

"And being friends with Mr. Google qualifies me for the job? If that's the case, anyone can do it."

"Not really. I trust you'll know how to find the right information. Basically, you're the one making sure we don't embarrass ourselves by getting history wrong. Your okay is needed on set before the scenes are filmed. The director and producers are perfectionists and aim for accurate, realistic replication of history. I'm convinced you can do it." He paused and listened. "Ava?

Hello!"

"I'm here," she replied pensively.

"What do you think?"

"Well, it sounds exciting. At least you sound really excited about it. But you still haven't said when. I need to know what I'm saying to make arrangements at work."

"So ... you'd start next Monday...?"

"Next Monday?! As in a week from today?" Ava snapped, floored.

"Yes, I know it's short notice..." he stuttered.

"Short?! Can you try *extremely* short notice?"

"You're right. Nobody planned this terrible accident, though. And if anyone can save our asses right now, it's you. Please, at least consider it," CJ pleaded, his tone still endearing.

"I didn't say 'no' either. For how long? I hope it won't be like that contract of yours, which started out as two weeks and turned into over two months." Ava wanted to know more.

"Two months. I promise you'll be home at the end of September. If we have to stay longer and still need your assistance, we'll find other ways. We have cellphones ... video calls. But hopefully, we'll know what we're doing by then."

"Hmm. I can't promise anything yet. I'll see what I can do and if I get permission to work from the US or take a leave of absence for that long. I'll let you know."

"When?"

"Um ... I don't know. Later today? Maybe tomorrow?"

"Yes! Yes! Thank you!"

"Don't thank me. I didn't say 'yes'. Not yet. I'll see what I can do."

"Well. I know you'll try, and that's a *yes* to me. You'll get a draft contract in your email with all the details. Get an idea ... see how you like it, okay?"

"Alright. I'll call when I have an answer. I need to get to work now. Talk to you later."

"Fantastic! I can't wait to hear from you! Bye now."

Excitement radiated from his voice, and Ava could only picture his expression beaming as well.

After she hung up, Ava wondered if it sounded like she had promised anything. She hated making promises. Especially when she wasn't sure she could actually do something. She'd rather have a plan first and then promise or surprise someone with an answer.

Now, she had to admit, this opportunity was kind of exciting. Like a blast from the past. *Hmm. Another shot at my previous life?!* She walked around with a smile glued to her lips for the rest of the day.

Working for the TV network was what she was born for. The rush of a live broadcast, the frantic whispers in her earpiece, the countdown ticking down on the teleprompter, the hectic schedule … She loved it all. The late-night script revisions, the buzz of a set coming to life—all challenging but rewarding in a way that still stuck with her many years later.

Even that morning, when she walked into a different season, with two feet of snow on the ground, after a long night of sound and video engineering. Exhausting? Yes. Chaotic? Always. But every time the cameras rolled, she felt like she belonged. It kept her sanity intact and salvaged her after loss. Well … she needed to recover again.

Maybe this is a sign! Another chance.

On Saturday afternoon, Ava landed in L.A. CJ met her at the airport, excited about seeing her.

"I'm so looking forward to working with you!" he said as he hugged her. Then he picked up her suitcase as if it weighed nothing and walked her to the airport exit. "We'll stop at the store so you can pick up some 'alien food'. There's food at the house, but I assume you'll want to pick out some items I may not have."

"Sounds good. Can you please choose a store with a cosmetics department? Also, has a package arrived for me yet? I ordered a few things. I hope you don't mind."

"I don't mind at all—*mi casa es su casa.* Nothing has arrived yet. Unless it has since I left to pick you up. What does the order confirmation say?"

"I was busy packing and didn't check. My phone is still in airplane mode. Roaming only kicks in tomorrow. I'll check when we get to the house. You have Wi-Fi, right?"

"We sure do. I'm glad you could join us," CJ said with a big smile as he glanced at Ava. "I thought the house was too big for just me, but it came in handy when they tried to find a place for you."

"Oh, so that was an ad-hoc arrangement. They're still looking, aren't they?"

"Why would they? You're staying with me. It's done."

"Are you sure you want me around? I'd hate to be in the way. Two months can be a long time. You'll need your privacy. You'll be sick of me in two weeks, tops." She giggled.

"Don't be silly," he snickered. "There are six bedrooms. One is taken. By me, of course. You can take any of the other five."

"Is it only you in this house?"

"Bella and me. And now, you. About Bella—she's nothing like Fox. Not sociable. She'll say 'hello', come and sniff you, she'll probably smell Fox on you, and then she'll ignore you completely. She barks like an idiot sometimes and chases squirrels, rabbits, or whatever small animals in range. I could swear there's a hunter gene in her."

"Sounds pretty much like Fox," Ava said.

"Worse. Anyway, unlike other huskies, she has no control when it comes to food. Then, she gets sick, and we don't want that. Therefore, her food is always in a cupboard, out of her reach. I'll show you where it is. Just in case I'm not around, and you'll maybe need to feed her. Although I suppose you won't have to. Oh, and she doesn't like to be petted by strangers. I mean, no one but me, and only when she wants. She basically asks. So, don't try to pet her if you don't want teeth marks on your beautiful hands.”

“Huh! Good to know. I’ll keep my hands in my pockets.”

“Don’t worry. She won’t take your hand off but will pinch you if you try.”

CJ pulled in front of the supermarket. “Here we are. I’ll drop you off right here, park, and meet you inside. Probably in the cosmetics department?”

“Or the whole foods section: veggies, meats ... Whichever is closer to the entrance. I’ll hang out around there. I don’t have a cellphone yet, so—” Ava said as she exited the car.

“Don’t worry, I’ll find you.”

Once inside, Ava completely forgot about her promise and headed to the other end. A yoga mat she spotted way in the back caught her attention. She grabbed it, only to realize she was missing something: a shopping cart. She made a full circle back to the entrance and was met by CJ, who had just entered the store.

“What is that?” he asked.

“What does it look like? I need to keep moving.”

He smirked with a knowing air. “You won’t need it.”

“Wow! And you know this ... how? It won’t take up too much space. And I promise I won’t leave it in your way.”

“That’s not what I meant. There’s a gym at the house. With a complete set of your favourites—dumbbells, barbells, and kettlebells, a bench press, a treadmill, some other machines, yoga mats, and— You’ll see. How about trying it out first, and if you need anything else, you can buy it later?”

“How do you know about my favourites? I don’t think I ever mentioned anything about that.”

“You don’t have to. I have a trained eye. I can tell just by looking at you,” CJ said teasingly. “Plus, I noticed the gym stuff in your basement when I helped you take the Christmas tree upstairs,” he added with a subtle smirk, the knowing air still there.

“Oh, that. You know, at one point, a guy lived in that

house..?." Ava smirked, swivelling to take the yoga mat back to where she'd got it.

"I have a trained eye!" CJ said again.

"Mm-hmm ... you do," Ava tossed over her shoulder, bobbing her head and smiling.

"Just, let's put it back for now," his reply trailed off.

As they pulled into the garage, Bella greeted her with a joyful bark and wagging tail. Ava remembered not to pet her, as she'd been warned.

Placing her hands between her knees, she leaned to look into Bella's eyes. "Well, hello there. I'm glad there's another girl in this house."

Bella barked again and sniffed at the guest, but ignoring didn't appear to be part of her plan. Not at all. She watched Ava's every move, following her everywhere, just like Fox did. *She probably didn't get the memo*—Ava mused.

"Go ahead! Make yourself at home. The bedrooms are all upstairs. The first on the right is mine. You can choose any of the others. I'll get your luggage. Oh! There's some stuff in the bedroom next to mine—my laptop and some scripts. I'll get it out of the way if you want that one. I'll need to take it to my trailer, anyway," CJ's voice boomed louder.

"Got it!" She was already halfway up the stairs after leaving her backpack and shoes by the door. Bella trailed behind her. Ava stopped and looked at the dog, who halted, glancing up at her. "You feel it too, eh, girl? I guess we are the majority in this house. Guys don't know the first thing about girls. He said you'd ignore me. Us, girls, must stick together. This is why you're following me, right?" asked Ava, and she continued up the stairs, Bella on her heels.

"She likes you," CJ smirked as he reached the top of the stairs, carrying Ava's suitcase and carry-on. "So? Which one?"

Ava was reeling out of the bedroom on the left at the end of the hall, with Bella right behind. The rooms on the right were an automatic 'dismiss'. *Nobody told me if I fucking snore, so the proximity might lead to annoyance,* she thought.

"I like the first one, right across from yours. There's a nice console that I could use as a desk for my laptop. Plus, the bathroom is quite a way. If I want to take a shower at an odd time, I hope it won't bother you if you're sleeping or rehearsing," Ava said as she pranced back and pushed the door open.

Swiftly, she grabbed the handle of her suitcase and rolled it into the bedroom. CJ followed with her carry-on.

When Ava turned around, she caught him smiling. "What are you smiling at?"

"Nothing," he replied, a playful grin on display.

"Do you often smile at 'nothing'? I need to know if we share this house for the next two months, so I won't ask again."

He chuckled, letting go of the carry-on handle. "It's just that this bedroom was my first choice. I changed my mind and took the other one, only because it had a balcony. That way, if I need a smoke while in the middle of work, I can step out and have one. I guess this one was meant for you."

"You had six bedrooms for your use only. You could've slept in one, had your office, or whatever you call it, in another, and used the balcony of this one to smoke." She pointed to the door across the hall.

"You're right, but remember? I'm a guy. I'm lazy. You're asking too much of me."

"Ha! What do you know, Ava?" She puffed, laughing. "Well, I guess I'll have to work out when I need a smoke."

"Make yourself at home. I'll get the groceries from the car and put them away. Take your time. I'll show you around later." He ran a hand through his hair, stopping at the back of his neck.

The gesture brought a faint smile to Ava's face. The military style cut, according to the new role, didn't match the motion at all.

10. And this is how you start rumours

Ava paused, eyes lingering over the inviting bed. Bed never looked so good. Then, she pouted. Despite her exhaustion and urgent need for sleep, the struggle always followed her. She had to go through an annoying hell when she slept in a new place for the first time. Hopefully, this time would be different. But it wasn't. Restless, she tossed and turned, waking up, trying to find that sweet spot where she could finally fall into a deep sleep.

Shifting from one side to the other, she opened her eyes briefly and jumped, startled. Bright, icy blue eyes sparkled strangely in the room's darkness. Somehow, Bella found her way into her bedroom and was now staring, her nose merely a couple of inches from Ava's.

"Girl, you're weird. You scared the shit out of me! Back off! Let me sleep," she grumbled in a low tone after glancing at the door and finding it was open.

The door to CJ's bedroom was also ajar. Somewhat considerate, Bella retreated beneath the console under the window and stood there.

Grunting in annoyance, Ava punched the pillow and flipped to the other side, falling back into a shallow sleep. It wasn't long before she shifted again. Briefly opening her eyes, she got startled again. Bella's eyes shone in the dark, from under the console this time, her stare pinned on Ava.

Somehow, Bella knew it wasn't right and finally walked away. Ava thought, or hoped, she would leave and return to CJ's room. But no, Bella was standing at the foot of the bed, still glaring. That's what Ava figured out when she tossed in bed and opened her eyes again.

"Oh, so you're still here. If that's what you want to do, instead of sleeping … your choice," she mumbled in a sleepy voice, this time without startling.

It was Sunday, and after a restless night, Ava wanted to sleep in. However, Bella's plans were quite different. Just before six in the morning, Bella began licking and gently chewing Ava's toes on the foot sticking out from beneath the covers. Annoyed, she drew it under the blanket.

Bella crawled and propped her chest against the edge of the bed. Then, her paws drummed along Ava's hairline at an unbelievable, annoying speed. In response, she pulled the blanket over her head. But now, her feet were sticking out. Bella returned to her feet. The hide-and-seek game continued for a few minutes until, frustrated, Ava spun around brusquely.

"What?! What do you want?" Startled, Bella sat and scratched the floor with her front paw, as if trying to tell something.

Ava craned her neck and caught a glimpse of Bella's leash on the floor. "Really?! It's six in the morning, you know?" Bella tilted her head, whining, puppy eyes pleading. "Whatever. I guess my options are limited. I can't get back to sleep now. Let me put something decent on," Ava muttered, flinging the covers and slipping out of bed.

Dashing into the bathroom, she splashed cold water on her face, pulled her fingers through her hair and twisted it into a messy bun. A pair of leggings, a T-shirt and runners completed her outfit. Then, she tumbled downstairs, managing to make no noise.

At about seven-thirty, Ava was out of the shower, still in the bathroom, dressed, just finishing putting on some makeup. A light knock on the door made her pause what she was doing.

"Yes," she answered.

"It's me. Have you seen Bella? I can't find her," CJ's voice called out through the door.

"I know. Come in."

"I don't want to bother you. She's my problem. I was just wondering if you've seen her."

"Oh, please come in. She's here."

He pushed the door, peering around, but failed to see Bella before Ava emerged from the bathroom. "Where is she?"

"Let me tell you, she's weird. Did you train her to do all that shit?"

"What did she do? Where is she?" His eyes continued sweeping the room.

"What can I say? She's tired. Sleeping. Right there." Ava pointed to the spot on the other side of her bed that CJ couldn't see from the doorway. "By the way, she sleeps like people."

"I know, she does. Why is she sleeping? She must be sick. Oh, no! That was the last thing I needed right now." He scampered around the bed to check on Bella.

"She's fine. She's just tired from watching me all night. Didn't sleep a wink."

He spun on his heels, turning a disbelieving gaze. "What?!"

"Like I said, she's weird. She bullied me into a walk, I caved, and now she's passed out. Let her be. She's fine."

"Why did she watch you? What did she do?"

"I can't tell you why, but—" Ava began telling the embedded story of last night in her own sarcastic way as she went downstairs to get her precious coffee. "—I hope Bella never meets Fox to tell him how I walked her before I had my coffee. Fox will never get that kind of sympathy," Ava wrapped up the tale.

Clutching his belly, CJ let out a roar of laughter. "I'm sorry she bothered you. This is totally out of her character. She's never done anything like this before. I don't know what to say, but I'll make sure it won't happen again."

"Well, she didn't really bother me. It was sort of unexpected since you said she'd ignore me. She also didn't seem bothered when I petted her briefly as I hooked the leash on her collar. However, I won't tempt fate again. I kinda like having ten fingers."

"Oh, my God!" CJ exclaimed, a mix of amusement and impressed lining his tone.

From the moment Ava stepped on the set, Jason Frank and Jessica LaSerre claimed her as their own. Maybe it was the shared homeland—three Albertans navigating Hollywood's chaos. But they adopted her fast.

Whenever they weren't on camera, they were by her side, trading stories, cracking jokes, hovering around her like moths attracted to a lamp. Even in the crowded cafeteria, they gravitated toward the same table, saving seats for each other, laughter and banter setting them apart from the rest of the cast.

One afternoon, Jason and CJ were alone at the snack bar, waiting as the espresso machine groaned through its cycle.

Leaning on the counter, Jason watched CJ with a knowing smirk. "So," he began, his voice laced with peculiar curiosity. "You and Ava ... Are you an item?"

Stirring his coffee, CJ didn't look up from the cup. "We're friends. Good friends."

"Right," Jason said, skepticism dripping from the single word. "What's about her? You know ... her past?"

CJ's grip tightened slightly around his cup. "She's a widow. She's lost her husband during the pandemic," he said, his voice steady.

Jason's smirk faded, his expression shifting to something softer. "Damn. That's rough."

"Yeah. Not sure she's ready to move on if that's what interests you."

Jason's smirk crept back. "So ... you're just hanging around for when she's ready, then?"

CJ exhaled sharply, shaking his head with a chuckle. "We're friends. That's all."

"Mm-hmm." Jason didn't appear convinced.

Only a few days in, once she slid into the car as they were leaving the movie set, Ava tossed her backpack onto the backseat. In the same motion, her elbow collided with CJ's shoulder just as he was about to put the keys in the ignition. The keys pinwheeled, pinged off the roof, and landed by Ava's feet.

Both dove for them simultaneously, heads crashing with a loud thud.

"Oh, for fuck's sake." CJ pressed his hand against his head. "I just saw my life flash before my eyes."

"What was your life doing on my side? Keys on my side? I get them. It's that simple." Ava winced, holding her forehead in her palm.

CJ blinked at her, still stunned. "Are you okay?"

"I'll survive." But her scowling face revealed something different.

"Let me see. Let me see!" he insisted, pulling her hand and assessing the damage. His eyes widened. "Uh-oh!"

"What uh-oh?" Ava yanked down the visor mirror. "Wow! This is real uh-oh." She stared in horror at the goose egg rising like a cursed soufflé before her very eyes.

"Stay right here. I'll go get some ice," CJ said, flying out the door. "The lunchroom still open?" he asked, bolting past Jason in the opposite direction.

"It was … but they were packing," Jason replied, CJ barely catching the last of his words. "Where is CJ running?" Jason asked Ava as he reached their car, his eyes still following CJ. "Holy cow! What happened?" He jolted back when Ava opened the door.

"He hit me! Now, he's fleeing the crime scene. Go get him," Ava deadpanned.

"What?!" Jason winced, utterly astonished.

"And, this is how you start rumours. Relax. I'm just kidding. He dropped the keys, and we both went for them, and … Bam! We butted heads. You're looking at the aftermath. He went to get some ice." She grimaced in pain, pressing her hand against her eyebrow.

"They might be closed. Wait! Take this!" Jason said, producing a can of soda out of his bag. "Stuck it in the freezer earlier and completely forgot about it. I took it out before someone else grabbed it, and they'd have a volcano in their hands when cracking it open."

"Thank you. This should do. But it's your drink," Ava paused, hesitant to take the can.

"I'm trying to cut down on sugary crap anyway. So, let's put it to better use," Jason replied as he looked up across the parking lot. "Here comes CJ, empty-handed. Take care and see you tomorrow." He patted the car canopy and left.

"Bummer! They closed. I'm so sorry," CJ groaned, opening the car's door. "Where did you get that?" He gawked at the can of pop stuck to Ava's forehead.

She threw him a one-eyed gaze from under the frozen can. "Jason!"

"Oooh … Jason came to the rescue—" he dragged out the words.

"What! He seemed concerned. It was very nice of him not to leave it behind and erupt in someone's face eventually. So, it came in handy, and he saved the day."

"Oooh … Jason saved the day—" the words dragged again.

"Luckily, he had a frozen drink in that bag, not pigeons."

"I think he likes you…" CJ's examining gaze tried to catch her reaction.

"Oh God, please! That's not why I'm here." She pointed to the goose egg on her forehead. "Now, this is why I'm here. Where else could I have gotten one of these, eh?"

Both burst into laughter, only to quickly whimper in pain as all the happy muscles contracted, a sharp reminder of their newly acquired goose eggs. CJ's hand shot to the top of his head, only then realizing that he, too, had a matching lump. His, was simply more strategically positioned—hidden beneath his hair.

"Let me see." She ran her fingers over the bump. "Not that bad. You might not even need extra time in 'makeup' tomorrow." She then flinched as if something had just come to mind. "Is there any wine left?"

"Come on now. I'm not sure drinking would help."

She scoffed. "Not for drinking. Helps prevent bruising. If I wake up with a black eye, *I'll* be the one stuck in makeup for an hour." She paused, then added casually, "By the way, I told him you hit me."

"What?! Who?" CJ snapped, taken aback.

Trying to raise an eyebrow proved painful, triggering another wince. "Jason...? I was joking."

"Did he understand you were joking?"

"I hope so," Ava's grin was anything but innocent.

"You are terrible. Oh, my! You're a piece of work! Hurt and still joking!" CJ laughed, holding his head.

"I can't help it." A wicked sneer accompanied her raised shoulders.

11. Who do you think you are? Superman?!

It was the weekend and, more than ever, Ava needed a break. Just to recharge her batteries. The new job was quite demanding. Juggling it alongside her main job, during breaks and downtime, proved an exhausting combo. She woke up early and stopped to put a load of laundry in the washer before hitting the gym.

As usual, Bella pranced behind her. So much for 'I'll make sure this won't happen again'. Bella won, and her bed took permanent residence in Ava's room. At least she was sleeping now. No creepy paranormal activity anymore.

After the gym, Ava moved her laundry to the dryer, made a coffee, and then off she went for a walk with Bella. Upon returning, she heard CJ fighting some iron beasts in the gym. She gathered the laundry and, hamper under her arm, climbed upstairs, starting the tedious process of folding and putting it away.

"Oh, shit!" She lost it. "I must've dropped it." After another quick, frantic inventory, she bolted back downstairs, scanning every inch of the way.

Barefoot, she cat-stepped into the basement, hoping to go unnoticed. As she reached the bottom of the stairs, eyes wide, and breath caught in her throat, she froze, hand gripping the banister. There he was. With his back turned and one arm raised, CJ was studying something. Something red, something lacy. Before he could even blink, Ava jumped like a tigress, snatching the item off his hand.

"Um ... I found it on the floor," CJ stuttered, what was supposed to be an excuse, his eyes just as wide as hers.

Ava shot him a dead stare. "Really?! Did it look like something that might be yours?"

"Um-I ... I didn't know what it was." Another faltering attempt at an excuse.

"Seriously?! A red, *lacy* piece of lingerie wasn't a clue?"

Shrugging, CJ opened his mouth, then closed it and exhaled. "Um ... I'm sorry. I didn't stop to think."

"Who do you think you are? Superman?! Even Superman wouldn't wear *lacy* lingerie! Next time you see something that doesn't remotely resemble anything you'd wear, why not just leave it alone? On the floor or wherever you found it," Ava fumed, heated and embarrassed.

CJ rubbed the back of his neck, chasing away a frog that was dwelling in his throat, appearing just as embarrassed as she did. "I said I'm sorry. I don't know what else to say."

"Whatever. I knew this living arrangement was a bad idea," she muttered, rolling her eyes before storming up the stairs.

"Ava, please," CJ called after her. "Let's not get carried away. It's just a bloody piece of lingerie, for God's sake! It was a mistake. I promise it won't happen again."

Halfway up the stairs, she suddenly turned, giving him a still troubled look. "Oh, I know it won't. And you know why? Because I'll be extra careful. I guess it was my fault. I didn't have to think about this kind of shit for far too long."

With a guilty sneer, he climbed two steps closer, holding his hand out. "So ... friends?"

Displaying a dramatic shrug and eye roll, she held out her right fist, still gripping the recovered underwear. "Yes, friends. And if you want to study this kind of stuff, I can recommend some reputable websites. And guess what? They come on fashion models. Much more entertaining and a better sight."

CJ groaned. "Oh, come on! Do you think I'm some kind of pervert?"

Ava tilted her head. "I didn't say that." She paused, then reconsidered. "Okay, maybe I implied it." He threw his hands up in exasperation. "Okay, I … overreacted. It's probably inevitable when you share the same space." She spun to leave, while tossing over her shoulder, "By the way, they were clean this time. But next time? Think twice."

CJ smirked. "I figured that much."

Both burst into spontaneous laughter as she vanished up the stairs.

The air crackled with tension, growing more intense, especially after a few nights ago when she had a strange hunch she chose to ignore.

It wasn't the first time she'd sensed CJ was just about to reach out and kiss her. Like that night in Victoria, when he leaned in too close. But then he pulled away, leaving only the ghost of his intention in the air and her breath caught in her throat.

And last Christmas, when CJ got stranded in Canada. He arrived last November. For work. The project was supposed to be wrapped up in about two weeks. But two months later, he was still stuck in Canada.

"Technical issues and other unforeseen delays," he said.

He declined other invitations. Christmas was for families, and Ava felt the closest—'almost like family', he said. And he dared to ask if she'd have him for Christmas. Ava was a bit too quick to say 'yes'.

It was the first year since Dan's passing that she felt like decorating a Christmas tree and her front lawn. For the past years, she felt like the Grinch of the neighbourhood. CJ just happened to be around when she spruced up the place last Christmas. He lent a firm hand with tasks that were beyond her strength.

Satisfied with the results, she placed her hands on her hips and browsed around, smiling. Then she sighed as her eyes continued scanning. "I guess I'll have to rethink and downscale my decorating style. I don't expect to have someone your height around to help next year."

The neighbourhood was known for the colossal decorating effort everybody put into their lavish displays. Too big a task for her to handle on her own.

Two nights ago, after dinner, they settled comfortably to watch a space show. Ava sat at one end of the couch while CJ took the other. The edge of the coffee table, where he'd put his feet up to relax after a long day, pressed into his ankles.

"Do you mind if I put my feet up on the couch? They're clean," he asked, still squirming and trying to find a more comfortable spot.

"I don't mind. Here!" She patted her lap, inviting him to put his feet up. Ava was a first-hand witness to his long, tiring day.

"Oh, no. My feet are clean, but I won't put them right under your nose."

"Then, how about I sit on the floor, and you can have the couch. The floor is my favourite spot to watch TV, anyway. And everybody's happy."

Ava plopped onto the floor, feet off the ground, holding her knees to her chest, in a balanced position.

"How can you do this?" CJ asked as he lounged on the couch, propped on his elbow.

"Do what?"

"Sit like that, balanced?"

"Practice, I guess. I don't know. I just do it."

Just a few minutes later, CJ sat up. "No! That's not right." He leapt to his feet. "I can't let you sit on the floor while I've taken over the entire couch. Come up here. I have a better idea. Come on," he insisted. With one quick, vigorous pull, he plucked Ava off the floor, and she resumed her previous spot. "Now ... this *is better, and everybody's happy.*"

He tossed a decorative pillow on the coffee table and sat beside her, feet up, stretching an arm along the back of the couch, behind her. That's when Ava sensed he was watching her more than the show. The proximity of their bodies felt strange, and she barely breathed as the image on the TV screen played out before her eyes.

Nah! It's all in my head. There's no way he's attracted to ... me?! Smarten up, Ava! Maybe he got carried away at some point. Tempted. I'm sure he knows it wasn't attraction. Just the proximity ... the convenience? Stop it! We're just friends—she dismissed the thought.

She swallowed quietly and let it slide, just as she had before, thinking that questioning, or even alluding to it, might make her sound ridiculous. But the doubt lingered, gnawing at her insides.

"Oh, shoot. I must call Nina." She jolted up after glancing at the clock on the wall, patting around as if she were looking for something.

"Now?" CJ asked, his voice heavy with disappointment. "I was feeling so good."

"Then keep feeling good. I have to call. Nina texted earlier. Something important, she said. I promised I'd call her. You should be happy, having the whole couch for yourself." She quickly tapped her fitness tracker, and her cellphone pinged.

Upon returning, she beamed with excitement. A sigh of relief, skillfully concealed, gathered in her throat when she found CJ sitting at the far end of the couch.

Even more good news—she thought.

"So, what was that important? Is she Romanian, too? I thought I'd heard you talking in another language."

"Yeah, you heard right. Nina is Romanian too." Ava flashed a radiant smile. "And I'm going to be a godmother."

"A grandmother!" CJ exclaimed, appalled.

"No, you silly boy!" She chuckled. "A godmother. Nina, my friend, is pregnant. That was the *important something* she wanted to tell me. I'm so happy for her."

With a sullen face on display, CJ played hurt. "Silly boy! I'm not a boy. Silly I am, though."

"That's right, you're not a boy. I'm sorry I called you a boy. And you're not silly either." Ava posed a guilty mien as she sat back on her end of the couch.

Driving to the grocery store was supposed to be a mindless task. That moment in the day, or week, when you don't need to stress over anything. Go with the flow, pick whatever catches your eye, or follow a shopping list. But her mind was racing a thousand miles an hour. The thick silence persisted on the way to the grocery store as Ava still struggled with the embarrassment from the earlier incident. The tension from that morning's near-confrontation lingered in the air.

"When I said you'd have enough of me in two weeks tops, I was wrong. I guess a week was more than enough," she broke the silence, avoiding eye contact.

"What?! What are you talking about?" He cocked a baffled eyebrow.

"I think this living arrangement, as temporary as it may be, doesn't work. I don't want to be in your way. And I feel like I am."

"Now you are being silly. Are you still talking about—? Because I already forgot what I saw."

"No, no! It's not only that. That only told me that you have needs ... Well, other needs, and I'm somehow invading your space ... your privacy. That I'm in the way of ... you know...? If you want to bring a girl home and have fun..." Ava stammered, still avoiding looking at him.

"Oh, my! No! I ... No. Really?! Is that what you think?"

She gulped her embarrassment. "Well ... I do. I ... I think I should move."

"Listen. If I wanted to ... whatever you think I'm being deprived of, I could." He flicked a hand. "I don't have to ask permission. I could let you know I have someone over, and that's it. Or I could go to her place ... get a hotel...? There are ways around it, you know? Please, get it out of your head that you are standing in the way of anything. I offered you to live here. I invited you. If I had any concerns about my space or privacy, I wouldn't have offered. Period," CJ said, as he gazed steadily at Ava.

"Can you please look at the road when you drive?"

"Only if you look at me when you talk nonsense." Ava looked at him for the first time since they left the house, and he grinned back. "This is better. Would be best if you could also throw a smile in there." She smiled. "Please promise me you won't bring up this topic again. And I promise to navigate around any objects that don't look like they could be mine. On the floor or anywhere else."

She started laughing softly, mostly inward, with only her eyes and her body vibrating as evidence. "Then, you have to promise that, if you ever feel like I'm in the way, you'll let me know. Or, even better, just ask whoever's in charge to make different living arrangements for me."

"That'll never happen, but ... okay. I'll keep it in mind."

The following week proved even more brutal and intense. The tension bubbled on set as everyone scrambled to wrap up one last scene before moving to a different location. Ava barely had time to breathe between tasks, exhaustion invading her bones.

Next Thursday morning, her cellphone dinged with a new email notification. Her pulse quickened as she read the email titled *Crew Housing Update*. They had a new place for her to move. Available on Saturday. Just a straightforward notice—no beating around the bush, no formalities. A mix of relief and unease took over her. *So, he did it.*

All she wanted was a quiet moment, and it was happening. At least now she wouldn't have to deal with the near-romantic hiccups, the accidental touches, or the assessing glances. She bit her lower lip, thinking how much she hated those infuriating butterflies tap-dancing in her stomach lately, whenever she sensed he was too interested. Like the other day, when she suspected he was about to kiss her.

"See you tonight," Jessica said when Ava and CJ got to their car.

"Yeah, see you tonight," CJ smiled brightly as Jessica wandered over to her car across the parking lot.

Oh, so this is why. I'm happy for him—Ava's mind raced as she buckled up, but she didn't give it another thought.

"I was thinking ... What if we stop somewhere and grab something to eat, so we can relax a bit before the party?" CJ asked once in the car.

"Party! What party?" Her tone carried a vague sense of surprise.

"The party tonight? The one that the producers and directors are throwing. And we're going."

"Well, you can go. I wasn't invited. It's probably a 'cast only' party," her reply fell dry.

"Have you checked your emails this afternoon? An email was sent to everyone."

She raised a shoulder as she checked her inbox. "No new emails. I guess it wasn't sent to everyone."

"Then, you're coming as my plus one." He paused and then shot her another look. "Your spams?"

"Yeah, spam folder." She skimmed through the message and exhaled. "But I'm not going."

"Why? It's a party. Nobody says *no* to a party."

"Well, I do. I have plans for tonight."

CJ scoffed. "You're seriously saying 'no' to a party?"

"Yes. That's exactly what I'm saying."

"We're off until Sunday night. Did anything happen today? Did anyone say anything out of place? I can tell something's bothering you," he insisted, taking another glimpse at her as they pulled out of the parking lot.

"No. I just have things to do." She forced a smile.

"Like what? Is it work?" He tilted his head, studying her with a more than charming smile. "Maybe I can help, just like you help me rehearse? Kill two birds with one stone?"

Ava squirmed, hesitating. "I need to start packing. Making sure I don't leave anything behind. So, you can't help. It's a *me-only* task."

CJ's smile faded. "Packing?"

"Yeah. They found a place for me," she said, her tone unaffected. "I'll be moving Saturday."

"Wait ... What?! Move?" Dismay equally lined his gaze and his tone as he almost shouted.

"Yes. I'll be moving Saturday." While Ava reiterated what she had just said, CJ veered off, pulling over in one quick motion.

Jaw clenched, and hands locked on the steering wheel, he looked ahead at nothing from under knitted brows, for a few eternity-long seconds.

Quiet, Ava struggled to regain her breath after the short and quick maneuver that brought the car to an abrupt stop. "What the hell! Was this necessary?" she asked, somewhat finding her nerve.

He shook his head in disbelief, finally looking at her. "I thought we were past this moving nonsense. I need you. I ... I mean, you've been an enormous help with rehearsals and everything. You have no clue what 'moving' means. You'll be dependent on others. You may have to get up earlier than necessary and spend more time in the car while the driver picks up others along the way." His voice was sharp, but there was something else beneath it. Something unspoken.

"Funny you should say that. Well, I guess I've got no choice, do I?"

Brows pulled together, his voice dropped a few notes when he spoke again. "Funny? It is not funny at all! And you do have a choice. But you chose to move—" he paused, shrugging. "You know what? It's your decision. Do as you want."

Ava fidgeted, biting her bottom lip. "What I want?! Anyway, I don't understand why you're acting upset. You asked, and they delivered."

"I asked! What have I asked?"

"Well … You asked. I was just hoping I'd hear it from you first, and it wouldn't come as a surprise. But I'm totally fine. I know I suggested it."

CJ's perplexed stare fixated on Ava. "Come again! You didn't ask to move?"

"No, I didn't. You did, right?!" she scowled, confusion evident in her expression.

"I didn't ask. I wouldn't. I thought I was quite clear the other day. Who told you you're moving?"

"I got an email this morning."

CJ reached out for his phone. "Does it have a number? I need to call and clarify this."

"—You can cancel. She's not moving anywhere," he ended the call and turned to Ava. "Well … lack of communication. Next time, please ask me, don't assume. And remember, I'd never do anything that affects you without telling you first. Now, let's get some food and then go to the bloody party."

He gazed at Ava, shaking his head, still upset about the mix-up. The brief conversation he had with the 'specific someone' who was simply doing their job left him jarred.

When he offered for Ava to live with him, someone failed to communicate that finding a place for her was no longer an issue. Whoever was in charge of staff housing continued the search.

12. Do we have a flat?

When CJ came downstairs, Ava was rummaging through the kitchen drawers, frantically looking for something. Or so it appeared. Seen from behind, she was wearing a peach-coloured silk housedress, barefoot, but her hair looked done.

"Oh, you're not ready," he said.

Startled, Ava turned around. She didn't hear him coming over her own clattering. "Um ... I was looking for something. But ... you're ready. I'll go change and be back in two minutes." Ava turned and headed towards the stairs.

"What's wrong with the dress you're wearing? It looks nice," he said, noticing the dress under the undone silk housecoat.

"Poor planning when I packed. I don't have time to make this work."

"What were you looking for? Maybe I can help."

"I was looking for a paper clip or something to pull up the zipper. I haven't worn this dress in a while. I forgot I needed an extra pair of hands. I'll slip into something else quickly and be right back."

"I have an extra pair of hands. I could help," CJ volunteered to make himself useful.

"Oh, no. It's okay. I have a backup plan."

"You always do. I won't look. I promise," he pressed.

She stopped on the second step and turned around, giving him a squinty-eyed look, like she evaluated the offer. "Oh-kay. Close your eyes."

Partially removing her housecoat, Ava turned around and swept her hair in front. Then she took his hand, guiding it to the zipper while holding the two ends together.

"Done?"

"I can adjust it from there. Thanks," she tossed over her shoulder as she ran up, the housecoat she was still half-wearing dragging behind her on the stairs.

"Where are you going now?"

"To get my shoes," she answered, already at the top of the staircase.

"Oh, okay."

When she returned, CJ was just getting up after tying his shoes. His look, one of astonishment, gazing at Ava as she floated down the stairs in her cream, simple A-line dress.

"Wow! You look ... stunning!" he muttered as something stirred in his stomach, making him feel as if he was indulging in a fantasy.

"Thank you. You don't look too shabby yourself," she tittered.

God bless whoever invented makeup—she didn't want him to see her blushing. Compliments coming from him made her stomach flutter lately. Her fingers clutched the handrail tightly as she came to a stop at the bottom of the stairs.

CJ's teeth bared in a wide smile, and he dashed to meet her, holding out a curled arm. "Here. Hold onto this. I don't think I have ever seen you in heels, and I'm not sure I should trust you in those. I feel responsible for your life."

"Is that right? I hate to burst your bubble, but I'm quite comfortable in heels. Probably not as comfortable as I'm in sneakers, but I'm pretty confident my life is not in danger."

"Hold onto my arm, please ... just in case," he added with a wink, while another humongous smile split his face.

"Okay! Just to humour you."

When they pulled into the club's parking lot, CJ exited the car, walked around, and opened the door on Ava's side, offering his arm again.

"I can do this on my own," she protested.

He pointed to the club's entrance, hissing as if someone could hear, although nobody was nearby. "If I hadn't seen you all dolled up before, I can only imagine the looks, and I don't want to miss that. I must be right here, by you, to see all the reactions when we walk through that door."

Ava puffed, rolling her eyes. "Oh, please stop it! What reactions? You're imagining things."

"Well, we'll see. Take my arm," he said, returning an expressive smile, and Ava wrapped her arm around his as they strolled in together.

Normally not paying attention to such things and oblivious to any reaction, if there had ever been one, this time she noticed. Probably just because she had been warned.

Quite some glances and double-takes turned toward them as they walked in. She quickly shrugged it off. CJ's appearance likely stirred those responses, she thought.

He looked as if he had just descended from a modern take on a Michelangelo painting. The deep, dark sea-green shirt and light blue-grey slacks he wore contrasted nicely with her cream-coloured dress. Let's say those were his colours and leave it at that.

"Wow! CJ, it looks like you brought your guardian angel with you tonight," Jason commented when he came over to greet and shake CJ's hand. Gallantly, Jason took Ava's hand and kissed it.

"Angel! I'm just a devil in disguise, you know? But I'm glad the chivalry didn't die," Ava replied, to CJ's dismay, who tossed her a surprised look as Jason left, laughing.

He then whispered in Ava's ear. "See? I told you."

"Get out of here," Ava pushed back with a crooked smile.

"And you like it. You're flirting," he whispered again.

She scoffed, flashing an offended gaze. "I am not! He was nice. It would be rude to be inconsiderate."

As the night progressed and people mingled and chatted, in a corner, Ava, Jessica, and Jason were just goofing off, tossing around the usual banter and laughter.

CJ headed to the bar to get some drinks. He paused briefly to exchange pleasantries with a few people before returning with Ava's gin and tonic and a beer for himself.

"I was just telling Ava this story. I believe Jessica already heard it," Jason resumed the tale. "I was about your age—"

"Why, Jason, thank you for including me. I'll take it as a compliment. Though I believe I belong to *your* age group rather than this one here," Ava interrupted, obviously amused, pointing towards Jessica and CJ. "I have a feeling that I might actually be the oldest of us all." All eyes turned to her, surprise evident on their faces.

Jason stopped mid-sentence, staring at Ava, confused. "Say what? And exactly how old do you think I am?" he asked, voice dripping with curiosity.

"Forty-ssseven-ish?" Ava guessed Jason's age.

"Right! I mean ... I'll be forty-seven next month... So, I don't get why you'd say you're in my age range...?"

"As guesstimated, it turns out that, indeed, I am the oldest, at forty-nine," Ava said, displaying a winning smile. "What? I am," she reacted after catching the disbelieving eyes staring at her.

"Is that true?" Jason asked CJ, waiting for his confirmation.

CJ looked from Jason to Ava, then back at Jason. Just as puzzled, he replied, "I don't know, man. Don't look at me. We never discussed age. You know it's not polite to ask a woman her age. And she's not a public figure, so ... how should I know?"

"Okay. I don't believe it. I mean, you don't look forty-nine. What am I saying? You don't even look forty. You look thirty-five

... thirty-seven, max. I'll need proof to believe it." The words poured at high speed, skepticism exuding from Jason's voice and gaze.

Ava chuckled, growing more amused. "I don't buy it. You can't possibly believe that I am— What?! Their age!" she snickered, gesturing towards Jessica and CJ.

"Look at our faces. I know we're all actors, but this is us outside work. Are our faces lying? Seriously! I need proof to believe. I do," Jason continued, his passion rising.

"Unfortunately, I don't have my passport with me. But think about it. What woman would lie about her age? I mean, pretending she's older than she actually is. Younger? Maybe. But older? I don't think so," Ava's logic kicked in.

"Then, you need to share what your secret is. What do you eat? I want to eat what you eat," Jason pressed.

"Gosh! How many times have we had lunch together? You must've seen what I eat. And—" She raised her glass. "I drink gin and tonic."

"She eats 'alien' food," CJ chimed in, just as his phone rang, and he excused himself to take the call.

Jason, who had hoped for some support in his request for proof, was now alone. The discussion about Ava's age didn't continue after CJ stepped away.

Minutes later, the club's atmosphere changed. Dance time. The music grew louder, and the conversations became difficult to follow. Mingling resumed in secluded corners and around the bar, and Ava joined the lively group on the dance floor.

When the call ended, CJ was hijacked into another conversation. The producers and the directors were part of the cluster. Probably discussing work, judging by their serious expressions. About an hour later, he joined Ava on the dance floor.

"You had too much fun while I missed it all. I'm probably the only guy who didn't dance with you tonight. You are a good dancer," he shouted, leaning closer, so she could hear over the loud music. His hot breath blew through her hair, sending shivers down her spine.

"How do you know? You just got here," she taunted.

"I've been watching."

"Oh, so you're one of those … standing by the bar, watching…? Okay. Good to know."

"I had to figure out if you knew how to dance before I put you on the spot," he said in a serious tone, swirling her on the dance floor and catching her in his arms. A bit too tight. A bit too close.

"Yeah, right," she gave a nervous chuckle.

On their drive home, Ava kept chatting excitedly, but CJ stayed quiet, glancing at her briefly and replying in short sentences.

That phone call probably wasn't good news—Ava thought. She reached over and searched for some music on Spotify, quickly tapping on a list of entertaining tracks that made her dance in her seat.

"Wow! Please cover your ears. This is my favourite song. I know I have no voice. That's why I have a day job. But I must," she said, and she began singing along, much to CJ's amusement.

He kept glancing at her.

Her performance didn't amuse him. But imagining the face Ava would pull when the song reached the part where Andrea Bocelli started singing in Italian brought a smile to the corner of his mouth. He knew the tune—a slightly different take on the original.

To his surprise, Ava switched to singing in Italian without missing a beat or mispronouncing a word. He cast quick, stunned glances at her. *What the hell?* he wondered.

"Sorry for killing your hearing, but I had to," Ava shrugged with a Cheshire cat smile when the song ended. "Okay. I promise I'll keep my day job, and you'll never hear me singing again. I'll save it for the shower," she continued in a witty tone, looking into his confused gaze.

As he grew more silent, his eyebrows knitted, and his incredulous stare turned to her. A million questions clashed in his mind at once, and about two miles later, he pulled over.

"Uh-oh. Do we have a flat?"

"No, we don't. I need to step out for a minute. Please stay in the car," he said as he exited, his tone intense.

"Oh, okay," Ava replied in a small voice, thinking the call of nature made him pull over.

She sat there, neither watching nor looking around. A quick movement reflected in the mirror beside her caught her eye, and she looked, but saw nothing. She dismissed it. Probably just an illusion from the headlights of the cars racing by. Then again, she thought she saw a flicker of movement. She looked, but this time kept her eyes on the mirror. *What if some wildlife is wandering nearby?*

Soon, the magic mirror showed CJ. He paced back and forth behind the car, stopping, clenching his fists, squatting, punching his knees, and raising his fists above his head. As her gaze remained locked in the mirror, Ava's eyebrows almost reached her hairline.

What the hell? It was her turn to ask, shaken by that image. *What on earth is he doing? He must've gotten some really shocking news.*

In just minutes, he returned, appearing almost peaceful but still extremely quiet. With slow, practiced moves, he buckled up and turned the engine on.

Lowered and curled up in her seat, Ava stared, extremely quiet.

"Do you want me to drive?" she asked cautiously.

"No. Why?" CJ finally looked at her.

That's when he saw she was curled up in her seat. Then, he noticed the mirror and realized she must've seen something, if not everything.

"Shit! What did you see?" he freaked out.

"I don't know ... Hulk?" she scrambled to sound funny. "Is

everything okay? Do you want to talk?"

"Not now. When we get home. We'll be home in about fifteen minutes."

"Are you sure you can drive? You seem quite ... upset."

"I can drive," CJ replied promptly.

"Okay," Ava said in a small voice, before reaching over and turning the sound system off.

13. Arguing her heart

Shoes in hand, Ava padded barefoot into the house, making a beeline for the stairs.

"Would you join me for a glass of wine?" CJ asked, striding in, just a few steps behind her.

"Yes, but I need to change first," she said, barely glancing back.

"Need help with that zipper?"

"Um, no, thanks. I've got my technique. I think I can manage."

When she returned, still barefoot and in more comfortable clothes, CJ was already pouring the wine.

His glance up, lax and steady, met hers. "I have red. Would you prefer white?"

"Red's fine," Ava said. "So ... What are we drinking for?" She rested her elbows on the island, chin propped on her fists, watching him.

Averting her eyes, his lips curved into something unreadable as he picked up the half-full glasses. Tracing around the island, he stopped before her and offered her one.

"I guess we drink for ... boys?!"

"So, for the boys, I suppose ... Cheers!" Ava forced a joyful tone, raising her glass and clinking it gently against his. CJ stood before her, his gaze intense. She took a sip and glanced up at him, only to be met by the look on his face. Slowly, she turned and placed the glass on the counter. "Why do we drink for boys? Forgive my ignorance. I think I'm missing the meaning," she asked, unsure what to make of his words, and especially that expression.

"For boys ... like me. Didn't you call me a boy not that long ago?" he asked, setting his glass next to hers.

Ava shifted her weight, an uncomfortable chuckle escaping her throat. "Oh! I said I was sorry. I didn't mean it. Gosh! Why are you bringing this up now? Is that why you were upset? You *are* upset...?"

She held his gaze as he moved closer, his stare fiery. Before she could react, his arm wrapped around her waist, and his lips brushed against hers. Soft at first, then locking into a passionate kiss. She kissed him back, butterflies and something else stirring in the pit of her stomach.

When his tongue glided between her lips, searching for hers, as if released from under a spell, Ava pulled away with a firm push. "CJ! What the hell! What's gotten into you?" She felt trapped between his body, his arms still wrapped around her, and the island blocking her from behind.

"Funny you should ask. You know exactly what. You've known since Paris. Ava, stop playing this game," he grumbled, his jaw tight, teeth nearly grinding.

Her pulse quickened, and words gathered in her throat as she stared at him before the words finally found their way out. "What game? And what does Paris have to do with it?"

"Ava, you're one of the smartest people I've ever met. Am I really just a boy to you? Because when you look at me, I don't think you see a boy. Please stop playing with me." He huffed, affected.

She gulped her own anxiety. "Listen. I'm sorry for calling you a boy. But I have no idea what you're talking about. You've got it all wrong."

His brows raised in mocking astonishment. "Really?! So, I imagined you kissing me back just now?"

"You don't have to mention it. I know what I did. It was a mistake. Please let me go. I don't feel comfortable."

His grip loosened slightly, but his voice remained steady. "We need to talk about this. About us ... About my feelings, which I figured you're already aware of. About your feelings, which you're trying to ignore...?"

"What feelings? You're confusing me. There's nothing to talk about. And why do you keep insinuating I know? What do I supposedly know?"

Eyes locked into hers, he slowly shook his head, puffing a quasi-smirk. "It occurred to me tonight that you speak Italian. And please, don't try to deny it. You didn't mispronounce a word when you sang along Andrea Bocelli."

She snorted. "Deny it? I speak a dozen languages, actually. Is it a crime?"

"And you just failed to mention that you speak Italian, correct?" The words rolled through still clenched jaws.

"Never came up, I guess. Can you imagine me going around, bragging, 'Hey! Do you know I speak a dozen languages? How many do you speak?' I really don't see what's wrong with not mentioning it," Ava countered, her intrigued gaze consuming the air between them.

"Huh ... You're probably right. There's nothing wrong. But it does bring up the fact that you knew I was into you since Paris. You understood everything I said to Paolo, not only the bits I translated for you."

She blinked. "Who?"

"Paolo, the taxi driver...?"

She scoffed, confusion painted on her face. "Oh, God! The meddler? No way! You just ... humoured him. That's what you did, right?"

"No, Ava. I wasn't." He slowly bobbed his head, a mix of frustration and dismay warping his expression. "I told the truth because I thought you didn't understand." His lips pressed against hers again. Gentler this time. "I wanted to do this right then and there. See? This," he grumbled and kissed her once more while she was still in shock, trying to compute.

"Fuck, CJ! This is so twisted. Please let me go." She placed her hands on his chest and pushed him. Unconvincing. That, or he was much stronger than her, since he didn't budge an inch.

"So, I'm just a boy to you. Here's another thing I learned about you tonight. Do you really think that I'm too young for you?"

"Please stop. I-um … I don't think you're too young. But *I know* I'm too old for you. Here! This is what I think." Ava almost shouted, struggling to break free from his arms, and he let her go.

Released from his embrace, she backed away along the kitchen island, coming to a halt as she came up against one of the barstools.

His gaze fixed on her, CJ closed the distance with two long strides, scooped her up in his arms and sat her down on the barstool. "Now, this is better. We can talk now."

"There's nothing to talk about!"

"Oh, there's plenty to talk about. Starting with your feelings. The ones you are suppressing." He nodded with a smug eyebrow and a matching sneer. "All this time, I was a fool who believed that you weren't ready for a new relationship. I thought you were still healing, still grieving— And I respected that. But you were playing me," he said bluntly, blocking her from getting off the barstool just by standing too close.

"I didn't play you," she uttered, her tone fierce.

In contrast, his voice arrived balanced. "I know you're scared. But I also know you care about me, more than you're willing to admit."

"Of course I care about you."

He grinned. "Aha! I knew it!"

"You're my friend— I care about all my friends."

"Bollocks!" he scoffed. "That's not what I see when you look at me!"

"Listen. We both had something to drink tonight, and this living arrangement … the proximity— All of this… is not ideal when you're confused—"

CJ let out a loud exhale, his hands gripping her arms just firm enough to hold her still. "I only had half a beer, and I'm not confused. This isn't about tonight. I was madly in love with you before you even left Ireland. You keep throwing numbers at me like they mean something. Like they change the way I feel about you. News flash, Ava: I don't give a damn how old you are. I just know I'm not spending another second pretending I don't want you." He let go of her arms, shaking his head, fingers brushing her cheek. "Ava, you deserve to be happy."

Her teeth tugged at her lower lip, and she avoided his gaze, uncertainty clouding her expression. *He is not completely wrong. But ... am I ready for another relationship? Not yet. And certainly not with him.*

"What do you expect me to say?" She exhaled a whimper before her voice levelled. "I'm not denying myself anything. *I* don't even know what I want. How *would you* know? But this? *I know* this won't work. How would it work? Somebody's gonna get hurt. And I don't want to be somebody. I'm nobody. I'd much rather stay that way."

"You're not nobody. Why did you imagine I kept following you, huh? Will you please stop this nonsense? It'll work. It will."

She tugged at her lower lip again, an inquisitive look on her face. "How?"

"The same way I've made it work so far. Why do you think I travelled halfway around the world *every few weeks*, to be with you?" he asked, not waiting for an answer before continuing. "I wanted to be near when you were ready. I didn't want to be too late. I didn't want anyone else to get you before me."

Disbelief etched all over her expression, Ava stared at him for a moment that stretched too long. "Well, technically, you didn't travel halfway around the world. You were already in Canada. So, you were halfway there..."

"That's what I led you to believe. I was in Canada the first two or three times, indeed. But each time after that, I flew from

London. Yes, technically, halfway around the world. *Every. Single. Fucking. Time.*"

"But you said—" Her back suddenly straightened. "You lied?"

CJ let out a rough breath. "I know what I said. I didn't lie. I always called from Canada before I boarded the flight to Edmonton. I just said I was in Montreal, Toronto, or Calgary, which was true. I was in Canada. I just didn't want to scare you. I wanted to wait for the right time and be there when the right time came." Ava pulled her upper lip with her teeth, gazing at him, lost. "You keep avoiding this like it's not real. Like I'm just some stupid crush you can ignore. Ava, I love you. And I know you love me too. So, stop pretending this is nothing. Please give yourself a chance to love again."

Her troubled gaze turned away. "Feelings are not enough. Let's not start something that has no future. It'll just be a waste of time. Your time ... mine... It'll most likely hurt when it's over. Badly. I don't want to hurt again," she said in a small voice.

In contrast, his tone fell firm. Determined. "This, right here ... getting to know each other first, as friends, without any other involvement... This is different. I already know. I want a future with you."

"Oh, please. You're completely insane!"

"I may sound like I'm insane. Do you think I haven't thought about this? About us? You think I haven't pictured waking up next to you every morning? Because I have. And I know exactly what I want. It's all new to you, I understand. When you know what you want—hopefully, soon, I can see us starting a family. Probably not too far from today."

"Come on, CJ! This is crazy talk. It'll never happen. I have nothing to offer. No hope ... no future ... I can't have kids... A family of two is not what you want. You can do better. You can do much more with your life. This is not meant to last. You don't know me..." A lump formed in her throat.

Determination was still there as he continued. "You are

what I want for myself. I know everything I need to know about you, and I love what I know. Kids? I'm okay with adoption, or getting a surrogate ... There are so many other ways. Can you stop listening to the logic in your beautiful brain, which I admire so much, by the way ... and listen to your heart? Just for a minute, please? What does your heart say?"

Ava gazed down at the space between them, kneading her lips, arguing her heart, not knowing what the right thing to do or say would be.

Follow her heart? Was this the right thing to do? Was this truly what her heart was telling her, or was he the one persuading her? She had feelings for him. She classified it as friendship, but she wasn't sure anymore.

He watched her, waiting, and her lashes finally lifted.

Her eyes flicked between his, searching for something. An escape, maybe? Or an answer? But all she found was sincerity and his pleading gaze. She bit her lower lip again, struggling with the emotions she had spent so long suppressing, as she asked for help from her logic. She needed help to figure it all out. When she finally released her lip, her pink, soft, moist mouth bloomed into a doubtful half-smile.

Slowly, she shook her head as if reacting to one of her unspoken thoughts. "This is so messed up. Why me?" she murmured.

"It's not messed up. And it is you, because you are you. This is just getting real," he grumbled in a low, deep voice, wrapping his arms around her, his lips finding hers once more.

Ava abandoned herself in his arms, allowing him to kiss her ... kissing him back. Her hands trembled with hesitation before touching his chest. Wary fingers traced the contour of his torso, feeling and exploring the sculpted muscles shifting beneath, hungrily chasing those hugs and kisses.

Soft lips traced along her jaw, nibbling on her earlobe, gently catching it between his teeth. His hot breath in her ear rolled within and reached those dormant sensors in her brain, lighting her up. She moaned, winding her body under his artful touch, and her logic completely switched off. There was no room for reason anymore.

It had been a while since she felt like this. Desire erupted, filling her inside. Electric shocks journeyed through her in waves, from that earlobe and all the way down to her toes. He pulled tightly against her, sliding and pressing his hips between her legs, as if intending to master an unimaginable metamorphosis into one.

Wood, spice, heat—his scent invaded her nostrils, her senses. She whimpered, her palm caressing the back of his neck, tracing up against the short haircut. It poked and tickled. It was like running in the park, freshly cut grass kissing the bottom of her feet. His fingers flirted a little with the hem of her housecoat before slipping beneath, claiming every inch they touched.

Releasing her earlobe from the tender, wet nibble, he whispered in her ear, "I so want to make love with you right now. Do you want to make love with me?" CJ's voice croaked, his hot breath lingering on her skin before he planted a wet kiss on her neck, just below her ear.

"Mm-hmm," she murmured, nodding slightly.

He pulled away, incredulously looking into her half-open eyes. "Was that a ... yes?"

"Yes," a half-whisper escaped her throat as her head leaned back, gazing into deep blue eyes.

Wasting no time, he scooped her up in his brawny arms and charged up the stairs. On the first landing, he paused and pinned her against the wall, his agile fingers ardently searching under the silk housecoat.

Breathing heavily, his hot lips inched along her neck, down below the neckline, chasing the scent of roses and ... maybe strawberries, for only a few seconds. Then swiftly, he hoisted her in his arms once more. Nearly running, he climbed the rest of the stairs, ready to discover her all.

At the top of the stairs, he stopped again for a second, grumbling impatiently, "My room or yours?"

"Mine," Ava panted.

With only one kick, the slightly ajar door swung open, and he stepped into her bedroom. Puzzled about the commotion, Bella jumped from her bed. With Ava's legs wrapped around his waist, his hand skimmed the wall, searching for the light switch.

Ava gripped his elbow. "Uh-uh. Please, don't."

"How will I find my way around?" he huffed, face buried in her neck.

"Put me down ... and I'll guide you. I hope you ... can find your ... way around ... the rest of it," she stammered, between teasing kisses peppered on her lips.

"You're so beautifully crazy! Don't you worry about the rest," CJ whispered against her skin, slowly placing her down.

In a quick, smooth motion, he peeled off his T-shirt, tossed it on the floor, and kept kissing her as his sweatpants came off. Ava's fingers tugged at the tie of her robe.

"Uh-uh! Not yet..." CJ growled deeply, holding her hands with one of his.

He then let go and nuzzled her hands aside, pulling on the ends of the tie. Her arms went slack, heat rushing through her trembling body. She bit her lower lip between her teeth and stood there, letting him reveal her.

Then, she noticed a faint movement out of the corner of her eye and looked to her left. Icy blue eyes flashed in the dark, observing the scene with keen interest. Wide-eyed and staring into CJ's eyes, Ava gasped, quickly bringing back the sides of her robe.

He winced before realizing the source of her startle. "Bella, out!" he commanded, and Bella obeyed. His foot reached behind and kicked the door. "Where were we? Oh, I remember—the best part. Discovering what I had only imagined so far," he muttered once the door clicked shut.

His gaze fixed on hers as he gently opened her arms, still

clutching the robe. He traced a parting line, smoothly slipping his hand beneath, feeling the silky skin of her under his palms, pulling her into him. Agile, warm, and moist lips descended lower and lower, seeking more of the smoothness. His hands continued exploring, pushing the garment over her chiselled shoulders, allowing it to slip until it softly folded onto the floor with a gentle swoosh.

He cupped her face between his hands, and blue eyes gazed into green eyes. His thumbs traced along her jaw before sliding down, following her silhouette, caressing her shoulders, then moving down her arms. Her chest suddenly felt too tight to hold her pounding heart as she succumbed to his touch.

Soft lips moved up her neck as he circled behind her, his tongue tracing along her shoulder. Her breathing slowed with anticipation as CJ's fingers fumbled slightly with her bra before it came undone, sending shivers down her spine.

Desire invaded her insides as he turned her to face him. Eager, Ava brought her hand up to finish the action and remove her bra. He shook his head slowly and stopped her again, gripping her hand and bringing it back down.

Nervous yet longing, Ava quietly gulped, then caught her lower lip between her teeth and nodded slightly. Her lashes fluttered, heat, longing, doubt—all tangled in her chest.

Something between intense desire and the feeling of wrong made her stomach twist. *Fuck! Why does it feel better than ever before?* His scent flooded her nostrils again. Wood, amber, and something spicy tickled her senses. Sliding one hand around her waist again, the other slipped down, gripping her buttock and pulling her body onto him.

Her eyes widened for a split second before being distracted by his other hand gliding up her ribcage. Sneaking under her undone bra, his fingers lingered under her breast, following its curve, stopping where her breasts met. His palm rested on her six-pack briefly. *Fuck, she feels so good!*

As if he's changed his mind, his hand darted under her

other buttock, lifting her in his arms. Lips still locked, he crossed the four steps to the bed and carefully placed her down. Only then did he remove her bra with unhurried, calculated moves. His eyes hovered over her, taking in the view of her perky breasts as he crawled onto the bed, pushing her further, caging her in.

Fuck! She must be lying about her age. She is too perfect. And nothing's perfect. As his eyes adjusted to the darkness, he could finally find his way around. Now, nothing could hold him back. In all his silence driving back, CJ's mind was only preoccupied with plotting how to get behind her shield and do it right. And slow.

Gifted fingers continued exploring the rest of her body. 'Discovering what he had only imagined so far'. His hand trailed down velvety skin, past her collarbone, until it met the silky texture below, lingering a bit too long. His tongue sluggishly dragged across her lower lip before plunging between her half-parted lips.

Their breaths intertwined in hot, passionate kisses, tongues dancing around, exploring each other. *Fuck, she's delicious. Strawberries, perfectly balanced with just a hint of tang.* His hand traced further below and cupped around her breast, a hard nipple arising against his thumb, slowly drawing little circles around it.

Her insides shuddered, and her breath quickened. Educated hands took their time to examine every spot. Checking, evaluating every little discovery, kissing it, feeling it, moaning in delight. Ava's body arched, twisted, and shifted beneath his transforming hands, and the tension inside her rose to a dangerous height.

She acknowledged how hard he was and longed to have him inside her. Then he paused, drawing back a little, staring into her eyes while his briefs came off one-handedly. A glance at the package made her stomach flutter with anticipation. She was in for a treat and grinned foolishly, craving the moment he fully claimed her.

Taking his sweet time, his lips skimmed from her stomach, locking on her breast. "You are perfect," he grumbled against her body. "Are you ready for me?"

"Yes, I'm ready," she responded a bit too quickly.

Taking in her beautiful face, he gently knelt up between her legs and removed her thong with a barely there smirk. They were just like the ones she had caught him looking at the other day, but in some very light colour he couldn't exactly make out in the dark. Then, casually, he dropped it on the floor.

He hooked his hands under her knees and adjusted her body to align with his. The tip of his pecker fondled her clit before sliding down, splitting her gently, teasing at the entrance. Soft and maddening. Hungry for his attention, her organs twitched at the thought of having him inside.

She was wet, ready for him, keen to receive what he was eager to offer. His gaze didn't leave hers as he penetrated her slightly, adjusting to her body. Shallow at first, each slow-motion thrust dove further into her depths, and breaths melted into a passionate kiss.

A guttural moan escaped her throat as her fingers clenched over the defined muscles on his back, nails digging in. Her body tensed under his touch—a different kind of tense.

He paused. "Are you okay?"

"Go slow, please. It's ... been a while. I'm ... out of practice. I don't know ... It's a little painful," she stuttered in a squeaky whisper.

"Okay, I'll be gentle. Let me know if the pain gets unbearable, and I'll pull out."

She brought one hand to her mouth, biting the back of it, her words muffled. "I guess what they say is true. Use it or lose it."

With only one gentle thumb placed in the cup of her hand, he pushed it out of the way, planting a tender kiss on her lips. His breath blew hot and deep. "Do you want me to—?"

"Keep going. I'll be fine," Ava rushed before he could finish.

"Now, if you allow me—" Reaching behind, he gently seized the hand still clawing at his back and brought it above her head next to the other, before resuming prudently.

Soon, the tension gave way to rhythm. Her body remembered what it meant to surrender. To ache. To want. Accepting the new experience, moulding around his roundness, yielding completely and meeting every thrust, actively immersed in the action.

Sweaty bodies swayed together, giving everything, taking everything, in a passionate harmony. He let go of her hands, and she quickly placed them on his buttocks, drawing him closer, pressing him into her, raising her hips to meet him. He pushed deeper, and a deep, loud moan left her throat, as if it weren't coming from her. The bed creaked beneath them. Their bodies moved like waves trying to reach the shore.

Unsparing kisses, searching hands and groans culminated in a series of short screams of triumph followed by a deep grunt. With a final double thrust, his warmth erupted in waves, filling her within. Wrapped around him, she pressed against him, spasms rippling through her body.

"You're fantastic. You're beyond my wildest dreams. I love you," he huffed, caressing her beautiful face with his fingers before capturing her lips in yet another passionate kiss. When their lips parted, Ava held his gaze, teeth tugging at her lower lip. CJ shook his head. "Don't! You don't have to say it. Not until you're sure," he muttered before catching her lips in yet another ardent kiss. She pressed her eyes shut as he fell onto his back at her side. Then she moved slightly, pressing her legs together. "Let's take a shower."

Without moving, she slightly scrunched up her nose with an inward flinch before she shook her head. "I ... no, I'm not taking a shower with you. You go. I'll go after."

Propped on an elbow, her incredulous eyes fixed on her. "Baby. You do realize we just made love. I touched every single inch of your body. I know you, inside and out."

"I know. I'm just ... not ready. Not yet. Not tonight," she purred.

"Okay. It's okay. Take your time. I'll take a shower in my bathroom, but I'll be back. I want to sleep with you ... hold you, breathe you..." He placed a quick kiss on her shoulder before leaping out of bed.

Plucking his clothes off the floor in one move, he nearly tripped over Bella, who barely managed to get out of the way when he stormed out the door, wearing a foolish grin.

Ava was still in the bathroom when CJ returned, humming, the foolish grin still present. The humming paused as he listened closely. A grunt and a sniffle, followed by a thump and a deep, muffled whimper, crossed from behind the door. The grin faded, and he cringed, inching closer to the bathroom door, listening.

"Ava? Baby! Are you okay?" he asked, worry flowing from his voice. "Ava, please open the door," he demanded after a few seconds, when she didn't answer.

"I'm fine. I need a few more minutes," she pushed to sound normal.

He gently lifted her face with just two fingers under her chin.

"What's wrong? Have you been crying?" CJ asked a few minutes later when she emerged from the bathroom.

She sniffled, forcing a smile. "I'm fine."

"You're not fine. Please tell me you don't think that what just happened was somehow against your will," his voice deep, and just as troubled as his gaze.

She scoffed. "Oh, God! Did it seem like I wasn't participating?"

"No, not really," he said with a subtle smirk and a sparkle in his eyes.

"Then, why do you have to ask?"

"Why did you cry?"

She chewed her lower lip. "I don't know."

"Listen. You don't strike me as someone who cries for no reason. I'd hate to think you're insecure about us. Look at me, please."

"I'm fine. I'll be fine," Ava replied softly, gazing into his eyes, her face settling into calm composure.

"I'll never hurt you. I would've given up long ago if I didn't know what I wanted. Do you understand that?" She nodded. CJ wrapped his muscular arm around her, drawing her into a tight embrace, holding her like that. "I love you," he reiterated, loosening the embrace enough so he could look into her deep green eyes.

Her lips trembled. "I love you. Here, I said it. That's why I cried," Ava whispered in one breath before she could turn it around in her head and think about it again.

A smile fired up his eyes before spreading across his face, as he leaned and planted a passionate kiss on her lips. *I knew it!*

They lay in bed, spooned together, unable to fall asleep, still processing their relationship's recent turn. Unexpected for her. Hoped for far too long by him.

"You're on the pill, right?" CJ's breath blew warm on her nape before setting a kiss.

"Pill! What pill?" Ava asked, half turning her head toward him.

He buried his face deeper in her hair, chasing the scent of roses and strawberries. "Right. Why would you be? You're not one to settle for a one-night stand. Please tell me you at least have a morning-after pill somewhere handy."

Swiftly, Ava turned to face him. "What part of 'I can't have children' did you not understand?"

"Well ... you haven't made love with me before," his husky mutter rumbled playfully.

"I'll say it again. I'm forty-nine, meaning I'm in menopause. The shop is closed. For good! I can't get pregnant. Not anymore. I don't know what you're thinking. I thought it was clear." A cloud shadowed her face.

"Okay. We'll look into other options."

"Other options?! Oh my God! You just expressed concern

that I might get pregnant ... Now you're talking about other options?!"

"I was thinking about you, not me. It wouldn't be ideal for you to get pregnant the first time we made love. Personally, I wouldn't mind. What can I say? A man can dream."

"Well then ... Tell that man there's nothing to worry about. Or dream about," Ava blustered, cutting the conversation short before flipping to the other side. CJ reached out and pulled her close, holding her tightly.

"I love you. Nothing else matters," he whispered into her ear.

"It will ... sooner or later," her response trailed off.

"Yeah. You'll see ... I can't wait to see everyone's faces when they find out."

"What?! No! I'm not looking forward to seeing anyone's face. I didn't sign up for that. Let's keep it to ourselves. At least for now."

He nodded. "Okay, as you wish."

14. Talking about bad timing

Bella showed up with the leash on Ava's side of the bed early in the morning. Same time as usual, and not really unexpected, but Ava fell asleep at almost two, after a rather eventful night. It was their day off, and she hoped she'd sleep longer. But Bella always gets what Bella wants, and Ava had been her favourite walker for the past two weeks.

Slowly, she dragged her weary body out of bed. She changed, managing to make no noise, and tiptoed out of the bedroom, shutting the door behind her.

"You'll have to give me five minutes. I can't leave, and I can't live without my coffee. I really need my coffee, if you understand what I mean," Ava replied to Bella's curious stare as she stepped into the kitchen instead of heading straight for the door.

She thought that today, of all days, this walk would help her clear her head and think about everything.

An hour later, Ava sat on the front deck, sipping her second cup of coffee with a cigarette in hand. Bella lay beside her, munching on her nibbles. A cab pulled up in front of the house. Discreetly, Ava craned her neck over the railing, wondering who it could be. *And who would show up this early anyway?* Then, she decided not to snoop.

After getting out of the cab, a woman pulling a carry-on began walking toward their house. Ava tried to peer between the bars surrounding the porch, but she couldn't see very well, and the woman's face was half-hidden behind sunglasses. As she climbed the small set of stairs leading up to the patio, Bella approached, barking and wagging her tail. The woman took off her sunglasses. That's when Ava recognized her—Jenna Larsen.

"Hi, Bella. How are you, girl?" Jenna's gaze turned to Ava, acknowledging her. "Hi. I am…"

"Jenna Larsen. I know who you are. Nice to meet you! Ava Martin." She smiled as she stood up.

She took Ava's hand. "Nice to meet you, too! I'm looking for CJ. I heard he's in L.A. I was here for a couple of days, and I thought I'd stop by to say 'hello' before leaving. I hope I didn't miss him. Is he already gone for the day?" Jenna tried a smile as she measured Ava with a keen eye.

"He might still be asleep. I could check."

"Asleep? I thought— Never mind. Please don't wake him. May I wait?"

"Sure. Would you like a coffee? Tea? A cold drink? Anything?" Ava offered.

"Coffee would be nice, thanks."

"Come on in. It's getting hot out here."

Once inside, Ava stumbled into the kitchen to make the coffee, with Bella on her heels, as usual. After leaving her carry-on in the lobby, Jenna followed and stopped on the other side of the island, climbing onto a barstool with measured nonchalance.

A love affair that lasted nearly three years, Jenna was CJ's girlfriend some years ago. Ava overheard the story from people gossiping. Just bits and pieces, like they were trying to allude to something. That was all. No details, no zing. She never searched online. And, who knows? All she could come across might be just spiced-up speculation, and she had zero interest. Even less now.

"Oh! I guess CJ's up. I hear the water running upstairs." Ava pointed a finger up at the ceiling. "He'll probably show up soon, tracking the scent of coffee."

When Jenna's coffee was ready, Ava pushed the cup across

the island.

"I'm sorry for showing up unannounced. If I'd known you were here, I wouldn't have come." Jenna's half-voice landed more like an apology. "I didn't know he had a new girlfriend, but I'm glad he found someone who Bella likes. CJ got her when we were together, but she's never been too attached to me. Not like this," she continued, gesturing towards Bella, who turned wherever Ava did.

"CJ's girlfriend? I'm not. We're just friends." She could still smell him on her, and she just lied.

"Oh, I'm sorry. Your looks made me think that— You're right up his alley, so I thought maybe you were." Jenna shrugged.

"Oh, no. It's nothing like that," Ava suppressed a wince, straining to keep her voice steady.

"Okay," Jenna's eyes narrowed a little, still unconvinced.

"Love!" CJ called from upstairs just minutes later, breaking the almost awkward silence between the two women.

Shaking her pre-workout, Ava's stomach clenched, and she hoped Jenna didn't hear. But she did.

Arching a curious brow, she looked straight into Ava's eyes with a vague smirk. "Love! Still saying you're not his girlfriend?"

Ava snickered. "Love? Is that what you heard? Oh, God! He said Av. Give a guy a three-letter name, and he'll come up with an even shorter nickname for you," she loudly dismissed Jenna's comment. CJ's cue that she was not alone. "We are in the kitchen!" she continued, even louder. Another cue—*we*.

"Who are you talking to?" CJ asked, rolling down the stairs.

"Jenna is here to say *hello*," Ava said.

"Yeah, I'm here," Jenna tittered, turning on the barstool to face the stairs, where CJ's voice came from.

"Jenna! What are you doing here?" he asked, eyes wide with surprise. *Fuck!*

She slid off the barstool and hugged him. "I was in L.A., and I heard you were here as well. Bumped into Jason the other day. He gave me your address. I thought I'd stop by to say 'hi'. Leaving for Arizona at noon."

"Oh! It's good to see you ... I guess," his tone plain, and a reserved hug barely touched her.

Jenna didn't miss his coldness. "You guess?" she asked, sounding a little offended.

"I ... am surprised. I wasn't expecting your visit, and Jason didn't say anything." His reply dropped curtly.

"I asked him not to. I wasn't sure I'd have time to stop by. But I made time. You didn't call in a while. You didn't answer my texts—"

"Been busy." He gave a casual shrug as he moved toward the espresso machine.

After their love affair ended, Jenna and CJ remained close, checking on each other occasionally. Less and less lately, since she rekindled with an old flame.

Pre-workout in hand, Ava reeled backward, toward the basement door, to blow off some steam in the gym. "Well, I'll leave you two. Nice to have met you, Jenna. By the way ... Love your work."

❧

"I'd like to say 'goodbye' to Ava. Where is she?" Jenna asked about an hour later when she was getting ready to leave.

"I'm sure she's killing that boxing sack in the gym. I'll tell her you said goodbye. She doesn't like anyone around when she's working out. And I respect that."

"You look happy. She seems really sweet. I'm glad you found someone who makes you happy."

He winced. "Ava?! We are just friends. She joined the crew at the last minute. I have a lot of extra space, so I invited her to stay. It's nothing, really. Just a living arrangement. That's all."

"Okay," Jenna replied, with a knowing smirk, glancing out the window. "I have to go now. My taxi's here. You look really happy," she said again, in a slightly suggestive tone, giving him a parting hug.

"Fuck! Talking about bad timing," CJ blasted as he closed the door behind Jenna.

Immediately, he dashed downstairs. As anticipated, Ava was killing that boxing sack in the gym, punching and kicking it like it was filled with all her poor decisions.

"Ava! Ava, Baby!" She didn't hear him. Nor did she expect him to come in. They had a deal.

Wow, she's good! And she's mad, thought CJ, pausing in the doorway for a second. He walked up behind and wrapped his arms around her, bringing all the action to a stop. "Baby! Enough! It's dead already. Stop kicking and punching it."

Ava, breathless and tense, stayed still, caught in his arms. When he finally let go, weighed down by a mix of emotions, Ava's shoulders sank in exhaustion. She gave up the fight and slowly took off her sparring gloves.

"Let me see," CJ took her hands, tracing his thumb across her knuckles. "You are so silly. Jenna and me? That's old news. Long ago. You, though … You're the only one who's ever mattered like this." He exhaled, shaking his head. "Well, I guess you're done here. Come with me." Holding her hand, he made her follow. "I'll make you a coffee."

"I already had two."

"Then, I'll make you breakfast."

"You know I don't eat breakfast. I wouldn't say no to a protein shake. But not right now."

"Okay," CJ walked back to her, around the kitchen island. "Look at me, please." He grabbed Ava around the waist and, in one swift move, lifted and placed her on the island's counter.

"You're crazy! Put me back down," she demanded.

"No, I won't. Not until you listen to me and understand that I love you." CJ exhaled sharply, rubbing the back of his neck. "Jenna's timing was complete shit. I didn't even know she was in L.A., nor that she'd show up unannounced. Had she called ahead, I wouldn't have invited her. I would have told her I was busy, not at home, or … whatever."

"It's not something that you had control over."

"Please stop being insecure. I'm really sorry."

"You don't have to be sorry, and I'm not insecure," Ava parried.

Forehead pressed against hers, he gazed into her eyes. A tender kiss landed on her lips as fingers skimmed behind her neck. His mouth grazed against her cheek and moved along her jawline, tracing down her neck, as if he intended to taste her. Discover more of her.

She squirmed slightly, trying to get away. "I'm all sweaty. I need a shower."

"Well, I haven't tasted this on you yet. All salty and spicy, and hot ... I love it," he grumbled between kisses, subtle mischief lacing his tone.

"Oh! This doesn't look like ... *nothing.*" With a slanted smirk on her face and the door still open behind her, Jenna stood in the lobby. "Sorry to interrupt. I forgot my cellphone."

Both jumped, startled. Muttering a "Fuck!" under his breath, CJ turned.

Flushed with embarrassment, Ava let herself slide off the countertop and hurried upstairs. Brows knitted together, CJ's gaze followed her while Jenna grabbed her cellphone, shaking her head and giving CJ a scolding look as she headed out.

"Jenna, please let me explain," he managed.

"You don't have to explain anything. I thought we were still friends, but I guess I was wrong. I probably can't be trusted anymore, and I don't blame you."

"No, it's not that. This ... all of this ... is new. *Last night— new*! Literally! Ava is not ready for us to be out there."

"Well, you must prepare her. You do realize this is going to get out, right?"

"It's too soon. It'll take time."

"You know...? Your happy puppy face will give you away in no time..."

His brows still furrowed, CJ swallowed. "It's ... complicated."

"Complicated? You love her, she loves you ... What's so complicated?" She paused. "Oh. My. God! She's married."

"No! Fuck no! She's not married. She's ... a widow. So, it's much more complicated. I know it'll come out, eventually. But please, keep it to yourself. She needs time to adjust to all of this. It's not easy being in the limelight ... I'm sure you can relate. Can I trust you? Please."

"Well, if it gets out, you can be sure it won't come from me. I can tell she's a good one. You're getting soft, and she's lucky to have your heart."

His jaw flexed. "*I am* the lucky one. Thank you, Jenna. I trust you'll do the right thing."

"Thank you for your vote of confidence. I have to go now. All the best ... to both of you. Now, go and talk to her."

Ava stood in the shower, punishing her body under hot and cold lashes of water. Lying in bed, CJ waited for her to come out.

"Are you okay?" he asked when she emerged from the bathroom.

"I don't know," Ava replied with a sad, lost look in her eyes.

"Come here," CJ patted the bed beside him. Obediently, she took a few steps, stopping halfway, a half-worried simper tugging at her lips. Leaping out of bed, CJ took her in his arms. "She's gone. She won't tell. She promised. And I locked the door this time."

A tentative smile briefly curled her lips. "Do you trust her?"

"Jenna can be many things, but she can also be discreet. She knows how things can go— Yes, I trust her," he finally answered Ava's question.

"Okay." Not a shred of enthusiasm in her voice.

"When did you wake up? You seem tired."

"Blame it on Bella. She woke me up at six. I'd probably still be asleep and missed all the fun, which would've been great. I'd feel rested, not restless."

"I'm glad you can still joke about it. Well, we were having some delicious fun when—" CJ said tauntingly, placing a gentle kiss on her lips while slipping a hand under her bathrobe.

"Hey!" Ava half-laughed, catching his wrist. "It's broad daylight."

"I know. You're even more beautiful in it," his voice low and raspy.

She hesitated just long enough for him to feel it. "I don't think I—"

"I must disclose something. I see better in the dark. So ... there's nothing I haven't seen already," he said with a naughty smirk as his lips brushed against the corner of her mouth.

"Oh, so you are one of those...? And you're only revealing this now?" Ava imitated his naughtiness.

"One of those...? Who else do you know?"

"Um ... Me?" she teased with a mysterious smile.

CJ grimaced, pretending to be shocked. "A-ha ... So, you think it's fair for you to see everything while keeping me in the dark?"

She let go of his wrist, and he pulled her flush to his body, rolling her over in a passionate kiss as his hand snuck under that bathrobe.

The robe slipped loose beneath his hands; her skin bathed in morning light. Daylight didn't lie. There were no shadows to hide behind, no dim corners to excuse the way her body moved toward his. Just them, bare and unsheltered in a room full of sun. It felt too exposed. Too clear. She flinched, not from shame but from the overwhelming tenderness of being viewed.

CJ's fingers glided around her waist like he was memorizing the shape of her trust. "I didn't think you could wreck me worse than last night. Then I see you in the daylight—" he whispered, as if daylight made her more real, more his.

But when CJ pulled her in, warm skin and familiar scent washing over her, Ava stopped thinking and allowed herself to want. Maybe this was a mistake. Maybe she'd cringe tomorrow.

But right now, her body wasn't asking for logic. It was asking to be held. Seen. Claimed.

His hands weren't in a rush, and that almost scared her even more. Her hand gripped the sheets. This wasn't lust clawing through clothes. This was CJ looking at her like she was something worth learning. His breath was hot. Heavy. His lips moved lower. Exploring ... demanding. Her body arched to meet him, a moan catching in her throat.

She let him touch her like that and allowed herself to forget how many ways she'd tried to talk herself out of this. Every time he pressed closer, she answered. Hesitant but hungry, wanting yet terrified. And still choosing him anyway.

15. I know you'll be fine

"**P**ack an overnight bag. We're not coming back here in the morning," CJ said before leaving for work the following Thursday.

"Where are we going?" Ava chirped, arching a curious eyebrow.

"You'll see. It's a surprise."

"What should I pack?"

"Whatever you think you'll need for the weekend. We'll be returning on Sunday. I suggest a swimsuit and sunscreen, and that's all I'll say." An enigmatic grin followed a quick smooch.

"Um ... I ... don't have a swimsuit."

Disbelief flowed from his stare. "You came to California and didn't pack a swimsuit? I don't believe."

"You better believe it. As someone who lived by the sea for a big chunk of her life, I happen to know that when you're working, you don't have much time to go to the beach. I'm here for work, so, yeah, I didn't pack a swimsuit."

"Then, we'll have to get you one," his tone final.

"I don't think so. I'm not going to the beach with you. That's not keeping it under our belts," Ava replied.

"We're not going to the beach."

"I don't do pools either. Chlorine kills my skin and my sinuses," she countered.

"Okay. You decide if you want to go in. You can stay by the pool. You'll still need a swimsuit. Or not. I don't really care." He smirked.

She rolled her eyes. "A pool! How does that go with keeping it under our belts?"

"It's a private pool. It'll be just you and me. You'll love it, I promise. Now, we'll have to leave about an hour early to stop somewhere so you can get a swimsuit. Although I'd prefer you without one." He smirked again.

When the final shooting night wrapped up, exhaustion hung over the entire cast and crew. The following morning, after everyone had hurriedly packed up and left, silence fell eerily over the set. While the others rushed away, CJ and Ava stayed behind. Set to stick to their plan, they lingered around a bit longer.

CJ kept an eye on their surroundings and, at last, they slipped away. Instead of taking the usual route, he veered in the opposite direction. The surprise destination? A private, gated property in a peaceful neighbourhood of Palm Springs.

It had been a long week of night shoots. The fatigue took hold of Ava as the cool desert night air summoned her body to relax. She drifted off to sleep. Didn't last long, though. She stirred awake with a pinch in her neck from the awkward position she had dozed off in. A sudden sense of worry washed over her. Maybe a dream she couldn't remember? Blinking away the sleep, her eyes gradually focused on the road. It took a moment for her groggy mind to process everything.

The headlights of the oncoming traffic flickered in the distance. Few cars ventured out this early. Her brain finally registered what was wrong with that picture. The painted line on the road was unmistakably on her right.

"CJ!" she gasped, panic seeping from her voice. "We're on the wrong side of the road!"

Without realizing, CJ fell back into his British driving

habits. Adrenaline surged through him. With a swift turn of the wheel, he swerved back into the right lane. In just seconds, a semi roared, passing in the opposite direction.

Ava's stomach knotted, the near-miss leaving her shaken and extremely quiet. Her fingers curled tightly around the seatbelt as she fought the nausea rising in her throat.

"I'm sorry, Baby." CJ's voice throttled as he reached for her hand. "We're okay."

She swallowed and gave a shaky nod, but decided sleep wasn't an option anymore. Acting as the co-pilot seemed like a much better idea. Just before seven in the morning, when they finally arrived, the world around them was as still and quiet as she was.

The property was the ideal getaway from the hustle and bustle of the busy city. The peaceful ambiance was exactly what they needed to relax and unwind after a long and tiring week.

A tall fence and gigantic palm trees surrounded the relatively modest property, providing much-needed privacy. At the back, a picture-perfect blue pool reflected an equally flawless sky, adding to the already perfect image. The well-deserved peace was only sporadically interrupted by the morning birds. And, of course, Bella, who, ever so social, started communicating with the neighbourhood dogs. Who knows what they were gossiping about?

It was just before seven in the morning when they reached their destination. Ava was still shaken. Prior to their arrival, CJ ensured the fridge was stocked with all her favourite 'alien foods', so they didn't need to go out for anything. Indulgence was included on the menu.

When they weren't by the pool, the kitchen was their gathering spot. Laughter, stolen kisses, and the occasional playful argument over who was to stir the sauce filled the air. CJ cooked like a chef, accepting Ava's help only when she insisted. And not just once, more wine ended up in their glasses than in the food.

The mornings began pretty quiet, with coffee in bed—courtesy of CJ. The afternoons turned into a lethargic haze, just lounging by the pool. And when the heat became too much and chased them inside, behind closed doors, the passion burned even hotter. At night, when the rest of the world had long succumbed to dreams, they wandered the quiet streets of Palm Springs. Hand in hand, they whispered secrets. And their only witnesses? The silver moon and Bella.

Yet, even in their perfect bubble, worry nudged Ava's heart. This was too much. Too intense. Moving too fast.

Deep down, she knew this moment wouldn't last forever. The stolen time together was precious, but reality rolled toward them like a threatening storm. The cruel world would catch up with them. Eventually.

Media, in all its forms, will find out and buzz. Rumours and gossip will spread like fire. Their privacy—this beautiful thing they had—will be ripped apart. And that's what terrified her the most.

CJ knew it too, and he tried to shield her from it, preparing her for what was to come. Inevitably.

"Things may settle before they figure out who you are," he told her one evening, his tone guarded, as if he read her mind, replying to her unspoken worries. "You're not a public figure, and it'll take time for them to put the pieces together. But when they do … it's best to say nothing. Make no comments. No reaction."

He asked her to stay away from the news, from social media, from the inevitable chaos that came with his fame. No posts. No likes or comments on his posts. Especially no lurking, no giving the press or social media anything to latch onto.

Ava listened, nodding. She understood. She also understood that all that only meant delaying the moment, not completely erasing it. And didn't stop the thoughts from creeping in, twisting her insides into knots.

Why her? Why did he choose her, out of all the women in the world? The question kept resurfacing. In the beginning, she convinced herself that his visits were out of kindness. Maybe guilt? Or, perhaps, he simply felt sorry for her. A fleeting interest, at best. Someone to fill the time, maybe?

Saturday evening, as they lay in the dim light of the retreat's bedroom, her head resting against his bare chest, Ava's thoughts swirled like a tornado refusing to settle.

"Why me?" she whispered the haunting question that had bothered her since all this started.

Casually tracing along her spine, CJ's fingers halted. "What do you mean?"

Ava exhaled, hesitating. "I just— I don't get it." She shifted, propping herself up on one elbow to look at him. "You could be with anyone. Someone younger, someone more glamorous, someone from your world." She let out a nervous chuckle as if saying it out loud made it sound less ridiculous. "I mean, look at me. I'm not—"

"Stop." His voice was firm yet gentle as his hand cupped her cheek, his thumb brushing just beneath her eye. "Do you think I give a fuck about any of that?" Ava averted her gaze, but CJ wouldn't let her retreat. Two fingers under her chin lifted her face, forcing her to meet his eyes. "You're everything I didn't know I needed, Ava," he murmured. "You're the only person who looks at me and sees me. Not the name, not the fame ... Just me."

She swallowed, but the words still escaped. "And what if it doesn't last?"

CJ's lips curved into a knowing smile. "And what if it does?"

Ava scrutinized his face, searching for hesitation. For uncertainty. She found none. Instead, she saw determination. Love.

"You drive me crazy," her voice barely above a whisper.

He chuckled, brushing a strand of hair from her face and tucking it behind her ear. "I'd be worried if I didn't." She forced a smile, but the tightness in her chest remained. As if sensing it, CJ leaned closer, pressing a slow, lingering kiss to her lips before murmuring against them, "I love you, Ava. And that's not gonna change."

She wanted to believe him. Desperately. But doubt still lingered, creeping in, even in the quietest of moments.

What Ava didn't know—or refused to believe—was that CJ

had never felt this way before. His past relationships? Fleeting. Easy. Built on shallow attraction and convenience. No one before had ever touched him the way Ava did.

She was different. Mature, wickedly funny, kind, in a way that felt effortless. And beautiful—though she didn't seem to realize it. She challenged and inspired him. She made him feel alive in ways he didn't know he needed.

With her, he wasn't just CJ Hamilton—the celebrity. He was a man in love. And he wasn't going to let her forget it.

She was his best friend. His greatest temptation. His soulmate. *Mine forever! If only she'd believe it.*

The last days before going home became hectic. Everybody looked forward to leaving, tension creeping in from around every corner. Over the past week, the pressure has escalated at an incredible rate. The last scenes, as well as retakes on a few that the directors weren't entirely satisfied with after reviewing the footage, were progressing at a slow pace. Or so it seemed. To top it all, someone came up with the 'brilliant' idea to take extras to extras ... just in case.

Exhausted, Ava began feeling queasy. An upset stomach and dizzy spells prevented her from being of much help. Whenever her brain turned to mush from what she classified as stress caused by permanent chaos, she would sneak into CJ's trailer for a nap.

That morning, she had another dizzy spell and charged into the bathroom to throw up after her first sip of coffee.

"You look pale. I think you need to see a doctor," CJ remarked when she returned.

"Oh, no. I probably ate something that my stomach didn't agree with, or I accidentally had gluten. It'll go away in a few days, and it's been a few days already. I'll be fine. It's not so bad that I need to see a doctor. I'm just feeling oddly tired, and I may be a bit dehydrated."

"Why don't you stay home if you don't feel well? We haven't needed you much these past few days, anyway. I'll call if we need anything from you. You'll get even more dehydrated in this heat if you come."

"I don't know … I'd feel bad for letting everyone down. I think I should come. I'm already feeling better."

"No. You're staying home," CJ decided for her. And she stayed.

"Shit!" CJ mumbled, scouring the car's glove compartment upon arriving at the location. He forgot to charge his cellphone the night before and just realized he didn't have a backup. *I may have one in the trailer.*

Running a little late, and with everyone eager to wrap up this project on time, he was rushed into makeup and getting dressed. As things got quite animated, the cellphone became a problem at the bottom of his list. No one asked about Ava after he said she was still not well, and she remained home. As predicted, everyone already knew what they were doing by now.

On the way home, CJ checked his cellphone. *Fuck!* He pressed the gas pedal. Without a spare second to check on Ava all day. And now he couldn't because the battery was dead.

Wheels screeching, he pulled up to the garage and rushed inside. As he stepped in, the atmosphere felt eerily off, as if something was missing. He looked around but couldn't quite pinpoint why the house felt deserted, why his stomach squeezed with a bad feeling.

She probably called an ambulance. Or maybe she's sleeping—CJ thought, after getting no response when he called her.

Bella was running around, agitated, as if trying to tell something. Two steps at a time, he bolted upstairs. Gingerly, he opened Ava's bedroom door. The bed, neatly made as if she had never been there. No clothing on the chair, no laptop on the console, and no clothes in her hamper. He dashed into the bathroom.

Other than an almost empty tube of toothpaste by the sink, and a few discarded cosmetic containers in the trash, nothing said she was ever there.

She left. She left me. He hunched, placing his hands on his knees. *Fuck! The damn cellphone is dead.* Grabbing the charger from the nightstand on his side of the bed, he darted back downstairs.

On the first landing, he stopped, staring at the void lobby. Ava's shoes and other belongings were missing. It must've been what struck him as odd, and the strange feeling of emptiness that crept up on him when he entered the house.

His shoulders slouched under the realization that she was gone. Knees buckling under his own weight, he placed a hand on the wall to his right, trying to remain upright. Staring at it, the memory of Ava against that very wall on their first night together invaded his mind.

Why? No, this can't be happening. Her flight isn't until the day after tomorrow. She must be in a hotel somewhere—his mind strained to make some sense out of her nonsense.

Once in the kitchen, CJ plugged in his cellphone and watched impatiently as it charged. Too slow. He fidgeted—a few minutes felt like a lifetime. Arms crossed, he turned his back to the counter and leaned against it, thinking the phone might charge faster if he didn't look at it.

Then he saw it. Across from where he stood, on the kitchen island, an envelope was staring at him. His jaw tightened as he stood up straight and sluggishly took the few steps to the island. Plucking the envelope, he tapped it on the counter a few times. In slow motion, he began tearing it, fearful of what was inside. He fished out a note. From Ava.

Dear CJ,

I'm sorry for doing this, but I have to go. Please don't try to find me or contact me. Please don't hate me or blame yourself. I love you, but I can't be with you. Please just forget me, and forgive me, if you find it in your heart.

You're a wonderful man, and I have no right to hold you back. You deserve to find a woman your age who you can love and who will love you back, someone who can give you what I can't: a family. You deserve to have a family. A family that I could never offer you.

You deserve to be happy and know what a real family is, with kids running around and the joy, and the worries that come with it. I'm too old for that.

Promise me you'll try to find someone you can spend the rest of your life with. Please take time to heal and time to love. Everything takes time, and time is on your side and ahead of you. My time is behind me.

I love you more than anything, but I can no longer be selfish. I can't hold you back from living your life. I must let you go.

Please take care of yourself and be happy.

Goodbye, my love,
Ava

A surge of anger bubbled inside him, and he groaned. *Be happy?! How? Really, Ava? Screw this! Anything but this? Why? Why! Why didn't I see it coming? Damn, woman! This is not the end. It can't end like this. It can't end, period!* Swiftly, he grabbed his cellphone. 5%. This should be enough. Frantically scrolling, he found Ava's number and dialled. The phone rang for what felt like forever.

That morning after CJ left, a wave of guilt and uncertainty washed over Ava. She sat on the edge of her bed, staring blankly at the wall, the weight of her choices bearing down on her. Arguing her

heart. Her thoughts kept swirling with doubt. *Am I being selfish?* Fragments of random conversations invaded her mind. In less than three days, they would part ways. No matter how she thought about it or how she tried to spin it in her mind, she couldn't see how their relationship could continue beyond that.

If this is the end … I'll have the last word. If my heart is to be broken … I'll do it myself. I'll rip my own heart apart, but no one else will. Never again! Then, she sat in front of her laptop for a few minutes, wondering what to do. *Leave?! Go where? Go home!* What awaited her home? More of the same. Sadness? Loneliness?

What makes me happy? What else has ever made me happy that doesn't involve heartache? Well … dolphins! Dolphins have always made me happy. San Diego … SeaWorld … Dolphins! This is it—her mind concocted at high speed. Fervently, she began searching for flights to San Diego. She booked a round-trip for the next few days, returning just in time to catch the flight that would take her home.

She made the bed, gathered all her belongings, and packed just enough for the next two days in her carry-on. Quickly, she poured her heart into a farewell note to CJ. Then, she left.

"I'm sorry, girl. I have to do this. Take care of him, okay?" Ava said to Bella, who followed her to the door as usual. Bella reached out and rubbed her head on Ava's hand—what Bella did whenever she wanted to be petted. That brought a smile to Ava's face as she petted Bella for the first and last time. "Well, goodbye. I guess I won't see you again."

Ava hopped into the taxi and left for the airport.

"Hello!" Already on the plane, she didn't want to annoy the other passengers and dismissed the idea of just hanging up with a default message.

"Ava. Where are you? I'll come pick you up."

"CJ. Did you get my letter?"

"Forget the bloody letter, Ava. Do you realize how foolish

what you did is? Why did you leave?"

"I explained why in the letter," she replied, trying hard to sound detached while her heart was in pieces and, just as anticipated, she was hurting. Badly.

"Tell me where you are, and I'll come get you so we can talk."

"I'm gone. I can't come back." Her shattered soul was profoundly bleeding.

"Tell me where you are, please."

"I'm on the plane."

"No, you're not. You're on the phone."

She remained quiet for a moment. Just enough so he could hear the announcement over the plane's public address system asking all the passengers to turn their phones off.

"I have to go. We're getting ready to taxi and take off."

He remained quiet for a moment, then said, "I'll call you when you get home. When do you get home?"

"Don't. I'll call you when I land, okay?"

She never did.

Ava spent the next day with the dolphins, getting splashed and wearing a mask of excitement. Suppressing her pain. Trying to forget. The other thing that made her happy? The penguins. She'd go on the moving walkway, then back in line for another round. The entire day, she wandered aimlessly around SeaWorld.

In her mind, she travelled back in time to when she was a carefree child, and problems of the heart were unknown to her. *Blissful times!*

That night, drained, she fell asleep before her head hit the pillow. She woke only when her alarm went off, signalling it was time to leave for the airport.

Back in L.A., after retrieving her suitcase from the rented locker, Ava went through the check-in and headed to the gate where her first flight to Seattle was scheduled to depart.

Breath caught in her throat, and she stopped in her tracks

as she spotted CJ, waiting for his flight, just two gates from where she needed to be. He appeared distraught and lost in thought. As if he hadn't slept. Looking out the window, he seemed to follow the planes as they taxied and took off. But his eyes were empty, staring at practically nothing. Hurting.

I know, Baby. It hurts right now, but it will go away. You'll forget. You'll be okay. I know you'll be fine. Better than fine. Abruptly, Ava turned and disappeared into a restroom. *It's a women's bathroom. He won't come here*—she reasoned to herself. She stood by the sink, staring at the water as it ran, swirled, and vanished down the drain. *Right now, I wish I were the water coming out of that faucet, fading down the drain*—she contemplated.

Feeling like throwing up, Ava took a few deep breaths and looked in the mirror. Anxiety taking over, she rushed into a stall and threw up. For a while, she leaned against the door, her back pressed against it. She had to get out of there, or she'd miss her flight.

When she finally gathered herself, Ava peeked out of the bathroom entrance to check the flight schedule. *Damn! His flight leaves after mine, meaning boarding for my plane will start before his. Shit! They'll call my name if I'm not there.*

She remembered the T-shirt and baseball cap she had bought at SeaWorld. With dolphins, of course. What else? Quickly, the two items came out of her carry-on, and just as quickly, she changed.

The only size they had in green was large, so the T-shirt looked oversized and baggy, not showing any shape. Otherwise, she was wearing a pair of black leggings. They all look the same, don't they?

She felt inspired when she kept that pair of sneakers for travelling. A trendy style. Probably every other woman in this airport was wearing the same kind. Or similar enough.

With one last look in the mirror, feeling satisfied with what she saw, Ava added a pair of sunglasses to the look—a backup she had never worn—and bravely stepped out. Her favourite backpack decided it had lived a long and glamorous life and died the previous day in San Diego. So, she bought a random, cheap, ordinary bag that would last her until she got home.

Without rushing, her pace slower than usual, she walked past CJ, toward the gate where her flight was leaving. Face down, pretending to look for something in her bag, her hands out of sight.

She sat in the waiting area with her back turned to the gate where he was waiting.

As the boarding began, Ava caught CJ gauging her as she stood in line, checking her out with an intrigued expression. She kept turning her head slowly, as if casually scanning her surroundings. No sign of acknowledgment.

Entranced, CJ began to get up when a group of youngsters came to her rescue. He found himself trapped as the teenagers circled him, asking questions, taking selfies, and demanding autographs. Initially appearing annoyed, he reconsidered and ultimately succumbed to their requests.

By the time the cluster dispersed, Ava was already on the plane. On her way home!

16. It was complicated

Ava had just finished folding tiny clothes. It was just an unusually quiet Saturday night, although a storm brewed within her soul. Her half-packed suitcase sat in the middle of the living room, the open lid gaping like her worst nightmare. Lips pursed, she slowly bobbed her head, gazing at the neatly folded wedding outfits that stared back at her from inside, like a warning.

Then she sprang to her feet and dashed into the kitchen, busying herself. Once everything was tidy, she collapsed back onto the couch. The images on the TV screen danced before her as the words faded into white noise. She wasn't actually watching.

Her gaze shifted once more to the suitcase, and she exhaled slowly, pressing a hand against her stomach. *It's just a wedding. Nothing to worry about.*

Oh, and one more thing she couldn't forget. She reached for her phone and added it to the list. The device slipped from her hand as her eyelids grew heavy, and she drifted off to sleep.

She jolted from her sleep, chest rising steeply, panting, desperately gasping for air. Her heart hammered against her ribs, sweat dripping from her hair as the nightmare still lingered in her mind. It's been a while since the nightmares ceased. Yet, the monsters found their way back.

It's just a dream. Just a dream. But the icicles running

through her veins said otherwise. Her mind was playing tricks on her. Again.

Travelling to London wouldn't be her first choice. Not even the last. But she couldn't say 'no' when Eliza asked her to fill in as the mother of the bride at her wedding. Her baby was getting married to... "It's a surprise," Eliza said.

A week is a long time. A lot can happen in a week. But I'll be busy with the wedding. No, not a chance I'd run into him. And who knows? He's probably not even in London—Ava reasoned, trying to calm herself down, as she had a thousand times before now. Getting up with a deep sigh, she turned the TV off and shuffled to bed.

In the early hours of Monday morning, she boarded her first flight to Toronto. From there, she flew to London, UK. Too late to change her mind. *Be brave, Ava! Eliza needs you. Be there for her, like in old times. It's your duty. You're fine! You're strong!* She kept telling herself.

As she got off the plane, she took a deep breath. *That's it. London, here I come! Please, be gracious to me.*

Before anything, she had to use the washroom. Like, immediately. She almost forgot how, on these international flights, people spend their time drinking beer and crowding the restroom lines. And she didn't get the chance to use the washroom for a few good hours.

Growing up in a communist country? Quite obnoxious. She spent most of her childhood waiting in line for almost everything. Now, she refuses to stand in line for anything—*maybe for coffee, but definitely not for the washroom. Well, if I can help it.*

At one point, a funny thought came to mind. What if she tells everyone this was an emergency? They'd have to let her use the bathroom, or they'll be stuck on a stinky airplane. Would they let her cut in front of the line? She stifled a laugh, and of course, she didn't ask. *I probably would've found wearing Depends pretty ... dependable*—another hilarious thought popped into her mind.

As she emerged from the washroom, the luggage from her flight appeared on the conveyor belt. Fortunately, she didn't have to wait too long for hers. The rest of the formalities? Just as breezy. And she finally stepped onto British soil.

Hard to miss, Eliza was jumping up and down, happy and loud, calling Lina's name. Lina was the name everybody knew Ava by before she called Canada home. With a humongous smile on display, she picked up the pace.

Eliza had changed since Ava, or Lina, last saw her. No trace of 'goth' remained in her appearance. Releasing the handle of her luggage, Ava opened her arms wide and embraced Eliza in a long, loving hug, holding her tightly.

Her gaze hovered over Eliza as she pulled back a little. "Let me look at you. Oh, you're so beautiful! And you look so happy. I missed you so much. I can't believe I'm here. For your wedding." She hoisted Eliza into yet another hug.

"Ava?" A very familiar voice resounded in her ears.

A shiver ran down her spine, and she slowly turned her gaze to where the voice came from. Right there, to her right, leaning in, CJ was trying to take a better look under the visor of her ball cap. Unsure if it was Ava he was looking at—his Ava.

"Oh! Hi, CJ. What a surprise!" she half-exclaimed, her heart racing.

"A surprise, indeed," he replied, looking puzzled at Eliza, then Ava, and back at Eliza.

"Oh, I'm not sure if you remember Eliza, my goddaughter. You met her in Edinburgh," Ava said in a self-controlled voice, misinterpreting his confusion.

"I hope he remembers me. He's marrying me," Eliza jumped to clarify. "This is the surprise I had for you," she chirped excitedly.

"Wow! Now, that ... um, indeed, is a surprise," Ava stuttered, an undefined smile warping her face. "Well, I guess congratulations are in order, then." She hugged Eliza again, then turned to CJ to embrace him, too. "You did amazing. I'm so happy for you," she whispered in CJ's ear.

Her stomach squeezed when his arm wrapped around her with an almost too-intimate pull.

"So, no Ayden?" Eliza asked.

"Oh, God. Of course not," Ava replied promptly, intending to get over the topic quickly.

"Who's Ayden?" CJ asked, an intrigued undertone in his voice.

Ava hesitated, but Eliza had the answer. "Her son, silly. How many times have I talked about him?" She sounded quite irritated. "He's never there when I talk to him." She complained to Ava.

CJ cocked a baffled eyebrow. "Your son?"

"Yes. Ayden is my son," her voice remained surprisingly steady.

"Um-I ... I didn't know you had a son."

"I do have a son," Ava replied, almost too sharply.

CJ's curiosity piqued. "How old is he?"

"Old enough to be staying home alone. I hope my home is still standing when I get back," Ava forced a giggle, trying progressively to put the topic off.

"Oh, my God! CJ, really!" Eliza intervened, her annoyance escalating. "He's two. The baby I keep talking about— I showed you pictures. The one you share the same birthday with. Remember all these details?"

"Wait ... Um ... who is Lina, then?" he asked, growing more inquisitive and confused.

"Guys, come on! I'm sure you have more important things to talk about right now. People are watching. Let's go," Ava said, aiming to smooth things over, eventually make a worked-up Eliza calm down.

But Eliza wouldn't give up. "Oh, allow me to introduce you. Lina—CJ, CJ—Lina. Now, when I mentioned Lina, and you said you remember her ... who exactly did you remember? I just realized that you know Lina as Ava. All this time, have you been pretending you remembered her?" Eliza asked, even more irritated.

"Yes, I have. I didn't know who you were talking about, and I didn't think it was that important. I don't know what you want me to say. I make a good living by pretending, so—" CJ became irascible, and Ava didn't miss the change.

"Eliza, honey, I don't think this is the right place to have this conversation. This is a discussion for your ears only. I really don't feel comfortable," Ava whispered in Romanian in Eliza's ear with a telling smile.

"Whatever." Eliza finally gave up, but not before she rolled her eyes. "I need to use the washroom before we leave. Do you want to come?" she asked Ava.

"I already was, while waiting for my luggage."

"CJ, would you take Lina to the car? It'll probably be a while. I see it's a long line," Eliza added before continuing toward Ava, "meaning, you'll have time for a smoke. I'm sure you need one after that long flight."

"Oh, I need one." Ava's stomach coiled, a fleeting smile curling her lips.

During the last part of the conversation, CJ glared at Ava while she avoided his gaze, and one could hear all the gears in his brain squeaking and screeching. His eyebrows furrowed as he looked down, appearing to deliberate.

That look when he raised his eyes and glared back at Ava, his gaze cutting through. That moment of realization, which Eliza completely missed. Only Ava and CJ were aware of the tension crackling in the air, unspoken questions intensifying.

His jaw ticked, and he didn't even try to hide it. "Let's go," he said rather abruptly, grabbing Ava's suitcase and trudging towards the airport's exit. Carry-on in tow, and purse on her shoulder, Ava kept up the pace, only a step behind him. Once outside the airport, heading to the parking lot, CJ hesitated for a moment before asking, trying to sound casual. "So ... Do you have any pictures of ... your son?"

"Of course I have," Ava replied in a steady voice, managing to remain composed. "In this day and age, I can't imagine a mother who doesn't have at least a thousand pictures of her baby on her cellphone." She sounded almost normal while expecting she'd soon be under attack. She paused briefly. "But I suppose this is not what you wanted to ask," she resumed, challenging CJ when he remained silent.

Her intention?—acknowledging the elephant in the room and moving on as quickly as possible.

CJ halted and turned brusquely, his gaze piercing. "Oh! And since you know so well, please enlighten me. Tell me, what is that I wanted to ask?"

"You wanted to ask if he's yours..." Ava replied bravely, holding his gaze.

He winced, scrutinizing Ava's face, convinced she'd try to avoid a concrete answer, just as she had been doing since she landed. "Well, is he?"

Ava swallowed and looked down, biting her lower lip. "Yes, he is."

"You— You're a mad woman, you know?" CJ roared between grinding teeth, his fingers tightening around the suitcase handle. "Why?"

"Why?!" she asked, tangled, looking back into his eyes.

"Yes, why! Why didn't you tell me?"

"It-um ... it was complicated." Her voice dropped, broken, as a ghostly forced smile twisted her lips.

"And who made it complicated? Do you remember?"

She revealed a faint grin, maintaining a calm look after glancing around and noticing people staring at them. "Smile. People are watching. Yes, I remember. I'll tell you. Just ... let's keep moving."

After a subtle look around, he started walking. "I listen."

"I wanted to. I swear to God. But there was never a good time, in my mind. I thought I'd tell you when and *if* he arrived. It wasn't sure I'd make it to term. It wasn't certain *he'd* make it at all. But he did. And when he was here ... I believed it was too late ... that you must've moved on. It turns out, you actually did. I knew I had no right to turn your life upside down."

He scowled. "Did you know you were pregnant when you left?"

"No, I didn't."

"Are you sure? I realize now that all the signs were there."

"You must believe me! All I knew was that I didn't get pregnant when I tried. Why would I think I may be pregnant when I was sure I was at menopause?"

"When did you find out?"

"About two weeks after I got home. I believed it was stress. I actually went looking for some stress-relieving supplements. At the pharmacy, I ended up in the wrong aisle. I walked past the pregnancy tests and kept going. Then I thought 'What if?' As ridiculous as it seemed, I went back and got one. If my peace of mind had only a few bucks tag, I decided to try. I forgot about it for a few days, and when I finally remembered. Well ... Ayden is now waiting for me to come home."

CJ glared at her, saying nothing for a few seconds that seemed to stretch too long, fighting the instinct to kiss her senselessly right then and there. Anger and all those old feelings he had for her spiralled and clashed together inside him.

"You promised you'd call," he reproached.

"I promised. But when I saw you at the airport ... when you were leaving ... You were looking distraught."

His eyebrows arched high, eyes wide. "The SeaWorld baseball cap?"

"Yeah, that was me," she admitted with an uncomfortable grin.

"Fuck! I thought I was losing my mind. I saw you in every other woman, everywhere I looked— Wait! You said you were on the plane two days before that."

"I was. Flying to San Diego. Hence, the SeaWorld hat. I left L.A. to go home on the day I was supposed to. After seeing you in that state, I couldn't bring myself to call. Wouldn't have done any good at that point."

Still frowning, he pursed his lips. "Where is Ayden now? Knowing you, I suppose he's not home alone, like you said."

She scoffed. "Of course, he's not home alone. He's staying with my friends."

"We need to talk about this. About your madness ... about everything. I want to meet him."

"No. No! What for? Leave him alone! Don't you dare even think to come after him! He is mine, do you understand? It was my decision to bring him into this world," Ava snapped fiercely. He kept walking.

When they reached the car, he tossed her suitcase into the trunk without a single word, his movements short and swift. Then he turned and reached for the carry-on she held. Probably to shove it next to her other luggage.

Her stare remained solid on him. "Do you understand what I asked you?" she pressed, exasperated. "You have a beautiful, extraordinary woman. You'll start your own family. You'll have your own kids ... many of them. I only have him. Let us be. Please. Please have a heart. He's all I have." When he said nothing, her tone shifted, almost begging now. "I shouldn't be here, and I wouldn't be here if I knew who Eliza was marrying. But don't worry. I'll find an excuse. I'll leave. Evidently, you don't want me in your wedding."

In silence, jaw clenched, CJ crammed her carry-on, which she eventually surrendered, into the trunk. He remained quiet while Ava was breaking inside. His stillness was killing her slowly, like he meant to torture her.

When he finally opened his mouth, "Sure. Run away. This

is what you're good at. I bet you had plenty of time to get even better." He paused, lips warped into a bitter smirk. "And ... what exactly makes you believe I'd come after him?" his tone set in irony.

"You just said you want to meet him. Forget about him. Just ... focus on your future. Please promise me you won't come after him. You're getting married in less than a week. What's the point?"

"Well, the good news is that I'm not married yet. You're mad. You are. You didn't even try to deny he's mine," he said, bitterness in his tone, head bobbing.

"Deny! Do you mean ... lie? I never lied to you. I don't know how to lie. And what for? It doesn't take a genius to figure it out. It's simple math. The face you made ... I knew you already figured it out. I hope to gain your sympathy and negotiate. Not make you angrier than you already are. Not that you don't have the right to be angry—"

"You didn't lie, but you kept it from me." His disappointed gaze narrowed at nothing, beyond her, before falling back on Ava. "I'll ask you again. Why do you believe I'd come after him?"

"Because ... people like you ... do?"

"People like me! What do you mean by people like me?"

"People with the means and the fame, and an army of law-yers ... I don't know. You hear things like that all the time."

"Aha. I see. I'm not sure who you're referring to. But I can tell you what I'll do. Just so you know, I'm not only coming after my son. I'm going for the whole package," his tone final.

"Whatever that means ... I'll fight. I'll die fighting if I have to. Hear me out. You may win. You may get him. But I swear to God, you won't see him. Ever! I'll take your eyes out before you get the chance to see him. I promise you that." Her chest tightened as a desperate cry rose from within her. "I can't afford to lose another child. I just can't."

She slouched, her heart crumbling under the perspective of losing her child. Another burden threatened to come her way.

CJ frowned, visibly perturbed. "Another child! What are you

talking about? What other child?"

Her shoulders quaked, hands clutching the handle of her purse, straining to hold back her tears. "I told you once ... You don't really know me. Not all of me. You only knew I was a widow. I was a widow not once but twice. With my first husband, I had a son, who I lost to cancer just a few years after we lost his father. I never talk about that part of my life. If you come after Ayden, you'll kill me." Her voice cracked, and tears she couldn't hold back anymore streamed down her face.

CJ flinched as if struck. His mouth parted slightly, but no words came. He dragged a hand through his hair, frustration flashing across his face, battling once more his first instinct to take her in his arms and hold her tight.

He stepped forward, then stopped, hesitant, his heart amid a crucial fight. Still furious, his entire being told him she should be punished right now, not comforted.

Divergent emotions and conflicting feelings sent mixed signals to his brain. He wanted to know. He had to know before he could trust her again. Before deciding which feelings win the battle.

A muscle flexed in his jaw. "Why didn't you tell me you were pregnant? Why didn't you tell me I have a son? You should've told me. I have the right to know. And please don't say it was complicated. You had three years. I refuse to believe these three years were all complicated. I just don't believe it."

Ava glanced past CJ, noticing someone approaching behind him. Quickly wiping away the tears, she put her sunglasses on. "Eliza is coming. Please don't tell her. She doesn't have to know. Think about you and her. Just don't complicate things more than I already did. Please make better decisions than I did."

17. What is worth fighting for

"**I** was just about to call you. I wasn't sure where you parked, but I remembered you had a favourite spot," Eliza joined them, her tone cheerful.

"That was quick. I didn't even have time for a smoke," Ava forced a chuckle, struggling to keep her composure and not crumble.

"I need one too. Let's have one before leaving." Eliza tilted her head as she noticed Ava sniffling. "I hope you didn't catch a cold. We have plans ... things to do."

Ava lit a cigarette. "I hope not. Feels like allergies. Probably the airplane air. You know how some people, instead of turning the air off when they don't need it, direct it towards the person sitting next to them? This is who I sat by."

"You should've said something," Eliza commented.

Ava scoffed. "Sure. Starting an argument with a Karen? By the way, her name was Karen. Try figure," she forced a giggle. "Plus, my contacts must be dry. I can't wait to get to the hotel, take my contacts off, shower, and hopefully, take a nap."

"What hotel? I hope you didn't book a hotel. I told you we'd take care of everything. You're staying with us," Eliza hurried to explain.

In silence, CJ took a drag from his cigarette, deeply lost in thought, while throwing occasional glimpses at Ava.

"Staying with you? I really don't think that's a good idea. You need your space right now."

"It's done. There's plenty of space. You're staying with us. Right, Hun?" Eliza concluded, seeking CJ's support.

"Right. You're staying with us," CJ confirmed, barely hiding a mischievous eyebrow raise and a similar smirk.

"Okay, let's get into action," Eliza tittered, clapping her hands and bouncing on her toes. "Final dress fitting. I need you and your expert eye there. I think those girls don't exactly know what they're doing. It was supposed to be delivered last week. I told them my mom is a designer, and she's coming today."

"Yeah, right. And they believed your designer mom didn't design a special dress for your special day?" Ava badgered her.

"I don't care what they believed. I'm glad you're here."

"I told you to go somewhere else. But you chose an ordinary bridal store," CJ chimed in.

"If there's one thing I learned from Lina, it's that if it looks good in pictures and you're happy, nobody's gonna know how much a damn wedding dress was. You only wear it once. All that matters is to be loved by your special one and feel like a princess, even if you are in rags. Plus, I wanted to give a chance to a small, local business," Eliza countered.

"Lina sounds like a brilliant and wise woman," CJ nearly mocked, as if he were talking about someone who wasn't there. "Ready to go?"

Everybody got in the car, and they drove off.

"Have they tried to adjust it from the shoulder?" Ava asked when Eliza went on, explaining what was wrong with the dress, and they couldn't figure it out.

"I think they only tried underarm, but what do I know? You'll see when we get there," Eliza replied before continuing toward CJ. "Hun, did you know Lina is a designer? My mom said Lina had the coolest clothes that she designed and made herself.

And she made my mom a bunch of pants, skirts, dresses…"

"Really? I didn't know you had this talent," CJ's tone softened as he looked at Ava's reflection in the rear-view mirror.

"Designer?! So pretentious!" Ava snickered. "Just dabbling. I had no clue what I was doing. I was lucky they turned out okay. Back then, under the communist regime, finding nice clothes was tough. I had to get creative. But nice, affordable fabrics were easy to find. Not to mention mom's stash, which often appealed to me. Oh, how many times I got in trouble for chopping her fabrics. Whatever caught my eye and seemed suitable for my ideas or projects— Those were good times. I wish it were the only thing I could get in trouble for today," and only two people in that car understood what she meant.

CJ peered at her reflection in the rearview mirror. "How about some background noise?" And he turned on some music.

"Wow. What?! Thank you. See? This is why I love you," Eliza squeaked, reaching out to kiss CJ.

"Ellie, please! I'm driving." He pushed her away.

The almost-too-abrupt gesture made Ava cringe in the back seat.

"Ouch! My grumpy bear," Eliza chirped. "I thought you hated his guts," she continued. Then she turned to Ava, as if trying to find an excuse for his abruptness. "He always asks me to skip it when this song comes on."

CJ looked at Ava through the mirror. "I don't hate his guts. Most of the time, I just don't feel like listening to his music, that's all."

The song that brought them together. His brows furrowed at the haunting memory of Ava's performance that night, on their way back from the party. The night when he was just as quiet as he is now. And just as tangled. That unforgettable night when they both explored and exposed their feelings and made love for the first time.

He glanced again at her reflection in the rear-view mirror. Ava turned her gaze, looking out the window, agonizing memories eating at her.

"Here we are. Call me when you're finished so I can pick you up. I'll grab some coffee. For all," CJ said as he pulled over in front of the bridal store.

"By the way, Lina takes her coffee—"

"Like me, I know. I remember that much."

"You are the best! I love you." Eliza reached to kiss him, but CJ turned his head, her lips landing on his jaw.

Already on the curb, Ava waited for Eliza to take the lead. CJ's eyes tracked her.

After only a few steps, Ava darted back to the car. "Eliza, you go inside. I left my purse in the car. I'll be right back." CJ's eyebrows lifted as she opened the door. "Here. Draw an 'U' to unlock it. I know. Not very creative. I mostly use my fingerprint. Check out my Facebook account. Look at Ayden's albums. See how happy he is. Think if you want to change that."

Then she grabbed her purse and joined Eliza in the bridal shop.

"Phew! One stressor down, a million more to go. I knew those girls had no clue what they were doing. Thank God you're here," Eliza said, turning to Ava as they got in the car, then she continued toward CJ, "Hun, Lina saved the day. I mean, she saved the wedding. Literally! I would've been miserable if they couldn't fix the dress to my liking. Well, it's done, thanks to Lina. They'll deliver it tomorrow. You're home, right? Lina and I are booked for a spa day."

"Yes, I'll be home," CJ's reply fell cold.

"Great! Let's go now," Eliza giggled. "Where is the coffee?"

"Um ... it ... was a long line and— We'll get home in twenty minutes."

Ava's cellphone was on the back seat, and a frowning CJ was throwing glimpses at her through the mirror.

When they pulled up in front of the house, Ava peeked out

the window, assessing the vast residence. Eliza grabbed her purse and Ava's and headed to the main entrance, while Ava stopped at the trunk to get her luggage. CJ picked up her carry-on, set it down, and went back to get the suitcase. Ava's hand was already on it.

"I got this. I got it," he insisted, gently nudging Ava when she didn't let go, his hand wrapped over hers on the suitcase handle.

"I hope you've made a good idea. Don't worry, I'll be out of your hair soon. Just playing along for now. Let's not muddy the waters. Think about what's worth fighting for. What matters to you. As for me, I already know what's worth fighting for," Ava hissed, a mixture of anguish and concern emanating from her stare.

"Yes. I have a very good idea. I know what is worth fighting for." His reply dropped sharply, like a dagger twisted in her insides.

The door to her designated bedroom for the week closed behind her, and Ava leaned against it, her breath laboured and her head spinning. Then, she stood brusquely, a visceral need for a thorough cleanse invading her being.

A long shower, she secretly hoped, might help remove all the evil karma from herself. On the outside and deep inside her soul.

She hunched, letting the hot water whip her body for a long time. Then, she turned off the hot water, standing for a few more minutes under icy-cold lashes, with the indescribable intention of punishing her body. Or probably yanking her mind out of a bad dream.

Of course, it didn't work as intended. *This is not a dream. It's a nightmare. My worst nightmare.*

Dissatisfied with the results, she stepped out of the shower. Her heart squeezed, feeling beat up. But not defeated. Not just yet. Her eyes shifted to her fitness tracker. Almost noon in

Edmonton.

She needed to see Ayden. Make sure he was okay. Hearing his little voice and all the excitement in it, she hoped it would give her strength. There's someone there, halfway around the world— as CJ once said—worth fighting for with every ounce of determination she could squeeze out of herself and put into this battle.

Was she planning to disclose anything about the disaster she had walked into? *Why open Pandora's Box now?* Ava was all a bag of hopes. She hoped that, with time, she'd find a better way to share the news. But what she mainly hoped for was that she wouldn't have to.

She promised she'd call her friends, with whom Ayden spent the week, when she arrived at her destination. And it had been a few hours since she had landed. They may have already started worrying.

She needed to see a familiar face and say 'sweet dreams' to Ayden before the kids went to bed. And, hopefully, just hopefully, extract some more strength from that interaction. The strength to fight and slay the wicked creatures lingering within this nightmare, waiting to consume her.

Ayden was her happy place, the primary source of strength she needed to stay afloat. Now, she had to put on a brave face. Born with a built-in distress detector, Ayden always knew when she wasn't okay. He wrapped his little arms around her neck and hugged her tightly whenever she was upset. More often than not, after dealing with idiots at work. A bitter smile curled her lips.

Before calling, Ava quickly checked her face in the mirror. Nothing unanticipated. And it wasn't great news. Her eyes were telling stories she wasn't ready to pour out of her battered soul.

Well ... I could come up with something. Just got out of the shower, no makeup, lacking sleep, long flight ... blah-blah. And, of course, I miss my baby. It's the first time we are apart for this long. It sounded like a pretty good and believable explanation. *And it's mostly true, not really make-believe.* She exhaled loudly.

Bella found her way into Ava's bedroom and was now

planted in front of the bathroom door, patiently waiting for her to come out. She stood up, wagging her tail. Just as she used to in the good old days. *Well, at least someone's happy to see me.*

Ava forced a half-smile and leaned, looking into Bella's eyes. "Hey, girl! I'm happy to see you, too." She remembered Bella didn't like to be petted, so she didn't think to try.

She sucked in a deep breath and called. 'Halfway around the world', others were living just another normal day. After an exciting morning at Telus Science Centre, filled with loads of fun, the kids had lunch and now enjoyed their favourite show before nap. Ava talked briefly with her friend, Nina, before Ayden figured out who was on the phone and ran eagerly to speak to 'Mama'.

Excited, he talked about his day. He made pancakes with the girls and ate them all. "But all of them, Mama." Ava smiled.

"I flew an airplane. To London. To be with you, Mama. I was the pilot." As always, his voice surged with enthusiasm. Her stomach flipped.

Anywhere but here, Baby! He was excited for the following day when they'd go to the zoo to see Lucy, the elephant, the camels, the zebras, and all the animals from around the world. She listened to his adorable rant, the smile not leaving her face, although her soul was in pieces.

Then, he remembered, "When you coming home, Mama? I miss you," asked Ayden, with the cutest smile and pout on his face.

"A couple more sleeps, Baby. I miss you, too. A lot. You be good and stay out of trouble. Okay? I can't wait to come home. You know Mama loves you very much." Her voice broke, along with her heart.

"I love you mo', Mama," said the little one in his own tongue.

She forced a smile while a lump in her throat threatened to suffocate her. "Guess what? I love you most, Baby."

It was their little game, always ending with a tickle on his belly and happy giggles. Eventually, the two cheerfully rolled on the floor, cuddling and laughing.

Ava just got off the phone, thinking of that tiny being waiting for her. Her heart swelled with love, only to suddenly sink into fear. She was glad he was not there with her, in the middle of this catastrophe.

18. *I'll talk some sense into him*

Ava's gaze turned toward the door, listening to voices from beyond. No intelligible words or conversations, just a muffled clamour. For someone attuned to the house's acoustics, it could mean something. In which room was the discussion taking place, at least? Then, it was likely Eliza who raised her voice. Ava didn't catch what she yelled. But moments later, what sounded like a slammed door shook the entire house. Or perhaps it was some other sound unique to this place, unknown to her.

She was still lying on her belly, sprawled across the bed, just as she had been when she made the call. On the floor, Bella's ears perked up, and she looked at Ava before shifting her gaze toward the door. She, too, listened to the same concerning sounds. Then, she glanced back at Ava as if to say, 'There's trouble.'

Promptly, Ava sprang to her feet, adjusting her bathrobe as the towel on her head still hung slightly to the side, ends falling over her shoulder. With wide eyes and a racing heart, she cautiously opened the door, peeking through the crack before stepping into the hallway.

Eliza stomped up the stairs, anger echoing from each step. Frozen at the top of the staircase, Ava's stomach twisted under the heavy feeling that something terrible must've happened. Worry pierced her heart, and her head spun.

Damn you, CJ. Why? All she could think about was that it was up to her to prevent the dread from spreading. She must shield her baby from being caught in this madness. She needed to protect her baby. *But how? Eliza is my baby, too.*

Ava's mission was greater than she had ever imagined. Her shoulders squared with determination. *I've been through way worse. I didn't make it to this day to give up now. This time, I have a chance. At least this time, it's people, not God!* She struggled for a deep breath.

I'll make it through this, too. Her fists clenched as if she were preparing to fight. However, this wasn't just a battle. *This is war!*

Only when she reached the top of the stairs did Eliza notice Ava standing there. Too frightened to ask.

But she asked anyway, "Eliza, baby. Is everything okay?" When their eyes met, Ava knew—'everything was not okay'.

The ice-cold, empty look Eliza gave her … Ava felt her heart shatter into a million pieces. Eliza knew. And she'd never forgive her. Ever! Ava's stomach dropped when she looked into those eyes, blurred from tears.

She was ready for war, but she was without a plan. She hadn't planned any of this. She dismissed the possibility of running into CJ as soon as the idea crossed her mind. *What are the actual chances? I'll be at a bridal shop, a Spa Day—mani-pedi and everything in between—as Eliza put it, rehearsal dinner, hair salon, and the wedding party. The chances of running into him in any of these places are slim to none.*

"Everything's not okay, and you know it all too well. You are so deceiving. Who are you, really?" A furious Eliza threw words at Ava that she felt she deserved. Perhaps. Or maybe she didn't.

Who knows what is right and what is wrong, actually? Everything's circumstantial.

Ava's teeth raked at her bottom lip as she swallowed the guilt rising from her core. "Baby, I swear to God, I wouldn't be here if I knew who you were marrying. I wouldn't. You ask who I am. I am the same Lina who has loved you since you were a baby and always will. The same Lina you grew up with. You have the right to be upset and hate me, but you need to know that—"

"Frankly? I don't need to know anything you have to say," Eliza interrupted sharply. "I already know a lot more than I bargained for. Now, if you don't mind, I need to pack and leave. Have a wonderful life!" she burst out, a bitter sneer warping her face.

"Wait! What?! Leave? No! No-no-no. You can't leave. I know it's a lot to take in, and you shouldn't have discovered this way. I begged him. I told him it wasn't a good time. Not before the wedding. Well, actually, not ever. Please, let's sit and talk," Ava implored.

"Talk?! I'm afraid there's nothing more to talk about. Everything that needed to be said has already been said," spat out an extremely hot-headed and annoyed Eliza.

Ava opened her mouth, but no words came out before she caught her upper lip between her teeth. Eliza trudged past her toward the bedroom she had shared with CJ for the last two years. Coming out of Ava's bedroom, Bella approached. She reached up and licked Ava's hand as if to say, 'I've got your back'. Looking down at her, Ava attempted a smile, running her hand along Bella's head.

As if she remembered something, Eliza halted and spun to face Ava. "And, by the way, there won't be a wedding anymore, so ... sorry for bothering you. At least you didn't come for nothing," another sour smirk twisted her face at the sight of Bella yielding to Ava's petting. "Knowing you, I think you had feelings for him. Do you still love him?" She continued after a moment of hesitation.

"What?! No..." Ava shook her head in confusion, uncertain of what to expect next.

Eliza seemed to reconsider. "Actually, that's none of my business. I don't need to know, and certainly, I don't want to know."

"Eliza, Honey, you have to understand, it's over. Whatever happened was long ago. Do yourself a favour. Leave the past behind and focus on the road ahead. I am the past. *You* are the future. You must fight for your future. Running away is not the answer."

"I'm not you. I'm not running. I'm leaving. It's a big difference, you know? And, by the way, there's no future here. At least not for me." Eliza paused, pride replacing the sarcasm in her voice. "You know what? You're absolutely right. I have a long road ahead of me, and I must keep my eyes on it. I also need to keep my eyes wide open for what and especially *who* is on that road."

Ava's gut told her that whatever happened just before this moment must've been more. More than just Eliza finding out that CJ was Ayden's father. *But what is 'more'? She obviously knows I ran. How much more, he said, that I probably can't even think of? What the fuck happened in the last ... about an hour?*

Ava shook her head, thinking it could all be her own imagination. *I'm probably just growing paranoid.* All Ava's mind could churn was that it was up to her to fix this mess if she was going to have any chance at keeping her baby.

"Eliza, believe me, I walked in your shoes. The week before the wedding is always stressful. Simple things can quickly spiral into craziness. I know all this shit doesn't fall under 'simple things', but it doesn't have to go like this," Ava pleaded, desperately trying to convince Eliza to change her mind. Immediately, she brought up something from her past, hoping to take some of the intensity out of the moment. "You know I sent Dan away just three days before our wedding? Like you, I said the wedding was off. We still got married, and we've been so happy. You were there. Don't do anything you'll regret later. Don't make big decisions when upset. Sleep on it and make your decision tomorrow." She struggled to craft a smile. "You must stay. Does he know you want to leave? I'll talk some sense into him."

Staggered, Eliza stared at Ava. She shook her head, puffing, as she began to understand the woman standing before her had no clue about what had happened only moments ago.

"Lina, you're wasting your time. The wedding is off. He

wants me to leave. And honestly, after what he just confessed, I must leave. I owe it to myself," Eliza's voice wavered with disappointment.

She had just had a revelation following CJ's confession about some terrible things he'd done. Her soul ached, and rotten denial was crawling under her skin. But deep down, she already knew they were past the point of no return.

"Ayden is my baby. And that will never change. Ever! I promise you! None of this was supposed to happen, but it did. And, in a way, I'm glad you found out. At least I can maintain some of my integrity by not having to lie about why I must leave now. I'll make sure I'm out of here before your big day. But you two need to talk. Not today. Maybe tomorrow, when I'm gone. Just the two of you!" Ava insisted.

"You're too late. Or, maybe I should say ... you're right on time? Otherwise, this charade would've gone on much longer. I should probably thank you," Eliza said, irony dripping from her voice.

Ava shook her head, unsure of what to make of Eliza's words. "Don't do anything stupid, please. I'll talk to him." She spun on her heels and bolted down the stairs in search of CJ.

In a split second, Bella followed, probably with the same intention—to have her back.

Eliza knew Ava's past, her burdens, and all about her lost battles in life. If Ava was going to save Ayden, she needed someone on her team. Eliza would be just her ally infiltrated into the enemy's territory.

She was an extraordinary young woman. And Ava hoped she'd be on her side. Even if it were just because ... *Let's face it: what woman would instantly embrace the idea of having to raise another woman's child, when it wasn't part of the original deal?*

As long as Ava had a chance to keep Ayden, the reasons didn't even matter. She was ready to accept any reason, take any risks, make any compromises, and pay any price. As she had promised CJ earlier, there wasn't one thing in the world she wouldn't do to keep her child. And keep him safe.

From the top of the stairs, Eliza watched the woman who, mere seconds earlier, had poured her heart out before her. A woman so determined to find a way to mend something that was beyond repair. Eliza shook her head slowly, a confused sneer tugging at the corner of her mouth as she realized Lina was the same human being she remembered.

This wasn't a conspiracy, as she first suspected. At least, Lina wasn't part of it. Selflessly, she was trying to fix things. As always. This was the same Lina—well, Ava—she had known since she could remember. This was the same Lina who was there for her and her mom when Eliza's dad left. Probably, the only one who cared enough not to tell her mom about her dad's infidelities. Who probably hoped more than her own mother that he'd make a comeback for Eliza's sake.

Lina knew things long before Eliza's mom began growing suspicious. The only person her mother confided in, when the inevitable happened. Even though Lina was going through the most challenging time of her life, she stood by them and cheered them up. She opened her home and offered them shelter, love, and a shoulder to cry on.

Well, I can't blame him for choosing her over me. She is ... kinda perfect. Even the flipping dog likes her—Eliza thought. *But the way he manipulated me, as if I were a character in one of his fucking video games*—was unacceptable to Eliza. *In my own way, I'm kinda perfect, too. At least he had the decency to admit it wasn't me whom he couldn't accept. It was Ava whom he wanted. It all boils down to: he was broken and hurting, and reached for the low-hanging fruit.*

She blew a deep sigh and muttered to herself, "You're so right about that part. It was you. Go to hell, CJ! I thought I was helping you heal. But all I did was help you play with my confidence. Now, I can be my perfect little self to someone who deserves me. I am me, and I am free! Fuck you!"

As Ava ran downstairs to 'talk some sense' into CJ, Eliza sucked in a breath and stepped into the bedroom. Without a coherent plan, random items were shoved into a suitcase. She paused, staring into the mirror as her mind once again wandered to what might go on downstairs.

"Not my circus, not my monkeys! But I certainly know the clowns," she muttered again.

She halted in her tracks, hair straightener in hand, her mind derailing to a different scenario. *Is Lina in for a big surprise? Is she aware of his intentions? Did they have enough time to—? They had only been alone when I went to the bloody bathroom at the airport.* She hummed. *How long was that? Fifteen? Twenty? Twenty-five minutes, tops. Not enough time to go through all that: shock, denial ... whatever-whatever... and make up his mind.*

Tossing the hair straightener into the suitcase, her mind buzzed, trying to identify the missing pieces in the puzzle. Discouraged and still incredulous, Eliza sat on the edge of the bed for a minute, struggling to process the whole thing.

This must be why he seemed preoccupied. Why he snapped and was cold and abrupt with me when we drove back. He was going through all those phases. I guess Lina will be taken by surprise, just like I was—Eliza thought. *Now, that would be interesting to watch.*

But no! Not her problem.

She had a different problem now. *I'll finish packing, and I'm out of here. But where the hell am I going? Tatiana—that's it! I'll have to tell her anyway. But I just fucking want to be alone, curl up and cry my sorrow, and not talk about it. What a circus! Well, Tatiana is my only option right now!*

Another deep exhale left her chest.

She stared at the door and listened. Fuzzy voices were coming from downstairs, and the tone in those voices wasn't the nicest. There was talking, and long silences. Probably trying to be civil, speaking in a lower voice. Then, shouting again, pausing again, and likely some sobbing was going on, too. *Who knows?* Shaking a tormenting thought, she resumed packing.

Ava found CJ in his study, his man cave, or whatever they call it here in the UK. His space—where he either played games, recharged or rehearsed when he had to. All the way at the far end of the semi-basement.

Not knowing the layout of the place, Ava wandered for a while. Bella pranced ahead of her, leading the way. Stopping before the door, she looked back at Ava as if to say, 'This is where you want to go'.

She could hear him talking. He sounded troubled. Probably still rambling in anger following what she imagined was a heated argument he had with Eliza.

He had his back turned to the door when she stormed into the room, shouting, "Do you know Eliza is packing? She's leaving! I thought we agreed not to tell her. Why on earth did you—?" She halted mid-sentence.

He calmly turned to face Ava, pointed to his earbuds, and shared a broad smile. With the same index finger and a nod of his head, he signalled for her to stay and wait until he finished the conversation. Then he motioned for her to come in and showed a chair. An invitation for her to sit.

She paused by the door, wincing slightly, a bit embarrassed about barging in, shouting. However, she wasn't about to accept his invitation to sit. *Absolutely not! If he stands, I'll stand too!*

Since he was nearly a foot taller, she would likely feel dominated by him during the discussion. At least if she stands, she won't feel like she's being 'talked to' but 'talked with'. This was her strategy to gain some advantage.

19. It is what I want

The towel wrapped around her head came loose, hanging limply on her right shoulder. In a desperate attempt to adjust it and keep it in place, Ava only managed to make things worse. The towel swirled and twirled and landed on her other shoulder, still hanging limp.

Another attempt at adjusting it, and again she wasn't successful. In one quick, fluid motion, she took it off and wrapped it around her arm, then she propped her hands on her hips, ready to face whatever came her way.

Her wet hair appeared darker than usual, loose strands falling around her face, wavy from the towel she had just unwrapped. She blinked, wincing, as she caught more of the discussion. On the phone, CJ sounded like he was speaking in some sort of code. His replies? Short and vague. That's what Ava realized when she finally finished wrestling with the stubborn towel, which somehow undermined her hope of how this discussion should go.

She couldn't hear the other side of the phone call. Yet, it sounded more than strange from her end. CJ appeared calm and pleasant. Conflicting. It wasn't what she thought she'd heard before walking in.

"So, this Lina is actually Ava? Your Ava! And you just found out that she had your child. And you're calling off the wedding?" In disbelief, Rob repeated all the information he'd just picked up from his brother's rant, struggling to understand what CJ was trying to convey. "Was that Ava?" he asked, hearing her shouting.

"You're correct … about everything."

"Wow! She sounds angry. How do you find her after three years?"

"Wonderful!"

"You're insane. Just wait until Mum finds out. She'll go ballistic. And I'm afraid Dad won't take it too well either, no matter how much he loves you. You know I have to tell them."

"No. I'll do it. Please get started on that list, and we can discuss the rest later."

"I don't get you. I understand you believe you still love her. Question is, does she still love you? You were in a dark place after she left. She'll leave again. Is that what you want? Is she still there?"

"Yes, still here. And no. Different circumstances."

"For me to understand … Do you want to get her back? Marry her, instead?"

"Exactly!"

"CJ, I know you have a child together. I understand you are shocked by the news, and you may feel you need to marry her. But this can be handled in a hundred other ways. She didn't even tell you that you were going to be a father. You don't have to marry her just because she chose to have your baby. It was her decision, and you had no say in the matter."

"Will you please trust me just this once? I don't have to, that's right. It's what I want, and you know it."

"Okay. I'll mind my own damn business. Fuck! What a mess, CJ! I'll have to get Lisa on board to help. We'll have to ask for read confirmation so there won't be any other surprises and cancel everything wedding-related."

"Yes, everything, but Wednesday evening," CJ said.

"So, the rehearsal dinner stays, but it'll be a 'meet my new future wife' dinner. It's so twisted," Rob puffed. "You probably won't get a refund for cancelling on such short notice."

"That's fine. Don't even ask."

"Have you proposed yet? Did she say yes?"

"I didn't yet!" CJ's jaw flexed.

"So, right now, you only hope she wants the same thing. You're totally messed up. You know what? Your mess, you clean it up. I'm just doing what you asked me to. I guess there's no point in trying to reason with you. It sounds like you've already made up your mind, and mending things with Ellie may no longer be an option."

CJ listened, gnawing at his cheek. "Don't worry about that. All I need from you is to start on what we discussed and help me control the damage. I'll take care of everything else. It'll be fine."

"Fuck it, man! What if Mum and Dad get suspicious? You know they are staying with us. The family might call and ask what's going on, why they've been uninvited. You know, things can go a million different ways. I'll have to tell them something at some point. Just ... the wedding is not happening, and you'll fill us in later?! They'll sound credible if anyone calls asking."

"No! Absolutely not! Give me a couple of hours. I promise I'll call you back to discuss the rest, okay?

"Then, I'll start drafting the message, but I won't send it just yet. I'll wait for your okay. Mum and Dad need to know before anyone else, or they'll panic."

"You're right. I have to go now. I need to handle something important."

"Well, good luck then. I hope you know what the hell you're doing."

"I'll call you later. And ... remember, not yet, okay? Talk to you. Bye now."

A slanted smile creased his face as CJ took a few steps towards Ava after the call ended. And his gaze? She saw in his eyes what she once believed was love. "Sorry. That was my brother. My oldest brother, Rob," he said now, that he was so close to her.

"Did you hear what I said?" she asked.

"Yes, I did," he replied in the most neutral tone.

Her head tilted to the side, and she stared into his eyes in an effort to understand what this calm was for. Where did it come from, and how, or why, could he act like this?

Pouting, Ava's head bobbed with each emphasized word. "Um— Eliza is packing. She wants to leave. Is that what you heard?"

"Yes, I know. I heard you."

"For God's sake, CJ! Why did you have to tell her? What's in it for you? Tell me!"

"Everything?"

"Really?! Your *everything* is up there, packing. She's leaving. Do you understand that? You must go and talk to her."

"We have already talked. Trust me, she'll be fine. And she's not my *everything*. She needs some time to process what I just admitted to, but she'll be fine once she has the chance to take it all in. In fact, she'll be better off away from me," CJ continued, his tone just as flat as before.

"You're not coming after Ayden. Ayden is mine, and that is final," she nearly shouted. Sad but hopeful eyes gazed at her, but he remained silent. "What in the world did you say to Eliza? You both speak in riddles. You're a monument to coolness while she's devastated. What the hell is going on?" asked Ava, scrambling to understand what had happened.

A muscle ticked in his jaw, and his throat worked. "She has every reason to be devastated. The wedding's off. This is what I discussed with my brother. Uninviting everyone and cancelling what needs to be cancelled. And just so you know, I don't feel cool. Not at all. But if we're both yelling, we won't get anywhere. There's a hurricane brewing inside me. I'm ashamed of what I've done. I'm ashamed of what I didn't do, but I should've. I'm confused and angry, and— Dammit, Ava! I just had to put on a face."

Ava's eyebrows shot up in shock. "So … you're actually playing! This is what you're doing right now? And what the hell is this play called? Do I have a part in it? You know what? Don't answer. I don't need to know. I have no idea what's going on in your head right now or what game you're playing. Everything's so messed up! I'll grab my shit and leave. But I'm warning you. Don't you dare come after Ayden! Do you understand me?" With that, Ava swivelled and headed towards the door.

Quickly moving around, CJ positioned himself between her and the door she had left slightly ajar. Bella, who had been sitting next to Ava all this time, moved to CJ's side, clearly having his back. He quickly reached behind and pushed the door shut.

"You're not going anywhere. Not this time. We need to talk. You're staying so we can discuss."

"What?! Am I a hostage now?" she asked, vexed by his move and choice of words.

"No, you're not a hostage. I'm just trying to stop you from doing something foolish again. Trying to reason with the Ava I once knew and, more importantly, with Ava, the mother. I get it. Believe me, I do. You always put others first, and I guess it's entirely normal to be upset about Ellie right now."

She snorted. "You guess!?"

"Well, I know you must be upset at the minute. All I ask is that you make an effort and channel that passion of yours towards yourself, our son … us," he continued, pushing to remain calm, though the hurricane still churned within him.

Tilting her head, she stared at him, bewildered. "Us! Who is 'us'? Do you mind—?"

"Us, as in you, Ayden, and I," he interrupted.

"Right now, I really think you need to fix something else," Ava said, pointing to the ceiling, somewhere beyond his shoulders, where she guessed Eliza might be. Then, in a jumble, she pointed in another direction, scrambling to guess which was the right one. The layout of the house was not something she paid attention to as she wandered around.

Nearly laughing at her confusion, CJ clutched her hand and pointed in the right direction. "It's over there," he said, arching a half-amused, half-sarcastic brow.

"Whatever! Point is, you need to fix that right now. Priorities, you know?" She jerked her hand free from his grip.

"Oh, I've got my priorities straight. Don't worry about it," he replied with a hint of sarcasm.

"Oh! You've got your priorities straight! Well then ... I suppose there's no reason for me to stick around any longer. So, I could just go, since I'm not a hostage, right?"

His jaw tightened as he struggled to stay calm and resisted the urge to grab Ava by the shoulders and shake her. Just to bring her back to reality.

"Under different circumstances, I'd say yes, you are free to go. Normally, I'd ask you to stay because you want to stay. However, I understand how hurt you must feel and, given your ... history, I may need to be a bit more ... *assertive*? I hope, though, you're still the same brilliant Ava I once knew, and you'll understand why we need to talk. So, you'll choose to stay of your own free will." He smirked, arching a brow, with an 'I'm waiting for an answer' look on his face.

Ava's gaze turned down. For a few stretched seconds, she glared at the space between them, saying nothing. Fists clenched, she chewed on her bottom lip, weighing her options. He would most likely come after Ayden if she left now, and her life could spiral into chaos. If she stayed, she felt she would betray Eliza's trust.

She was torn up inside, and it showed on the outside. On the other hand, this could be the perfect opportunity to clear things up once and for all, instead of prolonging this tormenting nightmare and the darkness of the unknown. Of ... *What's next, and when will he strike back?*

Ava wrestled with her own judgment. She needed to do this before leaving. Maybe that would help her forge a strategy. She'd know how to approach this ... mess. *My mess.*

Her duty was to protect her child. *Eliza is a grown, strong, independent woman who can care for herself. And if I am to lose Eliza's trust, so be it. Ayden depends on me. He is my primary responsibility.*

She huffed, an aggravated grimace spreading across her face as her lashes lifted. "I guess you win. I'm staying. But to be clear, I'm only staying because we need to talk. You're right about that. I need to get to the bottom of this," Ava agreed, evidently intending to hold her ground and not let him think he had already won. "After all, it sounds like you've already made up your mind to come after Ayden. I can't leave now and continue living in uncertainty while you gather your army of lawyers and prepare for war. I can't live in ignorance of what's to come, or keep asking myself, 'When will you come for him?' Let's discuss and reach an agreement. If after that you still want war ... Oh, you'll have some war, trust me!"

He listened, nodding. "Because people like me do this kind of stuff, I get it. Well ... Good! Actually, it's great. Is this the best decision you've made lately?"

"Oh, I've made some good decisions lately. But yeah, chances are this may turn out to be the best. I hope it'll bring me some peace of mind. I also hope I won't live to regret it!" she countered.

"You won't regret it. I swear. I promise not to come after Ayden, and I'll keep my promise. Here's some peace for your mind. However—"

"However?!" she interrupted, staring at him, petrified at the thought of what would come next.

She didn't want to hear the 'however' and ... However, nothing good can follow in a sentence that starts with 'however'.

20. So, he can still be funny

In the middle of their discussion, both paused and glanced toward the door, listening to the faint footsteps approaching. Eliza paused for a moment, not to eavesdrop but probably to regain her composure, before opening the door and stepping inside.

She was brave enough to plaster a smile on her face, trying to maintain appearances. But her eyes betrayed what was going on in her heart.

"I hope I'm not interrupting, but I must leave. I'll be just a minute," she said in a small voice, half-smiling at Ava while avoiding eye contact with CJ.

As far as she could read the scene, Ava appeared to be in distress. Given her earlier argument with CJ, Eliza was aware of the direction this conversation was heading. What she didn't know was Ava's position. *Did he reach that point yet?* Judging by the tension in the air, probably not. Or maybe Ava wasn't open to the idea?

Prolonging her stay and making the whole situation even more awkward wasn't in her plans. As Eliza walked past them, Ava glanced at CJ, signalling him to do or say something. Eliza continued to the desk, just a few steps across the room.

"Here we go. Your card, your keys ... both for the house and the car. Oh— and this," Eliza said as she slipped the engagement ring off her finger and set it on the desk next to the other items. "I guess this is goodbye," she continued, turning around and meeting Ava's gaze. "I'll probably reach out to Rob to meet and get the rest of my shit when you're away. I can't take everything now. I only packed enough to last me for a little while," she added, her words partially directed at CJ, but still avoiding eye contact.

Embarrassment and guilt seeped from his voice as he mumbled some kind of excuse, glaring at nothing specific. "Ellie, I'm terribly sorry. You'll be better off without me. You know that, right?"

"Oh, I know!" Eliza parried, squaring her shoulders. *If only there were another way out of this room, other than that goddamn door behind him*—she thought as she took a step to leave.

Speechless, Ava felt trapped in the worst situation she had ever encountered. Did she have the right to say anything now? And if so, what could she say? What would be the appropriate thing to say?

"Shit!" Ava blurted. "I can't possibly be the only one with a head still attached." Both CJ and Eliza stared at her, trying to make sense of what she meant. "So, let me get this straight. You have no job or income, you've lived here for the past two years, and you just left your bank card and car keys. You are at ... what? Two thousand kilometres, or more, away from home? I'm at a loss here. Where exactly are you going? How will you get anywhere? How are you going to get by?" As she equated all this, Ava's eyes flicked from Eliza to CJ and back to Eliza, an inquisitive look on her face perfectly synchronized with the tone in her voice.

"I'll be fine, Lina. I have somewhere to stay, for now. Eventually, am I still welcome to stay at your place?" asked Eliza in a subdued voice.

"Of course you are."

"No! Absolutely not!" thundered CJ.

"Oh, please stop being such an ass," Ava snapped. "This is between her and me." She then turned to Eliza and continued, "Baby, you can stay at my place. I'll transfer you money for the airfare too. But I'm sure you can't go there straight from here. I'm more interested in … Where are you going now? I could pay for a hotel for a few days. You probably want to be alone right now. How much do you need?" Ava asked, looking into Eliza's eyes, sensing she might not lose her after all.

"Oh no, there's no way I'm checking into a hotel! I'll crash at Tatiana's until I figure out which way to go," Eliza replied, her voice faltering.

Frowning, CJ's jaw clenched, simmering inside. He had his plans, and Ellie knew exactly what those plans were. Yet, Ellie asked Ava if she could stay at her place! *Really?! Ava's place! Out of all the places in the world, she chose Ava's!* His fingers clenched into fists, knuckles white with anger, carving with just his eyes and a beyond revolted look.

A quick glance at him for the first time since she entered the study, likely catching the vibes emanating from that direction, and Eliza knew. He must've misunderstood the entire conversation.

"Lina's apartment back home, in Romania," Ellie clarified, before CJ jumped at her throat. Eventually.

He blinked fast, as if he had just woken from a nightmare, and a controlled sigh of relief escaped him. "Oh, I-um, didn't know you had a place in Romania!" he stuttered toward Ava.

Still haunted by the 'Eliza situation', she missed everything, including CJ's reaction. "Who's Tatiana?" She then looked at each of them, as if waiting for an answer. A satisfactory one.

"She's my best friend. She was supposed to be my maid of honour." A bitter smirk twisted Eliza's expression. "So, I'll have to tell her, anyway."

"Oh! Is she to be trusted? I mean, I understand she's your friend. I'm sure you trust her. Just … I don't want all this to come out before I get home. Not asking for myself. I'm asking for Ayden. I need to know he's safe, at least until I go back. Could you keep some details to yourself when you break the news? Please. He's innocent. He's not to blame for any of this." Begging again, desperation obvious, Ava's hands clasped together as if in a prayer.

Her stomach clenched, and she suddenly felt weak, her eyes darting from one to the other, searching for sympathy. And hoping she'd get some.

A sudden realization struck CJ like a lightning bolt, jolting him out of his thoughts. "Crap! You can't go to Tatiana's. She'll get curious, inquisitive. You're in no emotional state to resist the pressure. Details might slip out before you even realize. I know you hate me right now, and I deserve it. I had it coming. Ava's right. The kid doesn't deserve to be caught in the middle of all this."

One could hear the wheels in his brain turning and squeaking as he scrambled for a solution.

"I have nowhere else to go. I'll keep my mouth shut. I promise. Not for you, but for Lina and Ayden. I don't know where to turn. Your family isn't an option, and all my other friends are either in Scotland or back home."

Clearly annoyed, Ava glared at CJ. "You must find a solution. I'm sure you don't want all this to get out. Not right now. Not this way. Or do you? Are you really willing to have a scandal on your hands?" her voice firm.

Obviously, she was the only one with a head still attached and a functioning brain.

"The flat! You can stay at the flat. For as long as you need," CJ said, hit by a moment of clarity.

"Cindy's staying there. She's already on her way to London. For— Well ... for the wedding," Eliza replied bitterly.

He fiddled, swallowing his uncertainty. Offering Eliza any kind of support right now? She'd reject it, for sure. Her pride wouldn't let her accept anything from him. Not under these circumstances. Still, he had to try.

"I'll take care of it. And ... here," he said, taking three rushed strides to his desk. "I believe I owe you this much. Keep the card. And the car. It was your birthday present. I can't take it back. I'll feed your card until you get back on your feet. I'll ask Ian if he can help you get a job. Probably at his law firm or—" he cut himself off, holding out the hand with the car keys and the bank card.

"So, you're buying my silence now? Seriously?! It's the last thing I expected you'd do. This is so beneath you. I'm doing it for Ayden. I don't need anything from you," Eliza shot back, her voice dripping with half-disappointment, half-disgust.

"Ellie, no. It's absolutely not like that. I owe you for all the shit I did before today. I can't just throw you out in the street. I hope that one day, when you look back, you'll realize that this, right here, is probably the best day of your life. What you thought we had was not what we actually had. It was a lie, not what you fantasized about. Not what you deserve. I take full responsibility for what I've done. But I can't let Ava pay for your survival. I was the dishonest one. I hope you'll let me do at least this much to make up for all the trouble I've caused," said CJ, aiming for it to be an apology. Maybe an expression of regret, not an attempt to buy her silence.

His hand remained out, holding the card and the car key. Silent, Ava was merely a witness to it all. She sensed the battle in Eliza's mind, although she didn't understand an iota of what they said.

Eliza's reluctance to accept what she already categorized as a 'handout' in her mind was more than clear. Ava had to step in. She knew she had to arbitrate. Convince Eliza to make a practical decision.

"Take it. Don't be foolish. Pride won't feed you. Nor would it put a roof above your head. I'm not exactly sure what happened here. However, by the sound of it, I can tell it wasn't a good ... 'marriage.' No pun intended. I'm sorry for insisting earlier to just get over it. From what was said, I realize there's no going back. But this money will help you move forward and not get stuck in one place. Don't think. Take it. I imagine you earned it."

With that, Ava stepped forward and took Eliza's hand. Her

other hand grasped CJ's, and she made the transfer happen. The card and the fell into Eliza's palm.

Until that moment, Eliza had stood tall and proud. Now, her shoulders slouched as she surrendered her pride. She accepted what she came to believe she earned and would buy her some time. She could afford to be picky and pursue the job of her dreams. Now more than ever, she needed some compensatory satisfaction in her life. *Well, this is something to look forward to,* Eliza thought.

For a fleeting moment, Ava's stomach rested as she slowly exhaled a breath of relief. Her own destiny remained uncertain. Still. At least for this one little battle, she felt satisfied with the outcome. Nobody lost, and nobody won. Just a stalemate. But it offered some gratification.

She finally could put the 'what ifs' out of her mind and prepare for the next battle. The decisive one—saving Ayden.

A defeated-looking CJ dragged his feet beside Eliza, accompanying her to the front door. Quiet, Ava trailed behind them. She wasn't even sure she needed to be there. But she sensed Eliza wanted her to be.

Her heart squeezed. She knew this wasn't the most challenging moment for her. The real battle was yet to come. And it would just be herself and CJ once Eliza is gone.

As the quiet, sad-looking trio made their way upstairs, CJ retrieved the keys to the flat from a drawer and handed them to Eliza. "Everything's paid for. All you have to do is live, and if you feel like hitting something, you can hit me. Those are just things, and they can be replaced. So, you won't hurt me, but you might hurt yourself, and I'm sure that's not what you want," CJ tried to sound funny.

He's still the same uptight Brit, and his attempts at making jokes are quite ... unique, thought Ava. *Brits can be funny as hell, but he's not one of the funny bunch.*

She almost smiled. She always smiled when he made his geeky jokes or at his clumsiness when he tried too hard to drop the stiffness. In time, he opened up. They laughed a lot, finished each other's sentences, and made silly jokes. *All that seemed to have reverted*—Ava made a mental note.

Eliza's hand was on the doorknob when the doorbell rang. A cab driver stood there, asking if they had called for a taxi.

CJ said, "Not us."

Eliza called for one, but she no longer needed it. It wasn't the first time a prankster had ordered a cab to their address. The unsuspecting cabbie walked away, muttering some profanity and waving the hat he had taken off in annoyance.

Despite the heavy tension, all three burst into laughter. The only amusing thing that happened all day.

Oh! So, he can still be funny, Ava thought.

Eliza's eyes lingered over CJ's as if silently asking something.

He shrugged and shook his head, mouthing, "I don't know yet."

When the laughter died down, Ava exhaled and, arms open, stepped toward Eliza. "Please don't be a stranger. Call me if you decide to go back home, and I'll put you in touch with Madam Popa to get the keys and prepare the place for you. Nothing's changed, so you might find it hard to go back there. But you can make any changes you want, okay?"

"I won't be a stranger. You are my second mother, you know?"

"Oh well, that'll never change. Take care of yourself. I love you. And keep in touch," Ava said, holding Eliza in a tight embrace.

That shoulder to cry on and those best-ever laughs have been the mortar and bricks of Gaby—Eliza's mother and Ava's friendship.

When Ava's first husband passed, the two besties drifted apart for a while. Gaby didn't know how to be around a broken Ava and how to comfort her, and Ava couldn't stand pity. Tacitly, they gave each other some space and time for healing.

When things returned to some sort of normalcy, they found their way back to each other. Laughter replaced the silence, and their friendship grew even stronger. Then Eliza was born, filling the empty space with giggles. She didn't know a world without Ava and Andy, Ava's son. They grew up together, closer than siblings.

When Ava moved to Canada. Gaby and Eliza filled her apartment with life and all the traits that come with. Until Gaby's sudden departure, just over three years ago.

With Eliza's mother gone, Ava left the apartment untouched, like a time capsule of memories. Exactly as Eliza left it after the funeral, when she returned to the UK to finish her Master's.

The memory of a sobbing Eliza by the Christmas tree was still vivid in Ava's mind. "Daddy left us." Tears of confusion sparkled in her eyes, the Christmas lights above starkly contrasting with her inner turmoil.

Christmas meant joy. Yet, that year, she unwrapped the bitter gift of abandonment. Eliza was only seven when her world shattered. Twenty years later, she still carried the heavy burden and the resentment of that day.

"You'll be lucky to have two mothers," her father said on the day he announced his new relationship, his voice dripping with the promise of a second mother.

Fierce, Eliza didn't let his lies hurt again. "Sorry, but the place is taken. I already have a second mother. Lina is my second mother." Her words arrived. Powerful, like an unexpected uppercut coming from a ten-year-old.

Right then and there, Ava knew Eliza would be fine. *You can't be that brilliant and not succeed in life.* A faint smile curled her lips, thinking back to those days.

As the door closed behind Eliza, Ava and CJ heard the car's engine start. Tires screeched, and she sped up, as if she wanted to be out of there, not just now, but a long time ago.

Eliza was gone, and it was time for Ava to get back to reality. And that reality didn't look too good. The idea of being alone with CJ? Not at all appealing. But she agreed to stay. She wasn't looking forward to what was coming next. However, she needed to do this so she could return to safety, reunited with her baby.

The last bastion, and then she'd be free to go home.

Back to her life.

CJ squinted at Ava, possibly scrambling to remember the status of their discussion before Eliza entered his study. That, or perhaps strategizing—looking for a way to navigate the conversation from here on.

21. You are the one

Exhaustion was slowly settling into her bones—probably the long flight, the recent events, or perhaps a combination of both. She barely caught a couple of hours of sleep on the plane, her ears still humming from the reverberating engines in the background.

Ava pressed her palms against tired eyes, still itchy even after removing her contacts. The previous night, she hadn't slept too well. She tossed and turned, her stomach in knots at the thought of being away from her baby for an entire week. Then she rolled out of bed several times to double-check whether a specific item had made its way into the suitcase.

And now, this! It felt like peace was never meant to find her.

Her shoulders slumped. With a silent sigh, she shuffled to a barstool by the large island separating the kitchen from the sitting room. Dropping the towel onto the stool, she turned, a concerned cringe on her expression. Arms crossed, she leaned against the island.

She didn't really expect to be attacked. In fact, she planned to strike first. But she didn't want to be caught off guard when CJ countered.

"I sensed that this breakup wasn't just about Ayden, and it

was somehow confirmed by both of you. Do you mind sharing what else you told Eliza?" she began, her tone firm.

"You don't want to know, trust me!" replied CJ, rather uncomfortable with her question.

"Oh, but I really do!" Ava mocked.

"Well, maybe one day— Right now, I just don't feel like sharing that part."

She snickered, her eyebrows arching high. "One day! What day? I'm afraid we don't have days, but merely hours. The moment we're done with this discussion, I'll be out of here. You need to get all your ducks in a row. You're a total mess. From what I understand, you've messed up that girl's life, too. What the hell happened to you? Tell me!" Lips pursed, Ava slowly bobbed her head in disappointment.

He winced, shifting his gaze for a moment before returning it, holding her inquisitive gaze. "I'm not sharing that part. Not yet. You probably already figured it out. That part doesn't paint me in a good light. It might sound like a load of rubbish to someone rational like you. I want to tell you about other things—everything—before we get to that part. It's been three years, Ava. Do you want me to only tell you the end? And then what? Just hope you'll understand how it all went down!" He shook his head. "No, I can't do that. I hope you'll see where I came from and why I messed up so badly. I trust you'll at least try to understand. I really messed up. I did."

"Was it my fault in any way?" Her gaze lingered on his uneasy expression.

"Absolutely not your fault. I've made my own choices—bad ones—one after another. I got caught up in my own web of lies. Before you jump to conclusions and start judging me. I never meant to hurt Ellie. I mainly lied to myself. She was one of the lies I came up with to make my life seem more ... acceptable, I guess...?" He paused his rant, lips forming a discouraged grin. "This sounds like an excuse, doesn't it?

"What the hell are you talking about? You've lost me already!

I don't get it. You had it all."

The sadness in his eyes deepened. "All, but you."

Her breath caught in her throat for a moment, and she looked at him through narrowed eyes. "It's only been three years..." she continued, shaking off his reply. "You and Eliza have been together ... how long? About two years? What happened in that one year?"

"After you left—"

"Oh, so it is because of me," Ava cut in. "This is why you want to punish me and come after Ayden?"

"No, no, please. You leaving was one thing, but what followed was because of the decisions I made, the decisions I didn't follow through with. So, *it was my fault*. And I've already said I'm not coming for Ayden. You didn't get it, did you?"

"Get what?"

"When I said I'm coming for the whole package—"

Again, he was talking in riddles. And she was way too tired for that.

Ava shrugged and shook her head, a baffled look on her face. "I guess if we need to talk, then let's talk like we used to. Openly. I'm exhausted, and all these riddles aren't helping. Tell me exactly what you're after. I don't want to have to guess what you're up to. I need to know. This is about me and, more importantly, about my baby. I can't take chances. Do you understand? I need meaningful words, not riddles. And, yes, I want to know what happened so I can understand," Ava blurted, irritated, before her voice softened. "I promise to listen. I won't jump to conclusions, and definitely, I won't judge. How about this? Is this fair enough?"

"Your baby...?! Shouldn't you rather say, our baby?" he asked, his voice subdued. Almost miserable.

"Our baby, that's right. I'm sorry. I've called him my baby his whole life. Now ... I'm listening," her tone as firm as she could feign it.

"Okay. Okay ... Fair enough. Here we go." CJ began

recounting the story of his past three years, with all its ups and downs. "Please don't get offended when I mention the day you left. I didn't understand why you left. I still don't ... But I never hated or blamed you for my actions or what I did to myself ... to those around me. I take full responsibility for being irresponsible. I hope we'll also get to you explaining why you left so suddenly. If I knew why, I probably ... I don't know. I'm tired of looking for excuses, trying to find signs where there were none. I'm tired of living a lie. Now I know what's worth fighting for. I know what I want, and I'm going for it."

Ava's heart skipped a beat. He was speaking in riddles again. She didn't have a good feeling about it. Not at all. Gnawing at her lower lip, she nodded patiently, letting him get past the introduction and, hopefully, to the point.

"I think I want to start with the end, though, with the present. With the 'right now', not with 'one hour ago'. When I said I'm coming for the whole package, I meant I'm coming for both of you. You and Ayden. I want you both. Or nothing."

Ava blinked fast, and her jaw dropped.

When she stopped blinking, her disbelieving stare stilled on CJ. "What are you talking about?"

"Like I said, I know what I want, and I'm going for it. I want you. I always have. I was a coward who turned into a liar. What a combo! But I'm not that person anymore. I realize it's been three years, and you may have moved on. I hope there's still a little flame in you, burning for me, buried deep somewhere in your heart. I won you once. I know I can do it once more. I'm ready to put in the work and win you over again." He spoke fast, eager to let it all out in one breath before she could react or object.

Her pulse quickened as she grappled to compute it all, her lip nearly bleeding from her teeth pressing into it. "Oh. My. God! Did Eliza know all of this when she left?" Ava's appalled question escaped her lips.

He let out a loud exhale. "Yes, I confessed everything. Ellie had to know and not think, just like you do, that it was her fault in any way. It was me. I was the jerk. I suppose I'll always be to her."

"Did you love her?"

"I-um ... loved the idea of you, in her," he stuttered, rubbing the back of his neck, discomfort swelling inside him.

"I'm sorry?!"

"When I returned from L.A., I was— Well, here we go. I promised the whole truth, so ... laugh all you want. I don't care anymore. So yes, I was heartbroken. Badly damaged. I was never like that, ever before you. I-um ... I admitted to a lot of things today. Bad things, mostly. I must admit to what could be the only good thing. When I saw you today, I realized I still love you. I always have. Always will. You are *the one*. My soulmate." His voice faltered. "I knew this all along, but I was an idiot. I tried to do what you asked me to. I tried. Only managed to make a fool out of myself and hurt others."

She pouted, incredulous. "So, it was my fault. Poor Eliza! She ended up in the middle of the mess I created."

"For fuck's sake, please. This is about us. You, me, and our child. Forget about Ellie for a second. I know you're upset. I know. I'm just as upset, but we need to figure this out. For us. All three of us. *I* created this mess, not you. I'll admit I need your help to get this sorted out, but it's not your fault."

Holding her spinning head in her hands, Ava's expression was one of confusion, and she wondered if she was ready to hear anything more beyond this point. This wasn't the CJ she once knew. But she wanted to listen to his confession. She had to. Hoping she'd understand.

"I need a coffee. And a smoke. Or ten," she uttered mechanically.

After placing an ashtray on the island in front of her, moving with the precision of a barista, CJ began making coffee. Distraught, Ava's mind wandered as she tried to process everything he had just confessed.

As he made the coffee, a thick, almost palpable quiet lingered in the air. Ava watched him. Her thoughts drifted back to L.A. when, knowing what a coffee snob she was, he surprised her with an expensive espresso machine. He wrapped it as though it was for him as well, not a favour for her.

When did that sweet guy turn into a jerk? Is the guy she used to know still in there somewhere? Shuffling into the lobby, she was trying to find the answer.

Maybe he still was. Perhaps he had been hurt. By her. Possibly, he started acting erratically and sank deeper and deeper until only the jerk resurfaced. He probably didn't know how to pull himself out of the darkness he mentioned.

CJ finished making the coffee just as Ava returned from the lobby with the cigarettes from her purse. "Can we go outside? I need some air."

"Sure. This way." He led the way to the back of the house.

They stepped out onto a vast balcony that hung above what Ava guessed was his study. From a different angle, she recognized the same view she had seen through the window of his man cave. A patio set, with a table, several comfortable chairs, and an enormous umbrella, added appeal to the space. While the morning promised a sunny, beautiful day, the afternoon turned out to be cloudy. Therefore, the umbrella remained closed.

Ava eased into a chair and took a sip of her coffee before lighting a cigarette. She exhaled a cloud of smoke to the side, then glanced at CJ, pressing him to continue, even though no words left her lips. And he did.

"So ... I returned to London and waited. Waited for you to call. You promised you would. I know you said you'd ring when you landed, and this was days later. I still hoped. Wanted to call you. Every day. And every day I'd read your letter, over and over, drinking myself to sleep. Every. Fucking. Night. Some days, well before five." He lit a smoke before continuing. "It got worse until it spiralled out of control. My family was already worried. Rob, my oldest brother, was the only one who sort of knew what was going on. Well, as much as I revealed. Then, about three months later, I had an audition scheduled quite early in the morning. Rob came over the day before to basically keep me away from the bottle. After he left, I still got drunk and passed out. You probably imagine, I missed the audition. This was yet another one. Rumours were already spreading about my drinking problems. Well, they weren't really rumours. Some studios were avoiding even considering me..." He paused, gazing at Ava. "Are you sure you didn't hear any of this?"

Tugging at her bottom lip, Ava shook her head, pensive. "You know I never followed you. After I left, I unfollowed everybody. In time, there were no suggestions about you, so..." She shrugged. "Then Ayden arrived, and I didn't have much time for social media, anyway. I hardly found time to sleep."

"So, what now?"

"Oh, I still don't spend much time on social media. Ayden is older now, indeed. But you know what they say: bigger kids, bigger problems. Well, not really problems. I simply don't have time. We spend a lot of time doing things, having fun— Kids grow up so fast. I just want to take advantage of the now."

Her excitement when speaking about Ayden brought a smile to CJ's lips. "I truly love your enthusiasm when talking about Ayden. I love what you shared about you and him. I was asking about us, though. What are we doing? I know what I want, and I just said it. Question is: what do you want? I recovered. I'm not a drunkard anymore. I can only promise I'll do all the work to win you over. I know, I have to learn to be a father. I've only been an uncle so far, and I'm not even sure how great I am at that. But I want what you have. I want my son. I want you both," he said, his voice dripping with determination.

"CJ, what do you want me to say? I don't know. Let's say I agree. How exactly will this work? You live here. We're about eight thousand kilometres away. An ocean and nearly a continent apart," she countered, uncertain of how they could make it work.

Her key priority was Ayden. Putting him through a chaotic situation? Definitely wasn't something she looked forward to.

"I'll make it work. I did it once, didn't I?"

"You don't understand. This isn't the same. Ayden is only two. We're going to confuse him. If you visit every few weeks, he'll forget you by next time. I can't agree to put him through this. Then you—" She scowled, flicking a hand. "—you'll grow frustrated. Like a never-ending story where you'd start building a connection with him for a few days, only to go away, and when you come back … poof, the connection is gone. And you'll have to start from scratch again."

His brows knitted. "How about you? What do you want for yourself?" he pressed.

"I only want what's best for my child. Nothing more. And what you're offering isn't it. I'm sorry, but I must decline. Perhaps in a year or so, when he's older, if you're still interested in getting to know him—" she swallowed, nibbling at her lower lip.

For a long moment, CJ stared at her, expressionless. When he snapped out of his thoughts, words poured out at high speed. "Stay right there. I'll be back in two minutes." Leaping to his feet, he ran inside.

Ava listened as the stomping faded up the stairs. *What did I say? He was just an uncle so far? The reality sank in, and the prospect of fatherhood must have hit him like a freight train,* she mused, a pang of sympathy nudging at her heart.

Moments later, the rhythmic thud of footsteps jolted her from her thoughts. This time, approaching, urgency clear in every footfall. Eyes wide and wild, he almost tumbled through the patio door.

Ava looked up from her coffee. "Whoa, slow down!" she said with a half-smile, just as he burst onto the balcony.

"You're here," he said, out of breath.

"Where would I be?"

"I thought you might try to … run again?"

"Huh?! Barefoot, in a bathrobe, and without my passport? I

wouldn't have gotten very far, would I now? I agreed to stay. Not for you, and not for me. I need everything about Ayden to be sorted out before going back. He is my responsibility, and his safety is part of that responsibility."

"I know-I know," he said, raising his hand and unfolding the envelope he was holding.

Ava thought she had seen it before.

"Is that—?" She began, squinting at his hand.

"Yes. Yes, it is." A sour-bitter sneer tugged at the corner of his mouth as he glanced at the frayed piece of paper between his fingers. "It's the note you left that day. I don't really need it right now. I've read it thousands of times. I know it from the top of my head. Now, unlike me, you didn't have the chance to read it again. So, in case you don't believe me, here it is for you to refer to what you wrote. Do you remember what you asked me in this letter?"

Dumbstruck, Ava glared at him. She now felt under attack, and she wasn't in a favourable position. Her eyes rounded, and her stomach churned as a painful gulp forced its way down. "Why in the world did you keep it? And you read it until you memorized it? CJ, why did you do this to yourself?"

"Ava, stop playing hard! Do you remember what you asked me in this letter?" he pressed.

She fiddled with her coffee cup. "Yes, vaguely ... Well, not much ... I'm sorry-um, I'm not sure what I wrote. I was upset and—" She groaned. "No, I don't remember." Here, she said it. She admitted it.

"I figured you were upset. Probably panicked. I still don't know why. Maybe because you felt insecure at times... The way you looked at me, the questions you asked, the way you dismissed certain things— That's why I kept talking about having a family." Again, he exhaled loudly. "In a nutshell, you are dismissing me one last time in this letter. You asked me to find someone I can love and who'll love me back. Someone who can give me a real family. That I deserve to know what a real family is like, with kids running around and the joy and worries that come with it." CJ recited from the letter Ava left behind on the day she vanished.

She gulped again, a guilty scowl taking over her expression. "I guess I said that. Sounds like something I would've said."

"Now, everything you said back then doesn't apply anymore, does it?" he asked. Ava glared at him, bewildered. *What does he mean?* Without waiting for her to answer or say anything, CJ continued, "To clarify, I already had someone I loved. You. Am I wrong to assume that you loved me, too? At least, this is what you said in this letter." He paused, staring at her inquisitively, waiting for a response.

Consumed by guilt, she lowered her lashes, biting into her lower lip. "No, you're not wrong," she said in a small voice, glancing back into CJ's blue eyes.

"Well, turns out, all this time, you had my kid, *my family*. Is this correct?"

"It is correct," Ava replied sluggishly, feeling her strength waning.

"And now, you're dismissing me again. Pushing me away from what you asked me to pursue in the first place."

She viciously bit her lip, the salty taste of her own blood sending her into a different emotional state. "I'm sorry," she sniffled, crying softly, as CJ knelt before her.

"Please— I didn't mean to make you cry. You said it. We must be honest with each other. All the way. We'll both need to adjust and take steps to make this work for Ayden's sake. And for us. I want you to know the rest of the story." Then he got up and started pacing. "The day I missed the audition, Rob tried to call all morning. When I passed out after he left, I forgot to plug my phone in the charger. So, no battery, no cellphone, hence no CJ. Around noon, I woke up with a terrible hangover. Rob eventually came over to wait for me, thinking I had turned my phone off, like I usually do when I'm working. Let's say that wasn't the case." CJ winced, shaking off the memory. "He found me literally weeping over your letter. Didn't need to ask. He knew exactly what happened. He was harsh. Didn't have good words to say about you that day. In his mind, it wasn't me doing all that to myself. It was you." Ava cringed. "I let him read this letter, so he'd understand who you truly are. He asked me what I wanted. What I really wanted. Do you want to know what my answer was?" He didn't wait for Ava's reply. "You. I said I wanted you."

She blinked, speechless, as he turned the envelope upside down, revealing a necklace in the palm of his hand.

"My rings!" Her eyes shone with excitement. "I thought I lost them. How come you have my rings?"

"I found them on the floor, between your nightstand and the bed. I thought they'd be my ticket back to you. I wanted to give you some time to maybe call. But you didn't. Then the plan changed because I fell into a pitfall. I had to give *myself* time to sober up."

A couple of days after they became an item, Ava removed the necklace and placed it on her nightstand. She didn't realize when it was gone. She convinced herself she must've tucked it somewhere safe, but couldn't find it after returning home.

Taking another sip from her coffee, their first encounter flashed in front of her eyes. She only now realized the coffee tasted exactly like the one in Paris.

22. I know what I need to do

Rob frowned, suppressing a groan, but bit his tongue when he stopped by to check on CJ and found him hunched over a single sheet of paper. Mopping. Ava's letter.

The family group chat had been on fire since all the leaked photos of the 'bad boy's latest adventures'. And pictures kept coming. Like clockwork. It got to where it wasn't a matter of whether he'd get drunk again tonight, but which club or bar he'd pick to get drunk at?

Rob had long suspected a woman was behind CJ's erratic behaviour. *The Canadian, maybe?*

"Who's the Canadian CJ's dating?" Lisa, his wife, asked Rob months ago.

He raised a puzzled brow. "What Canadian?"

"I have no clue. I thought you'd know. It's the third time in less than two months that he has asked me to book flights to Edmonton, Canada. This time, two. Three weeks apart. I guess it's a woman."

Brows knitted, Rob shrugged a shoulder. "I ... don't know. He didn't say anything."

Who was this woman? What was she like? One thing was for sure—CJ was an absolute mess. *So, this isn't just any woman. Must be one hell of a woman,* concluded Rob.

He'd seen CJ through plenty of breakups. But his youngest

brother had never been in such a deplorable state. Always bounced back quickly and moved on. It was only a couple of weeks ago when, a tad tipsy and loose-tongued, CJ revealed a name—Ava—along with very few details. Not much. Only that she was fantastic and older, but CJ didn't care. "I only want her," he confessed.

That morning, when he popped in to check on CJ, Rob had the chance to read the letter. The one Ava left behind on the day she vanished. Until now, to Rob, this woman was anything but fantastic.

She's not to be trusted—he decided. Nothing said she wouldn't leave again. But there was no way of reasoning with a CJ, who was blinded by who knows what. Probably by just being deeply lost in love! *Well, love can do this. And CJ is a wreck right now. Not a good time to even try reasoning with him. And … what would be the exact moment to start this conversation? When he's drunk or when he's hungover? With what chance of success?*

One can't help another when help is not accepted or wished for. First, CJ had to admit he had issues and take steps to address them. *That's when you can help someone. When they realize they have a problem. When they want help and are ready to accept the hand given to them.* Rob slouched, powerless. *Some things … well, there are things people need to figure out on their own.* CJ needed to sort this out on his own. Starting with putting his life in order and going from there.

When Rob finished reading the letter, he was under Ava's spell. His back straightened as he let out a controlled exhale, narrowed eyes glaring out the kitchen window at nothing in particular. Pondering.

"So?" asked CJ.

"I don't know if she's fantastic. She may be. I only read this one letter. She's … something else, though. If you believe she's the one, you need to smarten up, get clean and sober, and go get her. In this exact order. If you show up like this on her doorstep, you're doomed." When Rob reached over and dragged the envelope across the island to put the letter back in, Ava's rings spilled on the counter. "What is this?"

That's when he found out how Ava and CJ met, that she was a widow, and how his brother fell in love, and everything that followed. *Huh, the mysterious Canadian.* It became clear to Rob that this was more than just a fling. Knowing CJ, he realized his brother wouldn't do anything like he had just described unless he had serious intentions.

Rob remembered how he, himself, pursued Lisa, now his wife of many years. While sharing the story, CJ unconsciously fiddled with the necklace, rolling the rings between his fingers.

Tears played in his eyes when he finished the tale. "What should I do? What would you do?" His voice croaked.

"Well, little brother ... you're holding the answer in your hand. If you're sure *she is* who you truly want, you have her ring size right there. You know what you need to do. Get an engagement ring and propose. Unless she's really out of her mind, she won't say *no* when you put your true intentions concretely in front of her. Words are just words, and facts are facts. Trust me, women may be hard to guess, but they're not hard to please once you guess them. If she loves you—and after reading this letter, I believe she does—she won't say *no*."

"What if she does? This is what terrifies me. What if she says *no*? What then?" CJ asked, fidgeting with anxiety.

"From this letter, I can tell she's honest and down-to-earth. Did I get this right?"

"Why do you think I fell for her?"

"Then, ask her why she left. Try to reason with her. Worst-case scenario, you'll get closure, at least. It'll help you understand and, eventually, move on. This is what you want, right?"

CJ scowled at the rings in his hand, reflecting on his options. His eyes lit up, and he huffed, beaming a wide smile. "You're brilliant! I need to do this. Let's go! Come with me."

"Where are we going exactly? Like I said, you're not showing up at her door like this. And you must do it alone. I'm not coming with you," Rob shook his head.

"I know. I'm doing it myself. Just come with me to get a ring." He seemed to remember something. "Jeff! Did you keep in touch with Jeff?" CJ asked precipitously.

"Jeff?" Rob winced.

"Yes, Jeff, your high school buddy. He's a jeweller, right? Or his dad is. Didn't you say they opened a store in London?"

"Oh, Jeff. I haven't seen him in years. Yes, I believe he's still in London. His father retired. Jeff runs the business now. That's all I know."

Eager to get things moving, CJ pleaded, "Please help me pick out the perfect ring."

"Okay. Go take a shower. You kinda stink! I'll make a coffee and wait for you." Rob's eyes followed CJ, who was already running up the stairs two at a time.

He now had something to look forward to. The possibility she'd say *no* was still there, but ... *I know I can convince her. I did it once*—CJ concocted, enveloped in the steam of a refreshing shower.

Back in high school, Jeff and Rob were inseparable, always found side by side in the halls or causing mischief together. But that was about thirty years ago. One had traded late-night pranks for military discipline; the other for the steady routine of running his father's business. Life got in the way—families, careers—the usual drill. These days, they only saw each other by accident, a nod across a grocery aisle or a quick "How've you been?" at a mutual mate's barbecue.

Today, Rob wasn't leaving their next meeting to chance. He scoured the internet for Jeff's store location and dialled the number. The good news? Jeff still owned the place. Even better? He picked up. After a few polite catch-ups, Rob got to the point. Could they meet in about an hour?

Jeff greeted the two brothers after they stepped in, happy to discuss whatever matter brought them into his shiny store.

Behind the closed door of his office, he got straight to business. "Now, I understand this is a confidential matter. I assure you, no information leaves this office. How can I be of help?"

Rob glanced at his brother.

"An engagement ring! I need an engagement ring. The most perfect one," CJ uttered in one breath. Then, he added, "And yes, this must remain confidential. I'd appreciate it if it did."

"Oh, the perfect ring for the perfect lady of your heart," Jeff said.

He turned the screen toward CJ and, with a few practiced clicks, pulled up several sites for him to browse and decide.

Soon, CJ huffed a muted breath, running a hand through his hair. "I don't know … I can't tell the size." A discouraged look replaced his initial enthusiasm.

"Don't worry about the size. We can adjust that after you decide on the model," Jeff explained.

"I didn't mean the size of her finger. I already have that," CJ said, digging into his pocket.

With an indulgent smile, Jeff continued, "Okay. Tell me about your lady. How is she? What does she like? What kind of jewellery does she wear? I could narrow down your options if you tell me something about her."

After a moment of panic, CJ sighed, relieved, when he finally discovered Ava's ring tucked in a corner of his pocket. Fished-out ring in hand, he leaned over, holding it in front of Jeff. "Now, this is her. Size, and everything about her, is right here. But it has to be better. I want it to be better. Something that says *us*. Her and I."

"Oh, I see." Jeff narrowed one eye as he squeezed his jeweller's monocle to analyze the ring. "Discreet but sophisticated at the same time. Size J-and-a-half. Good. I think I know what you're looking for. I believe you should look at this section." He made a few clicks on the website's menu before turning the laptop back to CJ.

Immersed, he scrolled down, then clicked on the second page. And the third. He returned to the first page and looked closer at the one ring that had first caught his eye. It was perfect, just like her. That ring screamed Ava's name.

CJ leaned back in his chair with a satisfied grin, pointing at the ring on the screen. "Yes! This is it! That's her."

Jeff clicked on another website that listed diamonds.

"Hmm ... Diamond? Too boring. How about something else? Thinking ... an emerald, maybe?" CJ shrugged, his eyes sparkling.

"Excellent choice," Jeff simpered.

He peered through emeralds, each more vibrant than the last, and chose the perfect one. One rich and deep, like a forest after rain. Her birthstone. His, too. And very different from her other ring. Since the stone was not in stock, he had to wait six to eight long weeks for it to be ready.

When the two brothers left the store, Rob looked at CJ with a concerned smirk. "Well, the dice are rolling. That gives you enough time to clean up and be the man she fell in love with. Remember the order of these steps! Do you think you can do this?"

"I know what I need to do," CJ nearly snapped.

Rob cocked a brow. "Good!" No other comment.

Deep inside, the same question bothered both brothers. *What if she says 'no'?* CJ's mind was busy with different scenarios, like how to approach an eventual 'no' and turn it into a 'yes'. Or find some viable arguments for Ava to at least consider and say 'maybe'.

Rob's mind was cooking up completely different scenarios. *What if CJ won't take the 'no' too well? What if he relapses and makes an even bigger fool of himself?* These were all possibilities. He'd have to devise a strategy to help his 'little brother'. Oh, how CJ hated Rob calling him 'little brother'! He was not three anymore. When CJ was born, Rob was twelve, and he changed CJ's nappies quite a few times.

CJ set a date to begin the sobering-up process. He had to do it on his own.

Monday—he decided, adding to his calendar workouts and other goals, to keep himself on track and focused. The ultimate goal and primary motivator were to get Ava. But, first things first.

Now, that's something. I passed the test. I can do this—he thought later that night, when he managed to stop after only one drink.

The following day was Friday. Clubbing day. He went out and mastered the art of making a fool out of himself. Again.

23. Lina had a baby!

At the club, CJ bumped into Eliza. Foolishly, he started teasing her 'cute' accent.

Eliza shot back with a sharp joke, then she added, "I know you."

Squaring his shoulders, CJ sneered. "You're not alone. A lot of people do."

"I meant I know you … know you. Maybe you don't remember, but we met before. Through Lina. About a year ago, in Edinburgh." She kept feeding him details about their first encounter.

"Oh yes, I remember. You are…" He cringed, pretending to struggle for her name.

"Ellie," she extended her hand, their fingers barely brushing.

"Ellie, that's right! How are you, Ellie?"

"I'm fine. I live in London now."

"Good. Good for you."

The conversation flowed as the night went on, and alcohol kept pouring until even slurring words became a challenge for CJ.

Some rumours and speculation reached Ellie, but she didn't pay them any mind. *After all, rumours can be just that—rumours.* With her background in law, Ellie needed solid proof before she would believe anything. Hence, CJ got the benefit of the doubt.

Leaning against the bar, Ellie watched him with a mix of

amusement and concern. The way those so-called 'social midiots'—her favourite anagram for social media idiots hovered around him, snapping pictures, laughing too loudly—told her everything she needed to know. He wasn't just partying; he was drowning something.

Whatever brought him to this state, drinking is probably his only lifeline. And these midiots are feeding off his pain.

As he rocked on his feet, Ellie sighed. "Alright, that's enough." She grabbed his arm before he toppled over, steadying him. "Come on, let's get you out of here."

His weight leaned into her as they stumbled to the curb. She struggled to get him into a taxi and asked the cabbie to drive. By the time they pulled away, CJ was out cold.

"Well, where is home for you, mate?" With no address and only his password-protected cellphone on him, Eliza had to decide.

Holding onto her Good Samaritan side, she spelled her address to the cab driver and took him to her place. The cabbie helped carry the 'big guy' to her rented flat.

Inside, CJ took a few unbalanced steps across, mumbled something unintelligible, and sprawled flat across the bed, passing out. Again. Eliza rolled her eyes with a deep exhale and tossed a blanket on the only spot left for her to sleep—the couch.

The morning sun filtered through the blinds when CJ sat up slowly, head pounding like a war drum. His tongue felt like sandpaper, and for a split second, panic tightened his chest. *Where the hell am I?* Next thought flooding his mind? Ava. He looked around and remembered—*I need to clean up. This is too fucking much.*

Never before had he woken up hazy about where he was. *Last night was the first and the last time*—he promised. His eyes squinted, scanning around—small bedroom, scattered makeup, and other female items. He scowled. *A woman's place. At least, I hope it is.*

Some faint clattering and the smell of freshly made coffee wafted from beyond the slightly ajar door. *I so need coffee.* Timidly, he got out of bed and peered through the door crack, checking around, trying to remember something. Anything. He pressed his temples, wincing as if the motion alone might keep the pounding in check or his skull from splitting open.

In the tiny kitchen of the equally tiny flat, Ellie poured coffee into a mug, humming under her breath. She spun around at the rattling noise of CJ stumbling in the tangled blanket on the floor. The same blanket Ellie had slept under on the couch remained half-hanging when she got up.

"Good morning," she said with a knowing smirk.

"Um ... Good morning," he mumbled, looking around.

She responded to his puzzlement, explaining how and why he had ended up there, but he didn't appear to be processing. His eyes turned down, just to notice he was fully dressed. *That's good. It should be good,* he thought, pressing his temples even harder.

Amused, Ellie scoffed. "Nothing happened—in case you're wondering. You were too wasted for anything to happen. Other than probably pissing yourself. Coffee?" she asked, flicking a hand toward the coffeepot.

"Yes, please. I-um ... I must thank you, I suppose. You could've just abandoned me wherever it was that you collected me from. But you didn't," he said, still holding his head, like to prevent it from falling off.

Ellie smirked as she figured he didn't remember the conversation from the previous night. "Well, the friends of my friends are my friends. I couldn't have left you there, prey to the *social midiots.* So, I made an executive decision, and since you weren't in any condition to give your address, I brought you here." She shrugged.

He sipped from the coffee she poured for him. "Where is here?"

"My place. Not too fancy, but does the trick. I'm sure you are used to better, but this was all I could do. I hope you found the bed comfortable, though. I spent more than I could afford on it," Eliza giggled.

He winced, rubbing the back of his neck. "I must've caused a lot of trouble last night. I'm truly sorry. If you don't mind, do you have an aspirin?"

Eliza returned with the aspirin and a glass of water. He checked her out, trying to place where they'd met. There was something familiar about her. She spoke like Ava. Same gestures. And her remarks? Same style. The things she said and how she said those things pained and captivated him at the same time. *Exactly what Ava would say.*

"What did you mean by friends of your friends?" he asked, hesitation clear in his tone.

Eliza sensed his confusion and introduced herself again. Ellie—same as the night before. She mentioned Lina again, and CJ seemed to remember the day when they had met in Edinburgh. Well, he didn't remember shit, but he hoped he would. Eventually. Or ... who cares?

As he finished his coffee, he asked Eliza for her address so he could call a taxi. "Thank you. I really appreciate you looking out for me last night. Can I call you? I mean, I have to make it up to you somehow. After all, I took over your bed while you had to sleep on the couch," he said, moving his head towards the unmade couch. "I don't know ... May I take you out for coffee sometime? Just coffee. And I promise I'll be sober," he added, thinking that she might be in some kind of relationship, hence her reluctance, which didn't go unnoticed.

And that was the beginning. Coffee became lunch, then dinner. On his thirty-fifth birthday, Ellie moved in. From her little flat, into his immense house.

"What do you get the guy who has everything?" She asked, unsure what she could get him for his thirty-fifth birthday.

CJ grinned. "Just move in with the guy."

Everything was falling into place for him.

He took Ellie's entering his life as a sign. Their paths crossed just as he was about to go looking for Ava. In her letter, she asked him to promise he'd give himself time to heal and love again. And he did just that. *This must be it*—he decided.

When he picked up the ring ordered for Ava, CJ stared at its promising shimmer and his heart squeezed, sinking into the memory of her laughter for a moment. He had options now. He remembered Ava's words—*find someone you could love and will love you back.*

Ellie was here—warm, present, and undeniably real, bringing an effortless smile to his face. Each moment felt hopeful. And the way she seemed to draw him out of his pain was like a light peeking through the fog of his memories.

On the other hand, Ava was far away, and there was a possibility—a pretty high one—she'd say 'no'. The decision to spare himself from more pain and continue this relationship—with Ellie—seemed the right one.

He took a deep breath, feeling the weight of his options. *See where this is taking us.*

He shoved the box to the back of his nightstand drawer. Also pushed his doubts with it. Things were moving in the right direction, he felt. In the meantime, CJ remained consistent with his schedule, sobered up, and his career started to pick up again.

Though he didn't realize it at first, he didn't choose Ellie for Ellie, but for how much she resembled Ava. For how much of Ava Ellie had in herself. For how much of Ava he chose to see in Ellie. The cadence of her voice, the sharp wit that made him smile, the same playful remarks, the same fire in her eyes.

And for whatever part of Ellie didn't match Ava, CJ began pushing suggestions for change. As if he were adjusting a canvas, hoping to paint Ellie closer to an image he held in his mind. And he succeeded.

It started with a perfume. CJ bought it for Ellie as a birthday gift. "I'd like you to wear this instead of what you wear," he said.

He found her fragrance a little obnoxious, though he left out the *obnoxious* part.

Ellie agreed to a more sophisticated and expensive perfume. "He knows red carpets." She muttered to herself.

Then, he complained it didn't smell the same on her. Same as what? Same as on Ava. But he didn't mention Ava either. Poor thing, he didn't have a clue that—yes—the packaging looked almost identical, but this was a flanker of the perfume he knew. It smelled totally different. Even on Ava. Not that the scent was terrible or anything. His only problem was that Ellie didn't smell like Ava.

The comments about her clothing style came later, along with fashion tips—what to wear and, more importantly, what not to wear. When attending events, he chose her outfit based on ... What *would Ava wear?*

Just minor adjustments at first. The major ones crept in gradually. CJ constantly persuaded Ellie to change, and she went along with it. Oblivious, she played her part.

Ellie saw the transformation as something positive, shifting subtly beneath his gaze. Her essence slowly faded as she became a version of Ava that CJ desired. Subconsciously, or perhaps less so.

One evening, CJ leaned against the kitchen counter, watching Ellie prepare dinner. "I was thinking ... maybe you should quit your job."

Her stare lingered on him. "Quit my job?"

"Come with me when I film. Be with me, not just wait for me."

A lump formed in her throat, and her breath stopped, along with the knife halfway through chopping the onions. Her job ... her career ... wasn't just work. A challenging feat for someone from an Eastern European country, it took years of clawing her way up and proving herself in a country where no one handed out opportunities. She had built something. Alone. And now, with one request, he asked her to just drop it and leave it behind.

But when her gaze finally met his and saw the quiet plea behind his eyes, the decision took shape. As daunting as it felt, a spark of anticipation flickered within her. She nodded. Within a week, she handed in her resignation.

A year after Ellie moved in with CJ, he proposed, and she happily said 'yes'. A few months later, they set a date. A wedding date. Long hours went into planning the wedding as Ellie, Rob, and Lisa—Rob's wife—worked to make it perfect. Guest list, location, catering, flowers, and all the fine details for a small, family wedding. No big fuss. In reality, quite a big fuss, but on a smaller scale.

CJ insisted on keeping it private. He had zero interest in making a spectacle of himself. Not after the chaos that led to his downfall. After losing Ava. Then, his reputation. As he finally got back on his feet, he wanted something quiet. A private ceremony with just family and close friends. Ellie couldn't be happier.

When she called her father to tell him, Ellie already knew how this would go.

"A wedding?" Her father's voice carried the usual indifference. "I don't know if I can make it, Eliza. Finances are tight. Paying tutors for your sister … You know how it is."

Ellie's grip on the phone tightened. The words, somewhat expected, still burned. *Blah, blah. Of course. This is Dad.* A bitter laugh nearly escaped, but she stifled it. *I bet if I told him who I was marrying, he'd be on the next flight, ready to play the caring father. Just so he could brag about it to his friends.*

She hung up before she could say something she'd regret. Her jaw clenched, knuckles whitening as she whispered, "Jerk."

That night, she called Lina.

"Would you stand with me on my wedding day?" Ellie asked, her voice trembling more than she wanted. "You know … as my second mom?!"

Silence whirred on the other end, just long enough to make Ellie's stomach twist with anxiety. Then, Lina's voice came through, steady and warm. "Yes, of course."

She didn't ask why Ellie's father wasn't doing it. She didn't have to. Lina knew the kind of man he was. She knew it since the day he promised that, instead of paying alimony, he'd set up a bank account for Ellie. *Yeah. What account?* It was nothing more than words. A lie left to rot. Nobody saw or heard of the promised account.

Eliza almost told her everything. About the wedding. About CJ. But at the last moment, she decided against it.

"It's ... a surprise," she said instead, voice laced with mischief. "You'll see when you get here."

Lina had barely been in Ellie's life these past few years. Between raising her baby, chasing milestones, and collapsing into bed at the end of long days, social media had become an afterthought. Their interactions had faded to occasional check-ins, scattered hearts and likes on posts. Lina would sometimes share pictures of baby Ayden and short videos of gummy smiles and wobbly first steps. Ellie barely posted at all.

Probably too busy proving herself at that high-pressure job of hers—Lina assumed.

But none of that mattered now. The invitation was real, Lina was coming, and Ellie was ready. Aiming for a 'real surprise', Eliza pulled the official invitation from the batch.

Ellie and CJ kept their lives private and low-key, posting individual snapshots. Occasionally, brief mentions of events they attended as a couple have appeared only on CJ's social media. Not much of their life together. No wonder. Because of CJ's obsessive fans, Ellie likely chose to fly under the radar.

An enthusiastic Ellie shared all of Lina's pictures and videos with CJ. As the one taking the photos and videos, Lina remained behind the camera.

"O. M. G! Lina had a baby! His name is Ayden. Born yesterday. Hey, you and Lina's baby have the same birthday. Isn't that cool?" An overly excited Ellie shared the news the day after moving in with CJ. "I can't believe it. She's so brave to have a baby at her age! Look how cute the baby is."

"Yes, she's cute!"

"He. It's a boy!" A tad annoyed, Ellie corrected him.

"Yes, it's a boy. He's cute!" CJ said, not paying much attention.

He's never had the heart to tell Ellie that he only pretended to remember her. And whoever this Lina was. Not on the day they met at the club. Not even the following morning, when he woke up in her bed. And never since. He thought that not remembering wasn't a sin. And failing to mention something isn't, technically, a lie.

A few months later, Ellie showed him another 'cute' picture of baby Ayden. Then another. And one more on the day the baby just turned one. This time, CJ seemed to pay a little more attention.

He looked at Ellie and asked. "Do you want to have babies?"

"Oh, God, no! I mean, not right now. First, I must find the right man who really wants to be a father and not just one of those weekend dads, like … my dad." She scoffed. "It's probably too idealistic of me to dream about my kids growing up with two parents. Not shared custody rubbish, like three or five sets of confused kids. That's definitely not what I want."

"You turned out well," CJ said.

"Surprisingly. Yet, I have my own demons, and I have a jerk for a father." Ellie shrank the impact of her comment so he wouldn't take it as something that she expected from him.

A surprise private cruise on a sailing boat was the stage of the proposal. At one end of the reasonably small boat, the sun was setting. The sky was smeared with colours, as if it were on fire, while at the other end of the sailing boat, the moon was rising. Fat and bright. A rare sight you can't see but only in the middle of the ocean. Possibly on top of the mountains, too.

They stood there, mesmerized by the sunset, when CJ pointed to the moon rising behind them. Her eyes wide, Ellie turned to look, coming face-to-face with CJ. On one knee, holding a shiny diamond ring in a velvet box, his eyes glowed. Her heart pounded with hope, and a gasp of surprise caught in her throat.

"Ellie Dima, I plan to build a family with you. And I promise to be a forever father to our kids if you agree to marry me," he proposed, unpretentious but heartfelt.

Ellie's jaw dropped, tears stinging her eyes. Happy tears. "Yes! Yes, I agree to marry you!" she answered without hesitation.

He slipped the ring on her finger, planting a gentle kiss on her lips, under the sunset. Or under the moonrise, depending on where you looked from. But nobody was looking.

He kissed her knuckles. The diamond threw stars across the deck—not an emerald in sight. He didn't look in the drawer where the other box waited. Not since he placed it in the back of it.

They stood there watching the evening spectacle, kissing a bit more, admiring the sparkling diamond again.

The night completely took over, thousands of stars competing with the stone in her ring. It was nearly midnight and already quite chilly in the middle of the ocean when they went to bed.

24. Everything will be alright

"Three years ago, I had a better speech prepared. It's sort of obsolete now. So, I'll put it simply. I don't know what you want, but I know what I want. And I want to marry you." CJ knelt before Ava, slowly drawing out of his pocket the box with the ring he had made three years earlier.

Ava's jaw dropped, her eyes flying wide, nearly popping out of their sockets. "No, this can't be happening," she managed, dreading to breathe.

"You don't have to say *yes* right now," he said hurriedly.

"You're so damn right! I can't say 'yes'. It's hardly been an hour since Ellie left, and ... Darn, CJ! You're asking me this? Now, are you for real?" Ava blurted out. "You know very well I don't make big decisions when I'm upset. And, right now, I am beyond upset!"

"Would you let me finish? I'm not expecting a 'yes' right now. Not when you're upset. Just, please don't say 'no'. Let it sink in. I just don't want you to doubt me, grow insecure, and do anything stupid again. Coming up, I have over four months free. I'll come with you, meet Ayden, bond with him ... with you. Win you over again. When you know ... when you're ready ... You can give me your answer then. Let me just do the work. Give us a chance. Ayden deserves to know me, and I want to earn that," CJ stressed, his expression warped into a tentative, hopeful smile. "Here!

Please take the ring. Wear it, don't wear it … It's totally up to you. Just keep it. This way, you'll know what I want. I want you and our baby."

Ava sat quietly, pondering, staring at the box shaking in his hand. Was she considering his proposal? Worried, but hoping his speech reached her heart, CJ waited for her to finish balancing the pros and cons.

Her lashes slowly revealed her eyes as she looked into his. "Okay," she exhaled. "I agree with you to come and meet Ayden … bond with him. I guess I owe this to you both. But since I don't have any reason to stay in London until next Monday, I'll see if I can change my flight and leave as soon as possible. If I can catch a flight tomorrow, I'll leave tomorrow. Make your plans and let me know when you're coming." She glanced back at his extended hand, still trembling on the box with the ring. "This—" she said, taking the box. "—I won't wear it, but I won't *not* wear it."

She gasped quietly and stopped breathing for a moment as she opened the dark green velvet box. *Perfection!* The sparkling dark green emerald stared back at her like a reflection of her eyes.

He let out the breath he had held all this time. "Your birthstone. And mine. It's been waiting for you for a long time. Too long, I'd say."

"It's beautiful. If I have to give an answer now, you might not like it, and … who knows? I could regret it later myself. All I can say for now is that I'll consider your proposal." Her fingers trembling just as his did, she removed her old rings from the recently recovered necklace and slid the new one onto the chain.

CJ hurried to take it from her, clasping it around her neck, his breath hot against her skin. Then he knelt back, grinning, captivated, and leaned closer. His fists clenched as he stopped himself. *Fuck, no! No kissing. It could ruin everything.*

Instead, his fingers wrapped around her wrists, gently brushing his thumbs on her pulse points, relieved that she didn't say the word he feared the most. "Looks good on you. It matches your eyes. And—" Lips pressed together, he paused briefly. "—

you're not leaving tomorrow. I made plans for you to meet my family. Wednesday evening. Just two more days. I want them to meet my son's mother and, hopefully, my future wife. I'll have my brother get us on a flight anytime starting Thursday. I'm coming with you."

Ava flinched, visibly disturbed. "Meet your family? Do they know? I mean … about me? I figured they know about calling off the wedding, but have you told them why? Am I the witch…? The bitch, who broke your relationship?" She bit her lower lip.

A slanted smile hung in the corner of his mouth as he shifted closer, his fingers gripping reassuringly around her wrists. "Nope. The only ones who know at the minute are Rob, my brother, and probably Lisa, his wife. They were helping with the wedding and had all the contacts to cancel everything. Nobody else knows yet. This is something I must mediate personally. By the time I'm done, they'll know you're not the witch … nor the other one."

"Does anyone know I'm fifteen years older than you?"

"Yes."

She puffed a worried sneer, gnawing her upper lip. "And? I guess you've been lectured."

"Not entirely accurate. How many times have I said that age is just a number? Here's the 101 introductory class on my family: Mum is five years older than Dad. Rob is nearly four years younger than his wife, and Luke, my other brother, is nine years younger than Shannon, his wife. Even Finn, Emily's husband, is two years her junior. So, for my family, age really is just a number. I probably was the last one to follow in their footsteps."

"And you beat them all. Nice…!" Lips pursed, she locked her stare into his with a barely there shake of her head. "I bet your mom will have something to say about this. I don't want to be here when you have that discussion. I'll go try to get some sleep. I really need it. It's been a day!"

He gently held her down when she intended to get up and leave. "You don't know my mum. She only wants us, kids, to be happy. I promise you everything will be alright." His glance flicked over his shoulder at the screen of his cellphone, which started ringing on the coffee table behind. "Speaking of the devil. I need to answer this. I bet Mum found out the wedding was cancelled, and she must be freaking out."

"Yup. Everything will be alright. Alright," Ava mocked, her tone dripping with sarcasm. The same sarcasm that always served as her ally during stressful times. And this was certainly one of those times.

She shuffled inside, pulling away from a conversation she didn't want to witness.

The rush of adrenaline and cortisol left her feeling pumped, and despite being extremely tired to her bones, sleep refused to win over her whirling thoughts. *Meet his family!* That had some con-notation in Ava's universe. *Mothers of sons are unique. Well, I have a son, too. Does that make me unique?* She huffed a smirk, a mil-lion memories rushing into her mind.

Is it normal to think like this, or am I biased? But it wasn't her first time meeting guys' families. *Especially mothers*—she pressed her lips, twisting them in a displeased motion. Then she sighed. *My experiences—my conclusions. Others may disagree, but … Not putting my hopes up. You know one mother, you sort of know all of them.* She had been there before.

Dan was six years younger than her, and his mother hated it like it was personal. Until the last minute, his mom did everything she could to prevent their wedding from happening. She never said the words outright, but she didn't need to. Not when every glance, every pause, and every phone call said it louder. The resistance came in whispers and subtle interference. First, his mother tried to make it impossible for Dan to come to the wedding.

Still valid, Dan's Romanian passport would've been just a

few weeks shy of expiration by the wedding time. The renewal papers somehow ended up on someone's desk—someone conveniently on vacation. After countless calls, Ava tracked it down, and finally, the new passport was ready. But she knew better than to trust blind luck twice.

"Can you hold it in Romania?" she asked the authorities. "He'll pick it up when he arrives. Safer that way."

They agreed. Passport secured. Crisis averted. She should have left it at that. But no, like an amateur, Ava told Dan's parents. A harmless update, she thought. His mother nodded slowly. Two days later, the passport was mailed to Dan at his mother's insistence. By chance, the information fell into Ava's lap.

"It wasn't me," Dan's mother rushed to say when Ava, disappointed, only mentioned what she found out, but no names.

In reply, Ava smiled and remained silent. *For fuck's sake, I'm an investigative reporter, and that comes with some traits.*

Something's changed in Ava. She didn't expect a lie. She gave her future mother-in-law a chance to admit, hoping for a valid excuse or reason.

Well, mothers have more authority than fiancées.

Ava and Dan could only hope, as they held their breaths and crossed their fingers until he received his new passport. Only two days before flying to Romania to get married.

Ava never shared that, afterwards, she had called the Embassy and begged them to flag the passport 'urgent'. That she knew the ambassador personally. It remained her little secret.

Then, on the big day, after the wedding ceremony, everybody flocked to the designated location for staged photos. But Dan's parents were nowhere to be found.

"They didn't hear that part," Dan said with a shrug, though his jaw ticked with disappointment. Later, he joked that his favourite wedding pictures were those with his parents in them. "You know ... the invisible ones?"

Ava laughed, but her stomach squeezed. She remembered that moment more than their first kiss.

Eventually, his mother warmed up to her. Or maybe she learned to act better. More like a romantic, hopeful, resilient Ava, just needed to believe people change if you give them enough time.

Her eyes snapped wide open again as she tossed in bed. *Well, just don't give them enough rope. They'd probably just manage to hang themselves.*

And that wasn't the only time. Far from it. Ava flipped in bed again, unable to fall asleep. Her mind drifted to another chapter in her existence. She had seen this pattern creeping into her life before. She no longer judged based on a single moment. One mistake can be forgiven. A pattern, however...? That was something else entirely.

She was only twenty-two the first time grief left its mark on her. The Christmas lights flickered bitterly that year. On Christmas Day, a drunk driver stole her first husband away, leaving Ava to pick up the pieces and learn how to breathe again through pain. She became a widow with a nine-month-old baby before she even learned to live. The world blurred around her.

Years passed, and the sharp ache of her loss faded somewhat. She met someone new, allowing herself to dream again. Chris smelled like sunscreen and sea grass.

Andy, the son she lost some years later, adored him. At four, Andy clung to Chris as if they shared blood instead of boat rides and beach days. Ava worked at a bakery, and her hair smelled like sugar and vanilla.

Chris had a way of making the world feel possible again. He was gentle, funny, the kind of man who remembered your coffee order and fixed the dripping tap before she even asked. She thought maybe—just maybe—he was the one. When he proposed, she said 'yes'. *Everything will be alright*—she thought.

Then came Lavinia, his mother. At first, she smiled.

Pleasant. Polished. Not a hair out of place and perfect manicure. *A proper lady,* Ava thought. She called Ava "dear" and served her homemade strudel. Ava should've known. The ones with perfect crust always left the worst aftertaste.

On the day their families were supposed to meet, in her favourite red pants and a white shirt, simple and classic, Ava pulled into the driveway. Already dressed, Lavinia answered the door, then vanished upstairs 'to freshen up'. Twenty minutes later, she returned in the same damn outfit as Ava's. Same pants, but in white, and a red shirt. Same cut. Same everything. Ava blinked and forced a smile but said nothing.

Now, as the memory returned, she flipped onto her back and opened her eyes, looking at the ceiling. *What the fuck? Was it a test? A power move? A warning?* She still didn't know. But now, so many years later, she was convinced it meant something.

Later that same day, Lavinia took Ava for a smoke and a walk by the lake. She began talking about life with a husband who works abroad, just like Chris and his dad.

"You know," Lavinia said, taking a long drag, "it's not so bad having a husband who is away a lot. Gives you space to breathe. Do your own thing, live your own life ... Your marriage stays fresh."

Ava blinked and smiled politely. "I'm not that kind of woman."

Not exactly what Lavinia wanted to hear. Lavinia's eyes didn't narrow, but something behind them shifted. A flicker, a recalibration, and Ava felt it. Subtle, quiet, but final. Like a door closing.

"Oh," Lavinia reacted, as if Ava got the answer wrong on a test she didn't know she was taking.

An inexperienced Ava learned much later: Chris's mom lived promiscuously. Husband and son knew. Well, everybody knew, but Ava. Nevertheless, Ava's answer was definitely not the correct one. Not up to her future mother-in-law's 'standards'.

Lavinia wasn't just making conversation but was searching for a teammate. And Ava? She failed the test.

Eyes still glued to the ceiling, her lips puckered, and she huffed. "What kind of mother would wish for her son to be cheated on? The wrong kind, that's for sure," she muttered to herself.

Suddenly, Ava was no longer welcome at their place.

Fed up with his mom pressuring him, one day Chris told Lavinia, "I broke up with Ava."

They continued seeing each other in secret. Romantic dates meant running errands together, mostly. Or picking Ava up from work and dropping her off. Every other day, he'd return home at the same time. A pattern Lavinia didn't miss. Of course, she didn't.

Lavinia began whispering all kinds of nonsense in her son's ear. Someone 'trusted' saw Ava doing this or that. It wasn't long before the questioning began. It started slow.

Chris would look at her sideways and say something like, "You weren't at the store yesterday afternoon, right?" or "Did you mention anything about us to anyone?" Always casual. Always rehearsed.

Ava winced. "Why?"

He shrugged. "Just ... someone said they saw something. Probably nothing."

It was never *nothing*. Lavinia apparently had her spies. In fact, it was just her imagination. Either way, the rumours kept coming, and the accusations stacked like poker chips.

"You sure you're being honest with me?" Chris asked once, his voice filled with badly masked suspicion.

She didn't answer right away. Just looked at him. The same man who used to carry Andy on his shoulders and kiss the top of her head like she was everything, now doubted her. Day after day.

Dating in secret felt wrong. But dating someone who didn't

trust her? That felt worse.

Then came the ex.

Ava was rounding the corner of a café, arms full of groceries, when she saw them. Chris and his ex, seated outside, drinks half-full. Lavinia paced nearby, pretending to check her phone.

Startled, Chris stood when he saw her, turning crimson. Ava said, "Hi," and kept going. Lavinia smirked.

He called later. "Ava, that wasn't—"

"I know," she said, cutting him off with a forced smile, irony dripping from her voice. "She just dropped by, right? Eight hundred kilometres is just a short trip. Literally around the corner."

"Mom invited her over."

"Same mom who's telling you about my whereabouts?"

His jaw moved like he wanted to explain. But there was nothing left to say. In that moment, Ava didn't feel betrayed. She felt tired.

Lavinia had no intention of stepping back. And Chris? He wasn't going to make her. This wasn't a battle Ava signed up for. And she sure as hell wasn't going to keep showing up to a war she didn't start. She'd fought harder things in her life. Lavinia's nonsense wasn't going to make it on the list.

The atmosphere shifted. Chris still showed up, as if Lavinia hadn't already mapped his movements. He still kissed her like everything was alright. But the questions still lingered, and his silence stretched longer.

She caught him flipping through her phone book.

"Just curious," he said.

"About what?"

He didn't answer. That night, Ava lay awake, staring at the ceiling. Her gut squeezed. This wasn't the 'alright' she hoped for, trying to believe in new beginnings. It was something else entirely. It was cold. It was off.

She knew. Waiting for the next whisper or another doubt planted by Lavinia in his ear wasn't an option.

She met Chris at the edge of the park, where they used to take

Andy to feed the ducks. Her hands stayed steady, and her tone wasn't angry. Just done.

"I can't keep doing this. Your job takes you where it takes you, and without trust, we can't be. I don't want to go through the Inquisition every time you return home," she said. "Your mother's war with me? You've let it in. And now you bring it here. Into us." Chris blinked, mouth parting like he didn't expect her to speak first. "I need to know if you're in this with me. I need to know you trust me," she continued. "Truly. Fully. Without your mother's voice in your ear every time I breathe wrong."

He rubbed the back of his neck. "It's not that simple."

"It is," she said. "You have a week to figure it out. I won't be here for act two of Lavinia's circus."

She didn't wait for his answer. She just kissed his cheek. A ceremonial kind of goodbye. Then she walked away. It was the last time she ever spoke to him.

Hmm, mothers always win. She smirked, arching an ironic eyebrow and flipping in bed again. Sleep still refused to catch her, and her thoughts kept spiralling back when...

She remembered she had quit her job by the end of that week. Got a new one outside the city. That summer, she only came home a handful of times while her parents looked after Andy.

The shifts as a hotel receptionist were long, and the moments they spent sharing giggles and playtime were few and far between—whenever her parents brought Andy over.

It was just the two of them against a cruel world.

Her eyes wandered from the ceiling, and she blew a loud sigh, tossing in bed again. *Now I have Ayden to fight for—my fight against the world—if things won't be alright.*

After Chris, Ava refused to date anyone else. Somehow, they never bumped into each other, but news about Chris always found its way to her. "Chris had taken up drinking," she'd heard.

Another toss in bed as she frowned at the memory that crawled back into her mind. *Dang! What's wrong with the men around me? They turn to drinking when I walk out on them. Is it me? Am I doing this to them? Maybe there's something wrong with me. But I know what I want. Why don't they? Drinking never fixed anything.*

"Chris got married," the news reached her again, only a few years later.

"Good for him. I hope he found someone mom-approved, whom he could trust."

But she didn't have time for nonsense. She was on a new mission. Making her and her son's future better was her new goal.

She now had an excellent job as an anchor at a TV station and was accepted into the Communication and Public Relations program at the University.

Only a year later, the school had to take a backseat. After being diagnosed with osteosarcoma, Andy's struggle with cancer began. Ava found herself in the middle of yet another battle—saving her son.

Nearly two years later, they lost that battle. The same year, she'd lost her mom, and shortly after Andy's passing, her dad had gone to heaven. In less than a year, she buried all the people near and dear.

With her compass broken and a bleeding heart, she threw herself into work and school as her moral support, burying the pain deep between the pieces of her shattered soul.

She hoped she'd never hurt this badly again. *Never say never! I've seen more since, and the skies are not clear yet. Why? Will it ever end? They say what doesn't kill you makes you stronger. I don't want stronger. I'm strong enough. I had had enough. Just want a peaceful life. That's all I want. Is it too much to ask for just that?* The exhaustion settled deep in her bones. And in her soul.

Bella, who, unnoticed, made her way back into Ava's room, raised her head from where she lay on the floor. "What do you know, girl? Does history always repeat itself? What should I do?" Bella perked her ears, tilting her head. "Just like me, eh? You have no clue." She pouted.

Ava remembered how, in all her sorrow, an unexpected sense of resolution washed over her. She felt oddly comforted hearing news about Chris again, just a couple of years later.

"Chris is getting a divorce," Gina told Ava one day, out of the blue.

Gina, Chris's cousin, worked with Ava at the TV station. Same Gina, whom she'd heard from when Chris got married. Suddenly struck, Ava realized how odd it was that she had never met Gina, back when she was dating Chris.

"Oh! I'm sorry," she said, raising an apathetic shoulder.

"Don't be. Aunt Lavinia drove him straight to the bottle. His wife hoped he'd recover. Instead, it got worse. She kicked him out."

A little over a year later, Ava's phone rang. Her eyebrows rose in surprise at the voice on the other end. *Lavinia?!*

In one breath, brazen and quite jovial, she called Ava "sweetheart" and went on a rant about everything Ava already knew. How Chris got married and then divorced. The divorce was just finalized, and he hoped they'd get back together.

Ava listened intently, her eyebrows rising and falling. "I'm sorry, but the past, good or bad, must stay behind. I'm not going backwards. I moved on. I'm not interested in patching up an old coat and pretending it's new. That patch will always show. And I don't dream of a patched coat." Ava's sharp reply fell, hardly able to keep her voice level and her heart thudding, about to leap out of her chest.

Shaking from deep within her core, when the call ended, Ava blew a breath of relief. *The audacity! Well, Karma gave me this opportunity.*

What she actually wanted to say was, "You bitch! Guess what? I'm not the naïve young woman I used to be! Not anymore. Your son needs to grow a pair and call me himself if he wants me back. You fed your son poison, and now you want me to clean up the spill? Do you have any dignity left in you?"

In fact, that's what Ava said, but she said it in style. Eyes rolling and shaking her head, she smirked. At least Lavinia had the decency to call only after the divorce was final.

Not that she held a shred of care anymore. She had her moment of triumph. To her own standard, not Lavinia's. *Let's move forward. Living in the past is plain stupid.*

Married to Dan and living in Canada, a few years had gone by before she heard from Gina again. Chris passed away. Liver cancer.

Well, drinking never fixed anything. Only a few weeks later, his dad passed away, too. Enveloped in sadness, she winced, realizing her heart didn't ache, but her head buzzed with a strange satisfaction.

Karma is at work again! The thought that Lavinia must now feel exactly how she once felt kept swirling in her mind.

One simple question bothered her: *Had Lavinia ever loved anyone enough, so now she knows how it feels when it hurts? Let me check. See if I have any shits left to give about what Lavinia felt.*

History probably had a cruel way of repeating itself. Ava's mind raced a hundred miles an hour. Memories long buried stepped forward, taking centre stage.

Irritated under the effect of the loud, buzzing thoughts, she sprang to her feet. *Enough! All these stupid thoughts— Send them back to where they came from! History doesn't always repeat itself. There's good in people.* A deep breath left her chest.

She squinted, looking out the window, and scowled at the grey sky, mirroring the storm in her soul. *Can two storms cancel each other, or do they combine? Let's find out. A walk in that forest, back there, seems like a good distraction.*

She glanced at Bella, who cocked her head. "Hey girl, want to join for a walk?" Bella stood up and headed for the door, her tail wagging impatiently.

In a flash, Ava dressed and almost flew downstairs, looking for CJ. But he wasn't on the patio. The sound of a muffled conversation led her back to the semi-basement. A slightly ajar door caught her eye. Taking a step closer, she peeked inside. *A gym! Even better. I may settle for this. Let's ask*—a Plan B sprouted in her mind.

With Bella on her heels, she ended up by the door to his study once more. This time, she knocked.

When Emily walked into Rob's office and overheard the conversation about the catering cancellation, suspicion grew within her. In an instant, questioning spread like fire.

Rob struggled to keep things in check. Unsuccessfully. Emily was way too brilliant for him to even try hiding anything from her. Before he could even begin, Rob ran short of excuses.

Overhearing the discussion from the next room, Patti ambled in, and the tension only heightened. Her features twisted in displeasure. Not only because Patti and Emily had just returned from shoe shopping—shoes completely useless now.

Patti's words came from her son's ongoing childish and impulsive behaviour. It wasn't the first time he had broken an engagement.

"Terrible. Terrible. Only days before the wedding. Such a selfish, spoiled brat. I guess I raised him this way," Patti blustered, shaking her head.

Thankfully, he was smart enough, and since the wedding wasn't 'public news', only the family was aware. But still ... And who knows? It could transpire. She wasn't ready to face gazes and gossip. Not again.

First, CJ had a heated, brief argument with Emily.

"When you finally met someone half decent— I wasn't Ellie's biggest fan, but she was there for you when you needed someone most. You're making a fool of yourself again." Emily paused her rant. "You know what? It's your life. You make your bed; you sleep in it. I just hope you'll figure out soon what you really want in life," and she passed the phone to Patti.

CJ listened patiently until Patti paused, almost out of breath. "Mum, it's done, and it can't be undone. Ava would agree with you, but I don't." CJ's words flowed calmly but with determination.

"Well, that only means she's brilliant. I'll give her that. But you're terrible. You need to grow up and stop acting like a child. You clearly have commitment issues. This is the third engagement you're breaking. I hope it's not too late to fix things with Ellie."

"Mum! That's not my intention. Ellie is over for reasons you'll be horrified when I disclose. And one day I'll tell you. It was all me. My doing. My wrongdoing. Ultimately, it's about committing to the right person for the right reasons. Ava is a lot like you. Just get to know her. I know you'll love her just as much as I do. Please, Mum. Promise you'll treat her right, or I won't bring her to meet the family. We could elope, and you'll hear about it on the news. However, knowing her, I don't believe Ava would agree to it, but ... Do you remember that you've always encouraged us to reach for what makes us happy? Ava makes me happy. I love her. I want her and my son. Why is this so terrible?"

At the other end, Patti sighed. Her tone mellowed. "Choosing your child isn't terrible. I really hope she's wiser than you are, my dear. Well, you're putting us in an awkward position. Again. However, she sounds like a good woman. I can't wait to meet her. You say you love her, and she's my grandson's mother—"

"And my future wife..."

"So, you're serious about this one, huh?"

"Serious enough to cancel a wedding for."

"Have you proposed already?" Patti rushed to ask, anxiety returning in her tone.

"Yes, I did. No answer yet. But I hope I'll have good news soon. As you allegedly determined, wisdom is one of her strengths."

Patti sighed. "Oh, dear! So, you don't know yet."

"Just a second. I'll put you on hold. Don't hang up." CJ placed the call on hold. "You're not sleeping," he continued, swivelling in his chair and looking at Ava, who gingerly opened the door after she knocked.

"I can't," she shrugged. "I was wondering if I could take Bella for a walk in that forest there," she said, pointing out the window to the patch of trees.

"Oh! It's not as close as it seems. And it's off-limits, anyhow. Give me a few minutes to wrap up this conversation, and I'll make you a tea. Maybe something to eat? Alien food?" he asked with a big smile. Ava's lips arched slightly as old memories invaded her mind.

"I noticed you have a gym. I could blow off some steam. Do you mind if I—?"

"Absolutely! Here. I'll show you around," CJ said, springing off the chair and striding towards Ava.

"You've got someone on hold. Don't worry about me. I'll manage," she replied with a wry smile, her head motioning to the phone in his hand.

"I know you will. Thank you. Um … Let me feed you first. I need something to eat too. I'm starving. I'll see you upstairs in five?" CJ grinned, pointing to the cellphone in his hand. "It's my mum."

"Sounds good," Ava tossed over her shoulder as she left.

Given his serious and distracted demeanour, she sensed the conversation might not be for her ears. *Better this way,* she thought.

When Ava's steps dimmed, CJ returned to his conversation

with Patti. "Mum, can you please make sure Emily behaves? I'm afraid she may get hurt. Ava is unlike anyone else before, if you understand what I mean. She knows how to stand her ground."

"Don't you worry about Emily! I'll talk to her. Take care. See you both on Wednesday. Until then, send me some pictures of the little one if you can."

"That's up to Ava, Mum. Please be patient. I'm sure she'll share photos with you all. I'll see you on Wednesday. Love you."

"I love you too, dear."

25. I'm not going anywhere

"**Y**ou don't look so happy. Did your mom give you some tough love?" Ava couldn't help but ask when CJ joined her in the kitchen.

"No, not really. Mum wasn't impressed with the change … the wedding cancellation and all, but she can't wait to meet you."

Curious, Ava tilted her head. "Really? How about your sister? Has anything changed since you shared your concerns about how she was treating your … girlfriends? Not sure if I qualify as that, but should I be prepared for an attack?"

"I hope she'll behave. She has grown up quite a bit since becoming a mother. She probably wouldn't like it if her own daughter were treated that way. Emily didn't fully like Ellie, but she was nice to her. I believe she has no reason to attack you. I'll be there with you. For you. No need to worry about Emily."

"As you probably already know, I only worry about Ayden."

They looked at each other when the doorbell rang. The order Ellie placed online earlier was just delivered.

"I wonder what she's having for dinner. Should I send her some or order something?" he asked while checking the food.

"Trust me, she doesn't need anything right now. I'm not hungry, either, but you can eat. I'll have that tea you promised if you don't mind. Just show me where you keep the tea. I already put the kettle on," Ava said just as the kettle's blasting whistle

went off, triggering a wince from her.

Rob decided against using his own key to CJ's place. Not this time. He called from outside the house and had been cleared to come in.

"I thought the cleaning lady came on Thursdays," he commented as he entered the study.

CJ raised a confused eyebrow, failing to understand why his brother mentioned the housekeeper. "She comes on Thursdays, yes."

"Never mind. I just thought I heard some clunking in the gym. It's probably Bella." In the corner, hearing her name, Bella cocked her head.

Only then did Rob notice her. He looked baffled from Bella to CJ, who burst into laughter.

"It's Ava. She's in the gym. She'll probably be done in the next half hour, and I'll introduce you. Let's allow her to blow off some steam."

"Oh! Mum said she was sleeping."

"She couldn't. Too upset."

"Well then, it's good she's up. Just don't kill the messenger. I'm here under the pretext that I need Ava's info to book the flight. I know you'll say you could've texted me her info. I convinced Mum and Emily not to come over here." Rob smirked. "I compromised and promised I'd come myself. So, you're welcome. How is she?"

"Still upset, but she's holding up quite well. I hope she feels better after the gym."

As predicted, about half an hour later, the two brothers paused their conversation, listening to the faint steps coming from the hallway through the slightly ajar door. She was not approaching, but her steps were fading away.

CJ leapt from the top of the desk where he sat and stormed

out the door. "Ava!"

She turned, a spectre of a smile on her lips. "Yes."

"Feeling better?"

With a shadow of a pout, she lifted a shoulder. "Sort of. I've heard you talking. I thought you were on the phone and didn't want to interrupt."

"It's okay. I wasn't on the phone. Come with me. I want to introduce you to someone." Tilting her head, Ava's gaze expressed doubt about this being good news, while he continued in a comforting tone, "It's Rob, my brother."

"I'm all sweaty and out of breath. I'll need ten minutes to refresh and change into dry clothes. It's enough that one brother met me all damp and soaked in coffee."

"You made a good impression on that brother, and that's all that matters," CJ replied with a huge smile, reeling back. "Take your time. We'll be down here. And ... bring your passport. Rob needs your info to book our flight."

"Okay!" she said, already climbing upstairs, thinking how tired she was, to where she became non-belligerent, almost submissive.

She looked in the mirror and let out a sharp breath. *I need a good night's sleep and, hopefully—just hopefully—I'll wake up in a different reality.* Then, she hopped into the shower. A quick, five-minute one, just to rinse the sweat off. After, she put on some dry clothes. Nothing fancy, just a clean, dry pair of leggings and a T-shirt. With her hair still up in a messy bun, as she had it before the shower, she grabbed her passport and headed downstairs.

Although she was mentally preparing herself to meet CJ's family, this meeting caught Ava off guard. The two more days she thought she had to get ready for the encounter compressed fast. *On the bright side, meeting at least one family member before the others may work in my favour. If I leave a good impression on this one, it may help with the rest. For sure, right now, I'm the hottest topic—the only topic—in their family.*

Heart madly pounding, Ava bravely marched toward the study. Pausing before the door, she blew a long, controlled exhale, hoping to adjust her breath, feeling like she was about to crumple. When she confidently started pushing the door open, she nearly tumbled as CJ swiftly opened it for her from the other side. With quick reflexes, he caught her before she could regain her balance.

A half-smile on display, Ava released herself from CJ's arms with a slight wiggle, discreetly assessing her composure. "Well, I made some entrance."

Her gaze shifted to Rob, the older and somewhat shorter version of CJ, as she could now estimate when he was standing as well.

With one long stride toward her, Rob extended his hand. "Hi. It's a pleasure to finally meet you."

Her sweaty hand barely touched his, straining to remain poised while a dry swallow forced its way down. "Pleasure is mine. Rumour has it you don't really like me." She pushed a wide smile.

"That was sort of true at one point," he shrugged, a little embarrassed. "Though, if I may ... a hug would prove that's no longer true. We are family now." Rob heaved Ava into a hug, probably hoping it would warm up the atmosphere.

"Family!" Ava repeated when released from the big brother's embrace, somewhat surprised by his remark.

CJ's stomach flipped with unease, triggered by his brother's choice of words. His eyes widened, shooting a quick glance toward Rob, as he shook his head firmly, 'no'. Seeing Ava's face drop was the last thing he wanted.

"Well, you are my nephew's mother. This sort of makes us family, right?" Rob mumbled.

He cast a somewhat proud glimpse at CJ, who concealed a sigh of relief when his brother found the right words to undo his own gaffe.

"Sort of, yes. That's quite right," Ava agreed, to CJ's total relief.

His hand on the middle of her back, CJ guided Ava to the couch by the window. She squirmed, uneasy, holding a calm smile despite feeling like a bug under the giant magnifier of an old-school entomologist, who watched and studied her every move.

As he sat beside her, his fingers brushed the back of her forearm. A subtle message: 'I'm here for you.' Her lashes raised, and a smile encompassing appreciation bloomed on her lips as their gazes met.

Suddenly, she felt safe. Paris came to mind. When she panicked, realizing how many eyes were on them. And cameras. When CJ guided her to safety, having her back all the time. It was the very moment she started to trust him—she recalled.

Is he still to be trusted? She couldn't tell yet. *Well, he's probably asking himself the same about me. His entire family may be. And who's to blame them?*

Afraid to open her eyes and discover that the thoughts flooding her mind were not a continuation of a dream, she lay there for a few good seconds. Frozen. Hoping it was just another bad dream. Or was it good?

Then she felt the weight of what she thought was a hand on her hip. Hers? She wiggled her fingers and found the answer to her confusion. Not hers. Her eyes snapped open, vision still blurred, as if the dim morning light played tricks on her. But the warmth behind her, the steady rhythm of the breath rising and falling against her shoulder? Unmistakable! Familiar in a way that tightened her chest. *Definitely not a dream.*

Ever so slowly, she began dragging herself out of bed. Nearly sitting on the edge, CJ's chiselled arm reached out and wrapped around her waist, hauling her back.

His face buried in the small of her back as he growled in a deep, raspy, sleepy voice. "Where do you think you're going? Stay here, please. Just a bit longer."

Twisting her body, she purred, "I really need to use the

washroom. And I suggest you let me, if you don't want to spend a bit longer in a wet bed."

"But you're coming back," he grumbled.

His hot breath against her skin, through the fabric of her shirt, stirred some old feelings.

"Yeah, I will."

She hadn't eaten in almost forty hours, and her breath was telling stories. Before returning, she brushed her teeth and quickly pulled her fingers through her hair, amending the pillow hairdo.

When she emerged from the bathroom a few minutes later, Ava was met by CJ's face-splitting smile. He lay half-raised on the pillow, one arm under his head, peering at her through half-opened eyes.

After a couple of steps across the room, she abruptly halted, her eyes searching around as if lost. Frozen, her knees buckled, and she nearly collapsed. Livid fingers gripped the edge of the console to her left, while her other hand clutched the front of her oversized T-shirt, panic clear in her eyes.

Like chased by fire, CJ sprang out of bed. Strong arms scooped her up before she collapsed. His warmth wrapped around her as he carried her back to bed. "Ava, Baby. What's wrong?" He brushed a lock of hair away from her face, his eyes searching hers. "I'll call an ambulance."

"No-no, don't. I'm fine. It's just a stupid panic attack," she resisted, her voice still hazy.

"You sure? You look like you've seen a ghost. Turned whiter than these bedsheets. Since when you have these panic attacks?"

"Since now. Never had one before."

"What can I do? What triggered it?"

She hid a smile, biting her lower lip and avoiding his gaze as slowly, the colour returned to her cheeks. "Not saying. You'll laugh."

He crawled into bed, brawny arms wrapped around her in a steady, grounding embrace. "I promise I won't."

"It was just some silly nonsense, really. I'm fine."

"Ava, please. Nonsense, or whatever it is, I want to hear it. It'll make me feel better. If not, I'll call an ambulance."

"That's blackmailing," she pouted. "Promise you won't laugh?"

His hand stroked her hair as her head rested on his chest. "I promise."

She hesitated. Then sighed. "I warn you: it's pure nonsense. I don't even know how to explain it. It was like a déjà vu. Like we were back in L.A. I thought I was losing my mind, and I panicked."

CJ's arms tightened around her, and his voice softened, laced with something she couldn't quite pinpoint. "L.A. was the best time of my life." He paused, staring at the ceiling, as flickers of memories flashed through his mind. "And the worst. I lay on this very bed many times, thinking about L.A." His words dropped like a stone into still water.

To his disappointment, Ava drew away from his embrace without a word. She adjusted herself higher on the pillow, breaking the moment of intimacy. She disliked he brought up the 'worst part' in the conversation.

If we want to make this work, we must bury the past ... at least the 'worst' part of it. It will always be there. But talking about it again and again feels like twisting a knife in an open wound. They'll need to discuss this. *But not now. Not today.*

She cringed, scanning the room through half-squinted eyes. The déjà vu feeling returned with a vengeance, and she struggled not to show it. After a few seconds of silent browsing of her surroundings, she suddenly sat up and looked around the room, as if she had had a revelation.

With sudden exuberance and broad gestures, Ava spoke fast, her accent coming out stronger. "Okay-okay. I'm not losing my mind. Please tell me I'm not losing my mind."

He chuckled, seizing the opportunity to pull her into his arms once more, grumbling in her ear, his face buried in her hair. "Ava, you're not losing your mind. But it kinda sounds like you are, Baby. Though I don't think you are. Slow down, please. Do you mind explaining?"

"This room ... Look around. Tell me what you see!" A sense of relief that she finally figured it out rippled through her.

"Ava, Baby, I see my room. This was my bedroom for about eight years, before Ellie moved in. I can find my way around with my eyes closed. What should I see?"

Ava groaned. "You're impossible. Look around. The door, the dresser, the bathroom, the console under the window, the chair, the bed ... and the closet on the other side." CJ's brows knitted in confusion, his eyes following her finger pointing at each item. "Same layout as my bedroom in L.A.," she continued, twisting and looking into his baffled gaze.

CJ's brows furrowed. His eyes swept the room again, slower this time. The stark realization dawned on him. "This is—" His voice trailed off. He ran a hand through his hair. "It's the same. The same as your room."

Ava's grin stretched wider, and he let out a breath. A strange, conflicted look flashed across his face.

After their relationship began, they spent all their time in her bedroom. He had only now realized why it was so hard to find sense in his life after she left. Why the torment had only grown louder.

No wonder why—every night—he drowned himself, nursing a bottle to sleep. It probably felt easier to pass out on some couch, somewhere else in the house, than to sleep in his own bed. And, when he made it upstairs, he was most likely too wasted to know where he was and stir up more painful memories.

Mornings were even worse. Whenever he woke up in his bed, he looked around absent-mindedly, rolling her rings between his fingers. The letter sat on the nightstand, creased at the corners and worn from too many readings. His chest tensed every time he traced her signature; each word burned into his memory. This bedroom felt right for the first time since he returned from L.A.— because she was there.

His arms tightened around her, pulling her closer. "Come here. I need to hold you. Feel you."

The mystery of her dizzy spell now had an explanation. Silence settled between them.

"Have you slept here all night?" She asked, breaking the quiet.

"Not all night. I kept waking up, wondering if I had dreamt or if you were really here. I thought— Anyway, watching you sleep for a while felt good. Then you flipped to the other side."

"And ... you put your hand on me to make sure I'm not running away," she murmured, more like a conclusion to herself.

"Just so I know you're here, for real," he whispered softly in her ear.

His hot breath brushed through her hair, tickling her neck and sending shocks through her body. All her muscles and joints tensed in a quiet shiver as her body shifted from relaxed, cuddling in his arms, to tense and rigid.

He hoped she wouldn't notice. "What?"

"Um ... Something ... poked me?"

"Baby, this is the effect you have on me." He smirked. "Just give it a minute, and it'll go back to sleep, okay? I promised we'd take it slow this time. I'll keep my promise. I'll wait until you're ready." Ava turned slowly, scrutinizing the depth of his gaze for a few seconds. "You know I can wait. I chased you for ten long months and waited three more years. What's a bit longer?" CJ reassured, and he sounded believable.

"I'm sure you can wait ... Unlike you, I haven't ... in nearly three years. Since ... you know...? What if I don't want to wait? What if I'm ready? What then?"

For the first time in her life, she felt shameless, giving up common sense and letting desire lead her. As he was still processing, her body pulled against his, planting a soft kiss on his lips.

"What?! I can't believe you didn't— Why?" CJ asked, pulling away just enough to look into her eyes.

She snickered. "Are you really asking me why?"

"Well, I am. You're gorgeous, smart, funny. You're ravishing. I can't imagine you didn't have opportunities. Unless you didn't want to, or you just came across morons— Or maybe you loved me too much and couldn't find anyone to match me," he teased.

"Oh, God!" She puffed, her eyes rolling. "You are so full of yourself. Well, are you taking on the offer? Or I withdraw it."

"Oh, I'll take it." His eyes narrowed slightly. "Are you sure?"

"I'm sure," Ava whispered, her lips brushing against his.

"But first, please tell me why you refused to be with anyone. Not that I'm complaining. I can only imagine it was by choice, not because of the lack of good-looking men in Canada."

With a quick, incredulous headshake, she rolled her eyes. "You may want to try again."

"Seriously, Ava, I want to know."

"You're so ridiculous." She snickered. "Um ... Let me think about it. Maybe it was because, in the meantime, I was pregnant for about seven months. Getting rounder and plumper every day? What kind of creep do you think would want to sleep with a pregnant woman? Well ... not talking about the baby's father, who wasn't around, anyway."

"Shit! Baby, I'm so sorry. I shouldn't have— Please forget I asked."

"No. You wanted to know ... Buckle up, because I'll tell you. The first months were the hardest. You may not know, but pregnant women can get ... well, quite horny. However, I wouldn't have taken any chance to put Ayden's life at risk. Then, it was the last two months of the pregnancy, which I had to spend in bed. I was only allowed to go to the washroom, take a ten-minute shower, water, food, and bed again."

"If I only knew. I would've been there with you," his voice, nearly a whisper.

"Wait! There's more..." she tittered. "When Ayden arrived, I had even more fun. Caring, feeding, diapers, and ... leaky boobs? So, I'm asking you, what kind of freak do you think would want to sleep with a woman with leaky boobs?"

"My kind. Look at me! I jumped headfirst, not even thinking that you may not be available anymore."

"Yeah, your kind," she breathed. "You know? Men my age have grown-up kids. They have grandkids already. They are done. That chapter is over for them. I don't think they'd be willing to enter a relationship with a woman who has a baby. And how exactly was I to go about it? I need a babysitter so I can go out and play cougar?"

"Cougar?!" he scoffed.

"Isn't that what you call someone like me?"

"No, it isn't. You are so silly."

"Anyway, I didn't mention the sleepless nights. Ayden was the perfect baby. Healthy, happy, not fussy, never cried, he slept … well, like a baby. I breastfed him until a few months ago. I probably could've had some fun, but I didn't have any interest or time for that. I didn't want him to grow up meeting different … uncles. So, Ayden was the only man in my life lately. I chose to focus solely on him. It was my decision to become a mother and dedicate my life to my child." She paused for a moment. "Is my answer satisfactory to you?"

Wincing, he gazed at her, swallowing a lump that had suddenly formed in his throat. "Baby, I was a total ass. A ridiculous one, like you said. And I thought I had it tough. You put your life on hold to have and raise my baby. I'm … sorry."

"I'm not. And I didn't put my life on hold. I enriched it. My life is good. My life has been great since I had Ayden. I look forward to every day I get to spend with him." She paused, a half-bitter smile curling her lips. "You said L.A. was the best part of your life? It was the best part of my life, too. Without L.A., I wouldn't have Ayden. And he is the best thing that has ever happened to me. I have no regrets. I'd do it all over again in a heartbeat." She looked straight into CJ's still brooding eyes and added playfully, "Now, are you taking on the offer, or not? Third call, already."

"You're so wonderfully crazy. I love you. Let me just show

you how much I love you." He drew her close, his lips searching for hers, two bodies becoming one.

Oh, how he wanted to kiss her senselessly since she was back! His probing tongue tasted her lips, playing around before slipping all the way, chasing her tongue, swirling and dancing around her mouth. Agile hands began moving along her body in search of every place he knew so well.

His memory was rebuilding as their bodies relearned each other, passion rising at a dangerous height. Clever lips kissed all the rediscovered places. Agile hands moved lower and lower just as skillfully as she remembered.

Soft, guttural moans escaped Ava's slanted throat, and her body shifted under his touch. His hand snuck under her shirt and pulled it above her hips in search of that place. And then, he found it. As he seized her hips, his thumbs slipped under the waistband of her thong, passing twice over the scar.

He stuck his head from under the sheets, glazed-over eyes looking at her. "This is new. It wasn't there." He kept passing his fingers over the scar, feeling it, memorizing the new finding.

"That's ... Ayden," she half-whispered, biting her lower lip and gazing into his puzzled eyes.

"C-section?" Curiosity escalated in his tone.

"You're so silly. At my age, doctors wouldn't discuss any other options."

"Can I look at it?"

She nodded and nearly whispered. "You're already there."

Lost in wonder, he gaped at the still-pronounced scar. Soft fingers brushed over it, peppering tender kisses on Ava's belly, sliding his lips from one end of the pink mark to the other. "I'm the biggest idiot ever. I should've listened to my heart and come get you. I so fucking missed you." He exhaled a guttural mumble between kisses, his hands roving over her body, re-recording eve-rything.

His shirt came off in one rushed move. A hand traced from her bent knee, up her thigh, searching under her oversized T-shirt. With unrushed, gentle tugs, he pulled it over her arms and head, her hair falling over her shoulders in waves. Magnificently, her plump boobs slipped free from under the piece of clothing.

He tossed her shirt aside and resumed, pressing his face firmly against her neck. A deep, loud inhale—her scent. Roses and strawberries, lingering close to her skin. Teasing and inviting. His hand slowly skimmed from her waist and up her ribcage and cupped around her breast. Perfect fit, just as he remembered. His lips slowly moved over silky skin, locking onto a rosy nipple. She melted, arching beneath his touch as her nipples hardened. Responding to his strategically placed kisses, her body bowed, and her insides twitched with desire.

As if he's changed his mind, CJ's hand left her body, and one-handedly, he removed his boxers. Her core trembled with anticipation, chest heaving sharply. Her stomach twisted with eagerness, heat rippling through her body, and she thought he was taking too long.

CJ's hands and gifted lips fell back on her, touching, searching, kissing, promising, building momentum, leading to where she'd ask for more. She'd want more. Her fingers danced leisurely along his sides, mapping the muscles on his back, pulling him onto her.

His tongue sluggishly moved along her jaw, pausing under her ear, and her head tipped back. Hard and wanting, he rubbed against her. She longed to feel his hardness inside her pounding inner parts.

"Are you ... ready for me?" he grumbled in her ear.

"I thought you'd never ask," she whispered, and he pulled back. Surprised blue eyes looked into half-opened green eyes, suppressing a chuckle. "Go easy. It's ... been a while."

Breaking from her embrace, he knelt up and slipped his hands inside her thong, gliding behind and yanking her hips, muttering in a raspy, eager voice, "I know. Too long. I'll be gentle." With precise moves, the tiny piece of fabric still standing between them flew over his shoulder. "Let's give you what you crave," he rumbled, hovering over her and pushing his knees under her thighs, parting her legs wider, his pecker probing.

She reached between them, fingers wrapped around him, eager to guide.

Nipping at her earlobe, he slid a hand inside her elbow, tenderly pushing her arm. "I can find my way around, remember?" he growled, adjusting to line up with her.

Her fingers let go. His velvety tip split her, teased her clit, sliding and testing at her entrance, before shallowly gliding inside. The exploration elicited a deep moan from her.

Ava's limbs wrapped tightly around his waist and drew him close, deliberately taking him in, hungry, her slick softness moulding around his hardness. Her hips chased the rhythm, raising to meet each thrust. Then, her fingers found and gripped his firm buttocks, claiming his perfect length until he was swallowed fully inside.

A rumbling groan rolled from behind his throat. "Fuck, you are so hot! I'll never get enough of you."

The tempo intensified, each push eliciting sweet moans from her, bodies twisting and swinging, swaying between sheets, sharing unrestrained ... everything.

Almost on his knees, CJ lifted her in his arms, vigorously driving into her silky inside, aiming to reach her deepest depth, each thrust inviting gasps and moans from her.

"I'm coming!" she wailed, wrapping herself more tightly around him, shudders rippling through her body as short, intermittent panting cries escaped from her throat. "Oh, God!" she huffed a squeal, clutching as if she wanted to anchor. She gasped for breath as he gently placed her on the bed.

"I'm no God, Baby. I'm just a man who's madly in love with you." He huffed, pressing inside her, lost in her half-opened eyes and her throbbing insides. The tips of his fingers grazed her jawline as she shifted beneath him. "Don't! I'm not done with you yet." His hips pinned her against the bed.

As soon as her inner pulsing around him subsided, his hips

began moving again—slow, shallow, diving deeper, increasing the pace.

Five more orgasms later, he tried to lure Ava to take a shower together. Just like all those years ago, she declined with a short headshake, biting her bottom lip.

"Okay. I'll go take a shower. Then, I'll be downstairs starting the coffee. You take your time," CJ said, holding her tight, as if he didn't want to let go. Not yet. Then, as if he remembered something, he gazed back into her eyes. "You need to trust me and know everything will be alright. I don't want to see your beautiful eyes red from crying, okay!"

"You won't."

"Promise?"

"Now, I'd be a hypocrite if I cried, wouldn't I? I asked for it," she chirped with a naughty grin.

His gaze sank into her deep green eyes. "I'm happy you did." His lips hovered over hers before they finally touched for another kiss.

CJ's gaze paused on her neck with a slight cringe before he reached around, patting and searching for something. In the chaos of passion, the ring slipped, resting now on the pillow. He found it and slowly slid it onto the chain, gently laying it on her chest. A spark danced in his eyes as he looked into hers again.

"Don't push your luck. I'm not ready to make a life-changing decision yet."

"No rush. I'm not going anywhere. And if you do, I promise I'll come after you this time." He placed a quick kiss on her lips and sprang out of bed, running to the shower.

26. The Far-Far Away Kingdom

"**W**ow! Someone looks fresh and happy," said CJ, half an hour later, when Ava came downstairs, showered, dressed, wearing a bit of make-up and a huge smile. "Let me see." He cupped her face, searching her eyes.

"Stop it! I didn't cry," she said, lips curving into a soft smile. "You asked me to trust you. You probably need to start trusting me, too."

"Fair enough." He planted a tender kiss on her soft, pink lips.

Has anyone else noticed how the birds are noisier in the morning? The happy concert during her early walks always made them more enjoyable. It wasn't any different this morning. Otherwise, the patio was quiet. To Bella's annoyance, bursts of a cappella chirps interrupted the silence. Now and then, Bella raised her head, barking and whining at the trees surrounding the property where the chirping came from.

With a broad grin, CJ watched Ava sipping from her coffee, her smoke burning slowly as she stared at the trees. Her mind seemed far away.

"Can I ask you something?" he interrupted Ava's thoughts.

She turned with a serene smile. "Ask!"

"Why did you choose May 10th, my birth date, to have the C-section?"

"What makes you believe I chose May 10th?" Ava asked, a bit flustered.

"I just happen to know you can choose the date for an elective C-section. Because the doctors recommended it, I assumed it was scheduled. I'm just curious why May 10th?"

"Ah, you want to know how crazy I am. Do you really think I was so out of my mind to choose your birth date and be reminded of it for the rest of my life? Yes, I did choose a date. May 17th. My birth date. I thought I'd make myself the best gift ever. However, Bug decided to arrive a week early."

"Early?"

"Yeah. My water broke close to midnight on May 9th. Ayden was born a few minutes after 4 A.M. on May 10th. I'm not sure he arrived early, though. I suppose the math was off because of Ayden's size ... Also, I didn't have a last-period date to provide. I didn't have one for a while ... At birth, he weighed only four pounds and change. On a smaller scale for a full-term baby. I guess all this made it hard to be very precise. It's like it happened the very first time we ... you know—"

"First time we made love," CJ finished her sentence.

"I'll never know. All I know is that he ruined my birthday plans," Ava said, taking another sip of her coffee. "Now, can I ask you something?"

"Sure."

"Why did you pick our anniversary date for your wedding day?"

He winced, shaking his head. "Shit! Not me. Ellie picked the date. I didn't like it, but I couldn't figure out how to explain why I didn't want that date. I just played along. I thought that changing its meaning would help with the pain. But now you're here. Let's not talk about pain." Ava nodded. A moment later, after reflecting a bit, he added. "After coffee, would you give me a hand with something?" She gazed at him, quietly asking with just a raised brow.

"Would you help me pack Ellie's stuff? You may know what she needs from what she left behind. I doubt she'll want to come back here soon, and I'm sure she didn't pack everything she needs. I just noticed some stuff in the bathroom that I know she uses daily."

"Sure, I can help."

"Then, you and I must go shopping. I thought we could drop off her stuff at the flat on our way to the mall."

"I really don't feel like shopping."

"Baby, I'll meet my son for the first time. I must get something for Ayden. You know what he likes, his size ... I need you with me."

"Oh, my! He has everything he needs. And more."

"I'm sure he does. But nothing's from me. Nothing from his dad."

"Okay, but promise you won't go overboard. There's no room for more shit. I just gave away a whole load of toys a couple of weeks ago. A small toy, just to make Ayden open and bond ... You could probably get something at the airport, you know?"

"Airport? No way! Please tell me more about him. How is he? What's his favourite food? His favourite toy? What's his preferred kids' show? Is he shy? Is he chatty?" CJ shot all the questions in one breath.

"I wouldn't say he's shy. He is more ... cautious, I guess. He may appear shy or serious at first. Ayden is studying people, trying to guess what they're like. I believe he's actually trying to figure out how much he can get away with. After, he gets chatty." As she spoke, her face gleamed. "I guess he takes after me on that. He's quite rumbustious and smart ... you'll find him very funny. He plays pranks on me and makes friends easily. Although I step on toys all over, his favourite is Winnie the Pooh, and Winnie goes everywhere with us. We even have a backup for it. We lost Winnie once and had a bit of a meltdown. We recovered it, eventually, but I bought a backup, just in case. Ayden's favourite show is Paw Patrol, and recently, he developed a passion for Short Circuit. The first one."

CJ puffed a laugh. "Short Circuit? That's funny."

"Yeah. He was under the weather a few weeks ago, and I kept him home. I cuddled with him as he was fussy and watched Short Circuit, thinking he'd get bored and fall asleep. Kids his age don't stay put for a movie that long. He did, though. I thought he stayed because he wasn't feeling well, but he kept asking for it ever since. No complaints. I can always use a couple of hours of quiet time." She giggled. "I believe he's watched it five times already. Now he runs around asking for 'mo' input'. And, he goes nuts for sweet potatoes."

Amusement in his expression, CJ tilted his head as he listened. "Interesting. I was probably a bit older than Ayden when Mum took us to Short Circuit. She had my brothers take me again because I kept asking to see 'the robot'. I did the same. Ran around the house, driving Mum nuts, asking for *more input*."

Ava huffed a soft chuckle. "I guess, like father, like son, eh?"

"So, you don't feed him 'alien' food?"

"Well, he's an 'alien' breed, after all," Ava said, chuckling again, and she continued talking exuberantly about her favourite topic—Ayden. "He's not a fussy eater. Ayden eats what I eat. He even eats slightly spicy food. There's nothing wrong with home-cooked meals. He has protein, veggies, and fruit with every meal or snack. He may have been tiny when he was born, but now he's the tallest amongst the kids his age at the daycare. So, I guess I'm doing something right."

"You're so beautiful when you talk about Ayden! The vibrant energy you emanate when talking about him. And ... I see you're not upset anymore."

Ava sighed and smiled at her own thoughts. "I know he's safe and has lots of fun, and I was only to be away for a week, but I didn't realize I'd miss him so much; it hurts!" Her heart squeezed, tears shimmering in her eyes.

CJ pulled her into a hug and held her. "Two more days, Baby! We'll be with him! Does he know anything about me? Did he ever ask?" Curiosity laced his tone.

"He's only two. I'm his universe. However, a few weeks ago, he asked, 'Why don't we have a daddy?' He probably started noticing that other families are different. He spent a long weekend with my friends, which likely gave him more time to observe and think. My mind went bonkers. I knew the day would come when he'd start asking questions, but not in a million years would I have thought he'd ask now, when he's two."

"What did you come up with?"

"I didn't have to come up with anything. Ayden's question caught me off guard, but I told him the truth, in a way. He wouldn't understand if I told him everything. So, I told him that we have a daddy, which is true, but daddy lives far away, which was also true. Smart cookie that he is, he asked if Daddy lives in the 'Far-far Away Kingdom'. And that was true too. You live in a kingdom that's far-far away. I didn't lie to him, and it felt good." Her lips pressed into a thin line as she raised a nervous shoulder.

CJ smiled at Ava, lost in wonder. "I love to see you happy!"

"Happy?"

"You have a saying. Depending on your mood, your eyes change colour. When you're upset, sad, or worried, they turn a dark green, like the ocean's waters before a storm. When you're happy, your eyes are almost turquoise green, like clear oceans on a sunny day. And this is what I'm looking at right now."

"Ayden always makes me happy," Ava said in a dim voice.

"And I don't? I thought I played a part in it after this morning. You're pushing me away again, only one hour after you asked me to make love with you."

Ava shut her eyes, covering her face in embarrassment. "I did ask, didn't I? I can't believe I begged the way I did."

He clutched her wrists and gently tugged her hands, gazing into her eyes. "You didn't beg. You bargained, and I'm happy you did."

"Okay. You played a role. Now, let's get to work. Do you have any boxes? Plastic bags? Anything?" Ava's pragmatic side kicked in.

"I have. Why don't you head upstairs, and I'll bring boxes and bags. If you want to start in the bathroom … We may not be able to load everything in the car today. Let's pack what's most important first."

Meticulously, Ava began packing and sorting everything by category. CJ took Ellie's clothes out of the closet and placed them on the bed. He paused, pouting, as he stared at some perfume bottles and cosmetics on the dresser, by the mirror.

"I believe she won't want these," he muttered, just as Ava was coming out of the bathroom with another box.

"She won't want what?" she asked.

"The perfumes I bought for her, kinda hoping she'd smell like you," CJ displayed a disappointed grimace. "I admitted it to her. I guess she'll never wear them."

"She'll never wear those. I wouldn't if I were her." Ava got closer, inspecting the small collection of perfumes. "Oh. My. God! These are all the perfumes I had with me in L.A., except this one." She turned with a pink bottle in her hand after she sniffed it.

"You had it in L.A. I clearly remember the bottle. This was my favourite. I complimented you so many times until you only wore this one. However, it smelled totally different on Ellie."

"CJ, wasn't this one. I have it, but I'm sure I didn't bring it to L.A. I don't think I ever wore it around you. L.A. is hot, and this is not a perfume for hot weather. The bottles look too similar, but this is a different version. *I* even have to sniff them to tell which is which."

"What? No way!"

"Yes way! It smells different on anyone, not only on Ellie."

"Well, whatever. It doesn't matter anymore."

"Are you sure? It's one of my favourite perfumes, and I'd hate to give it up."

"No, don't. It bothered me how much I actually liked it. I was just disappointed that it smelled different on her. We could keep them for you."

"Well, I guess that's the last bit from the bathroom. There's still some room in this box. I can see a few things here by the mirror that aren't mirroring my stuff. No pun intended. I believe I can fit them in this box. I'll leave the perfumes out. We'll see about those," Ava said.

Within a couple of hours, with most of Ellie's stuff packed in the car, they left.

Appearing as if she hadn't slept or eaten, Ellie noticed Ava's necklace. Lips twisted into a bitter smile, she tilted her head when she saw the ring.

Ellie still remembered that one time when she forgot her phone charger in CJ's car. He was away. She looked for a spare and discovered the box with the ring in the back of his nightstand drawer. Curious, she opened it and looked inside. The sparkling emerald surrounded by blinking diamonds took her breath away. Her eyes glowed with excitement, and, just as any woman would, she believed CJ intended to propose. To her.

Only a few months later, Ellie had to conceal the surprise when CJ proposed, indeed, but with a completely different ring than the one she found that day. She brushed it off as probably being attached to a different story. A family heirloom, and he may save it for another occasion. Or he probably kept it safe for a friend. She only now realized it was something else. *It was for her. He had it planned, just as he said.*

"He proposed," Ellie said, half-smiling, her eyes on the necklace around Ava's neck.

"Yes, he did," Ava said in a small voice, fidgeting. "However, I didn't give him an answer. He insisted I keep the ring for now."

"I had time to think last night. Whatever you decide, remember that you deserve to be happy. I love you, Lina."

"I love you, too, Baby-Girl. Will you still love me if I say 'yes'?

I'm still pondering, but—" Ava shrugged, a demi-smile warping her lips.

"If this is the decision you want to make, go for it. I don't trust him, but that doesn't mean you shouldn't. He did what he did to me because he loves you so much. He was hurt and confused … He's not a bad guy. I can't even fucking hate him. And you'll still be my second mom. Always. Don't worry about me. I'll be fine." With a heavy heart, Ava nodded and embraced Ellie, holding her tight for a long minute.

Moments after stepping into the kids' store, CJ grabbed Ava's hand, hauling her and hunching behind a shelf.

"What?" Ava asked, bamboozled.

"Emily, my sister, and Cindy. You remember Cindy, right?" He peeked over the shelf to ensure no one was listening. His voice dropped to a whisper, his eyes darting nervously.

"Yes, I remember Cindy. What about her? And why are we whispering?"

"They're here. Let's go! We'll come back later."

They turned to leave and came face-to-face with Lisa, Rob's wife. Her eyebrows arched as she entered the store. Ava didn't know who the woman was. She only caught CJ's quick gesture to keep quiet with a finger to his lips. He squeezed past Lisa and hurried out of the store with Ava in tow, as she watched them leave with a puzzled look on her face. Even more confused, Ava blinked, stumbling behind CJ.

"What just happened?" she asked once they were reasonably far from the store.

"Phew! That was close."

"What was close?" Ava asked, still rattled.

"That was Lisa. Rob's wife. Rob was enough of a surprise for you last night. I didn't want you to meet them here. Not like this. You need time. They all need a bit more time."

"That was an odd coincidence," Ava said.

"I guess they are here for the same reason as we are." A pleased grin split his face from ear to ear. "Meaning they overcame the shock and denial and are now working on accepting my decision. And this is good news."

"Was your mom there too?"

"I haven't seen her. She probably wasn't. I'm sure Ayden will get something from my mum, though."

"That's not why I asked. I told you he doesn't need anything."

He cocked an eyebrow. "Don't try to say it to this family. We spoil our kids."

"Well, not my kid. Don't try to spoil him, okay? I don't want to break my feet or neck stepping on toys," Ava countered.

"Our kid," CJ corrected her with a half-sneer. "And I'll try not to spoil him. Just this once."

Early afternoon, on a Tuesday, the mall wasn't crowded. Lisa understood the assignment. She texted. The party had left the mall and was en route home. "BTW, she's gorgeous," Lisa's message ended.

After checking his messages nearly half an hour later, with a pleased smirk on display, CJ said, "They left. Let's go back."

Of course, he bounced like a kid in a toy store, his eyes eager for everything.

Arms crossed, Ava stayed firm in her stance, telling him there was a luggage limit and no extra space at home. "—plus, your family might've already bought a lot."

"Good point," CJ said. He shot a quick text to Lisa asking what they got, and she promptly replied with a photo.

After a brief, muttered argument, CJ prevailed. As per Ava's wish, a small toy made its way into their basket. But he also took home a full-size toy car for Ayden to drive.

"You do realize he's only two, right? He doesn't have good coordination yet. And it's too big for him, anyhow," she teased.

"He won't be two forever."

"He's not even able to reach all the gear, but he'll want to.

Plus, I don't have where to keep it for now," Ava tried to convince him it was a terrible idea.

"You have a big basement. Or in the garage."

"Well, you'll see."

"Well. He'll have it," CJ teased back. "Baby, I'm so excited about meeting Ayden. I promise I won't spoil him. Please understand me."

Her heart melted, and she caved. "Okay, but this car is not coming with us now. And this is final."

"He-he-he! You just said 'car' like a Brit."

"Ugh! You're impossible," she scoffed, rolling her eyes, amused, yet still not at peace with the expensive, 'ginormous' toy, which she found unnecessary.

Wednesday finally arrived. She wasn't looking forward to it, but she had to face it. On the verge of becoming a complete emotional wreck, Ava twiddled all morning as CJ tried everything to comfort her. His attempt to talk her out of her dread didn't fully work. He made her laugh. Yet, every single time, it ended in bursts of bittersweet memories from L.A., overcoming both.

L.A.—the apogee of their relationship. That time when their friendship blossomed into love, and they shared many good laughs over silly things. Those moments when their imagination ran wild. When the most unexpected little things had been embellished and twisted into incredible, fantastic scenarios. When genuinely pulling pranks on the cast, just for the fun of it.

"I haven't laughed so hard since L.A. Good old times," Ava sighed. "Well, I guess it's time. I have to get ready for the *unsettling encounter*." Suddenly, her eyes went wide as she bit her bottom lip. "Shit! What should I wear?"

"As far as I'm concerned, you can come like you are. You look beautiful in these leggings and tank top."

"You're not helping."

"Then let's see what you have." Of all the outfits Ava brought, without flinching, CJ squinted at a fitted lilac dress. "Definitely this one." He said, snatching it off her hand and holding it against her complexion.

Ava pouted, doubtful. "Mmm ... too fitted for the occasion?"

"Just perfect," he winked with a smirk.

Strangely enough, CJ's choice was one of the two options intended for the rehearsal dinner, originally scheduled for that exact evening, but she didn't mention it.

Nearly an hour later, pacing up and down, CJ waited. When Ava began down the stairs, he stopped in his tracks, jaw dropping. "Wow! You look ... like a goddess!" he exhaled in admiration, dashing to meet her at the bottom of the staircase, taking her hand. "And you smell so fucking sexy," he muffled in her ear, setting a kiss on her cheek.

"You cleaned up quite well, too." Her lips curled into a smile, her eyes resting on him. "Would you, please, help me with this necklace? My hands are all shaky and sweaty. It keeps slipping."

CJ took the purple pearl necklace from her hand and examined it, trying to figure out how it worked.

Ava turned, pulling her hair up. Brows knitted in concentration, he fastened the fine piece of jewellery in place. When she twirled to face him, CJ's admiration reignited for a short-lived moment before a sudden gasp escaped his throat. His expression betrayed a hint of shock, as if stirred by something unexpected.

"What?" Ava's eyes widened.

"Um, nothing."

"You say 'nothing', but your face says something else. Too fitted, eh? I'll change," she said as she turned toward the stairs.

CJ grabbed her hand with a failed smile on his face. "No. Um, everything's alright."

"No, it is not. Be honest."

"Okay! I know this necklace matches your dress. I was just hoping you'd wear the one with the ring, too. That's all. But it's okay." He tried a half smile, but behind his gaze, there was something else.

Her eyes lit up with a mysterious grin as she tucked a lock of hair behind her ear. "Is it? Really?!"

"Yes. I'm okay with it," he forced another smile.

"Well … I'm wearing it." Ava brought her left hand up with the ring sparkling on her finger.

"Wow! Um … um…" He gulped. "Does this mean—?" He stuttered, his voice wavering.

Her expression beamed with a broad smile. "Yes! It means *yes.*"

CJ swept her off her feet, sharing a passionate kiss. "Thank you." As he set her gently on the ground, their eyes locked, and he puffed a smile of relief. "Let's not go anywhere. I want us to stay right here. Just you and me. No one else."

"Well, that's not nice. It's sort of rude, if I may say so. You can't just let the most important people to you, waiting."

"Right now, you're the most important to me."

"Ha! I guess we should leave before I lose my nerve."

The entire ride, Ava played with the ring in a state of nervous anticipation. Silent.

CJ stole occasional glances at her. "I won't stray from your side," he kept reassuring her. "Everything will be alright."

She simply nodded in response, conjuring vague smiles. Finally, he pulled in front of his brother's house, already buzzing with family members.

"I'm frozen. I can't move," she whimpered, nearly panicked, when the engine stopped humming.

Turning towards her, CJ seized her hands. "Ava, please look at me. Breathe. Breathe in. Okay, now breathe out. Good! Again." Their gazes fastened, and she followed the directions.

Every curious soul inside the house clustered behind the semi-transparent curtains.

"What are they doing?" Shannon, Luke's wife, asked.

"I don't know. Come on already! Get out of that car! We're dying here!" Emily gushed out.

"Well, curiosity killed the cat. Boys! Girls! Away from the

window! What are you? Five? Waiting for Santa Claus? They'll be coming in," Patti said in a demanding voice as she barged into the room. Yet, she too craned her neck to glance out the window past all those tall boys.

After a few minutes, CJ exited the car and opened the door on Ava's side, lending a hand to help her out of the vehicle.

On the curb, facing each other, he looked into Ava's eyes, holding her hands. "Remember to breathe and remember I'm here. Grab my arm now. Don't you fall for me in front of everyone," he cracked a joke.

Ava wanted to laugh, but all she could manage was a faint smile. "Good thing we are still out here. Nobody will know unless I break something."

"You don't know my family. At this very moment, they are all bunched behind that window."

As CJ pointed to the said window, inside the house, Luke backed away. "Frack! He saw us!"

"He didn't see us. He knows us!" Emily uttered, engrossed. Then, she added, "Wow! When I grow up, I want to be her!" Brows raised with sheer surprise, all heads turned at her. "What?! What did I say? Did I say something wrong?" She asked, confused.

Lectured by Patti and Rob, the unbelievably genuine remark triggered instant wary stares.

"Actually, you said the right thing, for once. If you can keep this spirit for the rest of the evening, you'll make all of us happy." Patti seemed to recover and react first, and everyone tacitly agreed.

"Oh, God! You know what? That one right there ... She is the one for CJ. I can tell even from inside here. He's never had anyone like her. Why would I say something when there's nothing to say? Look out there! They are made for each other."

"Let's meet her first, and then we'll see," Don cut in. He was the cautious one.

"I believe I met her. Ava, right?" Cindy, who'd just arrived a few minutes earlier with Luke and Shannon, was curious. "Em, if you change your mind about when you grow up, I advise you not to be your old self, or you'll be put in your place. This one is one of a kind, trust me!" Cindy continued.

She only got a brief update. The wedding was off. CJ reconnected with the love of his life, and he had just found out he was a father.

"You met her? When?" Emily asked, her curiosity piqued.

"Yes, when?" Patti was just as curious.

"Um ... three or four years ago. Ava said there was nothing between them, but I know CJ. He was definitely interested. Actually, it was exactly when you broke your leg, Aunt Patti," Cindy said.

"This is where he was going every day ... Hmm. Don't you think she looks a bit like Louise? I believe this is who I saw him with."

"The 'just a friend' gal? I think he said Ava was her name," Don muttered, but nobody heard him.

"Mum! Louise? Ugh! Please don't say it! Look out there. Do you see 'class'? Because I see 'class'!" Emily added promptly as she turned and pointed out the window. Then, she quickly took another glance. "Okay! Here they come!" she chanted.

Rob opened the door. From what he saw through the window, he sensed Ava's anxiety—a familiar face would probably put her at ease.

Recognizing his brother's tactics, CJ smiled, content. Rob had always been the thoughtful one.

Ava smothered a laugh. They were watching. *How else would that door magically open before CJ even touched the doorbell button?*

She didn't miss the tail end of the entire party, rushing to look busy, away from the window. The sarcastic voice in Ava's head and her wild imagination were working overtime, spinning countless scenarios, each more hilarious than the last.

Then she spotted another familiar face peeking through the door—Cindy. As they exchanged a smile, Cindy winked and nodded as if she approved of something.

Then it was Lisa, whom Ava had seen for just a split second the day before at the mall. She pranced in to greet and meet Ava.

"Okay, everyone. We'll be there in a minute," CJ hollered loudly enough for everyone to hear him from wherever they had retreated.

"She wears the ring. Did she—?" Rob discreetly asked CJ while Ava and Lisa were exchanging pleasantries.

"Keen eye. Yes, she did." CJ's face lit up with a beaming smile and shining eyes.

"You're a lucky son of a gun! When?"

"Right before we left to come here. I was just about to call and cancel," he whispered.

"Ouch!" Rob nudged CJ, a crooked smile creeping across his lips.

Holding Ava's hand, CJ led her into the living room. Patti emerged from the kitchen, followed by Don and Emily. Cindy, her husband Sam, Luke, and his wife Shannon, and Finn, Emily's husband, were chatting in the living room.

Ava was introduced to everybody, and everyone who still needed to, was introduced to Ava.

She glanced around as if waiting for more. "No kids?"

"Not tonight. It's an adult-only event. Kids can be noisy and disruptive. Well, most are teenagers. We have some of those—the troublesome kind. You'll get there," Lisa tittered, winking.

"Where are they?" Ava was curious.

"We put them in kennels and locked them in the Tower of London," Emily teased.

Ava laughed. "You're my kind of girl."

"They're at our place, having fun, eating pizza, and staying up late," Shannon clarified.

"I assume that's better than the Tower of London," Ava commented, and everybody burst into laughter.

"Well, if nobody's asking, I'm going to," said Emily, and Ava felt CJ's thigh getting tense against hers. "I'm dying to see pictures with my nephew. I hope you have pictures," she continued, and CJ relaxed.

Ava's lips arched into an almost ecstatic smile. "Oh, only a few thousand. I know. I'm obsessed. I only have my cellphone, so it will be hard for everyone to see everything. But ... does everyone have Facebook?"

"We do, right? We all do," said Patti, looking around for everyone's approval.

"Let's connect on Facebook so you can access all of Ayden's albums. That way, you can take your time and browse the photos at your own pace."

As everyone was added to Ava's family list, they began scrolling through pictures. The atmosphere was filled with a mix of awe and quietness.

"Oh, my! Ayden looks exactly like CJ when he was a baby." Patti was the first to speak.

Of course, the women were all 'awe', 'wow', 'so cute' and 'adorable'. 'Look at this one' and 'look here'.

"CJ, have you seen them all?" Rob asked.

"I didn't get to see them all yet. But I will."

"Have you seen this one?"

"Which one?"

Rob turned the screen. "This. Mum! Dad! Look here! The pose, the look on his face— Remember that Christmas photo? CJ was probably the same age as Ayden in this shot."

"Oh, my!" exclaimed Don, tipping his glasses. "I know exactly which one you're talking about. Spitting image of CJ."

"Do you have it here? I'm curious," Ava said.

"You should have it, Rob. It must be in the album I made for you," Patti said. "CJ has it, too. I made an album for each of them," she continued towards Ava.

Returning to the room where they watched for their arrival, Lisa flipped through the album and found the picture.

Ava's jaw dropped, staring at CJ. "Oh, my God! He looks like you!"

He gently squeezed her waist. "I told you he does."

"Why did you choose Ayden for his name?" asked Patti, her voice dripping with more than just curiosity.

Ava squirmed a bit, hesitating. "Because of its meaning, 'little fire'. He arrived when I needed a purifying fire to change my life and make it meaningful again. I never thought I'd have another chance to have a baby. And then, there was hope again."

"CJ, have you told Ava that one of our twins is Aidan as well? With an I and an A," Rob asked, shifting his gaze from CJ to Ava.

"Really?" Ava's eyebrows raised in surprise; her voice tinged with anxiety.

"Our grandfather's name was Aidan. Mum's father," CJ clarified.

"Oh!" Ava's stomach twisted, worried that his family might not like the name she chose for her baby.

From what she could recall, CJ was fond of his grandparents. The chessboard—'the vintage piece of art'—he inherited from his grandfather, was in his study, displayed on a table that seemed custom-made.

"I'm honoured. Even more so, because you had the intuition to pick the name when you didn't know its meaning to our family. It's spelled differently, but it means just as much to me," Patti explained, noticing Ava's uncomfortable simper. "Now, let's all sit and have dinner. Forgive us if we seemed too inquisitive. We know you two are leaving tomorrow and just wanted to learn as much as possible about you and Ayden."

When all the officious questions ended, and everyone's curiosity was somewhat satisfied, the atmosphere changed. Feeling welcomed, Ava breathed better. CJ was right—his family was loving and lovable. Even Emily, whose reaction Ava feared the most.

To CJ's surprise, she called Ava—*sis,* and the two immediately hit it off. Although he didn't fully trust his sister's acting. He was more than prepared to pull the trigger if Emily dared to show her true colours. Couldn't stop thinking that, sooner or later, his sister's natural temperament would eventually re-emerge.

Earlier, when Ava asked for a glass of water, CJ dashed after Lisa into the kitchen. "What's up with Emily?"

"What do you mean? She's surprisingly sweet!" Lisa said, intending to temper him down.

"Too sweet. Surprisingly. Duh! That's a problem."

"She made some genuinely appreciative remarks before you two came in. I believe she truly likes Ava. Relax. Take it. Don't look for problems where they're not," Lisa said, her tone casual.

"I'm not too sure. We'll see," CJ frowned, fists clenched as if he were gearing up for a fight, no matter what Lisa said.

Before sitting for supper, Emily went to bring the appetizers, and CJ offered a hand.

"Who are you, and what have you done with my sister?" he whispered in Emily's ear once they were far enough down the stairs leading to the basement.

"What do you mean?" Emily grumbled, and she kept going.

CJ rushed past, stopping and blocking her. "You know exactly what I mean. Well, I have to admit I am pleased with the act you're putting on. I just hope you'll keep it up."

Emily rolled her eyes, vexed by his words, as she walked around him. "What act? I have no clue what you're talking about. *You* are acting weird."

"Please, leave Ava alone. All I ask is to be decent and treat her nicely. Don't attack her. Am I asking too much?" He continued, pivoting, his eyes following Emily, who kept rolling across the room to get the platters from the fridge.

She turned visibly bothered, holding the fridge door open. "Why would I attack her? You really are weird."

"I don't know your reasons, but you always attacked everyone I've been with before. Well, you treated Ellie quite okay, but … please. Ava is the one for me, and this won't change. It's a done deal. You'd better get used to the idea."

"You're totally right. Ava is definitely the one for you. I really like her. She's smart, beautiful, and classy. And I hope she'll have a good influence on you. Just don't screw up this time," Emily hurried to approve. "As for the other ones … well, they weren't right for you. I couldn't help but treat them as the gold diggers they were. I'm glad you figured them all out. Ellie was quite decent, and I don't agree with what I heard you've done. I'm happy that you chose the better version of Ellie, though. And definitely, Ava is the best for you."

CJ blinked, fogged. "What?"

"What-what? What did you think?"

"So, it wasn't—?"

"I don't know what you think it was," she interrupted. "I was just trying to make you open your eyes and see what we all did. The whole family, yes. No one liked them, but everyone has been too nice to say anything. However, I didn't want you to get burned. I was protecting you, believe it or not," said Emily, as she took the last platters out of the fridge. "And, why the hell are you living in the past? You have a wonderful woman up there. And a fantastic mother for your kid. Now, if you are here to help, get these and let's go," she said, dumping two platters with appetizers in a baffled CJ's hands. Grabbing the rest, she headed upstairs.

"Ava was right about you!" CJ muttered as he snapped out of his dazed state and scampered to catch up with Emily.

"What do you mean?" Emily tossed over her shoulder.

"A few years ago, I asked her opinion on what you were doing to my girlfriends."

"You did what? You never do this. You never talk about your ex-girlfriends with another woman. You're such a moron sometimes!" Emily whispered, spinning on the stairs and stopping right in his face with a challenging stare.

"We were just friends. And I was talking about you, basically. And the way I felt," CJ countered. "However, she guessed you without knowing you. Just like you did, Ava pointed out that I'm no longer with those girls. She said that women have an extra sense or something, and you may have sensed things I missed, so you may be protective of me," he whispered back.

Emily scoffed, cocking a brow. "Didn't I tell you she's smart?"

"Well, that I already knew!" CJ shot back, and both burst into laughter.

When CJ volunteered to help Emily, and until they returned, Patti held her breath, concerned that her two youngest children might get into an argument. To her relief, the two were still laughing when they entered the dining room.

At the table, Ava was chatting with Cindy. The others either listened to their conversation or helped in the kitchen.

"Ava dear, would you like some soup, for starters?" asked Patti.

"Mum, no!" CJ quickly responded on Ava's behalf. She stared at him, just as surprised as Patti. "Mum, Ava has some dietary restrictions!"

"If you can tell me what's in the soup—" Ava smiled, aiming to soothe the situation.

Being celiac was nobody's problem but hers. By now, she knew how to navigate food options without making others feel like they had to go the extra mile to accommodate her.

"Just beef broth and some veggies. I made it myself." Patti smiled at Ava, tossing a nearly scornful look at CJ.

"Sounds delicious. I'll have some, thank you," Ava said.

She missed CJ's exasperated grimace, but she noticed some smiles around the table that she couldn't make much of. Probably approving of her diplomacy. Who knows?

"Then, I'll have some too," CJ said.

So what? he thought. *Nobody passed Mum's test, and Ava has a great sense of humour. Well, this is it,* he grimaced, trying to convince himself that the outcome wouldn't make any difference.

An emotional package, Ava had barely eaten anything in the last few days. Surrounded by the warmth and kindness of this family, and since the tension dissipated simultaneously with her fears, she felt hungry for the first time in days. She most likely won't be able to eat much. But a warm bowl of soup, she'd definitely enjoy.

CJ didn't get the chance to warn her, and now, with everybody around, it was too late. Truth be told, he completely forgot about it. He never thought his mom would pull this with Ava. But Patti believed it would be fun.

As a guest, Ava got the first bowl of soup when it arrived.

She leaned over, inhaling the aroma. "Smells absolutely amazing. Thank you."

When everyone had their respective bowl of soup, they began eating. A starving Ava focused on the meal before her, savouring it. *Delicious.* After only a few spoons, obviously enjoying it, Ava glanced up and around the table. She winced. All the smirking gazes were on her, and she sensed it was more to them.

Still standing, Patti displayed a broad, proud smile. Arching a confused eyebrow, Ava blinked and looked around the table again. She wasn't sure why no one was eating, but they were staring at her instead.

She reached for the napkin and patted her chin to wipe away any potential mess on her face. Then she turned to CJ with a helpless look. "Do I have anything on my face?" she nearly whispered.

He was smiling, just as proud as his mom. "No, darling. You're wonderful," he said. "Now, everybody happy?" he continued with a satisfied smirk around the table.

"That's not fair. You warned her," Emily reproached.

CJ held her gaze. "Em, please, don't be ridiculous."

"Warn me? About what?" asked Ava, even more puzzled.

"Mum has this thing … It's a test. Um … not a proper test." CJ stumbled as he tried to explain.

"A test!" Ava exclaimed, mystified, peering around numbly. The last time she'd been tested, it didn't end well.

"Oh, dear! It's just for fun," Patti cut in. "Well, the good news is, and I'm proud to say that, from all these lads sitting around this table—" she gestured widely. "—I mean those who weren't born into our family— You are the only one who passed the said test. Congrats and welcome to our family. See? You all thought I made it up. There's a proper way to eat soup, and Ava knows it," Patti said, and Ava let out a breath of relief blended into a simper. "I thought it wouldn't be fair to the rest if I skipped you. This was my last chance. The last of my boys is getting married."

Everybody congratulated and welcomed Ava into the family.

"A test, eh? You didn't say I was supposed to pass a test," Ava admonished CJ in a fun way.

"I hoped my dear mum would spare you. And I forgot about this thing, which is … well, tradition. However, you did absolutely amazing. So, this will be a fun story to tell Ayden someday," CJ parried.

Those who weren't born into the family began sharing how they had failed the 'test'. Laughter filled the room. Of course, with each telling, every story gets better.

Ava smiled. She could only guess this wasn't the first time these stories had been bounced around.

This was a hilarious bunch. The atmosphere turned even more relaxed, warm, and alive. It was the right place to be, and Ava felt good. Once in a while, CJ touched her arm or shoulder as if he intended to reassure her. 'See? Everything's alright.'

It was past nine when Luke and Shannon asked Cindy and Sam if they should leave to check on the kids. 'Before they burn the house to the ground'. Since CJ's flat was not an option anymore, before reaching London, Cindy and Sam had been redirected to

Luke and Shannon's place.

"A change in plans," they have been told.

Ava appeared tired, and CJ didn't miss it when he glanced at her. "I guess we're leaving too. I still have to finish packing. Tomorrow will be a long day."

In the lobby, as they were all getting ready to leave, Patti embraced CJ and murmured something.

"Mum!" he exclaimed, wide-eyed, staring at Patti.

Then, she turned and affectionately hugged Ava, whispering in her ear, "Dear, take good care of our boys."

Ava nodded, sharing a glowing, face-splitting smile.

"What did Mum whisper to you before we left?" CJ's voice exuded curiosity as he glanced at her and asked while on their way home.

"I'll tell you if you tell me what she whispered to you. Do you think I missed that? Especially your reaction..." her tone teasing.

"You don't want to know."

She smirked. "Oh, but I do."

CJ hesitated a moment. "Okay, but you first..."

The love in CJ's eyes, looking at her when Ava shared what his mother asked of her! That gaze she treasured so much!

"Now, your turn."

"Well, basically, Mum asked me the same thing—to take care of you."

"Then, why did you look horrified? The idea isn't appealing to you?"

"The way she said it—" He paused, briefly, arching his upper lip. "See, sometimes, my mum can have quite a ... dirty mind. She was reserved tonight. But you'll get to know her."

"What did she say?" Ava challenged him.

"Um ... She basically told me to take you home and make love with you." His lips stretched into a peculiar smirk.

"What?!" Ava reacted, jarred, her hand to her mouth, eyes as big as saucers. "She didn't."

"She did. Mum said that starting tomorrow, things will be

much different with a toddler around. And I have to believe her. She had four of us around. So, I plan on taking her advice if you're not too tired. Besides, I haven't made love with my fiancée yet." He tossed an allusive sneer, reaching to take her hand.

"Well, you're right about that," Ava replied, glaring at the ring on her finger while CJ found her right hand and kissed it, holding it to his heart. "You should probably pay attention to the traffic. I need to make it home in one piece. Someone who needs me is waiting there!" She slowly withdrew her hand.

"Correct! I'll make sure you get home safe and sound, because I need you too. I love you, Baby!"

"I love you, too!" Ava's reply trailed off as she leaned her head on the headrest of her seat and closed her eyes.

That night, they made love, not rushed or hungry, but tender, like it meant everything, as if they discovered each other for the first time.

"Let's stay here. I was never this happy! I'll finish packing in the morning. And if I forget something, so be it. I just need to pack all the gifts for Ayden. Nothing else matters right now," CJ said, holding her in his arms.

"Not all. You'll need some if he ever comes here."

He was quiet for a moment, then said, "Baby! What would you say if I asked you and Ayden to move here with me? I don't want to push my luck, but—"

"Move here? But you said—"

"I know. I know what I said. I just believe it would work out much better. I'd feel like I left you behind if I travelled back and forth. We'll soon get married. We'll have to make some sort of decision, anyhow. Think about it. I know your house is just as big as mine ... We could try alternate living between London and Edmonton for a while, but always be together, wherever we are."

"That would be chaotic and confusing for Ayden. Well, you're right, in a way. But I also have my work, you know?"

"Think about it. And keep in mind that you won't need to work anymore. We could spend more time together, travel together, and you'd be with Ayden all the time."

"Oh, God! I don't want him to grow up being Mama's boy! I spend plenty of time with him, but he needs more than just me … us." She sighed. "I promise I'll think about it."

Ava's thoughts drifted, but she didn't want to spoil the magic of the moment.

There were things about herself she had never revealed. There was never a good time or the proper context, and she hated to brag.

And there was even more. Her 'big house' …?

Well … That's a tomorrow problem.

28. Daddy is funny

As soon as they fastened their seatbelts and the airplane took off, Ava drifted to sleep. After all the events and shifting emotions, she was finally going home—her safe and quiet place. To her baby—her happy place. The airplane's engines roaring and vibrating in the background didn't seem to bother her at all. If anything, it probably helped, like a lullaby soothing a baby to sleep.

Ava's anxiety only spread as they waited in the VIP area during a two-hour layover in Calgary. Her stomach in knots, she kept fidgeting, restless, her anxiety mounting.

"We are almost there. Two more hours, Baby. I know. My stomach's in knots, too. I'll meet my son for the first time, and I keep wondering, 'How will he react?' It's all new to me. Please stay strong for both of us," implored CJ, squeezing her hand.

"About that ... I hope you don't expect Ayden to run straight into your arms, calling you 'Daddy' right away. It's probably going to take some time for him to warm up. I wish I could tell how long, but I can't." Remorse threaded through her voice as she gazed into his eyes, sadness clouding her own.

"I know, Baby. I know. I'm trying to make a plan in my head, and I realize my plan may be worth nothing, but I'll do my best, and I need you there."

Ava sighed. "I'm sorry. It's my fault that we got here."

"No, don't blame yourself, please. Let's leave the past in the past and never mention it again. Okay? No guilt, no blaming … nothing. Let's just move forward and make the best of our future. How about this?" CJ asked, searching into her eyes for her accord.

"I suppose I like that. I'd hate to spend the rest of my life in the shadow of my past mistakes."

"*Our* past mistakes. You were not alone, remember? We both played a part in it. We both could've done things differently. And we both chose not to. Let's not allow the past to ruin the future. Ayden's future. We can't go back in time and fix it, but we can work together from here on and make better decisions, as you asked me. Promise?"

A dim smile arched her trembling lips, and she nodded, a sense of tranquillity enveloping her.

The flight to Edmonton was domestic. Passing through customs didn't take long. After she claimed her luggage, Ava nearly ran to get out of there and hold her baby. Ayden saw her first, the moment she passed through the doors. Small enough to slide under the lines delimitating the waiting area, he scurried toward her, calling, "Mama".

A rush of warmth flooded her chest. Releasing her suitcase, she dropped her carry-on and fell to her knees, arms open. Tears welled in her eyes as she squeezed him tightly, peppering endless kisses all over his face and tiny hands. Ayden's little arms wrapped around her neck, and he wouldn't let go.

Quickly peering around, Ava picked up Ayden and stepped aside, sharing a heartfelt embrace with Nina.

CJ paused for a moment, taking it all in. Jolting out of the moment, he picked up Ava's luggage, strapped it to his, and moved to the side. Waiting and watching.

It only took a subtle wiggle of her finger, flashing the ring, to draw a silent jaw drop mimic from Nina. Ava nodded in reply to her friend's mouthed, "Congrats!" eyes gleaming with happiness.

Two days earlier, Ava gathered her strength and revealed the entire truth, along with the more recent layers of the story.

"Change of plans. I'm coming home Thursday! Can you pick us up from the airport at six P.M.?"

"Why? What happened? And who's us?" Nina fired like a machine gun.

Voice wavering with hesitation, Ava continued, "Well ... the wedding is not happening. So, I'm coming home. There's more, and I need to tell you before I arrive, so you won't be shocked."

"How is the wedding not happening?" Nina raised a puzzled brow.

"I'll tell you everything. Long story. It's hard. Please, just listen," Ava's voice trailed off, small and cracking.

"Okay-okay! I'm all ears. Is everything alright? Are you alright?" Nina's tone carried a thick layer of concern.

Ava's eyes wandered before turning back to the camera. "Well, you have two girls ... I guess you're past the tale with the birds and the bees. You know Ayden has a father, right? I never discussed it because I wanted to protect Ayden. And his father."

"Okay! I think I know where you're getting to. Did you run into him? Or did you plan to look for him before you left?"

"Nina, what do you know?" Deep anxiety was equally reflected in Ava's tone and expression.

"Ava, I know where you were three years ago, and with whom. You came back pregnant. We respected your decision not to talk about it, but ... Honey, by looking at Ayden, it's quite obvious who his father is. It's not rocket science. I can only assume he didn't know he was the father ... A father. Have you told him?"

"Well, I had to. I mean ... I had to admit it. He knew right away. Listen! The wedding— Eliza was marrying him," Ava's voice faltered.

"What?!"

"Yes. Shocking, right? My nightmare began the second I

walked into him. Straight out of the airplane. Well, the very next minute, he found out about Ayden and kind of figured out Ayden was his. I tried to avoid the answer, but he insisted, and I couldn't lie. I was supposed to be here for a week. How long could I have kept it from him? Within hours, everything turned upside-down."

Reluctantly, Ava went on telling Nina about her ordeal.

Nina's brows remained arched high, taken aback by the twist in the story. "And ... what now?"

"He proposed," Ava replied, her voice still faded, her expression still worried.

"To you?!"

Her stomach scrunched, but she carried on. "Who do you think? To me, yes! I didn't give him an answer. I don't know ... I feel terrible for Eliza. I'm so confused right now."

"Listen! Eliza won't take him back after what you just told me. And if he wanted her, he would've gone ahead with the wedding. I'm not sure I am the right person to give you advice, but ... what will you tell Ayden a few years from now when he asks? You know he'll ask, right? That you turned down his dad? Twice? And why? Because you were too scared or too messed up?" Nina paused, her lips pursing with slight hesitation. "Or too proud? It is for you to decide, though. I don't want to interfere. I guess you loved him. Do you still feel anything for him?"

Ava blew a loud sigh. "Well, that was never a question. I left, but my heart stayed behind."

"Ava, give him the frigging answer he's waiting for," Nina blurted out, her voice rattling.

"Well, CJ is coming to Edmonton with me. He wants to meet Ayden and work on our relationship. Win me back, he said." Another sigh escaped her.

"Allow him. Don't push him away! Don't do anything you may regret later. You may not get a third chance." Nina gave an impromptu motivational speech.

Ava's clouded eyes stared into the camera. "I know. But I also know we are from different worlds. In his world, things can change at the drop of a hat. What if he wants to replace me with a newer model in a few years?"

"Didn't he just give up on a newer model to be with you? I don't know what you see from up close, but this is what I see from here."

"True. I'll see how things go with his family tomorrow," Ava mused out loud, slightly cringing.

"Why? You're not marrying his family. Follow your heart! Go back to where you left it." Nina's words hit right in her soul.

"You are a good friend, Nina. Please keep Ayden safe until I come back."

"What?! Is he in danger?" Nina's tone flipped to alarmed, and her shoulders squared as if ready to fight.

"No-no. It's just the mother in me worrying about everything. Kiss him 'good night' for me. I may not be able to call tomorrow. Unless anything changes, I'll see you Thursday."

"Make sure you bring back my bubbly, happy girlfriend. You don't sound great right now."

In response, a nervous laugh echoed from Ava's end.

Still standing to the side, behind all those waiting for a dear someone at the airport, intensely watching the scene, CJ's stomach coiled.

With Ayden clinging around her neck, Ava began walking alongside Nina to where he was. An unsteady mix of ecstasy, loss, terror, and overwhelming emotions twisted his expression. But his eyes mirrored his heart, full of hope and contentment. Overcome with joy, his jaw flexed as he swallowed hard.

Here I am! CJ thought, nervously chewing the inside of his cheek. He watched Ava and Ayden share tender embraces, affectionate kisses, and warm hugs. The most heartwarming sight he had ever witnessed. A strong feeling of fulfillment overwhelmed him.

Ava's eyes stayed on Ayden's expression, taking him in.

"I missed you, Mama!" Ayden cooed.

"I missed you, too, Baby!"

"But I missed you mo', Mama."

"Guess what? I missed you most, Baby."

"Mama..." He wiggled, giggling, and making the cutest face. "I missed you the most-est-est-est."

Ava chuckled, amused, tickling him. "Where did you learn to be so cute and outsmart me? Huh? Where?" She pouted, mocking an annoyed face.

Meanwhile, drawn by Ava and Ayden's happy, vibrant interaction, CJ inched closer, trying to catch a glimpse of his son's face.

Ayden noticed him. "Mama, who that?"

"This is your daddy, Baby!" said Ava after quickly checking behind her to see who Ayden was pointing to.

"You so silly, Mama. Ayden no daddy," and he wrapped his arms around Ava's neck, hiding his face.

Her heart dropped as she withdrew just slightly from Ayden's embrace and looked at him with a solemn face. "Why are you saying this, Baby?"

"Not me, Mama. Deea said."

"Hey! I'm sure Deea made a mistake. All kids have a daddy. And this is your daddy. You have to believe Mama, okay? Now, would you give Daddy a hug? He's got something for you. Do you want to see what Daddy brought you?"

After peeking at the 'stranger' again, Ayden quickly tucked his face back into Ava's neck. Her remorseful gaze turned to CJ.

Deea—Andrea—was Nina's oldest daughter.

Nina's expression warped into an uncomfortable grin, and she began apologizing, "I'm so sorry. The other night, Sean, my husband, was playing with Ayden. Allie, our youngest, had a bout of jealousy and told Ayden to go play with his own daddy." She shrugged, uneasy. "Deea explained to Allie that Ayden doesn't have a daddy, and we should all share ours. She meant well."

"It's okay. They're just kids. He'll forget, don't worry," Ava whispered, rubbing Ayden's back. "Come on, Baby. At least say 'hi' to Daddy! Please."

Ayden looked again at CJ, quickly said, "Hi," and hid his face again in Ava's neck.

"It's okay. You need some time to adjust. Let's go home now," Ava said, cuddling with Ayden.

About an hour later, after a ten-minute stop at a grocery store for Ava to grab something for dinner, Nina pulled in front of an apartment building.

"Did he fall asleep?" Ava asked CJ, who sat in the back seat, next to Ayden. He smiled with a nod. "Okay. I'll get him."

Turning the engine off, Nina slipped out of the car. While Ava unbuckled her seatbelt, CJ leaned and peered out the window.

With a raised eyebrow, he glared at Ava and asked, "What is this? Where are we?"

"Home. We're home," she replied with a vague smile, barely looking at him, her voice surprisingly steady.

CJ peered out again, his baffled gaze dropping on Ava as she opened the back door on Ayden's side and began undoing his seat. Her stare still avoided CJ's.

"Would you care to tell me what this is?" he pressed.

"We can talk inside. Let's get in," Ava replied, her tone unaffected.

"Unbelievable!" he mumbled, stumbling out of the car.

After opening the trunk, Nina stepped to the side. Her gaze sought Ava's as she stood up after placing Ayden's seat on the grass.

"You didn't tell him?" Nina mouthed.

Lips pursed, Ava shook her head.

With short, intense moves, CJ yanked the suitcases from the trunk. Jaw still clenched, he strapped the luggage into a train, in silence, before thanking Nina with a hug. Furious footsteps echoed as he continued toward the entrance without a word.

"Good luck with '*splaining*, my dear friend. You know he's right. You are a madwoman," Nina whispered in Ava's ear while embracing her.

Right then, Ayden woke up, calling, 'Mama'.

"Yes, Baby. We're home," Ava feigned a happy tone, even though happiness wasn't what she felt at that very moment. She then unbuckled Ayden from his car seat.

Once inside the building, CJ growled under his breath, "Do you mind explaining? What is this?"

Holding Ayden's hand and balancing the car seat on her other arm, Ava continued to the elevator. She glanced at Ayden, worried he might get upset. "Upstairs. Wait until you see. You need to see first."

Inside her 'flat', with a surprised arched brow, CJ scanned around. "This is really nice, but doesn't explain it."

"Explain what, exactly? It is where I live now," Ava replied promptly.

"You moved. If I hadn't insisted on you staying so we could talk … if you vanished again, I would've never found you."

Fury and something else—something more profound—fused in his tone.

"Depends on how hard you tried. CJ, there's no need to fret over something that never happened. It simply doesn't make any sense. And I didn't vanish. I stayed, didn't I?" She strained, but her tone stayed calm.

"You sold your lovely house so you could raise my kid. Of course, I fret! How could I have found you here? How? Tell me!" he insisted, his voice hitting up a few notes.

Ava's lips stretched into a composed smile. "What makes you believe I sold my house?"

"I suppose you did. Why are you living here, then?" CJ asked, browsing around. "Seems quite spacious, but it's not your house."

"Oh, please relax. This is home to us. And it's not what you think. Not at all," Ava parried, her tone just as calm, trying not to alarm Ayden. He now clung to her leg, nearly terrified, glaring at this 'mean Daddy'. Ava lifted him in her arms.

"Relax?"

"Can we have dinner now? I need to feed Ayden and get him ready for bed. We can discuss when he's asleep." She smiled at Ayden. "Baby, do you want to play with Daddy? He brought you many toys, and Daddy will tell you who all those toys are from, okay? Mama will be in the kitchen, making dinner." Then she turned toward CJ. "Can you please keep him busy and entertained? He's not allowed in the kitchen." CJ raised a curious eyebrow, wondering why Ayden wasn't allowed in the kitchen, and she went on, "Dangerous things around there, and I only have two hands."

Lips pressed, he nodded with peaceful acceptance.

She made a valid point. She stayed indeed. *I'm probably freaking out for nothing.* Yet, his heart sank. *She had to move so she could raise my child. Or maybe she rents the house out for much more than she pays for this apartment, to make ends meet.* Variations of the same idea kept looping in his mind.

Wearing a serene smile, Ava listened from the kitchen to CJ and Ayden's chatter. It took a hot minute for Ayden to warm up, but the new toys did the trick. He kept asking questions, curious about Grandma and Grandpa, Uncle Rob, and everyone who sent him toys. And why did they send him toys? He had toys. Full of energy, Ayden ran back and forth, arms full of toys, showing CJ his collection. Ava puffed a satisfied smile.

It didn't take long to put a salad together and air-fry some veggies for the roasted chicken she bought at the store.

"Dinner is ready," Ava announced, placing the plates on the table as Ayden returned from the bedroom with another round of toys, explaining in his own language. "Ayden! Dinner, baby! Let's wash your hands."

"But Mama—"

"But?" Ava asked with a severe look. They had rules, and

Ayden knew them. "You can show Daddy your toys after dinner, okay? Hands, now," her tone softened. Eagerly running to the bathroom, Ayden hopped on his little stepper to reach the sink. Ava followed to help him. Leaning against the doorframe, CJ watched, genuinely enjoying the view. "What are you smiling at? Wash your hands too, and let's eat! I'm starving," Ava said, holding a hand towel for Ayden to dry his hands.

After dinner, it was bath time for Ayden. Then, while she put away the dishes and leftovers, he was allowed to watch a bit of his favourite show.

Finally done, Ava stepped out of the kitchen. She halted in her tracks, smiling at what she'd found in her living room. Nestled on the couch, father and son sat side by side, in the exact same position, watching the show. Fascinated.

Bummer! Lips pursed, she suppressed a sigh, saddened to disrupt that view.

"Ayden! Time for your bedtime story, Baby."

"A bit mo', mama," Ayden tried to bargain his way out of another rule.

"Then, no bedtime story. Your choice," Ava replied, her tone firm.

"I want him to read story," Ayden nearly poked CJ in the eye as he spun to his knees.

"Sure thing. Let's read a story." CJ chuckled, seizing another opportunity to bond with his son. He was beginning to understand Ayden's language. Ava concealed an ecstatic smile as CJ proudly took Ayden in his arms and followed her. "See? Everything's fine. You worried for nothing," he nudged Ava, a gleeful grin splitting his face.

"I told you he's good," she whispered, opening the bedroom door.

"His crib is in your bedroom. So, Mum was right. Things will be different with a toddler around," CJ commented quietly after placing Ayden in his crib.

Ava gave him a playful look. "Well, you offered to make it work. The good news is, he sleeps through the night."

"This will have to change, though," his reply, barely a whisper.

"Not tonight. Too many changes for one day."

Meanwhile, Ayden picked a storybook from the pile on Ava's nightstand and handed it to CJ. To Ayden's delight, on the edge of the bed, CJ made voices and faces, putting on a show. In his crib, Ayden listened with wide eyes, mesmerized as if it were the first time he'd heard the story.

Ava lay in bed, listening, fascinated by the two's actions, interactions, and reactions. *It pays off to have an actor as a dad—* she smiled.

The 'show' ended, and Ayden sat up, craning his neck. "Mama?"

"Yes, Baby," Ava answered, propping herself on one elbow.

"Daddy is funny."

Ava's heart skipped a beat, and CJ slid, nearly falling off the edge of the bed. His son just called him 'Daddy'.

Radiating, Ava's relieved gaze met CJ's, tears gathering in her eyes. "Yes, Daddy is funny," she approved. "Now, it's time to sleep. Good night, Baby."

CJ's beyond-happy grin turned to Ayden. He got up and leaned over the crib, placing a kiss on his son's forehead as little arms clung briefly around his neck. "Good night now. Close your eyes."

Once he tucked Ayden in, CJ turned toward Ava. Eyes closed, she was smiling, surrounded by a happy aura.

He touched her hand, and her eyes snapped open. "What now?" he whispered.

Ava leaned in and mouthed softly, "We sit here in silence. He'll fall asleep in a few minutes. Unless your interpretation of the story got him too excited, and it'll take longer." She then shifted over, making room for him to lounge next to her.

Taking her hand, he brought it to his lips, whispering, "He's amazing. You did a great job with him."

A quick glance at the crib over CJ's body a few minutes later, and Ava knew Ayden was asleep.

29. So, you were looking for trouble in Paris

It was past nine. Back in the living room, Ava began searching for something worth watching on TV.

"What would you like to watch?" she looked at CJ.

"Is it now a good time?" he asked.

"A good time!" she chuckled. "It's a quiet time, so we can watch something for mature people."

"Baby, please. You know precisely what I'm talking about. Tell me exactly what you've been through so you can raise my kid. I need to know. I need to fix this. How bad is it?"

"Oh, God! There's nothing to be fixed. Everything's fine."

He quirked an eyebrow. "Then, why are you living in an apartment?"

"Convenience! And it's not an apartment. When you own it, it's called a condo in Canada. It is mine. And so is the house. I have renters living in it, but it's still mine." Ava's tone shifted from mocking to firm but warm.

Part of his suspicions confirmed, CJ pressed further. "What does convenience mean? I'm looking around, and I don't see any."

"Oh, you wouldn't, but it's quite simple. First of all, no stairs. No stairs for Ayden when he started crawling ... then walking. No stairs for me when I was pregnant with him, and I wasn't allowed to do anything. And ... bonus—less space to mess up or keep tidy and organized. I can keep a closer eye on Ayden while cooking, working, or ... whatever. Conveniently, shortly after I found out I was pregnant, the renters living here let me know they were moving. It became available, I made the decision, and, by that Christmas, I was living here," her tone, just as steady.

His bothered stare scrutinized her expression. "Christmas? So, if I came when I had planned to, I wouldn't have found you at your house."

"I guess you would've called first, like you always did," her reply dropped irritatingly chill.

"I was planning to just show up at your door. Not giving you the chance to reject me on the phone. You already said you'd call, and you didn't. So, no! I wasn't planning to call ahead. I probably would've gone back, defeated."

Ava looked down and didn't say a word. After a long minute, she continued, "If you asked around, you could've found me. My neighbours looked after the house for a few months before I could get it ready for renting. They also adopted Fox. Big dogs are not allowed in the building, and he couldn't come live with us. I rented the house only after Ayden was born. But where there is a will, there is a way. I'm sure you would've found a way if you really wanted. But you didn't even try. So, what are we talking about?"

"I suppose you're right. There's no way of knowing now what I would've done then. However, one question remains. By any chance, is the extra money from the rent for raising Ayden?" Concern persisted in his voice.

She slightly cringed with hesitation before continuing in the same flush voice, "Okay. I guess I'll have to tell you, anyhow."

"Tell me, and I'll fix it."

"There's nothing to be fixed, I already told you. Whatever you think, it's not that. I own this condo and the house. I sold 80% of my late husband's company for a good price. I still own 20% and get the profits from that. That money goes into an account for Ayden. I also have a well-paid job, which is more than enough for the two of us. So no, the money from rent is not for living. When I said we were fine, I meant it. Now you know." Her gaze averted his, slightly fidgeting, as if she were embarrassed about revealing her wealth.

He arched a brow, visibly perturbed by the news. "How much money are you talking about?"

"Not as much as you have, but enough so I don't need to work a day for the rest of my life if I choose to, and I'll still be okay. Also, there'll be enough money left for Ayden not to worry about his future when I'm gone."

"How much?" CJ insisted.

"I hate bragging—" She squirmed. "Well ... Okay! It's over thirty million Canadian dollars. Ayden's account and the assets come on top."

CJ's jaw dropped, beyond perplexed by the new perspective. "So, I'm marrying a rich woman!"

"Oh, please! Elon Musk is rich. I'm just better than others ... Well, most. I don't think of myself as rich. I'm living a normal life, I kept my job—" Ava fidgeted, uncomfortable, dreading he might think she was vain.

His eyes narrowed, and he blinked a few times, appearing to deliberate. "This is good. Nobody can accuse you of being a 'gold digger'. They'll probably blame me for being one. I mean ... I may have a bit more money than you. However, this makes the PR campaign much easier when we come out as a couple."

She chuckled, amused. "Well, if I move to UK, as you suggested—and I'm not saying I will, yet—I won't sound that rich anymore. It'll be much less in pounds. They'd still call me whatever they want, true or not."

"Trust me. For PR, it's excellent. This will fly. They won't have any reason to slay you."

"It's like they need reasons. They always find at least one. You know that, right? I can see you're still afraid of your fans."

"My life sort of depends on what they can say or do. Soon, it will be *our* life. And I'm not afraid of them. I just don't want you and Ayden to get hurt. Come live with me, please. I can't protect the two of you if we live apart. We'll get married next year. I just need to let the dust settle a bit. I'll have Lisa and Rob organize our wedding. They know the drill. Please stay as inactive as possible on social media and refrain from following my accounts. I'll handle everything on my end. You don't need to stress over or deal with any of it."

"How about your family? Are their accounts set up as private, so no strangers can find me?"

"Yes, I took care of that. Can I look at your accounts? I need to check a few settings."

"Sure." As she handed over her cellphone, her mind flew back to the day they first met in Paris, when he asked for her phone to enter his number.

CJ smiled with admiration. "You're good! I like that you changed your username to Lina Martin. I couldn't have found you either. Keep it like this."

She smiled. She knew it was right. It was very much intentional. And now, he knew it too. If something went wrong, her accounts would be clear of suspicion. No more secrets. From now on, there should be no room left for distrust.

"Will you think about what I asked you?" he continued.

"I will. I need to take a shower and go to bed now. You may be on a different time schedule, but I'm drained, and Bug wakes up early. Come with me." She got up from the couch and walked to the spare bedroom. He followed her. "Here! This side of the closet is available if you want to unpack. And you can use this bathroom. As you saw, the other one is sort of cluttered with Ayden's stuff and mine ... It's not off-limits, but I thought having your own space may be more convenient. So, you won't cut yourself when shaving or whatever business you're up to, with Ayden lingering, curious, and nosy. Although it probably wouldn't be bad for him to watch daddy shaving rather than me putting make-up on," she giggled.

He looked at her, cocking an intrigued eyebrow. "Does he follow you in the bathroom?"

"Well ... let's say I don't leave him out of sight. And when I have to, I'm in and out in a minute or less while he's playing or watching TV. By the time he figures out I'm not around, I'm out."

"So, all this time ... you didn't have a minute for yourself!"

A crooked smile spread across her face. "This is why he goes to daycare. You can find clean towels in here." She tapped on the door of the closet just outside the bathroom. "Now, unpack ... don't unpack— It's up to you. You could do it in the morning when I take Ayden to daycare."

"Wasn't he supposed to go back when you returned to work? Please, let's keep him home. I need him here. I'll look after him, I promise."

Her lips curled into another smile. "Okay. We'll keep him home until Tuesday. I'll hop in the shower now."

Twenty minutes later, when CJ returned to the bedroom, he found Ava smiling by Ayden's crib. He placed a tender kiss on her temple, running a gentle hand through her hair.

"He's wonderful. Thank you." His arms enveloped her as she stood there, above Ayden's crib, absorbing his little peaceful face. "You know, I've never made love with a filthy rich woman," he whispered.

Flashing a suggestive smile, she twirled to face him, diving into his eyes. "Um, I'm exhausted. Right now, I can put my legs up only one way, and it's not that way," she purred. "But I promise, tomorrow I'll be just as rich. Even more. My paycheck is being deposited at midnight."

"Sounds good. I'll wait for you to get richer, so I deserve to be called a gold digger," he said, leaning over and placing a soft kiss on her lips.

Another fifteen minutes passed, and none of them could drift to sleep.

"Are you sleeping?" CJ whispered.

"I'm afraid not. I suppose I'm feeling a bit on edge. A lot happened today. Lately—" Ava's response trailed off.

"A lot … Indeed."

Ava was preparing Ayden's breakfast when CJ waddled into the kitchen.

"Coffee is ready. Do you want breakfast?" she asked cheerfully.

"Coffee is good. Where is the closest store to get some essentials? I forgot my shaving kit, deodorant, and other stuff … I had it packed and ready, but I missed the last step—throwing it in my luggage. Or we could go to the mall. You scared me that winter was coming soon, so I got a cold-weather jacket, but I didn't realize it could still be scorching hot in Canada. I need some short-sleeve shirts."

Ava chuckled. "Gosh! I said winter could be here as early as October, and it could happen overnight. But it's only August."

He made a funny grimace. "I see this now."

Ava pressed the fork down, mashing the egg and avocado salad for Ayden. Then she squinted as if she remembered something.

After making sure the little one had everything he needed, she turned to CJ.

"There may be some stuff that could temporarily fix that. Come with me. Here! I'm pretty sure these will fit you," she said, opening the other side of the closet in the spare bedroom.

A few summer shirts were neatly hanging.

"Oh! These are nice." He turned a questioning stare. "May I ask why you have guys' stuff in your closet?" Then stopped and bit his tongue. "You know what? Don't. I don't care to know. Just recently, another wise woman told me to never talk about exes."

"You know I've been married. I hope you're not jealous of a dead man."

CJ blinked, confused. "But … you moved here not long ago."

"I know it sounds twisted. When I returned from Europe, I got rid of most of his stuff, but I kept some. I don't know why …

Still too broken, I guess. I probably wasn't much better when I moved here, so I brought it with me. You know—? Forget it. I'll pack it up and donate it to Goodwill."

"I don't mind if you want to keep it. I'm not jealous of him." A muscle twitched in his jaw as his fingers brushed against hers before taking her hand into his. "Actually, I am a bit jealous. He had you. He found you before I did. I just thought— Never mind. I was just being an idiot, and now I feel terrible." His gaze shifted, embarrassed for doubting her.

"It's okay. It must go. It's time to let go," Ava concluded in a faint voice, heading back to oversee Ayden.

What the hell was I thinking, offering him my deceased husband's shirts?

Quiet. CJ followed her. The atmosphere shifted, feeling utterly heavy and crackling with tension.

"He had good taste," he broke the nagging silence.

Yanked from her thoughts, Ava blinked, tangled, "Huh?"

"The shirts in the closet ... They're nice. High quality. He had good taste."

"Oh, that. That was me. I was the one who bought his clothes. If you like them, you can wear them. It's up to you. Just as a temporary solution, if they fit. I'm sure you didn't have any room left in your luggage after insisting on packing all of Ayden's toys."

CJ winced, shaking his head. "I really like the stuff, and I'd wear it, but ... it'll probably bring back terrible memories."

"Those memories are fading away. It's been over five years. I moved on. Besides, the things I kept were brand new. Dan probably only wore those shirts a couple of times. I don't really have any memories ... good or bad. If you change your mind, you know where they are."

"Before you give them away, I might take another look. I'd still need to go to the store for the rest of the stuff I need. I suppose you don't have a shaving kit, deodorant, or men's cologne stashed somewhere," CJ chuckled, attempting a joke, aiming to ease the dread hanging in the air.

"Um ... I plead guilty. I actually kept a bunch of cologne." A troubled smirk split her face. "You may want to check out the medicine cabinet in your bathroom before you buy anything. I threw away everything else, though. So, no razors and stuff like that."

"Wearing a couple of his shirts is one thing, but smelling like your late husband? No. That's a definite no."

"Would you check that cabinet first? You'll figure out what I'm talking about." Her lips stretched into an awkward smile.

"I'm not wearing his cologne," CJ pushed back, his voice low, so as not to alarm Ayden, who was eating his breakfast.

It was a steep learning curve, but he quickly picked up how to behave around his son.

"You already do, Baby. And I swear it doesn't bother me," Ava said, her tone even.

"What?!" CJ leapt off the chair and dashed to the bathroom. Ava followed him. "All my favourite ones!" He seemed just as taken aback as he sounded.

"I bought them. They are *my* favourites. Please stop acting all weird. If I didn't like you wearing them, I would've said something long ago, don't you think? I have a past, but I don't live in it. Should I have chosen not to have Ayden because I had a kid and lost him? However, if you want something else, you could try one of my unisex ones. Or layer two of these, and you'll smell very unique. But I love any of these on you, just as they are."

He snickered. "And you say I'm weird? Are you sure you don't mind? Just like you, I'd hate to give up on certain ones."

"Have you heard what I said? As bizarre as it sounds, smelling these scents on the street, on random guys, reminded me of *you* lately. Probably that's why I kept them. The real question here is ... why on earth did I unpack these when I moved, while some of *my* stuff is still in boxes? Now, you can continue being stubborn if you choose to. Just stop being silly. Come on now." Looking up at CJ with a reassuring smile, she took his hand, steering him back to the dining room.

He trailed behind, still perturbed and quite unsure.

Ava knew her perfumes. And her taste? Impeccable. What some would call 'a connoisseur'. Nothing too annoying or obnoxious. Always matching her feminine side, a casual outfit, or a special occasion.

Her scent was the first thing that drew him in. That's why he ended up behind her in that coffee shop in Paris. He was sniffing the air, trying to identify the source of that beautiful, haunting fragrance, faintly revealing itself among the usual bakery and coffee smells. He found it. He found her. Later, he picked up the same fragrance on her during one of his spontaneous visits just a few months later. That's when he asked what the name of the perfume was.

Her eyes wide, she parried a bit too quickly, "I can't tell."

"Why? Is it a secret?" he teased.

She wiggled in her chair, blushing. "Oh, no! It's just ... inappropriate."

"It's just a perfume. What could be inappropriate about it?"

"Well, you'd be surprised how many perfumes have truly unfortunate names. And this one? Trust me, sounds really inappropriate. So, I'm not saying it. Not to you. And don't try to make me." Ava's eyes flickered, raising a shoulder, with a nervous half-giggle.

"Ha. Okay!" he gave up, not entirely convinced.

When they started dating, CJ found the perfume in her bathroom.

If she only said the name when I asked, he thought after sniffing the bottle, just out of curiosity. The inappropriate name that Ava didn't want to give? *Voulez Vous Coucher Avec Moi?*— Would you sleep with me?

He remembered he dashed out of the bathroom after discovering the *unfortunate* name.

"Seriously!? This is the name of the perfume you didn't want to tell?" he asked, flashing a mischievous smile, holding the simple, dark bottle of perfume. Already under the blankets, Ava's eyes widened as she slid further down, pulling the sheets over her head. "So, you were looking for trouble in Paris," he teased, hopping into bed, crawling under the covers, and cuddling and kissing her.

"Well, it worked. I found trouble," Ava lifted a playful shoulder, looking into his eyes.

She always smelled out of this world. By then, he already knew she had a perfume collection ... or *addiction*, as she frivolously called it.

30. Make me another baby

Two weeks went by, and Ava still hadn't made a final decision about moving to the UK. Each passing day just brought them closer to the time CJ had to leave. He couldn't afford to back out of his previous commitments.

Through regular video calls, Ayden met his grandparents, uncles, aunts, and cousins. Everyone was thrilled to meet and talk to him, and Ayden wouldn't stop chatting as he got to know them.

One busy morning, as Ava was getting him ready for daycare, a rambunctious Ayden tried everything to evade the rules. Again.

"Ayden Matthew Martin, come here right now!" she called, her tone unwavering.

Buried in his laptop, going through emails, CJ's eyebrows lifted as he shot Ava a puzzled look. "Ayden's last name is Martin?"

Her shoulder lifted in a vague shrug. "Um … He has my last name, of course. This is how it works. I assumed … you knew," her voice nearly faltered.

"I um … I didn't think about this. How do we change it?"

"I have no clue. I suppose you have to do your homework. I won't say 'no' if you want him to have your last name."

"If I want to? He is my son. Of course, I want him to have

my last name."

After taking Ayden to the daycare, Ava shuffled to work. Just in the next room. The perks of working from home!

For a few days now, Ava has been trying to negotiate the possibility of keeping her job. Continue to work from the UK, eventually. She gave no other details but presented it as a prospective idea for the upper suite.

In the living room, CJ spent the entire day on the phone, either making calls or answering them. A couple of frantic and exasperated shouts passed through the door, while the rambling didn't seem to stop.

On the other side of the door, Ava faced her share of bad news. Or maybe it was good news? Whoever wanted to help didn't have the authority to make that kind of decision. And, of course, the CEO was conveniently on a five-week-long vacation. Ava could only hope he'd return from his European trip in a good mood and approve her request. With no other choice, she could only wait and cross her fingers. She hadn't told CJ anything about her intentions yet. Not before she had a solid answer.

When she emerged from her home office at lunchtime, CJ seemed preoccupied and ravaged. "What's your address? Rob has to send me some important documents via DHL, and I need the exact address."

Ava gave him the address and asked no questions. She could read his expression, clouded with a thousand thoughts and worries. Walking into the kitchen, she started making some lunch and called him when it was ready.

"I don't have time. I'm not hungry," his reply fell sharp, avoiding eye contact.

He kept pacing and checking the phone every twenty seconds, as if watching it would make it ring.

"Oh! You should probably eat something. You sound *hangry*," Ava countered. "That phone will ring when it rings. You could eat meanwhile." She attempted to find a silver lining in what bothered him.

Jaw clenched and brows knitted, CJ sat at the table. He stared at his plate, lost in his own thoughts, playing with the food. His gaze finally lifted and fixated on Ava, looking through and beyond her.

That look said a million words. It wasn't hard to guess he was itching to say something.

"Do you want to talk about what's bothering you?"

"According to Canadian law, I only had a year to claim Ayden after he was born. I'd prefer not to talk about it right now," his response dropped plain and heavy.

Ava's heart skipped a few beats. Suddenly, she didn't feel hungry anymore. It was her turn to stand up and pace. Without a word, she turned around and stopped behind the chair she had just gotten off of.

She opened her mouth, not exactly knowing what to say, but she said it anyway, "There must be something. Other ways? Different options?"

CJ slowly set the fork on the plate. The way he looked at her told another million words. Her mind only buzzed louder. All this was because of her own poor decisions. Her stomach coiled, and her entire being quaked, her petty soul ripping at the seams.

"Yes, there is. Adopting Ayden—that's how things stand right now. That's my option. Adopting my own child. I refuse to go down that path. I'm waiting to hear from my lawyers about other options. The lawyers you dreaded so much."

His words cut deeply, and he sounded and looked wounded. Crushed. Without even glancing her way.

Ava felt her knees weaken. Her fingers grasped the back of the chair, dragging herself around and sitting on its edge.

"I'm at a loss for words. I can't say how sorry I am. It's my fault. Tell me what I can do to fix this. Please, don't give me the silent treatment. There must be something we could do," she implored, her voice trembling with distress.

Right then, CJ's phone rang, and he raised a finger, signalling her to pause as he stood up and answered the call. The pacing started again.

Ava couldn't hear the rest of the conversation, but only CJ's part, which was mostly a lot of "a-ha," "okay," "and then?" "how would this go?" and "absolutely not". About twenty minutes later, when the conversation was finally over, he returned to the table, appearing calmer. Almost optimistic. Her heart? Still shrunken.

"It seems there was another case in Canada. The court decided in favour of the father. This is good news, according to my lawyers," he said, and the creases on his forehead loosened a bit.

"Precedence," Ava swallowed her anxiety. "It is good news, indeed. Courts go by precedence. I hope it wasn't in Quebec, though. Quebec has different laws." Concern made its way back, vibrating in her voice.

"It was in Ontario. My lawyers will try to find a Canadian lawyer specializing in these types of cases to represent us. It'll take time, though. Possibly a year or longer." It was only then that he raised his eyes and finally looked her way, noticing Ava was crying quietly. "Baby, I'm sorry!" He dashed to comfort her. "I was distraught … I know, I have no excuse for talking to you like that."

She sniffled, biting her lower lip. "I deserve it."

"Hey!" He grabbed her by the shoulders. "No! No, you don't. Look at me!" And he shook her gently. "Ava! I'm sorry. I needed to do this! I should've shaken you long ago, when I first sensed your insecurities. I need you. I can't get through this alone. Please, let's move on from the past. You need to understand that I'm here to stay. I'm not going anywhere. I love you, Baby." He held her in a long embrace until her remorseful crying finally ceased.

The weeks after the documents arrived were filled with legal meetings. Mostly CJ. He also took Ava along whenever she was available. One day, after coming from the lawyer's office, CJ handed her a pile of documents to sign.

"You're not taking him away from me," Ava erupted. Then, she added quickly, trying to soften her outburst, "I'll read and sign them after work."

"Baby, you're growing paranoid. Look, it's all about me acknowledging I'm Ayden's father. I'll never take him away from you. Never! I promised you. What's gotten into you? I thought you were past these worries." Lips pursed, he paused and nodded slowly. "I'll leave the papers on the table for whenever you're ready. Take your time."

When she finished work, Ava picked Ayden from daycare and started preparing dinner. She cleared the stack of documents from the dining table so they could eat. CJ watched her do it and kept quiet. It wasn't the right moment, and he might make her more suspicious if he pushed.

With Ayden finally in bed, Ava sank onto the couch. CJ slid from the other seat to cuddle with her. She offered a guilty smile, glancing at him, her teeth catching her upper lip. "I'm sorry for earlier. Could you please give me those papers to sign?"

"Right now, I just want to cuddle. Why don't you look at the damn papers tomorrow? It's your day off, right?"

"Yes, it is. And cuddling sounds tempting," she replied, wiggling and nestling into his arms. A rerun of their favourite space show was on the Discovery Channel—the same episode they watched together in L.A. years before.

A flash of another unsuccessful attempt to kiss Ava crossed his mind, and he sneered, pulling her closer. "I have to check on Ayden," she said, attempting to get up.

For nearly two weeks, Ayden slept in his own room, and Ava felt she needed to check on him every so often.

Tightening his grip around her, CJ tugged her back. "Oh, you're not going anywhere. Ayden is perfectly fine. And I need you here."

"You need me here? What for?"

"For this." He planted a wet kiss on her neck before flipping her over, making up for that time in L.A., when she tactfully said she had something else to do.

That one time when she got up to finish whatever it was she had just remembered. *Yeah, right! She had something to do exactly then.*

From her reaction earlier, he already knew Ava was edgy. The last few days had been quite intense. And he figured putting her at ease and reassuring her of his intentions had to be added to the menu. He was here to stay. He took her into the bedroom.

About an hour later, spooned together after passionate love-making, they were fighting to fall asleep. "Make me another baby!" CJ grumbled in her ear.

"What?!" She flinched, appalled by a request that seemingly came out of nowhere.

"Make me another baby. Please," he repeated.

Ava spun around suddenly, blurting, "You can't be serious." Her disbelieving gaze fixed on him. Those pleading puppy eyes. "Fuck, you are serious." She scowled. "You do understand this is not an option. Not anymore. The shop is closed. This time, for good."

"It's exactly what you said three years ago. Yet, right now, Ayden is sleeping in the other room."

Her breath quickened. "Three years ago was three years ago. Ayden got me on the last train to motherhood. Please don't put your hopes up. It won't happen again. Not now ... Not three years later."

"We could look into alternatives. All you need to do is be open to the idea of us having another baby."

She exhaled loudly, eyes rolling. "Oh, God. We're not having this conversation right now. Can we discuss it another time, please?"

The next day, without reading them, Ava signed the papers—initialling only where the lawyer had marked for her to.

"Done. Sorry for yesterday." She placed the pen down,

shrugging. "Would you please double-check and make sure I didn't miss any?"

If I don't trust him, how can I expect him to trust me? I am the one with a 'history'. Less likely to be trusted.

After reviewing the documents, CJ asked her to sign in a few more spots, which she 'missed'. She did.

31. Say 'I do'

The days settled into a rhythm, but CJ felt time pressing against him like an invisible weight. More often than he cared to admit, his gaze drifted to the calendar on his phone, his fingers tracing over it, counting down.

Each passing hour brought him closer to the day when he had to leave and honour previous engagements. Each passing day—another day without Ava making a decision.

His jaw flexed whenever the urge to bring it up nudged him. *Pressuring her wouldn't help.* Still, the waiting wore his patience thin. The countdown? Two months. Then, he had to fly back to the UK. He only clung to the hope that she'd decide before then. Give them both time to breathe. To plan. To settle. If not, he'd keep doing what he did before. Crossing oceans, chasing stolen moments 'halfway around the world', making a life in the in-between.

That morning, the scent of fresh coffee filled the kitchen as Ava stood by the counter, making Ayden's breakfast. Cross-legged, Ayden sat on the floor, eyes glued to the TV, giggling at his favourite show.

Ava took another sip of coffee, savouring it, until her stomach flipped, then flopped. Her fingers tightened around the mug as nausea clawed its way up her throat. She barely made it to the bathroom before the coffee came back up. *Not again.*

Huffing, she pressed a cool hand to her forehead. For days now, she had felt drained and off-balance. The fatigue, the nausea, the way food no longer sat right.

'Tis the season. The answer came automatically. She reached for her phone and added *vitamin D* to her shopping list. From September to April, vitamin D was always on the menu. All the months with an "R" in their name. But September had slipped away, and she hadn't even picked up a bottle yet.

CJ emerged from the bedroom. "Did you throw up again?"

"Yeah. Sorry, I woke you up." She pushed a smile. More of a sneer.

"Maybe you should see a doctor."

"Must be some bug Ayden gifted me. Why do you think I call him Bug? Just stay away from us, so you won't get it."

"That's going to be hard. You look so beautiful this morning," he said, stealing a kiss.

"Well, you've been warned. If you get sick, it's on you."

"Too late." He kissed her again, more passionately this time.

Right then, Ayden came running into the kitchen, squeezing between them and wrapping himself around Ava's leg.

Lately, whenever Ava and CJ cuddled around him, Ayden had spontaneous jealousy spells. He'd drop off whatever he did, climbing between them, claiming Ava's attention.

Instead of admonishing Ayden for coming into the kitchen, Ava hugged and comforted him. He was still adjusting, and she figured it wasn't the right moment to remind him of the rules.

"I guess we'll have to be more careful and reserved around this one." She hissed like a ventriloquist, lips not moving, words barely articulate.

"Or we continue until he gets used to it, and it will be part of life. He needs to know that Mama and Daddy love each other. We love him. We are a loving family. Showing our affection builds confidence and trust, and he'll feel safe," CJ murmured in Ava's ear.

"Or that!" she softly agreed, smiling.

Giving her one quick kiss, and then another, he whispered, "Nothing will stop me from kissing you whenever I feel like it. I can drop Ayden off at the daycare. What do you say, Bug?" he asked, taking Ayden in his arms before adding, "Then I'll hit the gym, and if you send me the shopping list, I could stop on the way back."

"There are a few items on that list that I'm very particular about. I don't want to make it too complicated for you. We could go together when you return."

"Okay. We'll go together," CJ agreed.

It was her day off, and it was chores day. With the boys away, Ava began doing laundry, organizing the toys, chopping and prepping to make lunch when CJ returned. Just removing the bedsheets felt like an exhausting task. She ended up lying on the stripped bed to rest for a minute and fell asleep.

When CJ came back, he found Ava still asleep. He pouted. She had said so many times before how envious she was of people who could nap. Worry grazed at him, thinking she might feel worse than when he left.

"Ava!" he called, touching her arm.

When she didn't react, he shook her gently.

"Huh! What?" she jumped, startled.

"Are you okay?"

"I'm fine. I don't know … I felt tired. I thought I'd rest for a couple of minutes— I must've fallen asleep. What time is it? I'm so hungry."

After loading the groceries for the following week into the shopping cart, Ava began toward the pharmacy department. Her shopping list detailed a few seasonal supplements for herself and Ayden. Leisurely pushing the shopping cart, CJ took his time, checking out all the aisles. He suddenly stopped and reeled back. Just a quick double-take, before calling out to Ava, who was a few good steps ahead.

"Yes." She swivelled on her heels.

"Come here. You must see this." She returned to where CJ was now leaning on the shopping cart's handle. "Look at that." His eyes glinted as his head motioned to his right.

"Where? What should I see?" she asked after failing to notice what might have caught his attention.

"Up there—the list of items on this aisle." He gave more specific directions, a mysterious grin flashing across his face.

She still couldn't see anything to justify his grin. "What is it? I see, but I don't understand what you find amusing. Feminine hygiene? Darling, it's not my aisle anymore." A patronizing sneer split her face.

"Read again. The one before last?" he insisted with an unspoilt look.

"Pregnancy tests? Fuck, CJ! You can't be serious. I told you. The shop is closed."

With an insinuating scorn, CJ tilted his head.

"You have thrown up almost every day in the last ... what? Almost a week? I found you napping—" He listed just a couple of pregnancy-specific symptoms she had shown in the last few days.

"Please, stop! It's just a bug. It'll go away. I already feel much better. I'll start taking my supplements. I'll be fine," Ava quickly dismissed the idea.

"It's only a few bucks, remember? Just so we can rule out this theory. Humour me, please."

"Fine! You and your theories—" Ava caved in, rolling her eyes.

She made a beeline down the aisle, grabbed a random test, and continued her quest for vitamins while CJ browsed other aisles.

"Have you put it back?" he asked when Ava returned to join him.

"What?"

He smirked. "The test?"

"Nope. I wouldn't miss the chance to humour you."

"Where is it?"

"In my backpack." She displayed an amused sneer. "I didn't steal it. I have already paid for it at the pharmacy counter. What do you think? I'm not walking with you at the main tills with a pregnancy test."

A satisfied smile split CJ's face. "Okay."

"Would you please wipe that smile off your face? You'll see. It's not what you think, Doctor Oz. I warned you not to put your hopes up." She rolled her eyes again.

Once home, before unloading the groceries and putting them away, Ava rushed to the washroom.

"Take your backpack with you," CJ shouted from the entrance.

"Why would I take my backpack in the bathroom?"

"The test? Didn't you say it's in your backpack?"

"Geez! You don't give up, do you?" she grimaced.

"You said you can't wait to humour me. So, humour me! Can I come with you?" He eagerly offered, scurrying behind her.

"Really?! You're going to watch me pee on this?" Ava swayed the test in his face. "Don't worry. It's not revealing right away. I'll call you when I'm done. You'll be there for the big reveal of 'here goes nothing', okay?" she blustered with frustration and ran into the bathroom. "Please go away! Stop lurking out there! I can't do it," she shouted a minute later.

Then she heard him snicker and imagined his brows wiggling. "Okay, I'm leaving. Call me when you're done."

"Duh!" Ava reacted, exasperated. "You can come in now," she called another minute later.

He stormed in, precipitated, only to find Ava sitting on the floor, her back against the bathtub.

"What? What is it? Where is it?"

"It's on the counter. Face down. You can do the honours. It takes ... well, here says one minute. Let's give it two," she said after a quick check of the instructions on the packaging.

"Okay, what should I look for?" he asked anxiously.

She flicked a hand. "A plus or a minus sign. To avoid any disappointment, please expect to see a minus. Negative. Meaning not pregnant."

"And the plus would be ... positive...? Pregnant?"

"It only goes with the logic, yes. But you won't see that."

"Why are you sitting on the floor?"

"You put things in my head. I need to be here, just in case."

"Okay ... Time's up?"

She shrugged, trying to keep in check the lump in her throat. "I think so."

Shaky, sweaty hands picked up the test from the counter and nearly dropped it, but managed to catch it.

He blinked at the test. "It's a minus, Baby!" he said with a disappointed grimace.

"See? I told you. No surprises there," Ava replied confidently, and began to get up.

"But ... It's crossed off," CJ added, a sneer spreading on his face.

"Crossed off? What?! Give it to me!" Incredulous, Ava jumped and snatched the test from his hand. "No. This can't be right." She dropped to the floor in disbelief, wide-eyed, glaring at the pregnancy test. "Fuck! You almost got me! I keep forgetting you're an actor!" she exclaimed through tears.

"Baby ... Please tell me these are happy tears. This is good, right?"

"What the hell? Why?! How is this even possible?" she ranted through tears, flustered.

"Baby, let's get you off the floor. Come here." Trembling and sulking, Ava grasped the hand he offered and got up. CJ pulled her into his arms, holding her tightly. "Look! I'm so frigging happy right now! I want another baby, you know it. I know you had a hard time when you were pregnant with Ayden, but I'm here now. I'll be here with you. All the way. However, it's entirely up to you, and if you don't want to have this baby, I'll be fine with whatever you decide."

She wiped the tears, looking at him in shock. "Absolutely not! Do you think I'd kill a baby? My baby? After I blamed God for taking a kid away from me? Probably He's testing me, watching me...? See what decision I make? I'll do everything in my power to have this baby. I realize things can go either way, and I'd be devastated if— But I won't start this journey with loss in mind. Most miscarriages happen early in the pregnancy. Let's not tell anyone yet. Not until a bit later. Not your family ... Nobody. Well ... Let's have another baby!" She said it all at high speed, as thoughts invaded her mind, looking to escape.

"Let's have another baby! I love you so much. We won't tell anyone." He agreed with a broad grin and set a delicate kiss on her lips. "Now, I won't leave you here. Not in your condition. Leaving you here is out of the question. You'll have to come live with me."

"Yeah ... It's in the works. I didn't tell you, but I'm pulling strings to get permission to work from UK. The CEO is returning from vacation on Monday, and I hope to get the okay."

"Do you think you'll be able to work? I won't let you continue working. No way! You need to take care of yourself and that baby. And I'll hire someone full-time to help with Ayden and the house."

"I'm just pregnant, not disabled. I can take care of my kid."

"I know, Baby. I know you can. But you'll need help. Didn't you say you weren't allowed to do anything when pregnant with Ayden? You can't possibly look after a two-year-old and not do much of anything at the same time. And, as much as I'd want to, my schedule in the next months won't allow me to be of much help."

"Well, no two pregnancies are the same. Besides, I hope there are better protocols now. Let's see what the doctor says first."

"Doctor? Shit! We have to leave and get you a doctor. I'll start making arrangements."

"Wow! Hold your horses! I can't just pick up and leave. I

already have a doctor. He can start me on whatever protocol, and when the time comes, I'll ask him to share my file with the doctor in UK. I need at least a month to prepare," Ava projected an ad hoc plan.

"A month! Why that long?"

"A month, yes. I need to organize and plan for our things to be shipped. Do you think I can leave with just a suitcase, like I'm going on vacation? I won't be able to travel back and forth while pregnant. And won't be any easier when the baby arrives. Let's not panic." Her brows shot up as she checked the time. "For fuck's sake! We're getting ahead of ourselves and forgot about Ayden! It's almost five. I have to pick him up."

"I'll go," CJ offered.

"No, you can't. Dropping him off is one thing, but picking him up is a different ballgame. The daycare won't release him to you. Your name is not on the list."

He stared at her in disbelief. "What? Really, Ava?!"

"I didn't think you'd want your name out there. This is the only reason I didn't update the emergency contact list. I swear."

Relieved that Ava was, once again, a step ahead of his impulsiveness, CJ puffed a smile. "Oh! That's ... that's good. You did the right thing. You always do."

The same evening, CJ posted on his social media:

"I wish to address a matter of personal significance. After careful consideration, I have decided to end my engagement with Ellie, which happened a couple of months ago. This decision was made privately and with the utmost respect for the relationship we shared. I ask that the privacy of all parties involved be respected as we move forward.

I remain grateful for the time we spent together and have nothing but the highest regard for Ellie. I will not be providing further details, as I believe it is a personal matter best left between us. I would appreciate your understanding during this difficult time."

A week later, Ava's heart rushed as CJ turned to her with a serious look. "Ava, can you call a babysitter? I'm taking you out on a date night!"

She cocked a surprised brow. "A date night?"

His grin widened. "Yes! A proper date night. We've spent too much time in the shadows. We haven't dined out since we were friends."

"I'm … not sure. But I guess it won't be any different than back then, right?"

CJ nodded with resolve. "I booked a private room. So, there's that."

Ava's eyes sparkled at his excitement. "I like that!"

As they prepared, CJ pointed at a simple but elegant off-white dress from her wardrobe.

"This one would accentuate your beauty," he said

Before they stepped inside the restaurant, he caught her arm gently, his expression turning serious. "Listen, Ava," he began, his words heavy with something intense. "I know you're a planner, and I act on impulse…" He paused, pressing his lips. "I want to prepare you for why we're here."

She winced, her eyes widening, as she stumbled on her own thoughts. An entire legion of thoughts.

"What do you mean?"

"Baby, we're here to get married," he said, his voice steady but almost cracking with passion. "All you have to do is say 'I do'. Unless, of course, you say 'hell no,' in which case, I'll take you to dinner and try again tomorrow." A charming grin spread across his face.

"Getting married? But … didn't you say…?" she stammered, still processing his words.

"Forget what I said before." He took a step closer, discreetly placing a tender hand on her belly. "Things have changed since. This baby will have my last name from the start. And I want us to share the same last name on the birth certificate. You haven't changed your mind about marrying me, right?"

She beamed a smile and shook her head, eyes locked into his.

"Okay, let's do this." Taking her hand, he hauled her inside.

As they entered, Ava gasped in surprise. Her eyes registered Nina and Sean. Rob and Lisa, who had flown in from the UK, were also there, chatting with Trent, their lawyer. All waiting. With a quick glance and thumbs up, CJ signalled all was good.

Shock clear in her eyes, Ava whispered beneath her hand. "Did you tell them?"

He leaned in with a hint of mischief in his eyes. "Just that we're getting married."

Her nose slightly crinkled as she returned a similar gaze and a subtle nod of approval.

During the ceremony, they were all smiles and, when their turn came, they rushed to say, 'I do', hardly processing any of the words. All that mattered? Their shared commitment and a future together, sealed in love and the promise of forever.

32. You must be a Superwoman

Ava remembered the house. She once waited for CJ in front of it. That day, only a few years back, when he drove her to Edinburgh to meet Eliza for lunch, seemed like a lifetime ago.

The pale November sun was performing at its best, warming the air and the ground. A mesmerizing kaleidoscope of colours adorned the path from the airport all the way up to the house, turning the countryside into a true art gallery.

The 'London party' started descending from the rented vehicles and Emily's car. She was the only family member to greet them at the airport.

It's been a busy week for Ava. Her mind felt like a scattered jigsaw puzzle. She had met her new doctor in London, spent hours unpacking boxes, and tried to charm Ayden into a new sleep schedule. All while battling the pregnancy fatigue that tried to stop her.

Today was important. They were ready to share the news with the family. All the news, with the entire family. Time was running short, and they knew this was the perfect moment to get everybody together. As witnesses to their wedding ceremony, Rob and Lisa were half-aware of the plan.

When the cars pulled up, the house seemed quiet. That changed pretty fast when Patti and the rest of the family emerged, loud and full of excitement. CJ knew his family really well. He quickly slipped out of the car, gesturing for them to quiet down.

"Ayden is sleeping," he said, as the commotion somewhat faded.

After a brief exchange of hugs and kisses, the women clustered around Emily's car, peering inside, curious to see the sleeping angel. A discreet hint from Ava, and CJ went to get Ayden out of the vehicle, dispersing the cluster of enthusiastic, curious women.

"I'm so glad he's sleeping. Ayden has been quite restless since we moved to London. You'll have the chance to interact with him when he wakes up, which should be in about an hour," Ava apologized to everyone.

"CJ, your room, dear. There's also a cot for Ayden." Patti rushed to give them some direction.

"So, this was your room?" Ava asked when she stepped in, looking around, scanning the place. "It's nice."

"Yes, my old room. Of course, there was no cot back then," he whispered, placing Ayden in the crib. "Let's go outside now."

"Oh, no. I'm staying here with Ayden. I don't want him to get scared when he wakes up and doesn't know where he is. But you go and apologize on my behalf. I think the other baby needs a nap, too. I'll come outside when Ayden wakes."

As estimated, about an hour later, with Ayden in her arms, Ava stepped outside. She paused on the deck for a moment, telling him about Grandma and Grandpa, and everyone waiting to meet him. They had met before through video chats, but this time was different.

CJ dashed over when he spotted them.

Carrying Ayden, Ava lost her balance as she stepped on a loose tile on the stairs. "Oh, shit!" CJ bolted to catch them and made it just in time. "For God's sake, Dad! I thought you fixed the bloody tile," he shouted, livid.

"Everybody knows and goes around it, so I didn't think about it anymore," Don replied.

"Well, obviously not everybody knows about it," CJ uttered, shaking his head. "Are you okay, Baby?" he asked Ava after placing Ayden down.

"I'm fine, and you're overreacting. You don't need to be a pain, you know? I'm not made of glass," Ava said, her voice low.

As easygoing as kids that age are, Ayden began playing and running around with his cousins. Patti showed the little ones to the small wooden hut that housed a family of fluffy bunnies. Meanwhile, Emily, Cindy, and Ava carried on a side conversation, sharing stories and laughter, while most guys hung around a charcoal grill.

"You say you're tired, but I don't know ... you look so beautiful and radiant! If I didn't know better, I might think you're pregnant," Emily made a frank remark in her own very distinct style.

Ava chuckled. "What?! Oh, God!" With a headshake, she deflected the comment.

"Only if I didn't know better. But I know better. So, I'd say you look happy!" Emily quickly changed direction.

"Well, I am happy!" Ava agreed, taking a brief glimpse at CJ, who was chatting by the grill with other family members.

After visiting the bunnies, Patti returned with the kids. "Ayden said something I couldn't quite understand..." she mentioned casually.

"What did he say?" Ava squatted and asked Ayden, "Baby, what did you tell Grandma?"

"You have a 'pool in you bey', Mama."

Ava snarled as if she didn't understand. "What?!"

"Mama, you have a 'pool in you' bey'. Here, mama," he insisted, pointing to Ava's middle.

Luckily, as she was crouched, what Ayden had pointed to wasn't very clear. Mystified, she stood back up. "Okay, Baby. You can go and play now," she dismissed him. When Ayden took off to play with the kids, Ava continued, "I have no clue what he's trying to say. He says new words every day, and he's started to get a very British accent since interacting with CJ. Half the time, I don't get what he says the first time he says it, anyhow. I guess we'll figure it out in time," she canned the incident, holding a straight face.

Phew, that was close!

There was only one person in the world with whom Ava and CJ shared the news—Ayden. After the first ultrasound, they told him he was going to be a big brother.

"Everything looks alright. You know how it goes. Stay off your feet as much as possible and follow the protocol. At seven weeks, the embryo is the size of a peanut," said Doctor Wong.

"Pearl," Ava corrected him promptly.

"Huh?" the doctor asked, tangled.

"The size of a pearl," Ava repeated. "My Peanut is right there, with his daddy." She pointed at CJ, sitting across from her, bouncing Ayden on his knees, neck stretched to look at the computer's screen.

Amused by her comment, Doctor Wong agreed, "Oh, yes, the size of a bigger pearl. That's correct."

To Ava, Ayden was 'Peanut' since he was in the womb, and for several months after birth. That changed one day, when she realized he might grow up believing his name was 'Peanut.' He was nearly three months when she began calling him by his given name.

About fourteen weeks into this pregnancy, the little life growing inside Ava already had a name: Pearl. Too early to tell the gender, but Ava and CJ previously decided they didn't even want to know. Not until the baby arrives. They'll be just as happy and grateful.

And knowing ahead of time ... why so much fuss about it? What is it for? It's not like there is a return policy if you don't like it. And this pregnancy was so unexpected! Why not go for more surprises? They only wanted to know a few things. Is everything going as it should? Is the baby fine and healthy? Is it only one? Yes, it was only one.

Ayden shared the news before Ava and CJ could. "Mama has a Pearl in her belly." Luckily, nobody spoke 'Ayden' fluently.

"What do you want to drink, my dear? A glass of wine? Red? White?" Patti asked Ava.

"Just water, thank you."

"Oh, dear! Water is plentiful and falls from the sky in Scotland. That's why Scots invented scotch, so they look fancy. Water's too plain for us," Patti chuckled. Ava laughed at her joke, referencing the reputed Scottish rain. "I see the boys are almost done with the grill. Let's get you a seat at the table. I'll gather the kids. Ask Emily to bring you a blankie if you find it cold."

"Thank you. I'm quite Canadian. I'll be fine," Ava chuckled. When Patti left to gather the kids, she signalled to CJ that she wanted to talk to him. "Bug, little traitor, almost gave away. Nobody understood what Ayden said, and I played dumb. Also, Emily made a remark earlier, but I brushed it off. I believe it's time."

CJ glanced around. Everybody was there. It was time. He nodded discreetly.

With their mouths full, the kids were quiet, probably looking forward to dessert. When everybody else had food on their plates and drinks in their glasses, still standing, CJ wrapped his arm around Ava's shoulders.

"Hey, everyone! Thank you for the homecoming party. Ava and I are truly grateful to all of you who showed up for us. I know I didn't apologize to everyone for certain things from the recent past ... but let's leave the past in the past, where it belongs. We have some news to share with all of you. Firstly, there will be a party—a *proper* wedding party. The news is ... I want to introduce my beautiful wife, Ava Lina Hamilton, to all of you. We got married a month ago, in Canada."

Patti gasped, looking around, scattered, trying to understand if she'd heard right.

"And I wasn't invited?" Emily reacted promptly.

"Oh, don't be upset. I wasn't invited either," Ava giggled.

"Well, you were there, though. You had to say, 'I do'. I guess it works the same way in Canada, right?"

"Oh, I just happened to be there. I was invited for a 'date night'. A proper one," Ava mocked, giving CJ a hilarious look.

He grinned. "Perfectly true. Ava didn't know until we got there. Huge thanks to Rob and Lisa, who were also present as our witnesses, and they are already planning the wedding. Here, in Scotland. So, please save the date—December 26th. I apologize for the short notice or almost no notice. But I'm not sorry. I needed to keep it as low and as secret as possible, and I hope you all understand why."

"I didn't believe you'd elope when you said it," Patti cut in, looking and sounding disappointed. "And ... a winter wedding? Why don't you wait until spring, at least?"

"Mum, there was no time for other arrangements. It had to be done because ... we have more exciting news." He paused and looked at Ava with a grin beyond cheerful. "We are expecting another baby. Hence, the winter wedding."

"I knew it! Oh. My. God! I don't know who's a better actor between you two!" Emily exclaimed, springing off her chair to welcome Ava into their family. "It's official now. You are family. You are my sister," she squeaked excitedly.

Congratulations poured in. Patti overcame her initial instinct and expressed genuine happiness for the couple. Don now understood why CJ had snapped earlier and apologized for the 'bloody tile', promising to fix it the next day.

Rob and Lisa looked at each other, somewhat taken aback. Trusted enough to be invited as witnesses when the two got married, the 'expecting another baby' part was deliberately skipped. Ava and CJ felt the need to explain why they had decided to wait.

"You two. How do you do this? You get together, and ... bam, a baby pops out," Cindy chuckled. "I'm so happy for you. I really am. And you, lady, you must share what your secret is."

"There's no secret. Or, if there is, then it really is a secret. Even *I* don't know it. I thought we were just having fun. And, as you said, *bam*," Ava giggled.

"I think I know your secret. You must be a Superwoman!" continued Cindy, her witty comment eliciting another chuckle from Ava.

"I was thinking the same. That's the only explanation, right?" Emily supported Cindy's theory, drawing a roar of laughter from the entire gathering. "When are you due, by the way?"

"Well, if I make it till the end, it should be May. Again. We'll be the Bulls'," Ava giggled.

A satisfied beam widened on CJ's face, sensing that everybody agreed with his decisions. And it wasn't hard at all. Ava's character fell right into place in this family.

Until now, Ava had never been curious, never asked how CJ went about submitting her part of the application for the marriage license.

"Who did you bribe to submit my part of the application? As I know, I should've done it in person." She only assumed he had snuck the application among the paternity papers.

"I did my homework, as you asked me. There are ways around it. If you *can't* do it, you can delegate. Don't you remember delegating Trent, our lawyer?" CJ asked with a complicit smile.

Completely unaware, Ava signed for Trent to represent her at the Registry.

The romantic story CJ shared sparked a lot of *awe*

reactions.

"I would've never thought my brother had a romantic bone in him. Well, nothing like this will ever happen to me," said Emily, in her emblematic style.

"Darling, you missed the opportunity. Besides, I didn't have such a good role model around when we got married," Finn, her husband, replied in a ridiculously genuine tone.

33. Three generations of Hamilton boys

The wedding was kept small and private. Family members only and a handful of CJ's trusted friends. All dedicated. And they managed to keep it under wraps. However, it was only a matter of time before the news came out. But CJ had everything under control. Fully prepared. After the wedding, he'll post pictures of his new family. The message to his fans was ready. Just waiting for the right moment to be pushed out.

He hoped many would take it as a 'done deal' and move on quickly. And, just as he expected, they embraced his decision. Most of them, anyway.

The wedding party took place at one of the castles where CJ took Ava when they first met. Once a backdrop for their budding romance, the castle stood as a testament to their love, and it felt surreal to see everyone celebrating.

"You should see Ayden. CJ did his hair. He looks like a little man," Lisa said, peering through the door as Emily and Eliza were helping Ava to get ready.

For her wedding day, Ava made a simple request to CJ—for both women to be her bridesmaids. Something wrenched in his stomach, but he caved.

Assisted by Eliza, Emily was fixing Ava's veil. Emily stilled for a second before suddenly dumping the lacy piece of fabric into Eliza's hands and rushing across the room to the restroom.

When she returned, Ava shot her a concerned gaze. "Em, is everything alright? Did you throw up?"

"I'm fine. Just a bit nervous," Emily replied.

Ava looked at Emily's reflection in the mirror. "Well, that would be my part. You know, right? Take five. You look pale." She stood up, helping Emily to the couch in the corner of the room. Then, she asked Eliza to bring some water. "Em, are you pregnant?" she continued when Eliza stepped out.

Emily avoided Ava's gaze. "What? No, I'm not."

It sounded, though, as if she were trying too hard to mask something.

"You're pregnant," concluded Ava. "Does anyone know?"

"I'm not pregnant."

"Please tell me at least Finn knows," Ava prompted Emily.

"Of course, Finn knows. Look. This is your moment. Let's enjoy your moment. I'll be just as pregnant tomorrow, and that's when I'll tell everyone, okay? Let's get you ready."

Ava hugged Emily. "Congratulations, Mama. Thank you! I truly appreciate it." Eliza returned with the water. "Eliza! Let's give Emily some space. Would you, please, help me?"

A faint knock on the door fifteen minutes later made Emily get up and open it. "What are you doing here?" She squeezed out quickly. "It is bad luck to see the bride before the wedding, don't you know? Shoo! Go away."

"Okay-okay! I'll go." CJ put his hands up, dragging his feet in slow motion. "How's Ava looking?" He flashed a grin, pivoting sharply after only a few steps.

"You'll see," Emily shot back, still standing in front of the door, fiercely guarding it. "Now go. Shoo." She waved him away. "Hey!" she called after he took a few more shuffled steps.

CJ turned swiftly, hope flickering in his eyes. "What?"

A blazing, broad smile illuminated her expression. "You look dapper. Love you."

"I love you, too, Em!"

"Who was it?" Ava asked when her sister-in-law returned.

"A curious cat," she replied.

Ava cast a funny look. "Do cats speak in Scotland?" All three burst out laughing.

"It was CJ," Emily said.

"Did he need anything? Is Ayden okay?" Ava turned, alarmed.

"Come on, sis. Please. It was only CJ. There are so many people out there to tend to Ayden. He's fine, or we'd know. Okay, final touch-ups. Five minutes left."

Leaning over, CJ was talking to Ayden when Ava started walking down the aisle alone. Behind him, Rob touched his elbow. Ayden's hand in his, CJ stood up and swung, his eyes flicking from Rob to Ava.

A wave of pride washed over him as he realized how far they had come. A grin spread across his face as he watched her glow in her elegant gown, happy tears glinting in his eyes. Ayden stared too, and it took him a few moments to realize who she was.

"Mama!" he called, pulling from CJ's hand and running to her.

Ava knelt and hugged him. "Look at you, how handsome you are! Let's walk together to Daddy."

"Hey, little man. Is it you giving your Mama away?" the priest taunted.

"No. My Mama." Ayden buried himself in Ava's gown, and every soul in the room burst into laughter.

"I guess I'll have to take both of you now," CJ teased, another wave of laughter filling the room.

He asked Ayden to pass him the rings and nodded for Cassie, his niece, to come and get Ayden.

Later that night, during the wedding party, when it was time for speeches, everyone took their turn according to the schedule. Ava thanked everyone for being there, especially CJ's family, who welcomed her and made her feel like one of their own.

"—I also want to thank my beautiful maids of honour. As you all know, this is not my first rodeo. And it's not Eliza's first rodeo by my side, either. She was once my flower girl, and she is today my maid of honour. Eliza, thank you for being you—the beautiful, smart, generous, wonderful woman you've become. I love you. Emily—my other wonderful maid of honour. Selflessly, Emily chose to keep a secret from almost everyone in this room, and I'm about to divulge it. Only three people know it, and I am honoured to be one of them. How did she put it? She didn't want to ruin my moment. She said the situation would be the same tomorrow. That's when she'll share her secret with everyone. Well, my moment is over, and … it's already tomorrow," Ava closed after glancing at the massive clock on the wall, its arms showing a few minutes past midnight. "Emily, the mic is yours." With a kind smile and a wink, she handed the microphone to Emily.

"Okay, I thought you were my sister, but you put me on the spot," Emily began, taking the mic. "Ava is an inspiration to me. She is amazing, smart, beautiful … Let's not forget her being wise, caring, brave, and I'm proud to call her my sister, not sister-in-law. Finn and I followed her and my baby brother's example—"

"Hey! Watch what you're saying! You are the baby of the family!" CJ cut in, eliciting a rush of laughter from everyone.

"Well, true, but this baby is going to have another baby. Here, the secret is out," Emily's eyes sparkled with happiness as she shared the news.

Everybody's attention switched to Emily and Finn.

"I'm so proud of you," CJ told Ava, and kissed her before whispering in her ear, "It looks like they can handle themselves and have fun without us. Let's sneak out of here."

"I want to have fun, too," Ava whined, making a funny grimace.

"Oh, you'll have. I promise." He returned a wicked look, wiggling his brows, before he planted yet another kiss on her lips.

The promise and his hot breath sent shivers down her spine. CJ grabbed the microphone and announced that they were leaving, but everyone was free to continue dancing, eating, drinking, and having fun.

In the hospital waiting room—outside the Operating Block—with Ayden asleep by her side, Ava wrapped her arms around herself, winding, her soul shaking. Restless.

Her past flashed through her mind. *Not again! Please, God! You took enough from me! If you want my life, take my life. Don't squeeze it out of me, one ounce at a time.*

Almost one hour passed. It felt like an eternity, and nobody came to tell her anything. *Well, if something went wrong, it would've happened already. I would've known by now*—Ava kept telling herself.

Rattled, Rob and Lisa rushed through the doors, running straight at Ava.

"What happened?" Rob asked.

"He was shot," Ava whimpered.

"By whom? Why?"

"I don't know who. It's my fault," Ava howled.

Lisa took Ava into her arms. "Shush. Don't say this. It's not your fault. Where is he?"

Ava wiped the tears streaming down her cheeks, moving her head towards the doors leading to the Operating Block. "Still in there. He was shot in the shoulder. It doesn't appear to be life-threatening, but the waiting is killing me," she wailed.

Until now, only her heart had roared as she held back her tears. With Ayden asleep, her emotions took charge and ran free.

"He'll be fine. We are here. Cassie's on her way to take Ayden to our place. She'll watch him."

Not coming from the operating block, a doctor approached

the group. "Missis Hamilton?" the doctor asked, looking at Lisa.

"I believe you want to talk to that Missis Hamilton," Lisa said, pointing to Ava.

With shaky hands, she wiped a new set of tears. She stood, her breath shallow, winding under a brief, dizzy spell, before Rob wrapped a supportive arm around her.

"I was told your husband is stable. The surgeons are still operating to remove the bullet from his shoulder, but he'll be fine. However, before going under, he asked that you be checked on. He mentioned you are expecting?" The doctor continued toward Ava.

A determined headshake contrasted with her half-voice when she spoke. "I'm fine. I'm good. I need to be here."

"Just a routine check. Blood pressure, EKG ... Just to make sure your stress level is under control and won't harm the baby. It will only take fifteen to twenty minutes."

"You go. We'll be here if Ayden wakes up," Lisa urged Ava.

One early January morning, London woke up to a white scenery. Overnight, it snowed just enough to cover the ground. The morning air was crisp, breaths curling into soft clouds as Ava and CJ walked toward the park, Ayden bundled up between them.

Ava's eyes sparkled with childlike excitement as she tugged on CJ's sleeve. "Come on! Before it melts!" she pressed CJ, literally bouncing on her toes.

He smirked. "Are you sure this is for Ayden and not for you?"

She shot him a playful gaze before turning to their son. "What do you think, Bug? Playground?"

Ayden barely needed the invitation. With a delighted squeal, he wriggled free from their hands and took off, his little boots squeaking over the snow. His giggles echoed as he ran toward the playground, arms outstretched, the puffball on his hat bobbing wildly.

Other children were already there, their laughter mixing

with Ayden's as he flopped onto the ground to make a snow angel. Ava crossed her arms, shivering slightly, but her smile never faded as she watched him play.

CJ slid an arm around her shoulders, pulling her close. "Happy now?"

She leaned into him, eyes still locked on Ayden. "Very."

The day was bright, the sun reflecting off the snow. A flash from a brighter object blinded Ava. Her gaze flicked upward, and in a split second, strength surged through her. She pushed CJ out of the way just as a blast of gunfire split the calm morning air. He fell, and she threw herself to the ground.

No other gunshots after that one.

"Are you okay? Have you been hit?" she asked, simultaneously, checking herself for eventual wounds.

Ava's eyes made a complete scan around, registering mothers and babysitters huddled in the snow. Kneeling on the cold ground, she glanced at Ayden and the other kids, still playing. Then she turned her attention back to CJ, eyes falling on the dark-coloured patch, gaining on the green of his jacket. A deep groan escaped CJ as he tried to get up. Moving fast, Ava stopped him with just a finger nudge, and she partly unzipped his coat to evaluate the severity of the wound. Her eyes stopped on the gushing wound in the right shoulder, under the collarbone.

"You'll be okay. Don't move," Ava demanded, swiftly pulling the scarf from around her neck and shoving it under his jacket, applying pressure. "Keep pressure on it and stay put," she barked, then crawled to where the kids continued playing, innocently unaware of what was going on.

Composed, she cradled as many kids as she could in her arms and ducked down to the ground, urging the others to dodge as well. Pretending it was just part of the game. Only a minute had ticked by on the clock, although it felt like an eternity.

Ava scrutinized the area where she had spotted the bright flash earlier and noticed the commotion. Bystanders had immobilized and disarmed the criminal. Ducked to the ground, one mother was already on the phone with the police, reporting the crime. Others checked on the babies in their strollers.

The sound of mixed sirens whined louder. Finally in handcuffs, the criminal was taken into custody, while another police crew began questioning everyone still hanging around. Most, just out of curiosity, when they figured out who the victim was.

With expert precision, the paramedics swarmed in, providing CJ with first aid. In no time, he was loaded into the ambulance. Sirens blaring, they drove off at full speed. Another police crew offered to take Ava and Ayden to the hospital, closely tailing the ambulance.

Terrified, Ayden was crying in Ava's arms, intimidated by the police uniforms and all the mayhem that underscored the seriousness of the situation.

"Mama. Where is Daddy?" Ayden whined as Ava wiped his tears, promising that everything was okay.

"Daddy is being taken to the hospital, so the good doctors will check on him. This nice lady is taking us to the hospital to be with Daddy."

She herself wasn't sure that 'everything will be okay'. She checked CJ's wound. Given its location, she knew it shouldn't be life-threatening. But the doctors will have the final say on that.

At the hospital, Ava rushed in with Ayden in her arms, trying to keep pace with the paramedics pushing the stretcher.

"Baby, I'll be fine. I love you," CJ said, trying to reach her.

As the gurney was hauled through the Operating Block doors, someone held Ava back, stopping her from going past. Her eyes stayed locked with his until the doors shut. The doctors and operating room staff were all on the clock, waiting for this case.

Crushed, she stood in front of the doors for a long time before stumbling to the chairs by the wall, slowly easing into one.

In court, Ava's heart ached as she felt a strange connection to the grieving father, his pain mirroring her own. They both carried the

burden of loss. The heartbreak of a child gone too soon.

When word spread that CJ had built a life for himself, complete with a wife and a son, the ripple effects reached far and wide. A teenage girl, infatuated with CJ, tragically ended her life, leaving her father's soul orphaned and seeking revenge.

The father stood before the cameras, hunched and defeated, eyes devastated with despair. "I should've seen it!" he cried out, his voice breaking. "I should've been her shield!"

His words touched Ava, stirring her own regrets and self-blame. She could see in his eyes the torment of what might have been if he had only paid attention to the signs.

When he turned toward Ava and CJ, guilt washed over him as he stuttered an apology. "I'm sorry," he choked.

Yet, even if he poured his soul and admitted to his crime, the spectre of justice was above and beyond all of them. Covering her eyes with both hands, Ava remained still as he was taken away from what used to be his life.

"Did you know?" she asked CJ.

Cringing, he nodded. "I promised I'll protect you."

"You're right. I don't need to know all the speculations, rumours, and gossip out there. But from now on, I want to know what I need to know. I'll leave it up to you to decide what I need to know."

Adamant that he was doing fine, CJ convinced Patti and Don that they didn't need to rush over. Maybe in a few weeks. Just not now. Weeks later, they flew in from Glasgow, ready to support. By then, his wound had healed, leaving a scar that would likely never fade. Back in the gym, as he eased into light workouts, CJ began to feel like himself again.

After dinner, everybody went to bed.

"What took you so long?" Patti asked Don when he returned with the glass of water.

"Well, I believe CJ has recovered well. They were going at it.

I had to wait downstairs and give them some time. I should've stayed longer, I guess. They were still at it."

"You, dirty old man! You didn't listen to your son making love to his wife."

"I didn't listen. But I'm not deaf."

In the morning, with Ayden's monitor in hand, CJ joined Patti and Don in the kitchen. "Good morning."

"Good morning," Patti greeted him. Don just mumbled something. "Somebody had a good night," Patti tittered. CJ squinted at her, trying to figure out if the subtle undertone he perceived meant something else. "I'll make your coffee. Is Ava coming too?"

"She's still sleeping."

Coffee was ready, but glancing at the monitor, CJ saw Ayden getting out of bed and rushed upstairs.

"Look, it snowed last night. After you eat breakfast and Daddy's coffee, we go outside and play in the snow," CJ told Ayden minutes later when they returned, dressed and ready for the day.

Outside, Don was sweeping the fresh snow off the stairs. While preparing Ayden's breakfast, Patti asked CJ if it was possible to have the bedroom downstairs.

"Why? The bed in that room is quite small."

"You two need your space, and my leg is bothering me."

CJ cast an interrogating look. "Mum! What did you hear?"

"Nothing," Patti answered a bit too rushed.

"Mum. Please don't say it to Ava. She'll be mortified."

"I didn't hear anything, personally."

"If it wasn't you ... Then who? Dad?!"

"It was my fault. I forgot to take a glass of water when I went to bed last night. I asked Don to bring me one. But he didn't listen. He just heard. You know? Ava is your wife. You are two adults living a normal life in your own home. I was pregnant four times. I sort of know how it goes."

"Oh, God! Mum, please. Let's change the topic," CJ said as he covered Ayden's ears, eyes rolling and shaking his head.

When Ava entered the kitchen, Patti was putting the dishes away. "Good morning."

"Good morning. Have you slept well?" Patti asked.

"Yes, I slept well, thank you. How about you? How did you find the bed in that room?"

"It was good. However, I asked CJ if we could move into the bedroom downstairs. My leg is bothering me. I can't do stairs."

"I don't see why not, since Marissa is away for another two weeks. But the bed is barely enough for her."

"I'll make your coffee. What do you want to eat?" Patti changed the topic.

"Eggs and bacon. Thank you," Ava answered, feeling spoiled. "Where are the boys?"

"Outside, playing in the fresh snow. It snowed quite a bit last night." Wrapped in her comfy poncho, Ava waddled to the window, sipping her coffee. "Ava, dear, your breakfast is ready." Patti joined her, and they both watched the happy party outside. You couldn't tell they belonged to three different generations. "A penny for your thoughts. What's troubling you?"

Ava puffed an anxious smile. "I got so excited when it snowed a few weeks ago. I convinced CJ to take Ayden to the playground, afraid he wouldn't remember our good times playing in the snow in Canada. I'm watching now, and he's playing in the snow for the first time. Well, I feared for nothing." She sighed. "He won't remember this snow until the next, just as he doesn't remember that one from a few weeks ago. Instead, we almost lost CJ. I wonder where the bullet would've hit if I hadn't pushed him. How good a shooter that guy was—?"

"Oh, dear! Don't. It's too stressful ... And you'll never know the answer. You don't need this right now. What's important, is that CJ is doing well. This is what you should see when you look out this window. This is what I choose to see."

"Three generations of Hamilton 'boys' playing in the snow

for the first time," Ava let her thoughts out, nodding quietly.

"Now, that's the spirit. Come and eat. It's getting cold."

Marissa was the nanny CJ hired. Her bright smile and warm presence instantly made their home feel livelier. As she settled in, Ava discovered a heart-wrenching truth. Marissa hadn't seen her family or children for over six long years.

Six years! Just thinking about it made Ava's stomach drop. *I was sick just being away from Ayden for less than six days.* The thought of being separated from her child for that long was beyond her comprehension. The idea of leaving behind young children and returning to teenagers struck Ava like a nightmare.

Determined to help, she approached CJ and tried to persuade him to buy Marissa a flight ticket to Honduras.

"We'll be busy with the wedding anyway, and she deserves this. Especially at Christmas. Another year will go by before we can be without her," Ava insisted, her voice laced with empathy.

CJ nodded. "I'll ask Lisa to buy her a ticket."

"It was my idea. I should pay for it."

"No way."

He took on the role of caring for Ayden, ensuring everything ran smoothly while Marissa was away.

Then tragedy struck. The shooting changed their lives, casting a shadow over their happy plans. Rob, Lisa, and their daughter Cassie have been their steadfast allies, lending a supportive hand in those frantic weeks.

When the news reached Honduras, Marissa wanted to return. But Ava remained firm. "We're fine. Everything's under control."

That night, CJ snuggled up to Ava in bed, feeling cozy and happy. "I missed you. Last night was terrific. Tonight will be even better, with Mum and Dad downstairs."

"You know? I was thinking— I found it strange that Patti asked to move into Marissa's bedroom. She says her leg bothers her and she can't do stairs. But their bedroom, at their house, is upstairs," Ava remarked.

"Probably her leg bothers her. Mum's not getting any younger," CJ replied nonchalantly.

"Just like the rest of us. It must be something else, though. What do you make of it?"

"Baby, please! You are overthinking, and you're killing the mood," CJ said, caressing and peppering kisses on her protruding baby bump.

"Babe. You didn't recover completely. I know you were in pain last night. Let's take it slow. Do you think they heard us when ... you know—?" Her voice dropped, lined with concern.

"I don't know. And I don't care. It's our home. We are adults, and you're my wife. We're not doing anything wrong. We're doing what a husband should do with his wife." He maintained the same nonchalant tone.

"Oh, my God! They heard us. I mean, me. They heard me."

"Why are you saying this?"

"And you know they did. What you just said ... It sounded like something Patti would say."

"So what? Why do you care?"

"I can't believe you. You kept this from me, and now you want to— Ugh! Stop acting with me!" Ava turned her back, pushing his examining hand off her.

"Baby, I'm sorry. I didn't want you to feel like you do right now. This is why I didn't tell you. To protect your feelings."

"Was I that loud?"

"You were loud ... and I loved it," he smirked.

Ava scoffed at the naughtiness in his voice. Although she couldn't see his face, she pictured the wiggling brows pairing that tone. "Was it Don? He didn't look in my eyes all day today."

"Honey, please don't ask questions you don't want to know the answer to."

Ava covered her face, horrified. "Good grief! It was Don."

"Do you think we are the only couple that has had this happen to them? I walked into my parents doing it when I was ... I don't know ... four or five? I had no clue what they were doing. But I do now." She could hear his grin through the words as he spoke.

"Why did you have to tell me this? You know I have a wild imagination," Ava shot back, her voice muffled from under the covers she pulled over her head.

"Good. Now you're even. You can start feeling better about it." Propped on his left elbow, leaning above her, CJ kissed her shoulder.

"You're terrible, you know?" she said, turning and glaring into his eyes.

He pinned her to the mattress, placing an ardent kiss on her lips. "This terrible guy loves you so much."

34. That thing was demanding a life

Out of all the seasons, spring was Ava's favourite, and this year it coincided once again with the last few months of her pregnancy. Aiming to keep it away from the world's prying eyes, she didn't venture out anymore.

"Come with me tonight," CJ tried to entice Ava.

"To the show? I'm not coming, but I'll watch it," she countered, convinced that now, when she was showing even through bulkier winter coats, spending more than a few brief minutes anywhere wasn't a good idea. It's a TV station—the incubator of gossip—and she'd have to take her coat off. So, that was an absolute 'no'.

"A lot has happened lately in your life. You are a married man now. It came as an enormous surprise to your fans. Everybody knew you were engaged and, only a few months later, you're married … to another woman. Wait! What?! What did we miss?" the show's host began.

"I know. Yes, I am now a happily married man with a wonderful family. It was just as unanticipated to me, but I made my choice, and I expect my fans will support my decision," CJ answered, sensing that he might get cornered.

"Your son … Rumour has it you're going through the

adoption process for your wife's son. How is that going for you?"

"My wife's son?" CJ scoffed, shaking his head. "Ayden is *my* son. Nearly four years ago, my wife and I were in a relationship. Ayden is the result of our love story. Things happened, and ... we've been apart for three years. Ava wanted to protect me, and— Well, I didn't know I had a son. But fate brought us back together. Indeed, it is quite a process to get Ayden to have my last name. We're not talking about an adoption process, though. According to Canadian laws, I only had one year to show up and claim him as being mine. I missed that window, and now the court must decide on it. But I'm optimistic. Ayden is my biological son, and I'm convinced the court will decide, rightfully, in my favour."

"Oh, I see. Tell us about your wife. I believe everyone wants to learn more about Ava. How did she sweep you off your feet, snatching one of the most eligible bachelors in Hollywood? What makes her special to you?"

"I don't even know where to begin." He paused, his expression radiating happiness. "Ava is fantastic. I could sum up everything about my wife in just a few words. Ava is brilliant, fun, kind, thoughtful, supportive, loving, and lovable. She's ... everything! She's my best friend, my beacon, and my soulmate."

"Some say that you acted on impulse; that you may not know each other too well. What would you say to those who believe this?"

CJ scoffed. "It is my belief that we know each other very well. We've been friends before anything else. Our relationship, as convoluted as it was, didn't involve arguments or fights. It was and still is pure harmony. And you probably would want to know why it ended then." His voice softened. "Well, it ended because we've both been a bit confused and strong-natured. She feared the limelight, and I was a blockhead who didn't get it. Somehow, our pride got in the way, and we failed to do what was right. Both of us. We talked about our errors ... All is fine now. We knew we still loved each other. That was the easy part."

"Is she still terrified of the limelight?"

"I believe she still is. Sometimes. Well, my fervent fans don't make it any easier for us. But Ava is not active on social media, and she doesn't follow me. This is what we agreed upon. She only knows what I feel she needs to know or be aware of. I must protect my family, and I believe nobody should blame me for taking care of my family."

"You are doing the right thing. It is our duty, as the heads of our families, to protect our loved ones." The host's voice carried empathy.

CJ's gaze looked straight at a camera lens, casting a wide smile. "I only hope everybody understands it."

"The shooting—"

"That's something I don't like to talk about," CJ's voice rose slightly as he interrupted the show's host, irritation clear in the tightening of his jaw and the fire in his eyes.

"I understand. So far, we have only talked about the matching aspects of your and Ava's personalities. In my experience, however perfect a relationship may appear, some things don't align completely. Could you name something your wife does, but you don't like or don't fully agree with?"

"Well ... Like I said, she's perfect." CJ tossed a laughter-inducing, wicked smirk toward the audience. "No, really, I don't know. There was something ... and it's not that I didn't like or agree with it. It was more that, in the beginning, I couldn't understand it. Ava likes olives. Let's make it clear. She doesn't eat two olives or just a few. She can eat a full bowl of olives in one sitting. Like popcorn. I recall a time three years ago, when we lived together. We went shopping, and she picked a humongous jar of olives. A three or five-kilo jar. I don't remember exactly. My first thought? She must be drinking a lot of Martinis." The audience roared with laughter. "I remember suggesting a smaller one because I don't eat olives. Her reply?! The olives were for her, not for me. And let me tell you, that jar was gone in less than two weeks." Laughter filled the space once more. "However, olives started to grow on me. I never did before, but I now eat olives. Not like she does, but I do," CJ resumed.

"Now, we have your wife on the line ... to approve or disapprove your answer to the next question. Good evening, Ava." CJ blinked, surprised.

She beamed a wide smile. "Good evening."

"How is your night going?"

"I'm having fun watching your show and eating olives as any respectable Olive Monster should."

Laughter erupted from the audience again.

"Is Ayden with you?"

"It's quite late. Ayden is in bed, already asleep."

"Ava, here are the rules. I'll ask your husband a question, and he must be the one answering. You only need to approve if he answers correctly or disapprove if the answer is incorrect. Would you take on this challenge? We are live."

A composed smile arched Ava's lips before she spoke. "If I can watch you while I talk to you, then I know we're live. Sure, I'll take the challenge."

"Do you trust your husband will know the answer to the next question?"

"I trust him, yes."

"So, CJ ... What is one thing that you do, and you suspect Ava doesn't like, but she never told you?"

"Oh!" She raised an inquisitive brow. The question was more than she had expected.

"Um, I'll have to guess here—if it's something she'd never told me, I can only guess, right? I believe Ava doesn't like me riding my motorcycle. Whenever I leave on my motorcycle, Ava looks at me like she sees me for the last time. And she asks me at least five times to call her when I get wherever I'm going."

"Ava, is CJ's answer correct?"

Her gaze deepened, and her voice wavered. "Um ... somewhat. I don't feel comfortable knowing he's on that thing. I lost two very close friends in motorcycle accidents, so, yeah. I guess I don't like it, but—"

"Then the motorcycle will have to go," CJ decided right then.

"No … I know how much you love it. I'd never ask you to give it up," Ava's voice wavered again.

"You should've told me, but we can discuss when I come home."

"Thank you, Ava. Enjoy the rest of your evening. Now, CJ, I think you're good on your own with the next question. What is something that you do, and Ava doesn't like, but she told you?" the show host closed.

CJ dipped his head, puffing a smile. "She is the wise one. The calculated one. The planner and the logical one. And I'm the impulsive one. More often than I'd like to admit, I don't stop to think or plan ahead. She has a way of tempering me whenever I tend to go … overboard. And it has happened so many times. I'd need an entire show to give you examples. However, all those times, I'm absolutely sure she didn't like what I was doing or what I was about to do. She looks at me and starts: 'Hold your horses' or 'Easy cowboy'." The audience giggled. "And I know I must slow down or stop and think twice, eventually. We communicate and plan everything together. Since we became friends, she was the one I called when I needed honest advice or support in making a decision, and she never imposed her thoughts on me. She's not telling me 'Do this' or 'Do that'. She asks me questions, helping me find my answers and make my own decisions. In short, she is my best friend, my beacon, and my soulmate."

"CJ, I know you don't like to talk about the shooting, but this is about Ava. She saved your life. Witnesses say that you could've been fatally shot if she didn't push you out of the way."

CJ fidgeted before answering. "I believe that's true. Though Ava doesn't like it when I say it. She insists we don't know how good a shooter the guy was, and he would've missed, and probably I wouldn't have been shot at all if she hadn't pushed me. But I know which way she pushed me and where the wound is. I could've been dead, indeed. I'll be forever grateful for her presence of spirit in that moment. We don't talk about this because, for some reason, Ava feels it was her fault, and I don't want to perpetuate her fears. You can't be guarded enough, nor feel responsible for every lost soul out there. We can only hope decent people surround us, but we can't be certain. We all go to bed in our safe homes every night, but we're not sure we'll wake up the next morning."

In the kitchen, Marissa was tidying up after dinner. Lounged on the couch in the family room, Ava cheered for Ayden, who played with CJ on the floor. From where she sat, her eyes flicked to the window, suspiciously squinting at the unfamiliar car that had just pulled in front of their house. More cautious and alert since the shooting, her stomach churned. It always did whenever something unusual appeared on the horizon.

"Are you waiting for anyone?" she asked CJ.

"No. Why?"

"A car I don't know just pulled out front."

CJ stretched his neck to look outside. "Oh, I know who that is. I'll talk to him. You can stay where you are. He won't come inside."

She smiled, grateful that she didn't have to leave the couch and 'go into hiding', as she usually did when someone outside the family came over.

Fifteen minutes later, she shook her head in disappointment, sighing when she glanced out the same window and saw CJ leaving on the motorcycle. Her heart sank for a minute before CJ returned inside.

"I thought you left," she said, pushing to sound casual.

"I would have told you if I had left."

"Was that—? I could swear I saw you leaving on your motorcycle."

"Oh, you saw my motorcycle ... which, by the way, is not mine anymore. I sold it. It was the new owner riding it. The guy you saw—Ben."

"You sold it! Why?"

"I told you it had to go. It's gone."

"You said we'd talk about it," Ava muttered, tugging at her lower lip.

CJ sat by her, pulling her into a caring hug. "Why talk? It's mine. I mean, it was mine. I don't want you to stress over it. I decided I wouldn't ride it anymore. Why keep it? Listen. I made this decision, and I'm fine with it. Now you don't have to worry anymore, okay?"

Earlier that day at the studios, CJ ran into a stuntman he had worked with. "Hi, Ben. How are things going?"

"Hi, CJ. All good. Listen. I wanted to ask you something," Ben said.

"Sure. What is it?"

"I watched the show last night."

"Oh."

"It was amazing. You were great, as always. I was talking to my wife, and..." Ben hesitated. "If you ever decide to sell the motorcycle, just know I'm interested. I'm not sure I have the money right now, depending on how much you ask, but I'll figure it out."

"You know what? Come and get it whenever you want. For you, it's free."

"Oh, no! I'll pay. We have some savings, and— Thank you, man. You are the best!" Beyond enthusiastic, Ben shook CJ's hand.

That very evening, Ben showed up to get the motorcycle, insisting that CJ accept the money. Their savings. All of it. Overly excited, Ben decided he'd ride it immediately.

Driving around the area, on their way home, Rob and Lisa spotted 'CJ' on the motorcycle. After watching the show the previous night, like everyone else, their first thought was to check on Ava.

"Your brother's crazy. He said the motorcycle has to go, and what does he do the very next day?" Lisa shook her head. "And he's riding like a maniac. No wonder Ava doesn't like it. Let's swing by. She might be worried sick right now." She shot Ava a quick message announcing their visit.

Eyebrows raised, Rob and Lisa exchanged glances, surprised to find CJ home when they walked inside. The couple figured he might have just gone for a quick ride and returned before they arrived. *At that speed, of course!* Lisa thought. Nothing was said aloud. *Maybe CJ had slipped out quietly, and Ava had no clue.*

As usual, at eight precisely, Ava's fitness tracker alarm went off. Time to take Ayden to bed. They said, "Good night," and walked out of the family room. The doorbell rang.

"I'll get it," Ava said, detouring to the door to open it while concealing her belly under a poncho.

To her surprise, two police officers stood at the entrance. The woman, the same female officer who had driven her and Ayden to the hospital over a month ago, took the lead.

"Good evening, Madam," she began. "I got this," she added, glancing at her partner after her sharp eye caught Ava's baby bump when the poncho briefly unwrapped.

"Good evening, officers. How can I help you?" Ava asked, unsure why the police had shown up at their door. *What could've happened?* She tried to peek past the officers, searching for clues.

"Madam, may we come in? I believe it would be better if we sit."

Ayden clung to Ava's leg, intimidated by the uniforms and the weight in the officer's voice.

"Should I call my husband? I assume you want to talk to him."

After a moment of hesitation, "I'm afraid that's not possible, Madam. We are not bringing good news. Your husband is in the hospital, fighting for his life. We could drive you to the hospital," the female officer said.

The male officer swiftly stepped inside, meaning to catch Ava if she collapsed.

With a distressed grin, Ava's voice rattled as she flicked her hand, pointing somewhere behind her. "Must be a mistake. My ... my husband is home."

"Madam, I'm really sorry. We can take you to the hospital right away. We'll wait here for you to get dressed."

"No, you don't understand. This is a mistake. I'm telling you, my husband is home," Ava continued, her voice firm this time. "CJ!" she called.

"Yes, darling."

The police officers stared at each other, puzzled, at the sound of CJ's unmistakable voice.

"Could you come here, please?"

Sensing the urgency in Ava's voice, CJ materialized in no time.

The female officer seemed to bounce back from the perplexity quicker than her partner. "Good evening, Mister. Mister, do you know where your motorcycle is? We have reasons to believe it may have been stolen."

Ava gasped. "Oh, no! Poor boy!" she wailed, clutching CJ's arm.

"It wasn't stolen. I sold it earlier today. We haven't closed the deal formally yet, but the guy is legit. He didn't steal anything," CJ clarified.

"Do you have any of the buyer's information? He was in an accident and had no documents on him."

"Accident? Oh, no!" CJ reacted.

"He's in the hospital in critical condition. We believed it was you riding the motorcycle, that's why we're here. What's his name? Do you know where he lives? Does he have a family? Any details could help."

"Um, his name is Ben Smith. I work with him. I know he has a family. A wife and two young kids, but I have no idea where he lives."

"Over forty hits on Ben Smith. Try figure!" The other police officer said after running the name in the system.

"Oh! That car, out there … is his. He left with the motorcycle. How bad is it?" CJ asked, voice dripping with concern.

"I'm not going to lie to you, sir. The doctors aren't optimistic. They're not sure he's going to last the night. Sorry to have bothered you. He's the same build as you, riding your motorcycle … that's what threw us off. And the face … well, there's not really a face left to tell," the female police officer revealed.

Before CJ could brace her, Ava nearly collapsed.

"Okay. This must be our Ben Smith," the male police officer said as he returned after looking up the registration plates on Ben's car.

CJ confirmed.

"Sorry again. We must go. Have a good night, Mister. Madam," the female police officer said, giving a brief nod before they left.

Right then, breaking news was talking about CJ Hamilton in the hospital, in critical condition, after a motorcycle accident.

"What the heck?" Lisa shouted just as Ava entered the family room, supported by CJ.

"Poor boy," Ava kept mumbling as CJ took her to the couch.

"What's going on?" Rob asked, stumped.

"I'll need you to switch to 'damage control' mode. We gotta go. I'll fill you in on the way. I'll get Marissa to take Ayden to bed, I'll change and come back in a few minutes," CJ pouted, troubled. "Baby, will you be alright?" Limp, on the couch, Ava nodded. "Lisa, can you please stay with Ava until we come back? If the doorbell rings, don't answer. Rob, we'll ride in your car and go undetected." His words flowed with urgency.

"What happened?" Lisa asked after CJ left, voice thick and conflicted.

"Just before you arrived, CJ sold his motorcycle to this guy, Ben, and he was involved in an accident. The police mistook him for CJ," Ava's voice came out shaky and faint, barely above a whisper.

"So, it wasn't CJ who we saw," Lisa concluded more for

herself.

Rob frowned, connecting the dots in his mind. "Ben! Ben Smith? CJ's stunt?"

"Yes, Ben Smith," Ava mumbled. "CJ's stunt?" She didn't know the last detail.

"Yes, Ben's doing CJ's stunts," Rob confirmed. "How bad is it if they couldn't tell it wasn't CJ? He's built almost the same, a bit shorter, but he looks completely different."

In a small voice, Ava explained what she had just heard. "It's bad. The police said he may not make it."

Rob's brows remained knit in concern. "Fuck! Oops, sorry," he apologized, realizing Ayden was still there.

"Thank you, Marissa," Ava said when the nanny came in to get Ayden, who was still clinging to her. "Baby, please go with Marissa. She'll tuck you in."

"Mama, story."

"Not tonight, baby. Mama is not feeling well. You'll be a good boy. Marissa will tell you a story, okay? Nighty-night!" Ava kissed and hugged Ayden tightly before letting him go. Her stomach squeezed as her eyes followed the two until they turned to go upstairs. "He has two young kids," Ava murmured, turning back to Lisa and Rob. "I mean, Ben has," she added, noticing their confused faces. "I shouldn't have admitted last night to CJ about not liking him riding the damn motorcycle. Dang! That thing ... That thing was demanding a life. I couldn't even look at it in the garage."

"Oh, my! Let me tell you. This is why we stopped by. That Ben guy was riding like a maniac. It was bound to happen. I thought it was CJ, and I told Rob we had to swing by and check on you. I couldn't believe CJ would do that to you," Lisa said.

Ava sighed. "Well, he promised, and he delivered. He always does. He didn't even tell me until the guy left with the motorcycle. Just like you, I thought it was CJ when Ben left. Last night, he said we'd discuss, but we didn't. He said it was his, decided it had to go, and it's gone. I guess it's really gone now. I don't imagine there's anything left of it."

The doorbell rang again, and CJ stormed down the stairs. His jaw stiffened, instantly turning livid at the sight of their front yard trampled by reporters and cameramen.

"You guys are like vultures. I have nothing to say. A good friend of mine is fighting for his life right now. Why are you even here? If it were me, you'd be here for what? Feeding off my wife's pain? You have no respect. Shame on you!" CJ's biting words lashed at the reporters.

Shortly, a few police cars whined in to keep order.

"CJ, who was riding your motorcycle?" a more daring reporter asked, taking a step forward.

He cringed, struggling to keep his temper in check. "It is not my story to tell. I'm sure the police will have a report for the public soon. All I can say is that, as you all can see, I am shaken and hurting for my friend, but I'm alive and quite well. Now you can all leave. There's nothing more here to see."

"The hospital! Let's go back to the hospital," someone shouted, and the cohort of reporters scattered, clearing their front yard.

"Now, let's go to the hospital," CJ said to Rob as he returned inside. "Baby, I believe they won't come back. However, don't answer the door. I'm not sure how long it will take. I must be there to offer my support to Ben's family. You go to bed and don't wait for me up, okay?" he continued, setting a kiss on the top of Ava's head.

"Okay! Take care, you two. Don't worry about me. I'll be fine," Ava replied, her voice dim.

CJ signalled Lisa to look after Ava, and she confirmed with a nod.

"Ava dear, why don't you go to bed? You need to rest," Lisa

said after the two men left.

"Do you think I can sleep now? I keep thinking about those kids."

"Yes, I know. It's sad. But my God, that guy— Well, I guess it must be a job requirement. I don't think these stunts know what fear is. The concept of danger must be unknown to them. Well, you can't do anything about it. CJ is there to offer support. Do you want me to make you a calming tea? Look! You go to bed, and I'll bring you a tea."

"My back hurts. I guess I could stay in bed, at least. Thank you, Lisa."

35. You are an angel

CJ stood among the sea of mourners, his hands clasped in front, shoulders heavy with grief. The weight of the loss pressed down on him, but he wasn't the only one carrying it. Ava couldn't be there, but her absence didn't mean she didn't care. As the crowd began to thin, he stepped away, pulling out his phone. He dialled Ava.

"I believe Ashley could use some of your kindness," he said quietly.

A soft exhale arrived from the other end. "Is she there? Put her on."

CJ passed the phone to Ashley, watching as her tear-streaked face relaxed a bit when she heard Ava's voice.

She nodded briefly, murmuring, "Thank you," and her grip tightened on the phone as she listened.

"—If you ever feel your friends or family don't know how to support you through your pain and be there for you, please call me. I'd gladly offer a shoulder to cry on. I've walked in your shoes, and I understand how it feels. Feel free to come over anytime. I'm home most of the time. I've rarely left my house lately, and I don't expect to go out much in the coming months. You'll see what I mean if you decide to come over. We could have a play date for the kids."

When the call ended, Ashley wiped her cheeks and looked

at CJ. "Ava wants to meet us," she said, her voice breaking with emotion. "Whenever we're ready."

Lips pressed, CJ nodded. "Whenever you are."

"So ... Ayden's father died? Did I get this right?" Ashley asked, returning CJ his phone.

He shook his head. "Please don't believe all the rumours. Ayden is my son. My wife, however, lost two husbands and a son. I met Ava and fell in love with her not too long after her second husband passed away."

"Oh, I'm sorry to hear that."

"Grieving and healing ... well, it's a process. I was completely smitten with Ava, but I knew any chance of being with her was nonexistent until she was ready to let go of her past. We've been just friends for quite a while before we graduated and moved to the next level."

"Oh, my God! Tell Ava I'd love to meet her. She sounds like an incredible woman."

"That's my Ava. Between you and me ... Nobody has to know if you know what I mean. She's pregnant. That's why she's not here today. Only the family knows. And now, you. We want to keep it this way for as long as possible. Eventually, until the baby arrives. About two more months."

"Oh, no! I understand the police came to your place first. They mistook Ben for you. Was she home?"

"She's been home a lot lately, so yeah. Luckily, I was home too. Still, she was completely shaken."

"Last month, the shooting, now this? And she's pregnant? How is she holding up?"

"She's strong, wise, and worth meeting. Please take the time to get to know her. She's kind, caring, knows how to listen, and has a wicked sense of humour—probably not fitting to mention right now. I sense you two will get along very well."

Ashley nodded, her lips arching into a bitter smile. "I don't think you know how much Ben appreciated you. Working with you... He was thrilled to have your motorcycle. That's all he talked about that night, after the show. He wanted it so badly. Just like Ava, I didn't have a good feeling about it." A tear rolled down her cheek. "And exactly how she couldn't tell you, I couldn't tell Ben. He was so excited when you said he could have the flipping motorcycle. But Ben? He didn't have a realistic sense of danger. I knew he was speeding before I read the police report. I knew Ben," Ashley wiped her tears.

"Here. Ava and I decided this belongs to you. We believe you could use it right now," CJ said, returning the envelope with the money that Ben insisted on paying for the motorcycle.

"But ... Ben wanted to pay for it. He told me you said it was free for him, but his ego was bigger than Buckingham Palace. He didn't want it for free. This was all we had left of our savings after we moved here before the baby arrived."

"It's still yours, and the motorcycle is gone. It wouldn't feel right to keep it. Ava and I have more ideas we'd like to discuss with you, but I don't think now is the right time. When you feel better, please call Ava. Her number's inside."

"I will, for sure. I promise. Thank you for this." Another bitter smirk tugged at the corner of her mouth as Ashley accepted the envelope.

A few weeks later, Ava's phone buzzed, and she glanced at the screen.

"Hey, Ava, it's Ashley. I was wondering if this would be a good time to stop by. The kids would love to meet Ayden and play."

Ava's eyes flashed toward Ayden, who was playing on her bed.

He was finally back to his usual energetic self after a few days of sniffles, but she kept him home for one more day, just to be safe.

"Sounds perfect," she said, already pushing back the covers.

If nothing else, it was a good reason to drag herself out of bed.

Nearly an hour later, Ashley stepped in, balancing seven-month-old Brian on her hip while Simone, her three-year-old, clutched her other hand. CJ was out, running errands. Talk about perfect timing.

"Come on in," Ava smiled warmly, crouching to Simone's level. "I bet Ayden's going to be so excited to meet you."

Simone peeked up at her shyly before catching sight of the toys scattered on the floor. Without hesitation, she let go of Ashley's hand and scooted inside. Ava laughed, stepping aside to welcome them in, already feeling the warmth of much-needed company.

As Simone played with Ayden in the family room under Marissa's watchful eye, the two enjoyed tea and chatted mostly about kids.

Ava snuggled and played with baby Brian. "He's such a good baby. I can't wait for little Pearl to be born."

"Oh, is it a girl?" Ashley asked.

"No. I mean, we don't know. We didn't want to know. It's a surprise baby. A real surprise," Ava replied to Ashley's curious question, going on about how the name Pearl stuck.

"Oh, a real surprise. I see. Ben said—" Ashley halted, shaking her head as if chasing away a troubling thought. "Never mind. He said a lot of silly things. I don't know where he was hearing or coming up with all that stuff," she said, tears shining in her eyes.

"Did he say I'm much older than CJ?"

Ashley winced in discomfort. "I can see now all that was pure speculation. I'm sitting here with you, and I can tell you're not."

"Look closer. Not everything out there is speculation. I'm much older than CJ, actually. Fifteen years. You do the math, and you'll understand why my babies are surprises or miracle babies. Both of them."

As she said that, CJ strolled in, and Ashley began getting ready to leave. "Leave? Why? Is it because I came home? The kids appear to have such a good time." Placing the grocery bags in a corner, he turned to Ava, "Darling, have you shared your ideas with Ashley yet?" He took baby Brian off Ava's arms, bouncing and playing with him.

"Ideas?" Ashley's brows arched with curiosity.

"Yes. We want to do something for the kids," Ava revealed. "I'm thinking about an education savings account. For each."

"No ... No. You don't have to. I couldn't—" Ashley stammered.

"But we want to. All you need to do is open the accounts, and I'll deposit the money monthly," Ava continued.

"Ben's family won't like this. They still refuse to believe the accident was all Ben's doing. Somehow, in their pained minds, they still believe it was CJ's fault. I'm sorry, CJ. They'll think I'm selling my kids ... my soul. I can't."

"Pain is a strange animal. I fought it many times. There's nothing more painful than losing a child. Try to understand them. I suppose sometimes it's easier to blame others than your own. Ashley, we're not buying your kids. They are and will always be your kids. Nobody needs to know where the money is coming from or that there's money coming. Look! The money is mine, not CJ's. I lost a son to cancer, and currently, I donate to a charity for kids fighting cancer. All I'll do is redirect it. This way, I'll know exactly where the money is going. We're not buying, and you're not selling anything. It's just repurposing, that's all. I don't want to force this on you. Take your time. Consider this carefully and let me know. Think about their future." Ava tried to persuade Ashley.

Only a few days later, Ashley called again. As she considered the offer, she couldn't help but think about her children's future. After reflecting, Ashley realized they deserved more opportunities. Determined to give her kids the best possible chance for success, free from any financial limitations, she made her decision.

Ava smiled. "Now, this is very wise of you. Have you opened the accounts?"

"Not yet. I'll meet with someone at the bank tomorrow."

"Excellent. Let me know when it's done. I'm really happy you

made this decision. Don't ever feel bad when you know you're doing the right thing for your kids."

"Thank you, Ava. You have no idea how deeply grateful I am.
CJ was right about you," Ashley's voice trembled.

"Was he?! Huh, I wonder what he said."

"You can ask him. He missed mentioning one thing, though.
You are an angel."

Ava chuckled. "Ha! Thanks. Take care, and please visit us.
Bring the kids. Soon enough, there will be four of them playing ...
Or just cooing."

"Good morning, sleepy head. Happy Birthday!" CJ met Ava when
she woke up.

He lay next to her, watching and waiting for her to open her
eyes.

"Good morning. Thank you, Babe! You know, you need to
stop doing this," Ava purred.

He beamed with a naughty grin. "Doing what? Loving you?"

"I don't mind if you keep doing that, but watching me while
I sleep is kinda creepy. I now know where Bella's got it from. Remember when she watched me all night in L.A.?" she asked, her
voice still sleepy.

The grin widened on his face. "She didn't get it from me. *I*
got it from her. I suppose she was playing matchmaker. I sort of
confessed to her that I loved you." CJ reached to plant a kiss on
her lips. "How do you feel today?"

"Like a huge Orca, ready to give up, but not really. Do you
know female Orcas are the leaders in their communities? When
they get ready to retire, they pass the role down to their daugh-
ters." CJ cringed, confused. "When in San Diego, this old Orca
was preparing to retire, training her daughter to take on the role.
The daughter took it too seriously and thought she was already
the boss. Mama Orca wasn't ready to give up on her status yet,
and she didn't like the attitude. They got into a bit of an argument,

and the trainers had to stop the show, separate the two and give them time to chill." Ava paused, groaning loudly as she tried to move. "Anyway—unrelated topic. All this Mama Orca wants is for this baby to be out of there and in my arms," she said, lazily rubbing her belly.

"Three more days, Baby. Three more days."

She groaned again. "Orca needs a coffee. Is everyone up yet?"

"They are. Messing up your kitchen. Making you a birthday cake."

Ava scoffed. "Marissa's kitchen. Haven't been there in a while. They'll have to report to Marissa for the mess. I don't give a damn about the kitchen right now."

Patti and Don flew down to London with Emily and Finn for the baby's arrival, but also for CJ, Ayden, and Ava's birthdays. They've been celebrating birthdays for over a week already.

"Okay. You stay here. I'll make you a cuppa, and we can have coffee in bed."

Ava flung a mischievous sneer. "I'm numb. I need to get out of this ridiculous bed. I'm coming downstairs. I'll have coffee with everybody there and have fun watching them destroy my kitchen. Sorry, Marissa's kitchen."

"Oh-kay ... Are you sure this is a good idea?"

"Hey! Don't put up with Mama Orca, okay? I'm coming downstairs. The worst that can happen right now is to give birth a few days early. It's probably time for me to get a baby for my birthday," Ava countered with the same funny, playful grin.

Downstairs, the cake was already in the oven, baking.

"Yum-yum, smells good. Good morning," Ava acknowledged everyone as she swayed into the kitchen.

"Happy Birthday, my dear!" Patti pranced to hug her.

A choir of wishes and more hugs and kisses followed.

"With all these babies and bellies between us, we must look like Sumo wrestlers." Ava chuckled, hugging Emily, who was only about two months behind with her pregnancy.

Everyone burst into laughter at her witty remark.

"We made you a baby-cake too, so you can have it with your coffee and give the okay. Cindy tweaked this recipe to match your dietary restrictions. I made it with her once, so I kinda know what I'm doing," Emily's nose creased as she slightly shrugged.

"It smells amazing. You already have my 'okay'. I can't eat anything right now, though. This little Brat is already up, tap dancing, kicking, and boxing all my organs," Ava grimaced, rubbing her belly.

She huffed and lay on the couch in the family room, chatting with everybody while having her coffee.

After, she returned to the 'boring' bed. "I can tell I'm close. My back hurts so badly," Ava uttered with a deep grunt.

For the last two months, she had been confined to bed. Total rest. After the shooting, she only got out of the house for the weekly visits to the doctor. The reason? Nothing, but just keeping the secret. Otherwise, she felt well, no different from any other pregnant woman. But now, she was so done.

The house filled with laughter and cheer as the rest of the family, 'the London party', joined for an early birthday dinner. Ava sat at the table, her hand resting on her belly as she absently poked at her food. Each bite felt like a chore, her appetite fading as the baby pushed against her stomach, and she probably ate less than Ayden.

"You must have cake, at least," Patti tempted her.

"I'll have a bite." Literally, a bite was all she could have. "I'll go check on the kids," Ava said, getting up.

"I'll go," CJ offered, and promptly jumped to his feet.

"I can do it. I need to move a bit." Slowly, she began up the stairs, followed by CJ. "I need to go to the washroom first," she said once at the top of the staircase and veered to her right.

Alarmed by the urgency in her voice, when Ava called a minute later, CJ bolted to tend to her. "What happened?"

His gaze flicked between Ava and the puddle she stood in.

Eyes wide, Ava exhaled, "My water just broke."

Eyes wider than hers, CJ freaked. "Fuck! What now?"

"Now you breathe and keep breathing. Please get that towel and throw it on the floor. Then bring me a clean one. I'll hop in the shower. Call Doctor Moussa and tell him it's happening. And … do you remember that bag, ready to go, in the closet by the door? Put it in the car. When I'm out of the shower, we go to the hospital. And … do you have a name picked out yet?"

"I do. I do. So, towel … Okay, what's next? CJ precipitated, scattered.

"Breathe."

"Okay, yes. Breathe," he repeated automatically. "Darn, Ava! I breathe! What else?"

"Clean towel, Doctor Moussa, bag … closet, by the door."

"I'm calling Mum."

"Good. Call Mum. She knows the drill. And breathe. I'm taking a shower."

Hands clutching his head as if worried he might lose it, CJ ran in circles, terrified. "Mum! Ava's water just broke," his voice boomed as he hollered from the top of the stairs, and all the women rushed up.

"Okay, dear. Calm down. There's time. Where is Ava?"

"In the shower," he said, eyes wide and wild.

"Well, dear, you get in there, help her," Patti said before she turned to the other women. "Emily, Shannon. You two get something for Ava to wear when she's out of the shower. Lisa, you come with me to get Ava's hospital bag. I know where it is. She showed me." With the precision of a military general, her orders continued to arrive. "CJ, have you called the doctor?" she asked out loud before leaving, so he could hear her from the bathroom.

"Calling him now." His answer came promptly.

One evening, months ago, they sat together, scribbling names.

One list for a boy, one for a girl.

When they compared their choices, Ava raised a brow, amused. "Well, that's kinda unexpected."

Many of their choices matched.

CJ grinned. "I guess we're more in sync than we thought."

"You get to pick this time," she reminded him. "I chose Ayden's name."

CJ tapped the paper with the matching names. "Then, I'll choose from these. We both like them, so no complaints later."

Ava smirked. "I wouldn't dream of it."

True to her promise, she never asked what names he picked, and CJ never revealed. She'd find out when the baby arrives.

It was past midnight when Ava woke up, her eyes trying to conquer the bright light in the hospital room. Disoriented, she scrambled to focus and finally saw CJ at her bedside, his head resting on its edge. Stirred by the soft rustle of the sheets, he lifted his gaze.

"Hey, beautiful. You did it," he greeted her, eyes tired but bright.

"What is it?" she asked, her mouth dry.

"It's a baby girl, and she looks just like you." Through a tired smile, his voice oozed with happiness.

Groggily, Ava tried to look around. "Where is she?"

CJ helped her sit up before picking up the baby from the bassinet, bringing her to the impatient mother. "Allow me to introduce you to our daughter, Victoria Pearl Hamilton."

"Pearl!" Ava arched a surprised eyebrow.

Placing the baby comfortably in her arms, he added, "She is your Victory, hence Victoria, and our Pearl. It's a beautiful name, and we could continue to call her Pearl. Thank you, my love. There's no man on Earth happier than I am right now. Tell me you are happy, too."

"Can't you tell?" she asked, preoccupied with checking the

baby and counting Pearl's fingers and toes for the fifth time already.

"They are all accounted for. All ten of them. She's perfect. Like her mother."

"You're finally here. This old clam made quite a cute Pearl. This must be that little fist you kept punching Mama's liver with, right? Welcome to the world! I love you, my Pearl," Ava cooed, then she looked at CJ. "I love you, Babe."

He set a tender kiss on her lips.

In the morning, the rest of the family invaded her hospital room, bringing Ayden to meet his baby sister.

"Mama!" Ayden scurried enthusiastically, keen to climb onto Ava's hospital bed as Patti struggled to hold him.

CJ took baby Pearl from Ava's arms so she could make room for Ayden.

He studied Pearl with curiosity and kissed her. "She's cute, Mama," Ayden said, cuddling baby Pearl. "Mama. We take her home?"

"Of course, Baby. She's ours. We take her home. You were smaller than her when I took you home. And look at you now!" Ava said, kissing Ayden.

A week later, mother and baby were adjusting to a new routine.

CJ came home early that day. "Where is Ava?" he asked the moment he stormed in.

"She's nursing Pearl," Patti said. "We're making her lunch. Did you eat?" she continued, but he was already halfway up the stairs, taking two at a time.

"No, I didn't," he replied, scattered. "Baby, I've got good news!" CJ said, stopping in the nursery's doorframe, enthusiasm lining his voice, as if something extraordinary had just happened.

In Pearl's room, Ava was burping her after a copious lunch. "Easy, cowboy! You startled her." She looked at CJ, trying to soothe Pearl. "What news?"

"We got a court date. An early one. July 3rd. Ayden will have my last name." CJ conveyed, his tone softer, but still excited.

"July 3rd! That soon? But I can't travel with Pearl," she replied, her voice filled with concern.

"Relax. Trent's an excellent lawyer. He presented our case to the judge, and our request was granted. Only *I* have to show up in person. You can join online. I could take Ayden with me if that's okay with you," he reassured Ava, stepping into the room. "Will you trust me with him?"

"Of course, I trust you with him. Just make sure he's allowed in the courtroom before you leave. What if they don't allow small kids? Where will you leave him?" Ava asked while checking on the baby.

CJ took Pearl from Ava's arms. "I'm sure they can make an exception, especially since this is all about Ayden."

"You have a case plea right there," Ava commented, her eyes glowing.

"I think she's almost asleep," he said, lending Ava a hand to help her get off the recliner. Slowly, he placed Pearl in her cot. "I have a confession to make." CJ displayed a guilty pout as he turned and looked at Ava, who joined him by the cot.

"A confession?" Ava wondered, glaring up at him.

"Yes. Please don't freak out. I panicked. I thought, what if the court asked for more? For proof. I don't know ... I thought I should be prepared, and I ordered a Paternity DNA Test."

"Okay. And? Have they asked for it?"

"No, they haven't," his voice croaked. "And because they haven't, it is somewhere in the house. I just wanted you to know if you found it, so you won't question why I had it done."

"Good."

CJ arched a confused brow. "This is all you have to say?"

"What should I say? Should I ask if he's yours? I know he's yours. You knew he was yours," Ava replied plainly.

"Sorry. I acted on impulse. I should destroy it." CJ decided.

"Why? Is there still speculation about adoption out there?"

"Yup," he sighed. "They are calling us liars."

"Well, then ... keep it. You never know when it'll come in handy. Your fans can be relentless. We don't need to prove anything to them, but one day, Ayden may start hearing things ... asking questions ... You'll have the proof. Now, let's eat something. I'm hungry," Ava grabbed the baby monitor, taking another glimpse at Pearl, sleeping peacefully in her crib.

Epilogue

Through narrowed eyes, the judge glanced over his glasses, analyzing CJ's interaction with Ayden as he looked over the papers. He asked CJ and Ava a few questions. It didn't sound or feel very official. More like a conversation.

From the questions, the judge appeared mostly interested in their personal relationship, family dynamics, and childcare.

"Mr. Hamilton. Ayden is your son," he declared, knocking the gavel on the court bench.

CJ blinked, surprised by how simple it all felt. "This is it?"

"What else? This was your request, correct?"

"Yes. I just ... Well, I also had a Paternity DNA Test done. Just in case—"

The judge shared a kind smile. "Mr. Hamilton, I wish all my cases were like yours. Unfortunately, most of the fathers I see in this courtroom deny paternity. Even when a DNA test proves it. I don't know, and frankly don't want to know, how you ended up before my court. I can only assume it was complicated, but it's clear to me that your family has already overcome a lot. What matters most is that Ayden is in good hands, surrounded by love and stability. That's all I care about. And that's exactly what I've seen here today." He paused. "You're a good father, Mr. Hamilton. And a good husband. Take care of them."

Tears streamed down Ava's cheeks.

CJ turned and waved to the camera. "Say hi to Mama," he whispered to Ayden, beaming with happiness. "I love you, Baby," he told Ava. "We're coming home."

It was late at night when Rob picked up CJ and Ayden from the airport. When they arrived, only the night light in Pearl's room was glowing. Ayden had fallen asleep before the airplane landed, and CJ carried him straight to his room, changed him and tucked him into bed. Then, he quietly stepped into Pearl's room. He missed her. A lot. With a satisfied smile, he crossed the hallway to their bedroom.

Ava was peacefully asleep. She stayed up, waiting for them to come home. But she didn't last.

Without a sound, CJ grabbed clean clothes from the closet and tiptoed out of the room. He returned after a quick shower in the gym and slipped into bed, resting a hand on Ava's hip. Just a few minutes later, Pearl fussed on the baby monitor.

Sleepy, Ava struggled to get up, and she stopped for a second on the edge of the bed. A brawny arm reached from behind, wrapping around her, pulling her back.

"You stay here. I'll bring her," he whispered.

"You're home!" Ava smiled, blinking the sleep away. "Where is Ayden?"

"Sleeping," CJ said in a low voice, already rolling across the hallway to get Pearl.

In the morning, CJ rose early. When Pearl woke up, he took her downstairs to Marissa to be fed.

"Ava is tired. We'll let her sleep," he said.

Along with Marissa, they figured out Ava's breast milk stash in the fridge, and Pearl was changed, fed, and was now happy. Then he returned upstairs to get Ayden ready for daycare. When everyone was set, Marissa headed out with Ayden and Pearl.

"Unless the house is on fire, we are not to be disturbed," CJ told Marissa before she left with the kids.

Ten minutes later, when Ava stirred in bed, he was already by her side, watching her. Waiting.

"Good morning, Baby."

"Good morning. You're doing that thing again."

"What thing?"

"Watching me when I sleep," Ava replied, trying to check the time on her fitness tracker. It was dead. "What time is it?" she asked.

CJ leaned in and kissed her. "It's time to make love, darling."

"CJ, I need to feed Pearl. What time is it?"

"Kids are not an acceptable excuse, Baby. Besides, they've been taken care of. Marissa is out with both of them, taking Ayden to the nursery. It's just us." He kissed her again, deeper this time. "I missed you so much."

"I need a shower," Ava said.

"Nope. You don't."

"I really do. I haven't showered in two days. Pearl was really fussy."

"Okay, let's give you a shower then."

Slippery, dripping bodies, wet hair and giggles ... holding, kissing, rediscovering ... CJ carried her back to bed, where the rhythm built until their bodies moved as one, twisting, swaying, gasping. A soft cry, a deep moan, and the kind of silence that follows only after the loudest kind of love.

Breathless, Ava's fingers still clenched on the sheets. "That judge was wrong," she panted a whisper. "You're not a *good* father. You're a *great* one. And an even better husband. I could get used to this," she teased.

CJ looked at her, smiling. His eyes glowed with something deep and steady. "You better," he said. "I love you, Mrs. Hamilton. The most-est-est-est. To the moon and back. Speaking of ... It just hit me that we never had a honeymoon."

"I shouldn't have trusted you when you said you won't stalk

me," she taunted.

He grinned with mischief. "I didn't stalk you. I pursued you."

"Mm-hmm ... I guarded my heart like a national secret. I argued it. Then you waltzed in, awkward, clueless, and somehow irresistible with your British accent. And you kept showing up like a bad penny. Only ... shinier. And I fucking like shiny things. And sleep-deprived morning sex."

He held her tight. "Love, not just sex."

She curled into his chest, her smile decadent but steady. "Yeah, whatever you call it."

"Well, that's what I call it. Anyway, I know you once said you're not planning to go back there anytime soon, but it's been a while. So, how about Paris? Taking the kids to see where we first met?"

Ava grinned, her heart racing with anticipation. "Hmm, Paris?" She let it sink in for a second.

"Well?"

"Yeah, why not? I feel like I'm living backwards lately."

CJ rolled her over with another ardent kiss.

Arguing her Heart

Prologue   1

1. That bad, huh?   4

2. So, you really are an actor…   17

3. She's walking with a purpose   27

4. Where have you been my whole life?   36

5. We don't like stalkers around here   51

6. You must be an alien   59

7. It's not about the bloody doll   67

8. I guess we are friends   77

9. I have a trained eye   89

10. And this is how you start rumours   99

11. Who do you think you are? Superman?!   106

12. Do we have a flat?   116

13. Arguing her heart   124

14. Talking about bad timing   140

15. I know you'll be fine   149

16. It was complicated   162

17. What is worth fighting for   172

18. I'll talk some sense into him   180

19. It is what I want   188

20. So, he can still be funny   195

21. You are the one   204

22. I know what I need to do   215

23. Lina had a baby!   222

24. Everything will be alright   232

25. I'm not going anywhere   249

26. The Far-Far Away Kingdom   264

27. It's a 'test'   274

28. Daddy is funny   290

29. So, you were looking for trouble in Paris   302

30. Make me another baby   312

31. Say 'I do'   319

32. You must be a Superwoman   329

33. Three generations of Hamilton boys   337

34. That thing was demanding a life   351

35. You are an angel   364

Epilogue   377